A ROLE TO DIE FOR

"No. I don't need money that badly," I said.

"You can act," Condé said. "And that old-fashioned accent of yours is a bonus. A lot of Column posts are held by old-school types."

"Sorry."

"I'm not an actor myself. When I said I was prepared to frame you for theft, I meant it." Condé raised his hand to the console. "The Shadowmen can start working you over within two hours. Or you can earn a fat, painless fee posing as the new sub-commissioner. What's it to be?"

When I left the office, shaken and sweating, the director stood in front of the floating mask of playwright Evan Larkspur—me, a hundred years earlier. "Art is what survives," he was saying complacently, "and Larkspur is immortal."

Fools who impersonate Column officials, on the other hand, are invariably put to death.

THE UNWOUND WAY

Bill Adams
and Cecil Brooks

A Del Rey Book
BALLANTINE BOOKS • NEW YORK

A Del Rey Book
Published by Ballantine Books

 Published in the United States of America by Ballantine Books, a division of Random House, Inc., New York, and simultaneously in Canada by Random House of Canada Limited, Toronto.

Library of Congress Catalog Card Number: 91-92109

ISBN 0-345-37238-7

Manufactured in the United States of America

First Edition: November 1991

Cover Art by Richard Hescox

To our mothers and aunts
GEORGIA and GENEVA
and to our fathers and uncles
EDWARD and EDWIN
with gratitude and with love.

This is as strange a maze as e'er men trod,
And there is in this business more than nature
Was ever conduct of. Some oracle
Must rectify our knowledge.

The Tempest V, i.

Part One

The Mask

Chapter One

I EMERGED FROM the sun's dazzle into a new world, night and stars. The vivid greens and raw-meat reds of the rain forest outside, the humidity and cascading bird calls, were tucked behind me by an airlock door. Humans can't follow the three-week days of the planet Zenobia. Indoors, they keep their own calendars and clocks, and within Condé's manor house it was just past midnight. All the scarlet-curtained windows had been polarized black, a hologram image of Zenobia's night sky projected within the frames.

After the heat outside, the air-conditioning was like the brandied kiss of the young woman who met me at the door—a pleasant shock, a new dazzlement. I think she introduced herself as our patron's niece, hostess for our cast party, but she was already pretty badly dazzled herself. I followed the flow of guests into the great hall, cheerfully resigned to the decadence of the occasion.

The actor, the smuggler, the fugitive—each lives for a successful run. I was all three that night, and felt I deserved a triple crown. The play was done. The contraband had been delivered. And my new identity appeared to be better-connected than usual.

I relaxed and took in the panelings of native wood and the wine-red carpets, my fellow players in flamboyant costumes and the local gentry in formal dress. I found another ostentation less amusing—human servants, in livery designed to make fools of them. But man must drink, even if the serving tray is strapped to some page boy's head, and I had just snagged an extra glass when I reached the entrance to the buffet room, and saw it.

For a moment I thought I'd begun one of my special dreams, those torments that rip me out of reality and leave the torn edges flapping. It was real, though. Not quite the sword of Damocles, perhaps, but hanging over my place at dinner just the same. The bust, the mask, the mocking face of bronze. Always bringing me down to earth, and back to beginnings.

* * *

The Blue Swathe—that's what they called this distant fringe of the human sphere, still nearly as far as you could get from the central stars ruled directly by the Column. At least three different waves of colonization had rolled through the Swathe, turning up rich new worlds every time, and even in this age of the Column regime an air of frontier freedom remained. Here you could buy a cup of coffee without submitting to an automatic identity and credit check; vote for local officials in a secret ballot; write an outspoken letter to a news service. A cynic might point out that this looser leash had been procured by special and rather dirty services to the state, for the region was also home to half the arms factories and naval shipyards that maintained the central power. But meanwhile, the Swathe's Sodality had recently voted in civil libertarian reforms—optimistically anticipating a rumored policy shift by the Column's shadowy Consultant. This had attracted me.

I'd entered the region as one act in a small carnival—a conjuror, the real me in a way, despite the fanciful alias: "Praku Ras." The outfit had folded unexpectedly on a mudball of a mining planet. I'd been stranded, no salary saved and no theaters to fall back on.

Fortunately I was only seven years out of naval service, and the universe remains abrasive enough to keep my martial skills polished. Shiphandling, for instance. Under the name Lars Park, I soon picked up a pilot's job with the Hermes Line, the only courier service franchised to operate within the Swathe.

I started at the bottom—probational half-pay, and an obsolescent boat that burned up half its backups on every sunplunge. But part of me had always wanted to experience faster-than-light travel just that way: alone, solely responsible, free to feel the immensity and insanity of it.

We sling ourselves into the curved space at the very rim of a star, protected from its energies only by wrapping them around ourselves. The stronger our bootstrap shield grows, the steeper we make our descent. And *if* we are not deflected into a dangerous spin, and *if* we do not take in energy too fast and burn out, and *if* the force field curves to singularity against the slope of the gravity well—we squeeze ourselves out of space entirely, following a geodesic through praeterspace into the domain of a new star.

And yet, I finally learned, the sense of wonder slips away. The job turned into a dull grind as I transported messages, packages, and news dispatches from star to star throughout the

Swathe's Six and Thirty Sodality. Only the smuggling kept me aware and alive.

My dispatchers insisted that if I didn't play along as the other pilots did, I would never be promoted to the permanent list. Anyway, I rationalized, smuggling is not a crime against people, only their Customs—bad manners, in other words, and no more.

But when I demanded an overdue raise the Hermes Line kicked me out, using evidence of the "misconduct" they'd forced on me as their excuse. It was obviously a racket. I wasn't arrested, for one thing; a trial would have exposed the smuggling as company policy.

But the company gave me a good scare and, to get rid of me, a letter of introduction to a Swathe labor exchange. I used it, too, which meant not changing my name again—two mistakes, but I couldn't see that at the time.

Once the labor exchange found me a part in a play, I couldn't see past the footlights. I had originally signed on as an understudy, but when the lead had an attack of temperament—something about wanting to be paid—I picked up his role. *Odysseus in Phaiacia*—by Larkspur, of course. I'm not a first-rate actor, but a great part can make you look great if you understand it, and I understand that one better than any man living. The interstellar craze for live theater and Larkspur had just reached the Swathe, in what was billed as the *Odysseus* play's centennial year. Our production moved from triumph to triumph, feted afterward by local society; something about verse plays always brings out the rich.

I enjoyed the tour—hell, I reveled in it. But I was irked because our canny impresario paid me only scale, putting me off with vague promises of a tour-end bonus. I don't live for money, mind you, I live for experience—but that *costs* money. It's the bait that never stales; it draws us back to old and obvious traps.

One night on Woodvyl a man named T'ung came backstage and introduced himself as another exploited ex-pilot for the Hermes Line. He said he had a plan to cheat them out of a fat smuggling fee. So revenge as well as greed demanded I help him.

My part in the scam was to be simple. All I had to do was wear a certain bracelet to the troupe's next port of call, Zenobia. The dull gray band didn't look like much. But it had belonged to a Discocephalic alien once, and like every other nonhuman intelligence of which the human race had ever found traces, the Discocephalics had been extinct for millennia; that made the artifact extremely valuable. A Zenobian would pick it up on behalf of one Maximilien Condé—a big-time defense contractor who hadn't wanted to be involved with a more professional smuggler.

The risks seemed slight, since the iron-alloy bracelet had no face value and could be worn openly. But I think I was surprised, given this perverse universe, when everything went off without a hitch.

The contact man showed up the evening of our first Zenobian performance, relieved me of the contraband, and paid me in full. For the next few weeks I had nothing to worry about except our leading lady's boyfriend, and perhaps the continual whine of our troupe's director: "Why are you *tampering*, Freeman Park?"—his stubborn refusal to take my word for it that if Larkspur had lived past twenty-two, he'd have fixed Odysseus's closing speech. And meanwhile the play rolled across the Zenobian landscape like a great golden engine, with cheering crowds to greet it at every stop.

I hadn't been surprised when we received invitations to hold our cast party at Condé's manor and Condé's expense. The contact man had implied that this was coming, and I'd looked forward to the role of secret guest of honor. And here I was. Only that bronze face—my own dark side, the shadow of the past—could bring me down now, I reminded myself. But in fact a future had already been hung and honed for me; a winding hall of mirrors, and an upraised axe.

I entered the room and faced the damned thing. They had it rigged to float head-high in the air, above a little table between the smorgasbords, with passage on either side to go around and view the back. I assumed at first it was a hologram, sharper than most. I'd seen such copies before; they were so commonplace you'd have thought the wealthy would pass them up as vulgar.

But someday I would have to visit Schaelus's original bronze, in his subject's restored dorm room at Nexus University—the Larkspur Museum. The piece has the crazy virtue of Jacques-Louis David's Napoleonic paintings: neoclassic lines so clean that they make the romantic seem realistic.

Face-on, it appears to be the bust of a young man. He's just begun to turn and look upward at something surprising and inspiring. His hair is worn long and unbound, to the shoulders. Styles come and go, and when we wore our hair that way it didn't seem effeminate; but here it emphasizes the slenderness of the subject's neck. The eyes and their lashes also conflict with the otherwise virile cast of the face. I wonder why people like to see their poets as androgynous. Perhaps it's an attempt to picture the Muse as well as the man; here, it does work.

Then you walk around the bronze, and discover that it's not a simple bust, but a hollowed facade, like a death mask. And it shares an optical illusion with death masks: under the right lighting, the concave inner side begins to appear convex, another outward face; it's like the drawing of a transparent cube, which you can mentally flip back and forth as you decide which end is toward you. Schaelus deliberately spent as much effort on the inner side as on the facade, to maximize the illusion, the uncertainty.

What is it meant to suggest? We peek beyond the young man's enigmatic face to find—nothing, except an opportunity to see through his eyes. But if we attempt this, we find the eyeholes opaque and the face unexpectedly confronting us again. A cool comment on a legend, and also a fine work of romantic art. But I hate it for the lie on the little plaque in front:

EVAN LARKSPUR
1594–1616
If Light is but a wave, then why not surf?
The Enchanted Isle

I don't mind the choice of quotation, apt or not. But I object to the name—the pretense that this is a portrait, when there is no resemblance at all. That's what I was thinking when a female voice whispered in my ear, "He's you," and maybe that's when the evening began to turn on me, maybe that's when I entered the mirror maze behind the mask.

"What?" I said, looking to see who had followed me around the table—an attractive blonde. The alcohol gleam in her eyes made it impossible to guess whether her shoulder straps were supposed to fall that way or not; I couldn't give the problem the attention it deserved, because she hit me with it again: "He's you."

But she went on, smiling now that she had my attention: "He's *me*. That's what Schaelus is saying. Everyone wants to put on that mask, and see himself as Larkspur. Everyone likes to imagine . . . taking off the way Larkspur did, seeing something better out there, and just turning his back on all this . . . crap." On the last word she gestured to indicate the room, the planet, or the Column and its Consultancy ruling over us all—a fling of the arm that settled the shoulder-strap question, anyway.

An older, soberer, richer-looking gentleman came up behind her, turned her around, and readjusted her dress; she raised her arms and took it for granted, like a six-year-old. "Romantic nonsense, of course," the boyfriend—if that's what he was—said to me. "This whole notion the young have, of Larkspur as a social critic."

"Uh-hunh," I said, and started to move away, but he acted as though I were arguing with him.

"Oh, he was a fringe colonial, true," he went on, "but he must have had aristocratic ties. He got into Nexus U. itself, was accepted into one of the 'exclusive' secret societies there—a Kanalist fraternity, of course; *The Enchanted Isle* is full of their symbolism—"

"Hans is jealous," the blonde pointed out, turning only her head. "Hans was blackballed."

"Envy," Hans said. "Nouveau types are the worst snobs. Like Larkspur himself," he went on, for public benefit now; a few other guests, china and silver in their hands, had drifted into distant listening positions. "His plays were obviously written for a coterie audience. Can't you just see the colonial boy trying to fit in with the old guard at Nexus, learning Ur-Linguish to smarten up his accent? That's what led him into the treasure trove of forgotten Earth literature. He was no genius. Homer, Shakespeare, Cervantes, Rostand—those are the geniuses. People say 'adaptation' and '*hommage*,' but the right word is 'plagiarism.' "

"Totally unfair," said another woman, looking on, and her companion added, "What about the *Satires*?"

Hans ignored them. "Larkspur would be forgotten today if not for a romantic death—and the rise of nouveau snobbery under the Consultancy."

"Watch it," someone said in a low voice, but we were far from the Column's central worlds and its Shadow Tribunal, and everyone just laughed.

"Oh yes, we're all supposed to be good Ur-Linguophiles now," Hans said, shaking a finger at me as though I had been arguing with him. "Even in the Swathe, our class is supposed to speak with a central-sphere accent. Where better to pick it up than in memorable verses? And if the plays are full of the sort of heroic, larger-than-life characters the Consultancy would like to have in the Column navy, all the better for recruitment, eh?''

''Totally unfair,'' repeated the outriding woman, an intense brunette in a conservative dinner gown. ''Larkspur can't be blamed for the way his work's been used since his death. He was an individualist, an old Alignment Federalist. I think that's why he ran away and joined the navy—the last bulwark of the old order. He was an Old Rite Kanalist, too, and he saw that the Reformed Rite lodges were selling out to the Column. He saw—''

''He saw *The Enchanted Isle* flop within the elite community that was supporting him,'' Hans said, swooping to the kill, ''so he decided to give up amateur theater, accept a commission in a nearlight survey, and make a vast vulgar fortune, like—''

''Like me,'' said a self-assured voice at my side. There was another general laugh, as the speaker wedged his way into the center of the group. By the time he clapped me on the shoulder I'd guessed that he was our host, Sir Maximilien Condé.

I regained my composure. Wherever Larkspur is played, they gossip about his life. As the lead player, I was a natural target; no doubt our director would have to listen to the same literary yattering when he arrived. But there had been something about the way they'd gathered around me . . . Of course, in Condé's case I was the secret guest of honor, a colorful character who had done him a favor. No doubt that explained the look of hidden knowledge in his eyes.

''So Larkspur took an easy way out, is that what you're saying, Hans?'' Condé's voice didn't boom, but it did carry. Tanned, taut, and energetic, he could have passed for eighty years old, but a closer look said a hundred, the end of middle age; the great shock of white hair was no clue, probably dyed from a duller gray. ''But surveys weren't short private hops in those days, remember. Only big navy ships like the *Barbarossa* could control the scoop-fields. You had to sign up for a five-year cruise with only twenty mates for company. Suspend-sleep most of the time, and sixty or seventy years passing for the folks you left behind—relativity effect. *You* try kissing that much of your background good-bye. Don't forget, too, that many ships still just disappear, like Larkspur's. Not an easy way out, when you don't come back.''

''But Larkspur still *could*,'' said the blonde suddenly, and the childishness of her drunken voice seemed fey, oracular. ''He could come back tomorrow, couldn't he? If the *Barbarossa* had just . . . overshot a few months, that would be another few decades, our time. He could come back tomorrow, still in his early twenties . . . find himself appreciated at last . . ."

"Not for long," I said—all too easily. "A century has been kind to the seven plays you have. It's glossed over their faults, and quoted all the best lines into your ears from childhood. If Larkspur came back, all his new plays would only seem thin by comparison. And once Larkspur started showing off at the same parties as your other writers, stealing the prettiest girls from your critics—they'd have to tear him down to human size."

"But the quality is there," the brunette insisted. "The talent behind the legend. He could start over from scratch, under a pseudonym. If anyone could write like that now—"

"We'd tell him to stop imitating the sentimental style of a hundred years ago," Hans insisted, and when someone playfully booed, he added, "Tell me you don't see that phrase twice a month in the reviews!"

Only I could know how right he was. Objectively, it was a funny scene—but no fun to play. God is one of the more heavy-handed ironists.

"He couldn't conceal his identity anyway," Condé said. "Not if he cashed in the *Barbarossa*'s data record. It would be one of the largest fortunes in history, even split twenty ways after the navy's cut. Look how many planets Del Mehta and I discovered with only a ten-light-year baseline. If anyone ever did make it back from a *hundred*-year circle, tangent to the fringe like that, they'd be able to fill in the p-space access data for thousands of stars. The revenues would be fantastic. Unimaginable."

"But I wonder if Larkspur cared much about money," the brunette said.

"That much money cares about you," Condé said with conviction. "Ever hear the 'selfish gene' theory—humans are just the vehicles that genes use to perpetuate themselves? Well, a fortune is selfish, too. It doesn't want to be broken up, so it buys its owner a defensive arsenal of banks and lawyers and senators. And you use them. Because by then you're in the arena, and the only way out is on a stretcher."

"Oh, *poor Sir Max*," Hans said, and everyone laughed again. The scene was breaking up, I suddenly knew; God is also pretty pacey. "These self-made men—who would have thought? I can assure you that when the fortune *comes with* the genes, one doesn't feel so insecure."

"Just twice as selfish?" I asked—no malice, just the pull of the ad lib.

"And the representative of Art scores in the final round," the blonde concluded dully. ". . . Where can I throw up, anyway?"

"She's all yours, Hans," Condé said. "Anyway, I was hoping for a private talk with my fellow peasant here."

They didn't wheel away at his word, of course, but a few minutes later we were alone with the mask. He gestured toward it. "Can't expect a worm like Hans to identify with a man like that. Not even sure why I do, sometimes. But Larkspur and I were born the same year. And there's *Odysseus in Phaiacia*; I think I understand that character better than any man alive . . . Terrific likeness, isn't it?"

I tried to shake the illogical feeling that he was on to me. After all, if a shrewdie like Condé did suspect my real identity, he wouldn't coach his friends to play cat and mouse with me in public. No, he'd do what half the powerful men in the galaxy would be willing to do, given a clue—take me to some very private place and have me torn apart brain cell by brain cell until I answered the questions: *Where is the* Barbarossa *and her crew? Why haven't you used her data? What's the big secret?*

But there aren't enough answers to satisfy them. So Larkspur must remain a hollow name, and I a nameless man.

"Terrific likeness," I agreed solemnly. "Didn't know holograms came that sharp."

"Oh, it's not a holo." He reached out and rapped his knuckles against what I had taken to be the empty air between us and the mask. "A simulacrum. One of our Blue Swathe specialities. A column of luminotrope glass. The outer layer has the same index of refraction as air. The rest of the mix casts an image whose sharpness always optimizes to the ambient light—no projector or display lamps necessary. Unfortunately, the volume of glass necessary to cast an image is much greater than the size of the image itself, and heavy as hell—that's the export drawback. You and I prefer more portable wealth, don't we?"

There it was again—or no, of course; he was just talking about the bracelet.

"That's old business. I'm happy."

"But so am I, Park. Always happy to find someone I can do business with. And I have a new proposition for you—if we could talk about it now, before more people arrive?"

He raised one hand to a blank wall in the shadow of the mask;

it changed color and slid aside. I followed him through the portal, glad for the change of scene. I'd had enough exposure to the public for one night.

The next room was a large office, all dark reds and browns, smelling of leather, cigars, and the oddly peppery local wood. The door became solid wall behind me as I backed into it, trapped.

Before me stood a tall young man in a crisp white Column uniform. His expression was uncertain, but the pistol in his hand was definitely aimed at my head.

Chapter Two

WHEN EVERYTHING FALLS apart, I don't panic. Not any more; it happens too often. In this case the cop—or whatever he was—looked as trapped as I felt, and that made it easier to keep a poker face.

Condé seated himself behind an impressive desk and mocked us with an introduction. "Freeman Lars Park—Citizen Bunny Velasquez, of the Commission on Non-Human Artifacts. As you may know, Freeman Park, local governments have to yield all alien relics they discover to the care of the Column."

I adopted an expression of courteous boredom and took a chair. Velasquez shifted his feet nervously for a moment, then followed suit, handling the pistol as though it were a prop he hadn't rehearsed with yet. He was as thin as he was tall, pale-haired, pink-faced, and blue-eyed, with an overbred look—somewhere between petulance and bafflement—that brought back my Nexus University days. He appeared to be just out of college himself, and the white tunic's upright collar bore no silver tabs of rank; probably just an aide of some sort.

With hammy slowness, Condé pulled something from the top drawer of his desk. I was not surprised to see the bracelet I'd smuggled for him.

"Some weeks ago," he said, "this artifact was stolen from an official repository on Woodvyl. Soon Citizen Velasquez of the Artifacts Commission heard that the thieves were offering it for sale. He asked a local citizen known for his archaeological pursuits—myself—to pose as an interested buyer. Ten days ago, my agent contacted the gang's middleman—that's you—and bought back the item."

His fingers were hovering over a small console on the desk, but I took an actor's deep breath—the kind you can't see—and cut in before he could activate it.

"You can skip the replay of whatever recording your agent made," I said. "I'm sure it does sound as if he were making a purchase from a thief. So what? We both know better. Velasquez isn't an investigator, he's a flunky. And you're no honest citizen. You must have heard of me through the Hermes Line, and if you have any ownership in that, I can tie you to their smuggling operations. It's a nice try at a frame, Sir Max, but I'd make you unhappy if it actually came to a Column court. Why don't you simply tell me what you want me to do, minus the blackmail? Maybe you can afford to just pay me."

Condé barely hesitated. Then he laughed. "Nice try yourself. But I calculated the value of this bracelet carefully. Your genetic pattern would be checked against outstanding Column warrants, I suppose, but then you'd be remanded to a local court—where I have influence. Slandering me there would only add years to your time, believe me.

"Still—what do you say, Bunny? Didn't I tell you he'd handle himself well? You're right, Park. The Hermes Line disposes of troublesome pilots through my labor exchange, which screens them for talents I can use. I've discovered a number of exceptional employees that way, over the years. To our mutual benefit. As you said, I can afford to pay.

"So let's start over. You seem to be a sharp operator. I'll put my problem to you as a paid consultant, and we'll see if you can come up with a better solution than I have. Fair enough?"

"Fair enough." On the one hand, he was more scared of a Column investigation than he'd let on; I could smell it. But on the other, heavier hand, I could never afford to call his bluff. The Column's Shadow Tribunal would almost certainly match my genetic pattern to my old navy file. And then they'd cheerfully break me to extract the secrets Evan Larkspur would be expected to have—not just the star data, but the location of a missing navy ship as well.

I hadn't trusted the First Column a hundred years before, when it was just one group of powerful worlds within the Federal Alignment, and I hadn't been astonished, when I returned to the human sphere four—or rather, ninety-two—years later, to find the word *Column* synonymous with the new central government. I was still puzzled as to how an outside Consultant had come to hold dictatorship over the Column-world oligarchs, but that addition in no way improved the picture. The civil liberties of Alignment days were gone, at least in the central sphere. I wouldn't plead my case there.

But it could have been worse. Condé would have put me through the wringer himself, if he'd had an inkling who I really was. Blinded by his own secrets, he went on blandly.

"My story is simple. You heard some of it a few minutes ago. Ninety years back—in standard time scale—I was a young kid of thirty. An engineer, fresh out of the new navy, which didn't make me very popular, even though there hadn't been much resistance to the Column out this way. I had plans in my head for the best deepspace war machines anyone had ever seen, but no way to finance their construction, no family connections. All I had was brains and guts and a few ex-navy friends my own age. One of these was Delip Mehta, second son of a big landowner on Woodvyl. He was ambitious and—in those days—pretty honest. I let him bankroll a scheme I had in mind . . . What do you know about nearlight surveys?"

"Nothing," I said—a protective reflex.

"Well, you're a sunplunger. You know that when you squeeze yourself out of the plenum, you have to reappear *someplace*, someplace where the mass-energy pattern of your inertia and shield distortions will 'mesh' with local space-time. It almost has to be within the curved space near another star, but which one? You pilots don't have to worry about it; you feed the right access data to your computer, and field adjustments automatically fit you to the target sun. That access data is what makes interstellar civilization possible.

"But a star's access data is its mass, density, composition, output, Main Sequence stage—a hundred factors. Only a tiny fraction of all stars reveal that much to a one-point observer; the first sunplungers were restricted to those systems. To fill in the blanks and get access to all the skipped regions between, you have to take repeated readings along an extensive baseline. Since we're talking about distances in the light-years, you want to push as close to lightspeed as you can handle. That's a survey.

"And for more than twelve centuries, only big governments could run them, with big, clumsy ships. They'd fly huge circles, many light-years. Home worlds would wait decades for their return, but the crews would only age three or four years. Relativity, you know. The time displacement was murder on the crews, but they were always paid enormous bounties. Kept them from taking their data treasures elsewhere, for one thing. You with me so far?''

''Sure.''

''Okay, the next generation of hydrogen drives didn't require as much shielding. Suddenly you could build a much smaller, more maneuverable nearlight ship—make money on shorter surveys. My idea: run out a quick ten light-years toward a neutron star, and use its gravity to double back tightly along the same course. A short baseline, but twice the data along it. Make your trip in the skipped-over part of an area like the Swathe, unusually high in Sol-like stars and Earth-like planets.

''That's what Del Mehta and I did. I had the plan, and knew how to modify the ship. He had the money. Dropped out of history for twenty years and came back the discoverers of two hundred worlds. Eighty exploitable, fifteen terraformable. The Column took a bigger cut than we expected, but it was still a bonanza. We'd reopened our own home region, and we settled down as the two richest men in the Blue Swathe. Happy ending, right?''

''No?''

''No such thing.'' He looked meditative, and cracked his knuckles—one by one, too. ''I don't know, maybe we just built that ship too small. Three subjective years in each other's company. No privacy. No relief. Give you an idea: there was this disgusting noise Delip used to make instead of blowing his nose like a normal human being, a sort of hawking sniffle . . . Well, just saying that, just remembering it, makes me want to . . . smash him, to obliterate even his memory. That's how intense it gets. And he has the same hatred for me, of course. Didn't cheat me on the initial split, we had a contract. But he's kept the lid on me ever since. He can build, he can grow, he's Senator Mehta now and *the* liaison between the Swathe and the Column. Not that he represents the great families who settled the area—he's always pandering to the mob and their 'rights.'

''Meanwhile, I can buy citizenship and a knighthood, I'm allowed to spend my money, but make a mark? Never. The only active position I was ever allowed, reserve admiral in the Swathe's militia navy, was stripped from me this year. Mehta's doing; he was open about it. But Newcount Two is the last straw."

"Newcount Two?"

"It's a small Earthlike planet, uninhabited. Mine, I always believed. One of the first I scouted out personally, after Del and I filed the data claim.

"A peculiar, haunted place. Must have had its own unique biosphere once, but sometime in the last twelve hundred years other humans touched down there, contaminated it. Part of the first wave of settlers in this fringe, I would guess; they must have passed it up for a larger world, more surface area. Anyway, we gave it a full-scale life bombing forty years ago, and now it's a green little Terra, with exotic offshoots.

"And there are the Stone Huts. Alien spacefarers—one of the extinct kind we call Titans—touched down on Newcount Two eight or nine hundred thousand years ago. Left a few temporary structures behind. Archaeologically, the find is worthless; the Column's experts declassified it long ago. But to an amateur like me—a little hobby I picked up from Del, as a matter of fact—the site is still interesting. Every now and then I've camped out there and poked around the Stone Huts . . . And somehow, Del got word that I valued this little place. So he decided to take it—build a summer palace and maybe retire there. And rub our mutual hobby in my nose, too . . . Right now he's got a team of archaeologists picking through the Stone Huts to find decorative motifs he can build into his palace. Get the picture?"

"Sure." His reference to an entire empty planet as "this little place" had boggled my mind only slightly. "But you say that Newcount Two isn't really his?"

"That's right, he's misreading the Column's record of our claims. And I'll have proven that, within a month or two. They will evict him. The trouble is, he might find the barrow first."

"The barrow?"

"An underground extension to the Stone Hut site. Just a small supply cache, but archaeologically priceless! I stumbled onto it only a month before Del's invasion. Park, it's my one chance of going down in history; and without even knowing it's there, Del is trying to take it away from me."

"You couldn't just lift it?"

"Load the artifacts into a shuttle, you mean? No, of course not; remember how ancient it all is. It would take months to remove everything safely. And it would take only minutes to destroy it."

"What do you mean?"

"If he found it before he's forced to leave. He'd destroy it to spite me. Even if I could prove it, he can pay any fine the commissioners name. He'd do anything to keep me from making a mark, especially in his own precious field."

And I believed him. It must have been the detail about Mehta's way of sniffling; that crazy hate sounded real, and if it was, any sort of craziness could follow from it.

"But he doesn't know the barrow's there."

"No, not yet. The entrance was originally disguised, and I restored that. But with all those archaeologists on the site, one of them will stumble across it eventually. So that's my problem. To keep them away from my barrow for a lousy six or eight weeks."

"Sounds hopeless," I said. "I mean, if *you* found it, working alone, you have to expect a team of professionals will."

"But they're not!" Condé said eagerly. "Even if you could interest professionals, Del wouldn't have hired them. They would have taken all the fun out of it, don't you see; they wouldn't have let him participate. No, my spies tell me that these are just more amateurs, enthusiasts he's met at parties, amiable cranks. Court jesters for his palace. An easy group to infiltrate, if only I'd known in advance, but it's too late for that now. There has to be some other way to get at them, stall them away from my find."

Condé smiled at me, as if to say that the ball was in my court.

The one part of his performance that had never rung true—and he'd made the mistake of repeating it—was this "little hobby" line of his. If this driven, hawk-faced man had anything to do with archaeology, it would be on an imperial scale, like the European pirate-scholars who'd raped whole dynasties from Egypt in classical times. Without challenging his story, I pried for some truth. "Where does Velasquez here fit in? Is he really from the Commission on Non-Human Artifacts?"

Condé waited a moment for Velasquez to reply. Then he sighed. "Yes. 'Flunky' was not quite fair. Bunny was the aide-de-camp to the Swathe's last sub-commissioner."

"Have you thought of using the Commission? Surely that's the most direct way to stop progress at the dig. You know, tell Mehta's people they're working too fast, endangering the artifacts, have to proceed more carefully, and so forth. Amateurs would have to do as they're told."

Condé's eyes glowed. I didn't like his smile. "Yes, I thought of that. The sub-commissioner himself was too risky to bribe, too closely allied to Del's political party. But I've managed to grease the right palms to have him recalled. The post will be vacant until his replacement arrives."

"Then, wouldn't it be natural for his assistant to act in his place?" I asked. "Since he does seem to be on your payroll."

Condé nodded. "Citizen Velasquez has gambling debts so huge that he can look to no one but me for help. You've hit on the same plan I have, Park. Except that you don't know Bunny." As Condé went on about him, Velasquez's lip curled unreadably. "He's not stupid or anything, and I've convinced him that he has to play the aide, lend a little verisimilitude, but he's not capable of carrying off the main con by himself. It would take guts, you see, sunplunger's guts. He doesn't have them. More importantly . . . *he just isn't an actor.*"

"No good," I said. "No. I don't need money that badly."

"You can act. I flew out to see you perform as soon as I read the labor exchange's report. You're good enough. And that old-fashioned accent of yours is a bonus. A lot of lesser Column posts are held by old-school types."

"Sorry," I said.

"I'm not an actor myself. When I said I was prepared to frame you for theft, I meant it." He raised his hand to the console again. "I can have a Tribune here in ten minutes. The Shadowmen can start working you over within two hours. Or I can call it off, and you can earn a fat, painless fee on Newcount Two. You can be the new sub-commissioner, with all the perks of Column officialdom. In and out before anyone could possibly discover you're a phony, screwing up their dig without actually shutting it down—Del might complain to the Column if you went that far. But currently, the distinguished senator isn't even on the planet. Fooling his underlings will be a piece of cake. I hope you can see that, because you'll have to decide right now, while you're in my control. What's it to be, Park?"

Fifteen minutes later I left the office, shaken and sweating, as Condé cracked his knuckles cheerfully at my side.

The play's director had arrived, and stood with Hans and that gang around the floating mask.

"Art is what survives," the director was saying complacently, "and Larkspur is immortal."

Fools who impersonate Column officials, on the other hand, are invariably put to death.

Chapter Three

YOU GO TO *bed and you dream your pallid, hazy dreams, and maybe now and then one frightens you, but you can wake up and know instantly, by the density and intensity of sensory detail, that you are back in reality, and safe. How I envy that, who lost all certainty long ago, asleep between the stars. If your dreaming self should happen to think, "This is just a dream!" you wake up. Proof. But I never do, not since the suspend-sleep tanks failed—or did they?—a decade or century ago . . .*

Thunderclap. I was falling in stormy darkness, through rain which I could hear but not feel, protected in an invisible bubble from the lightning and the wind. Not alone; a trapped animal moaned at my side, the sort of blatant symbol that gives my dreams away but does not end them; I felt the whimpering creature's warmth but could not see it. Falling, falling, helpless, and I *knew* it was a dream, I could consciously compare it to the other sense-perfect dreams that haunt me—the recurrent ones I've sometimes thought of numbering and writing out, like Stephen Vincent Benét—and still I was at its mercy, falling, wanting to scream, braced for the impact I could not avoid.

But even when I can't wake up, there is an out. If I can't get back to reality, I try history. I have a poet's trick memory; I can bring back details in almost lifelike profusion; I can close my dream-self's eyes and escape to that era before the survey, to my student days, when I held the passing moment cheap . . .

"Daydreaming again?" Even with the morning sun blazing back from the mica of the Great Plaza all around us, Summerisle seemed to glow with his own mysterious source of power. One never noticed the color of his eyes—only that they were bright. "You can get lost in dreams, Odysseus," he went on, even though the waiter hadn't yet gone back inside the cafe. Master of the Nexus University chapter of the Kanalist fraternity, Summerisle didn't consider its pseudonyms the slightest bit corny himself. I tried to catch the waiter's reaction, but found his face almost entirely hidden in a great red beard; then he left us.

"Since when," I said, "have we been known as realists, *O Daedalus?*" Actually, I wouldn't have minded if I'd been initiated as Orpheus, since Domina Wintergrin had preceded me as Eurydice. But Summerisle had insisted that among the transient undergraduate members there must always be one Odysseus, and the pseudonym was especially apt for one who might someday become a Master in his own right. And he had judged me correctly; now, after three years, I was second only to him as a student and custodian of the frat's traditions.

"You talk like an outsider," he said. "Mysticism isn't about dreaming, it's about being more awake than other people. While you daydream, the real world is walking past you." He pointed.

I turned to see some workmen headed toward the center of the plaza, dragging ladders, scaffolding, and their own long shadows.

"What are they up to?"

Summerisle looked amused. "Pay attention, Odysseus, and you'll find out. Of course, if you'd rather go back to picturing future generations enraptured by a revival of Larkspur's *Cyrano* . . ."

I was irritated. "I'm not quite as conceited as you think. I look forward to the day when my undergraduate plays are buried in a single volume marked 'Juvenilia.' If I didn't know I can do a great deal better, I'd never write another line."

"Oh, now," Summerisle said. "*The Enchanted Isle* has greatness in it."

"Of course you and I think so," I said. "It's a hymn to Kanalism, and the rest is stolen from the greatest dramatist in Ur-Linguish. It's . . . academic, like all my others."

For the first time, I had his real attention and sympathy. "It *will* move them, Evan. I once asked you to be the poet of a Kanalist Renaissance, and I want you to know . . . you haven't let me down. If anything could bring our so-called Reformers back into the fold, it is your play. Only a few days away now, and everyone plans to attend."

I hadn't meant to expose my *post scriptum* blues, my preperformance jitters. But I couldn't recapture the elation I'd felt the night I'd finished writing; I didn't even want to discuss it, instead muttering, "We shouldn't talk about frat business here."

"On the contrary," Summerisle said. "This is the perfect setting. Look around. Don't you see anything familiar?"

I didn't get it. I'd assumed he'd chosen this meeting place precisely for its distance from the university and all the people there who had been our brothers and sisters once. But Summerisle never spoke without a reason. I took a good look at the old government buildings around the plaza's circular rim.

Nothing caught my eye except the workmen, who had put on false red beards like the waiter's. I assumed that their strange getup, and the scaffold they were constructing across the way, had something to do with one of Nexus's obscure local holidays. Certainly nothing familiar about them.

"I give up."

"You're resting your foot on it."

I drew back my boot from the base of the small fountain that marked the north compass-point of the plaza's circle.

"This old relic?" I said—but then, "Wait a minute. It's the same style as—"

"No," Summerisle said, shaking his head, "not just the same style. It's the *twin* of the fountain at the end of our Labyrinth. Two hundred years ago, the architect of the plaza was a brother Kanalist. He smuggled this piece into his design for symbolic reasons, as a way of secretly infusing the planet's government with our ideals—from the very fount."

"It's not quite the same as our fountain," I insisted.

He sighed with exasperation. "The esoteric markings were sanded off, of course. It had to be secret. The man on the street doesn't know that we're his friends, that half the signers of the Alignment Charter were Kanalists; he thinks we're a sinister conspiracy of the superrich."

"And isn't that true—now?" I said. "If Kostain and Von Bülow have their way, our fraternity will publicly come out for Reform. And what a reform! The entire human sphere to be run from a central government like one of the Column worlds. Chartered monopolies, oligarchy, and to hell with liberty."

Summerisle's gaunt face suddenly looked its fifty years. "If I really believed it . . . but the other chapters will never join that movement if ours repudiates it; they've always looked to us. And we can still turn around the 'Reformers' in our ranks."

"But if they choose to call themselves the 'true' Kanalists," I countered, "who would believe otherwise? Hasn't our frat always argued against the state?"

"Not limited states like the Alignment," he said. "An endless war against *all* government would only be another form of slavery. We do accept the normal human desire for organization, a state, a ruling class." He looked as earnest as if I were the one who had to be convinced. I didn't interrupt, but turned away to watch the workmen across the plaza. Their ladders and scaffolds went higher and higher, with no apparent object.

"But to safeguard the important thing, individual liberty," Summerisle went on, "there has to be a circulation of rulers. Natural leaders must be free to rise from whatever level they're born into, to replace incompetents born into the ruling class. Otherwise, right-wing dictatorships build on entrenched power, left-wing dictatorships on the frustration that results. But where power circulates freely, right and left check and balance; the apolitical majority is left in peace.

"That's why our predecessors placed such an emphasis on recruiting the younger ruling classes. On getting them to join the search for natural leaders among the underprivileged—who also became members, grateful to their new patrons. You, for instance, a rude colonial. Cliquish, I admit, but it's made for peaceful transitions of power, and something like meritocracy, for so many centuries—"

"Oh, come on," I said. "Not that again. I realize that all secret societies have done the 'ancient origin' bit. The Rosicrucians and the Masons pretended to have built the Pyramids. But don't you think the true history of Kanalism would be more interesting than the one we've made up?"

"The true history?"

"Spare me. Four, even three hundred years ago, no one had ever heard of Kanalism. It must have arisen among refugees, on one of the melting-pot worlds. There was an Earthborn Polish enclave on Volkhaven, for instance, called Sewer-Town—and 'sewer' is 'kanal' in Polska. Some place like that, where people would want to say, 'We're not just refugees without a world, we're a Folk, we have a Tradition.' They synthesized something out of memories of Earth's Western Civilization, but why should we be ashamed, since it was something good? Wouldn't it give Kanalism more legitimacy to drop this Minoan Crete myth and search out our real roots on Volkhaven, or Bonaventure, or Cath—"

Summerisle raised his hand for silence. "I applaud your skepticism and your research, but there are things you don't know. An older tradition, with no public membership like ours. I've read its history, passed down to me by the last Master of our chapter, and I believe in it."

"Where is it?" I asked. "All you received from the old Master was your ring, the scarf pins, and . . . oh, come on! The Book?"

We called it the Vice Book. Kanalist initiates were not hazed, but they were required to meet with the Master, in a drug-induced semihypnotic state, to confess their most harrowing sin or personal secret, which was added to a Book that only the Master might read. Every cult from Roman Catholicism to Chinese Communism has had some version of this ritual to level down, and bind together, its followers; but . . .

"Wasn't it you who thought that there was something un-Kanalist about our confessional?" Summerisle said. "You were right. It's a relatively recent practice. And unique to our Nexus University chapter. A tradition started only a few hundred years ago to conceal the real value of the Book from other chapters, which do not have one."

"We have the only Vice Book?"

"The only complete history of the Kanalist order from its founding," he said slowly and with satisfaction, "including secrets, esoteric lore of great power, for which humankind is not yet prepared."

"Oh yeah?" I said. "So ours is the only true chapter, and you the only true Master, is that it?"

"Not at all. Every individual Kanalist is his own spiritual sovereign. I do happen to have the one original Book, but I've also sworn never to forget that my Master's ring—like every chapter-master's ring—is only a copy of the original. If they were all destroyed, nothing essential would be lost. If all the Masters were corrupted, Kanalism itself would remain pure. 'The sun is new every day.' The entire Kanalist order could be reconstituted on the authority of the original Master's ring. And that ring is waiting, it will always be there, where Kanalism really started. Near the Labyrinth, in a mountain cave, on the isle of Crete, on Earth. That's the truth, Evan."

Summerisle wouldn't lie, but I didn't know what to make of this.

"Earth is gone, Master. Our chapter has sold out, and the others are following its lead. We've told them they're the enlightened ones, and now they want to rule the human sphere."

" 'The sun is new every day,' " he repeated, pointing at the fiery disc hanging above the workmen's rig. "We may yet turn them around. Perhaps your play will do it. Perhaps my Book."

"Oh, you have some bit of 'esoteric lore' that—"

"I was thinking of the vices recorded there. It would mean breaking a dozen oaths, but I do hold the power of blackmail over many of the Reformers."

I was astounded. But on second thought: "People wouldn't give up galactic hegemony for a bit of kiss-and-tell, Master."

He smiled sadly. "The scions of the great families have more interesting secrets than yours, Evan. Among the personal pecadilloes are perversion, rape, and manslaughter. Then there's the illegal trade or stolen patent or fraudulent deed behind the family fortune. And finally the political stuff: assassinations, treasonous alliances, crimes their parents and grandparents would kill to keep buried. Not everyone is so unlucky, of course; but there are key members of the cabal whom I could destroy—and they know it. But they also know I'd be violating everything I hold sacred if I did it."

"And can you do it?"

He sighed. "I think not. I'll fight them, if I have to, but not that way. And you, Odysseus? What'll you do if your play fails?"

"I've been thinking about it," I began.

"Daydreaming, you mean—"

"And I've found the perfect solution," I said. "I'll join a navy survey."

I could see that Summerisle didn't like it. He turned away to watch the workmen. They seemed to have finished their scaffold to nowhere, and stood on its various ladders watching as one man at the top level, just beneath our view of the sun, crouched over a small vat of liquid and stirred it. Baffling. Even more so, when his false beard slipped, and for a disquieting moment I thought I recognized him—Esterhazy, some name like that?—but I had to explain myself:

"Don't you see? In time, this Reform extremism will divide into factions and destroy itself, like all campus movements. Working people in the real world have too much sense to give up the Federal Alignment. Meanwhile I'll go on a long survey tour, and come back wealthy to a world that's forgotten both big government *and* my early plays. And I'll be making a statement by doing it, too. The navy is Federalist, and I'll stand with it."

For a long time Summerisle said nothing. We just sat and

watched the workman as he swished a metal hoop in the vat and began to blow bubbles.

"Some sort of holiday celebration?" I asked finally.

Summerisle turned back to me. "You're Odysseus, and must wander," he said. "You're a poet, and must dream. But if you can't tell dreams from reality, you will wander forever. 'The waking follow a common path, but the dreamer enters a universe of his own.' Old Kanalist proverb."

"The hell you say! Heraclitus, by way of Plutarch. I know, I know—both early Kanalists. Save it for the freshmen."

He wasn't diverted from his course. "You play the tough guy who wants to make a fortune and build a new career, but I see the daydreams behind this. A shipboard emergency; the captain gone; everyone looking to you; the fate of the ship, of the Alignment, of the universe itself hanging on your coolness and quick wits. It's the child in you, Evan, which we all love—but it can lead you into danger. Are you serious about this plan?"

"As a matter of fact, I am."

"Then there's something you should know. I can't name names, because of the oaths I've taken, but among the confessions in the Vice Book I have pieced together a story. I think I can honorably tell you its bare outline. The navy is steadfast for the Alignment, it's true. In part that's because the cream of its officers are sent to Nexus U. for advanced studies, and our chapter of the fraternity often recruits them and molds their ideals. But that cuts both ways. Just as the oligarchs of the Column worlds have infiltrated our chapter this past year, there is a power-seeking cabal within the navy which has been trying to do the same thing for over a century. They are known only as the Few, and they would put the human sphere under a military dictatorship. Sometimes we convert them, sometimes they convert us. I believe that eighty or ninety years ago, a Master of our chapter allowed them access to some of the most powerful secrets in the Book, and that they have been exploiting this forbidden lore ever since."

"Ah, the forbidden lore again." There's a child in every guru, too, and as much as I respected Summerisle's genuine spiritual attainments, I'd long since learned to discount his rumors of Vast Forces Out There.

"Take this seriously, Evan! The Few still exist, and nothing is beyond them. Not murder, not the hijacking of naval vessels to build their own secret fleet—nothing. I suspect they are supporting Reform, for their own purposes. That strong central government would be a lot easier to take over, when the time came, than all the Alignment's autonomous planets. So don't be sure you can avoid the Reform struggle in the navy. If you put ten years and twenty parsecs behind you—keep watching your back."

At the top of the scaffold, the workman kept blowing large bubbles, but most of them broke immediately.

"Okay, Master," I said gently. "But you're the one who should worry. You've got that Book, and the Reformers know it. I don't have any real family left; my home world never understood me; the woman I loved considers me a political enemy. I've nothing to hold me in this decade except you, my friend. Do you need help—someone to share your secrets, or—"

He shook his head, smiling. "I've already taught you too much. 'A little learning is a dangerous thing.' Trust me, as Pope of our little order, to do what's best, even if it means abjuring the mystical lore forever, like your Prospero. If necessary, I can hide the Book in a place where it will be safe for centuries, until the next Master comes to find it." He looked at me intently. "And he will know where to look."

Those words always come back so precisely, the clue I wasn't able to read. Near the Labyrinth, in a mountain cave, on the isle of Crete, on Earth? No, he wouldn't have spelled it out that way . . . But what's this next part?

Summerisle turns, and signals to the man on top of the scaffold, who blows a bigger bubble than all the rest, and this one hangs in the sky next to the sun, glowing nacreously. And suddenly I've had enough of this game, and cry out, "I give up! What holiday is it?"

But Summerisle says nothing, as the man on the scaffold reaches to one side of the glowing bubble—and plucks down the sun. It's just a disc of brass.

And the sky goes black, except for the sickly glow of the suspended bubble, and the men become shadow-men, black silhouettes except for the stupid red beards. They climb down from their rickety structure and come solemnly toward us in funeral procession, the bearer of the brass sun in the lead. Thunder sounds in the distance like the muffled drum of a dead march.

"This didn't happen," I say. "It was a spring morning. What day is this?"

And as the procession reaches us, black rain begins to fall in torrents. The beards are washed from the shadow faces; for a moment I see Entzwame again, and recognize him for the chief petty officer he was. And then the shadow-men are all washed away, as Summerisle presses the brass-colored data disk into my hand, and I see the name of the ship engraved in it, and he speaks with compassion but no mercy:

"It's Barbarossa Day."

Thunder, lightning, the rain slicing down, as he stands to slap me heavily across the face, shouting, "Every day is Barbarossa Day, *for the man who lives in the past! Anything is possible, you can always start over, but only in the present, Odysseus!"* Slap! *"Only if you wake up"*—Whap!—*"to what's real!"*

Thunderclap. I was falling in stormy darkness, through rain which I could hear but not feel, protected in an invisible bubble from the lightning and the wind. Not alone; a trapped animal moaned at my side, the sort of blatant symbol that gives my dreams away but does not end them; I felt the whimpering creature's warmth but could not see it. Falling, falling, helpless, and this time I knew it was not a dream . . .

Chapter Four

IT WAS NOT a dream, it was an aerofoil shuttle plunging through a lightning storm. I found myself in a Column uniform and an upright seat, with Bunny Velasquez moaning and whimpering like a trapped animal next to me.

The blinding flash was silent, but I jerked against the straps that held me to the framework couch, and a boom of thunder followed. The usual moment of traumatic amnesia had passed; I could reel in a whole, if flimsy, skein of connective memories.

Up to this point, our journey from Zenobia to Newcount Two had been speedy and uneventful. After the previous Non-Human Artifacts sub-commissioner's uniform had been retailored for me in the orbital mall off Orlo, we took a suite on a luxury liner, and Condé's agent T'ung stopped tailing us. Condé knew I could never turn state's evidence once I'd publicly appeared in Column whites. I was committed for the duration.

I'd come up with the new sub-commissioner's name myself: "Alun Parker," very old-worlds. I'd tried to pump Velasquez on the duties expected of me, but he wasn't much help. Sometimes he insisted that as aide-de-camp he'd done all the sub-commissioner's work for him; sometimes he admitted listlessly that there was nothing to it anyway—just hosting dinners along the museum circuit and reporting any new alien finds to more competent, nonpolitical authorities.

That was Bunny's style in a nutshell. He couldn't accept the role of underling, in or out of the impersonation, but his attempts to assert his own importance were always halfhearted and pathetic. The spoiled child of minor nobility, he'd never had to learn how to get along with lesser humans, keeping us all at a distance with his exhaustive arsenal of sneers and shrugs.

I never did manage to get a full briefing out of him. He couldn't summon enough interest to describe the Stone Hut ruins on Newcount Two, for instance, but I gathered that there was nothing to them anyway—aside from Condé's barrow, and the new sub-commissioner wasn't supposed to know about that. The new sub-commissioner didn't know much else, either.

The job manual in the previous sub-commissioner's kit included a full chapter on inspecting a dig—which medals to wear, a seating chart for dinner, and similar vital details. But there were also indications that a sub-commissioner might actually have a little background in archaeology. Complete ignorance was presumably reserved for full commissioners. I would just have to fake my way somehow. At least I'd had a good classical education, ancient languages and history.

For the last leg of the trip we requisitioned a packet boat from the nearest Swathe mail depot—our first perk as Column officials, our first big step as impostors.

Having undergone bio-decon and omniphylaxis en route, we weren't delayed by class-three quarantine restrictions. But we had to check in at one of Newcount Two's defense outposts—a station Mehta's contractors were still completing—in rotosynchronous orbit above the only large continent. There we commanded a shuttle to take us down.

The shuttle pilot had objected to the unexpected trip. And when I woke up he was taking it out on us.

The g force indicated that we had to pay for his initial overspeed with heavy deceleration now, even though already deep in the lower atmosphere, the viewpoot shields peeled back to provide a scarier view. Lightning flickered without letup amid anvil-shaped clouds, while thunder shock-waves rolled in from near and far to provide syncopation and suspense.

But in the end an insanely relaxed voice from the cockpit informed us that we were coming in to land, and that the local time at our destination would be early afternoon, in a twenty-two-hour day. The usual synchronization tones were played for the benefit of our wristcomps: a local minute in local seconds.

I'd had less than an hour's sleep. That meant flight lag on top of everything else—with a life-or-death performance only minutes away, and my assistant reduced to jelly at my side. Fed up and furious, I decided that the sub-commissioner would be fed up, too; I held on to my anger through touchdown and rollout.

The last few drops of cold rain rattled on the exit ramp, hissed against the hot skin of the shuttle. Bunny had wobbled down ahead of me, and stood, still green-faced, staring at his watch and tapping his foot impatiently, as though his own aide-de-camp were holding him up. This seemed to puzzle the woman standing next to him. She looked toward me as I stepped out of the shuttle. A sudden break in the clouds lit a golden nimbus around her head; the moment would pass, but the impression would linger.

"Your Excellency," Bunny said while I was still on the ramp, "let me present Freem'ss Ariel Nimitz, the managing director here. Freem'ss Nimitz, His Excellency Alun Parker, Sub-Commissioner for Non-Human Artifacts."

The clouds healed and I remembered to scowl. A tropical breeze, freshened by rain, played in the undisciplined blonde hair of a compact and shapely young woman in a severe business tunic. There was a large groundcar behind her, and as I said, "How do you do?" another one approached us from the direction of a small structure which, judging by its satellite dish, served the field as a control tower.

"Very well, thank you, Excellency," Ariel replied as I reached ground level. Now her face was framed by a rainbow on the horizon, artistically off-center. Bright blue eyes discreetly looked me up and down. Something in the set of her mouth, soft and generous in an otherwise businesslike face, led me to believe that I was making an impression, too. Not difficult, given a snow-white Column uniform in these gloomy surroundings—a gray basalt landing field, dirty green bowl of hills in every distance, gray-green storm clouds overhead.

"I'm one of Senator Mehta's executive assistants," she was saying. "I've planned a small—"

Screeching to a halt on the wet pavement, the arriving car overshot the nose of the shuttle. A tall, dark man emerged from the driver's seat and headed for the ramp. He checked himself before me and unclenched his fists.

Ariel hesitated. "Excellency, may I present Citizen Wu Arsenovich, Chief Contractor. Citizen, this is—"

"Excellency." He bowed stiffly, his angry face frozen. "An honor, sir. I hope you'll forgive me, but a disciplinary matter requires immediate attention."

We both looked in the direction of the shuttle's cockpit.

"Don't let me detain you," I said.

The chief contractor muttered thanks, flew up the steps, and slammed the hatch closed.

Ariel took a controlled breath and started over. "I've planned a small dinner at the hotel this evening. Just Your Excellency, Citizen Velasquez, Chief Arsenovich, myself of course, and Citizen Foyle to speak for the archaeologists. She's put together a quick overview of the Stone Hut site—a rather dry dig, I think they call it—so that you can lift off again tomorrow. I know these levy ships don't like to hang around long, and—"

It was no good. True, I wanted nothing more than to clear the system, space the uniform, and concoct a new identity. But the simplest, safest course was to play out Condé's game, fast and hard. For one thing, I needed his payment as getaway money.

"Freem'ss Nimitz," I said, "*I* will decide what I shall do here, and when to leave. What you call a 'rather dry dig' might be a dangerously incompetent one. And there's no point in plying me with dinner, since—to me—this is still two hours into a sleep cycle. As for the levy ship, it will of course wait in orbit for as long as I require."

Speechless, she began to pale. I paused a moment for effect, and to consider. Condé's spies had estimated Mehta's next arrival on Newcount to be a month or two away. A guess only; Mehta was fanatically secretive. But once the senator did show up, it would be too risky to interfere with his excavation. All Mehta had to do was send a courier Columnward, complaining about "this Nosy Parker you've sent here," and Velasquez and I would be exposed as frauds.

The plan was for me to brake the dig hard, install Bunny as overseer, and leave, within as few days as I could manage. Bunny was willing to stay on longer, but only if I'd convinced the locals he bore my authority—and if I could supply a reliable margin of safety by learning the exact date of Mehta's next visit.

I'd never have a better opportunity.

"I'd hoped that Senator Mehta would be here to meet me," I said. "Certainly, as someone engaged in a *private* excavation, he would be wise—"

"Excellency, we were given no notice of this visit prior to yesterday's transmission. Senator Mehta isn't even in this system, and I am not at liberty to divulge—"

"When might I see him, then? I assume he does take an interest in the work here—in the palace you're building for him, if nothing else. When's his next inspection?"

"As far as exact arrival times, Excellency, there are certain security concerns—"

"Which the Column shares. But I assume it's not the *Column* that the senator fears?"

She exhaled heavily. "Of course not, Excellency. And of course we'll be glad if you wish to stay with us for the next ten days, until the senator's arrival. I know he'd want you to spend that time in his personal hotel suite. I'd planned a briefer visit only for your convenience. After all," she added in a reasonable tone, while I thought *Ten days!* and tried to catch Bunny's eye, "the previous sub-commissioner saw the Stone Huts, and approved our plans some months ago, and Citizen Velasquez was with him. A quick update was all we thought you'd want."

I did have what I wanted, and if I wanted anything else, I'd have to quit towering and glowering.

"I see your point, Freem'ss. I'm sure I owe you an apology—which I can make more sincerely after I've had a little sleep. Meanwhile, please feel free to drop the 'Your Excellency.' Those formalities are just too unwieldy out here in the field." Antierotic, too. Why limit the potential of my role? "And I do want to meet with the archaeologists as soon as possible. I know their workday begins at sunrise, but if I went to bed now, we might be able to fly out and meet them for breakfast. Could you please arrange that?"

"Certainly . . . sir," she said, with a relieved smile. "And you may call me Ariel."

"Thank you. You mentioned a hotel?"

"Yes, sir." She gestured at the largest of a few low buildings at the tarmac's edge. "For the senator's guests, at least until the palace is completed. There's also a small office building, and we're putting up some apartment blocks for the workers—"

"A whole town?"

"Not really, sir. Senator Mehta intends to retire here. The planet will remain undeveloped, peaceful. A retreat."

Chief Contractor Arsenovich, looking much more peaceful himself, clattered heavily down the ramp.

"Chief," Ariel said, "We'll need one of Construction's flitters tomorrow morning, around four. We may be gone all day."

"Impossible."

"Oh, I think you'll manage," she said with weighty quietness, and he broke stride long enough to give in. He seemed used to it. A young woman for her responsibilities, and as overawed by Column whites as anyone, but competent and sharp. Attractive, but a potential danger. And aren't they all?

Despite what I'd said to Ariel, I didn't expect to sleep—or want to. The trauma dreams had been more frequent and more vicious ever since I'd entered the Blue Swathe. Reminders, perhaps, that even in this least-oppressed of the Column's domains, I did not deserve to be free. I lay sleepless for a few hours, occasionally massaging the last joint of my left hand's ring finger. That segment of bone is artificial, a repository for the information once stored on the data disk of the survey cruiser *Barbarossa*, the lost *Barbarossa*, my ship.

Chapter Five

THE NEXT MORNING I showered, shaved, and dressed in the senatorial suite's huge bathroom, and when I came out into the foyer I saw a cold-eyed official of the Column come striding through the door at the other end. His sinister smile gave way to surprise like my own. I stopped dead, and so did he.

It was a "rightway mirror" fitted to the back of the door; I hadn't noticed it earlier, entering from the corridor. Not the usual, recognizable mirror image, but re-reversed as in a photograph. I'd always hated that effect.

But this time I paused to see myself as others saw me, thinking about the sky-blue eyes I'd been introduced to nine hours before. And let the worst be admitted. Evan Larkspur, author of the *New Satires*, last true (Old Rite) Kanalist, enemy of all dictatorships—and yes, that smirking fellow in the glass—loved his Column uniform, from the patent-leather half boots to the gold piping on the erect collar.

A comic-opera costume, sure. At Nexus U. we used to mock the "self-defense forces" of the so-called First Column worlds for having to wear it. But if a cluster of local governments wanted to play Prussian, well, that was the price of our tolerant federal system, and a good joke at least. And then, at one of those interminable bottle parties at the Kanalist lodge, someone—Kostain, de Bourbon?—had suggested similar white tunics as perfect for the new central government the Reform group was pushing: "Like blank pages for a new constitution." And I'd laughed it off, until I'd realized that everyone was staring at me, that politics had taken an ominous turn while I'd been immersed in my rewrite of *Cyrano* . . . A hundred years ago; no one dares to laugh now. But.

But the outfit flattered me unmercifully. I'd had to shave my black Odyssean beard before the trip—too un-Column—but in white the resulting pallor looked pink and healthy. Physical fitness, in me owed entirely to a life on the run, makes the most of military tailoring. My face, nondescript when it's not unpleasantly sardonic, looks aristocratic and knowing above the trappings of power. And the touch of theater I'd insisted upon, the streaks of gray at the temples, completed the picture: some archangel just a little too clever to fall, the one who'd inherited Lucifer's place and expense account.

Which reminded me. I had urgent business to discuss with Bunny Velasquez.

He was waiting in the lobby of the hotel, next to travel bags packed for the day's field trip. The building was dead, even the lights seeming pale and exhausted an hour before dawn; there appeared to be no other guests, and the servants were still asleep. It was like a stage set, and we lowered our voices as if afraid of the audience.

"Only ten days," I said. "Too bad, but it does simplify things."

"Now just look," Bunny rushed, as if he'd been nerving himself up to it for hours. "We can't leave, understand?"

"Oh, we'll try to do the job first," I said. "Whatever we can to bring the dig to a standstill. But Mehta's just as likely to be a week early. And if I leave in forty-eight hours, you'll have to go, too; there's no way to summon another ship in time."

He reached up, with the astounding unself-consciousness of the very rich, to pull on his lower lip as an aid to thought. Maddening. Too timid to come here alone, but too afraid of Condé to leave.

"Arrange it right now," I insisted. "Call the packet boat and tell the captain to hang on another forty-eight hours, because we're leaving with him."

"I don't see how I could," Bunny said.

"Well, let's not argue," I said reasonably, and, grabbing him by belt and collar, backed him up against the nearest wall. "Let's just do what I say, and review the decision in the maturity of old age. All right?"

Limp, but glaring down at me from his greater height, he hissed, "Don't get physical with me, playactor! At school I won two ribbons in Shih Ho!"

After enough of a pause I let him go. You never know—prep schools do offer the martial arts, while my own repertoire is limited to basic military stuff and a few dirty tricks.

"I could call the ship myself," I said, "but our cover requires my aide to do it for me. Now get this: later today, in front of everyone, I'm going to ask you if you've made the call I ordered. The cover binds you, too."

His face was sullen, but he said, "All right, all right. I'll take care of it now and join you at the flitter. The radio is in the manager's office." I didn't think to ask how he knew this. He wandered off without my bag, and I had to remind him to carry it.

Ariel found me soon after that. She suggested some tea to tide us over until breakfast at the Stone Hut site, and led me outside, through warm darkness and a jasmine-scented garden, toward the commissary. I noted with appreciation that she was less severely dressed today, her black slacks tailored to show off the tidy curves of her legs. Apologizing for my strategic bad temper of the day before, I said I hoped I'd be less of a bear this morning.

"Bear?"

Unsure whether it was the animal or the idiom that was unfamiliar, I tried "Grouch."

She laughed so merrily that I wondered about that one, too. The fringe worlds just barely speak the same Interlingua, for all the efforts of universal education. And despite seven years in this century and a talent for mimicry, I still dated myself at times.

The garden path at our feet glowed dimly with guide lights, and she pointed out a few flowers; we exchanged the different names we knew them by. She remained attentive and amused.

All very ingratiating. She must have been an ambitious girl to have reached her present position in her late twenties, but she didn't strike me as a sycophant. Just a healthy young woman marooned for months on a planet where the only men were off-limits, under her command. And I had something else going for me; I'd sensed it the day before when she looked over my uniform, and now, electrically, when she inquired about one of "my" service medals, actually brushing her fingers against it. Hint of a fetish? That entertaining possibility sent the blood rushing to my brain and elsewhere. Forty-eight hours would still leave tonight free. *Screw everything up,* Condé had said, *in and out.*

The commissary's tea was as bracing as tea ever is. Ariel gave a lusty yawn. "I guess I'm ready to face Foyle now," she said as we went outside again, heading for the lit end of the complex's landing field.

"Foyle?"

"No first name, or at least she doesn't use it. She's the archaeologist you . . . didn't care to see last night. Sir. Very bright, very talented. A wonderful person once you get to know her, but she can be hard to handle." Some sleepy process of free association made her add, "A widow, I think."

"She's in charge of the dig?"

Ariel frowned. "No one's in charge that I can see. They're just guests, sir, amateurs on vacation." She seemed a little embarrassed. "I asked Foyle to make the presentation because she's the only one who might do it . . . coherently."

The flitter stood in the center of a ring of bright lights, its blowers and foils trimmed in a military fashion. It was a heavy workhorse model, not the sleek executive bird I'd been expecting, with an extra impeller on each stubby wing for cargo lifts. And it was old, two or three times rebuilt; no advance on the military jobs I'd trained in so many years before. Bunny was making himself useful by kicking one of the tires.

A side access panel hung open, and as we approached, a pair of long legs emerged, feet first. When they found the tarmac, an equally lithe and slender torso followed, in a form-fitting dove-gray jumpsuit stained here and there with oil. The whole woman, when finally unfolded, was tall enough to look me level in the eyes, and I am not short. Her own eyes, above high cheekbones and an assertive straight nose, flashed green in the bright lights; their lids lent them a slight tilt that seemed to go with the touch of copper in her complexion.

I believe in first impressions, emblems, and omens. Foyle held a torque driver and a work light as if they were sword and scepter. Handsome rather than beautiful in her early thirties, she was still a little too good to be true, and I was almost relieved when she unpeeled her protective rubber skullcap and a wealth of glossy hair fell to her shoulders, surprisingly red. I was saved. My tastes are broad, but I have a definite aversion to redheads. Think of it as a conditioned response—or a dueling scar.

"Citizen Foyle, I take it." She just nodded, and the curl of her upper lip said *go to hell*. A much more rational reaction to the Column uniform than Ariel's, actually, but it was going to be hard not to take it personally.

"Archaeologist and mechanic, too?" I said.

"I *told* her she should let the locals handle all repairs, Excellency," Bunny said.

"He told me that," Foyle said dryly. "It was just a few bolt heads that the computer considered too tight. Ground crews tend to ignore those." She racked the tools, closed the access port, and shot the cams home. "I don't fly what I can't fix," she added. Then she ascended as lightly, and claimed the pilot's seat as definitely, as any cat.

Bunny took the other front seat without asking, but I was just as glad to sit with Ariel in back. As I pulled down the overhead door, Foyle checked her repair work on the diagnostic box. I noted with approval that she had pushed the Standard F dash over to Bunny's side, out of her way, and had brought the manual controls forward instead. She knew how to use them; our liftoff was as smooth as Ariel's cheek—

Which, not too long afterward, came to rest against my shoulder. Ariel had fallen sound asleep. The cabin was nearly dark, the white noise of the impellers as lulling as silence. The frame of renegade blonde curls—some executive cut outgrown, so far from civilization—still lent her an adolescent air. But her other features were so faint in the starlight as to suggest only the generalized female. *Another Dark Lady, another mystery, though never the same.* Pale skin unblemished, fine nose uptilted, gullwinged brows delicately traced.

Not quite the same line of jaw. Nor neck, nor ears, nor time to argue the finer points, my love," I said, "so long as we agree on emotions, principles, aesthetics."

"But do we?" Domina asked in the lower range of that spine-tingling contralto, and would have finished buttoning her dress if I hadn't slipped my hands in again. We swayed together lip to lip until we were propped against our own flickering shadows on the wall of the Labyrinth entrance. But when she finally pulled away, her face was cool and ironical, only the flare of her aristocratic nostrils suggesting the hammering heartbeat I'd just felt beneath my fingers. "You're all emotion, darling. Aesthetics are your *only* principles."

Somehow I'd lost the topic of conversation. Wild contrasts in the candlelight: the whiteness of her skin, the darkness of her eyes and nipples; the quintessentially female neck, the almost soldierly haircut; the seductive softness, the will to power.

"But it's all here," I said, trying to lead her inside the maze. "It's not just a game and a joke to me. It's our whole heritage. If I could get them all to understand it, to feel it, just to see it as they walk it. Do the ritual for real, the way it was intended . . ."

"The way you will know it?" Domina said, her voice like mocking music. "They must grope their way along the Shining Fare, but it's all right for you to sneak in at night and memorize it."

"I told you, it has to be part of my play—"

"In other words, you have to give away the deepest secret of the fraternity, have to be above it all, master of the game. No, don't defend yourself. This is the Larkspur I love. Why don't you just wake up? Admit you're one of us, the natural rulers of the human sphere?"

"I want to wake *you* up, Domina. Let me show you something."

"*I've* been through it, darling. Properly. I *know* what lies at the center of things."

But I thought that if I took the candle, she would have to follow me into the maze . . .

Image of Odysseus, disguised in a beggar's rags. The suitors surround him, no longer laughing, for he has strung the great bow and suddenly looks capable of sending the arrow down the line of double axes, threading that narrow channel between the recurving upper blades.

". . . or Labyrinth, possibly named for the Labrys, or sacred double axe, by people who couldn't spell very well,'' droned my guide.

''And here is the first wall mosaic,'' he went on. '' 'The Return of Odysseus'—I see you came in costume for this, sir.''

I looked down and discovered that I was indeed wearing my *Odysseus in Phaiacia* outfit. When I looked around for Domina, the other tourists, always nebulous figures, faded away entirely.

The guide, a gaunt, fiery-eyed man in chiton and sandals, shifted back into his spiel as we continued walking: ''. . . symbolizing the Kanalist belief in the perpetual possibility of spiritual rebirth, of beginning anew, of . . . of—''

''Starting over?'' I suggested.

''Guess I'll have to,'' he said. ''I've lost my place.''

''Damn. Weren't we supposed to unwind a ball of string or something behind us?''

''Lost my place in the *speech*,'' he said. ''I never lose my place in the *Labyrinth*, you fool. I designed it.''

''Oh, then you're . . . ?''

''*Daedalus* is the name you're pretending you could remember,'' he said. ''A minor myth—like you.''

At this point, perhaps, he was strapping me into my wings. He was already wearing his—a kitelike framework out of a Da Vinci drawing, eagle feathers affixed with wax paste.

''But I do remember you,'' I said as we took flight. ''You built the Labyrinth for King Minos of Crete, to conceal his wife's son, the Minotaur. But then he began to sacrifice children from your home city to the monster. You turned against him and were imprisoned in the maze yourself, along with your own child, Whatsisname.''

''Icarus,'' Daedalus said sadly.

There'd been no ceiling to the maze, and now we were flying hundreds of meters above it, able to make out the spiraling crenellations of its scheme. We circled its center, something silvery—a pool?

''I forget what happens after that,'' I admitted, uncomfortable. It was hot up there, so close to the sun. ''Could be a play in it for me, though.''

''I made us artificial wings, and we flew away, Icarus and I.''

''Just like that?'' I said. ''Isn't that a little—''

''Escapist? But isn't that the sort of thing you're famous for, Lieutenant Larkspur?''

I flew a little higher than he, to change the subject. ''Tell me, were you really the first Kanalist? Frat mythology aside, I mean. Were you really . . . spiritually reborn?"

He nodded slowly. "Yes. But I had to die first. I had to lose my son, my son."

And then the wax in my wings melted, of course, feathers swirling down, and with a sickening lurch the air that had been buoying me up gave way. I heard a mocking contralto laugh and fell, slowly and flutteringly for a moment, then like a stone, and facefirst. I was directly over the center of the maze, the pool of water that turned out not to be water, now that it hurtled closer and larger. Glass. A glass coffin with razor-sharp edges and a mirrored bottom that reflected a dot that became a blob that became a screaming face, a face that shattered—

As I jerked awake, sweating tears. Of the recurring ones, Nightmare Number Two. The same old memories, the same lost Dark Lady, sensing that another woman had touched me, however lightly. Ariel had shifted against the window at my sudden move, but she was still asleep, still caught up in the dying night. I waited for the flitter to carry us east and clear of it.

Gloomy minutes passed. I perched on the end of my seat and leaned forward into the red and green instrument lights.

"I'm glad to see you prefer the manual controls," I said. "I never trust an emulator board myself."

But Foyle looked surprised. "You have to trust them most of the time," she said. "It's that or earn a new set of licenses, every planet you go to."

I saw her point. One wouldn't want to live the way they did in classical times: model variations from nation to nation, and technology remaking the world beneath everyone's feet every twenty years. But the Standard Flitter solution insults the integrity of well-made machines. One admires the classic simplicity of the Rawlins-Kurosawa flitter control panel, but no one's made an RK chassis in five hundred years. The emulator board has to translate RK commands into whatever applies to the model you're actually flying, and—

"The problem arises," I said, "when things go wrong. The malfunctions are reported to you in Standard F terms that may have little to do with your actual machine. You respond, and sure, your command is supposed to be translated into something appropriate to the situation, but how precise can an analogy be? I always fly bare-stick when I can."

Foyle sounded appalled. "You must have run into some incredibly archaic equipment somewhere. They fixed those interface bugs decades ago. I just prefer the feel of the manuals, that's all. I don't think they're any safer."

"Less safe, if anything," Bunny insisted.

"What is he *for*, anyway?" she asked me.

"Now, now," I said.

"Remind him that I have licenses in five classes. I fly my own freighter, for God's sake. Don't pretend you haven't both read the Shadow file on me."

I saw Bunny sit up straighter in his seat. So she had a record of some kind. She still retained full citizenship, though, so it couldn't be too bad. It was typical of her generation to think that every last branch and twig of the Column's clumsy bureaucracy had access to secret police files. The naïveté of cynicism.

"I'm sure the senator checked you out," I said. "But it's not really our department."

She made an unbelieving noise.

"How does a private citizen come to own a freighter?" I asked. "And what does it have to do with archaeology?"

She was silent for a long time. I watched her fingers move among the red and green instrument lights.

"I spent . . . the family fortune on it," she said finally. "It's my livelihood now. Charter transport. I've no unpaid bills, and I break even. I'd do better, but I like to stick to the art and archaeology trade. Newcount Two is the fieldwork I need for my doctorate. That will open the way toward more specialized contracts. Though I must say, if I'd known how little there was here . . ."

"Yes, there's not much to it, is there? I don't suppose the site will be visible from the air?"

"What? There'll be enough light by the time we arrive, if that's what you mean. Look at the horizon."

"The stars are still bright, though." I pointed behind her left shoulder. "Unless that's one of the defense satellites."

"That's Catharensis," she said. "Only a few light-years away. Remember it, if you get lost on the ground at night here. It's more or less a polestar in the north."

"*The* Catharensis? I've always wanted to visit Catharensis Five."

"Strange choice for a Column official. The cradle of so many heresies—the Green Church, the Sisterhood of Astarte. All those freedom-loving survivals from colonial times."

"Political Virtue fascinated by Vice," I said, and won an

honest laugh from her. I leaned back into my seat, afraid of falling out of character.

And what *about* the site? I thought. Stone Huts. A few crumbled stone walls inside a hole in the ground. Presumably several months' worth of hole. Shored up, like a mine shaft, maybe? Cave it in somehow, and set their whole schedule back to zero?

Ariel was awake again, nose pressed to her window. "There's the marsh," she said. "Getting close now."

I leaned over her shoulder. The sky continued to lighten, but the ground immediately below was still black in the shadow of a ridge to the east.

"Marsh lights, three thirty degrees low," Foyle announced.

At first I saw nothing. Then I discerned a general glow that soon resolved itself into a number of phosphorescent blue wraiths, flickering elusively in a greener field of radiance.

"What is this?" I asked.

"Bioluminescence from the marsh algae," Foyle said. "Nothing mysterious there. The bluer lights are probably methane flares. But every now and then—and only from the air—we see an especially bright one. There, look!"

I tried to get a fix on the white flash, but was distracted—our running lights had gone out. They came back on again in an instant.

"I'm piloting this boat," Foyle snapped. "Do not touch the controls."

"You did it! You slapped my hand!" Velasquez said incredulously. "And watch how you address me, you—"

"Bunny," I warned.

"You may care nothing for your own dignity, *Excellency*," he said, "but when she addresses me, she—"

"She does so as the captain of the vessel," I said. "The rank has privileges. And that reminds me." The occasion was public enough, and it would put him in his place. "What did the captain of the levy ship say when you told him to wait for us?"

Bunny turned, to let me see his smile. "It was as I feared, Excellency. I couldn't catch him."

"Catch him?"

"A victim of my own promptness, I'm afraid. I'd radioed our permission to leave last night, as soon as we arrived. So he had nine hours to reach the sun before Your Excellency changed his mind this morning."

"Must have gone to two-percent lightspeed," Foyle commented. "Hard on the converters."

"He had mail to deliver." Bunny was still grinning—as though it wouldn't be his head in the noose, too, if we stayed too long.

"We expect a parts boat in a week or two," Ariel offered. "If there's a problem."

I didn't say anything. One week might get us out before Mehta arrived. Two?

"And here's the site," Foyle said as we cleared the ridge. "You wanted to see it."

The first light of dawn disclosed a vast prairie. Dotted about it were some crude structures. Imagine a simple card house, only made with thick black dominoes. Now imagine dozens of them, scores, and scattered over several square kilometers. And the smallest was over twenty meters tall.

"Those are the Stone Huts?" I asked.

"You sound . . . surprised," said Foyle.

I leaned back and closed my eyes. "Thought they'd be bigger."

Chapter Six

"THOSE MYSTERIOUS LIGHTS in the marsh?" said Helen Hogg-Smythe, passing her stuffed quail with a good cook's confidence. "*Ignis fatuus*, Commissioner: 'foolish fire.' The original meaning of the Ur-Linguish expression 'will-of-the-wisp.' Not to be confused with 'foxfire'—the glow of the marsh algae, or of fungi in rotting wood."

"Or with 'false fire,' " I said, watching Bunny's face closely across the breakfast table. "A covert signal flashed by night." He did not meet my eyes.

" 'What, frighted with false fire?' " the old woman quoted, not quite knocking over Ariel's glass with one sleeve of her elaborate safari costume. "And then there's the 'cold fire' of the glowworm. 'Pale and ineffectual,' as the same poet says."

"*Romeo and Juliet*," I noted. "Act One?"

"A fellow classicist—what splendid luck! The current generation," she said darkly, "recognizes nothing but song lyrics and Larkspur."

Polite laughter and objections went around the table, adding to the dinner-party atmosphere. The archaeologists must have turned out of bed earlier than we had, to lay on such a feast for their sub-commissioner.

The camp had come into view as soon as we'd flown over the ridge. Just beyond the crest—a tiny plateau crowned with a weird balancing-rock formation—paths led down to a flat break in the wooded hillside overlooking the prairie. There a few prefabricated canvas buildings with metal frames, ugly but serviceable, stood next to a landing pad sketched out with flares. Nothing on the outside had prepared me for the dim but well-stocked cookhouse, its trestle table dolled up with a linen cloth, real glasses, and candles.

Citizen Hogg-Smythe—the surname pronounced, perversely, as if it were a synonym for "pork"—took credit for the bird's mushroom stuffing, the fruit salad, and the sauce for the quail's eggs on rice, all excellent. She apparently considered herself old enough to indulge a penchant for prosiness and eccentric dress. One hundred twenty-odd, I guessed, despite her wiry energy—perhaps the final decade left to her. But it was clear that she remained good at whatever she put her hand to, and retained keener wits than most of the younger members of the party.

There were six of these, five males and Foyle, mostly academics in fields other than archaeology. The one who had baked the breads, a short, fat sociologist named Ruy Lagado, had brought along his adolescent son Harry; otherwise the ages appeared to range between thirty and sixty—no one save Hogg-Smythe much older than I might be, with the dyed streaks in my hair. This made their constant deference feel less unnatural, though I still quashed the 'Excellency' business in favor of 'Commissioner' or 'Sir.'

I'd managed to keep the small talk away from archaeology, though the threat couldn't be warded off much longer.

"But the flare I saw in the marsh was so *bright*," I said. "I would expect gas discharges to be, as you say, wisps. Like this."

I made a fluttering conjuror's pass above one of the candles, and a half-dozen tiny ghost flames danced in midair beneath my fingers, to disappear as suddenly.

"How did you *do* that, sir?" gawky young Harry Lagado asked, surprised out of boredom. He wasn't the only one. Ariel applauded lightly, tongue in cheek, and Foyle aimed a narrow-eyed stare that caught me up short.

"Just a trick," I said, and shrugged. "We're all amateurs at something."

I can't resist table magic. It's so easy, for one thing, with everyone distracted and no one expecting it. Props are always at hand—in this case, a pinch of fine flour from one of the storage cans stacked under the table; the trick is to release it thinly enough to be both invisible and flammable. And I'd wanted to further my designs on Ariel. Card tricks bore women, but sleight-of-hand suggests a certain useful dexterity.

"Well. The marsh is a magician, too," said Citizen Piet Wongama. Dark-haired and heavily freckled, he was so tall that his athletic body looked skinny. He was on sabbatical from teaching one of the physical sciences, and spoke with the dogmatic assurance of a full professor. "We shall have to let it keep its secrets."

"But I wouldn't want the commissioner to think we've ignored it," Foyle said. She looked earnestly at me. "We've glanced over all the territory adjoining our site.

"Those wetlands fan westward from that lifeless lake just over the ridge. The water chemistry is poisonously alkaline, making the area an unlikely campsite for any past visitor. That's why we've concentrated our efforts on this side of the ridge."

That was good news. Condé had not entrusted me with the exact location of his precious "barrow," but the two areas he wanted me to steer the archaeologists away from were the marsh and the intervening ridge—especially the balancing rocks on the summit, which he'd called "an important clue."

Friar Francisco cleared his throat to speak. On leave from his order's seminary, where he taught biology and zoology, he wore the robe and cowl of the Green Church in an olive-drab shade matched to his personality. "I know what you're thinking," he told me. His eyes shone in his dark brown face.

"Indeed?"

"We know our aliens landed here roughly nine hundred thousand years ago. You are thinking, climates change in such a period; perhaps there was no poisonous marsh then. Perhaps we should check that area for artifacts after all."

"Oh, I don't know," I began.

"And of course you're right! One would normally expect all sorts of shifts and changes in that length of time. But not here."

"No?" I said.

There were rueful smiles around the table.

"We call it the sleeping planet," said Helen Hogg-Smythe.

"Newcount Two is pretty dense to hold an Earthlike atmosphere despite its size," Foyle said. "Which suggests plenty of heavy metals and a hot core. And if you go back far enough—say, a million point two years—you see evidence of all the volcanism and tectonic activity you'd expect.

"The whole central mountain chain of this continent is that recent, or even younger; it's so anomalous, geologically, that I wish I could doubt the rock dates. And there was a lot of magnetic field activity at about the same time they were formed, a bizarre upswing in intensity."

"If we can trust the sedimentary evidence, since the life bombing," Hogg-Smythe pointed out.

"There's room for doubt," Foyle agreed. "But the picture we have shows a period of anomalous field strength beginning about a million years ago, accompanied by just as dramatic a *decline* in the rate of geologic and climatic change. Overnight, this became an old, tired planet. Within the last thousand years even the magnetic field has settled down, currently about Terran strength, and unusual only for its regularity."

"Don't forget your *clays*," Lagado senior said with his usual trailing gasp. His delivery was that of a man who had to get his remarks in before people started ignoring him again.

"And the clays," Foyle continued. "Even normal clay has some surprising electromagnetic properties, you know, but here the strata interactions have our subsoil scanners baffled. That leaves us no way to check the other things that puzzle us. Some of the seismological echoes, for instance . . ."

"And as I keep reminding my less experienced friends, Commissioner," Wongama said, "none of this is really unusual. Because geology, when you come right down to it, is just the science of pretending that other planets are like Old Earth. And that's the one thing they never are."

"True," I said.

"But that's why I agree with *you*, Commissioner," Foyle said. "We shouldn't neglect the marsh. Planetary differences may be confusing the climate record. We'll never know unless we look."

"Oh, I don't—" I began, and Wongama interrupted obliviously.

"This is an old argument with us, sir. I contend that even if there were antiquities beyond the ridge, they'd have been lost when the lake appeared. It looks to be a large sinkhole, of relatively recent origin."

I put down my coffee—which, like the food, was first-rate; if you have to rough it, rough it with amateurs—and did my best to drag them out of the marsh and back to generalities. "Is all this data from the original survey record?"

Hogg-Smythe snorted. "Hardly. The terraformers don't memorialize what they mean to destroy."

"You blame them?" came a quiet voice from the other end of the table. "Creation has imperatives, and killing clears the way. To bend a world to your will, you must stand outside history." But the speaker, Freeman Ken Mishima, had been introduced as a lecturer on history, military and diplomatic; a latecomer to the dig, I'd been told, arriving with a letter of introduction from Mehta only a week or two before.

"You can also bend your will to a world," Hogg-Smythe said. "Enter in, and understand it."

"Stand down, you mean," Mishima said. "The weaker must give way. That is the nature of the dance, and all war." A big, soft-spoken man in his late fifties, he carried a slight paunch with the powerful unconcern of a tiger. His straight black hair was close-cropped, shaven away above his ears; his jet-black eyes were watchful but expressionless. Tan work clothes hung on him like the uniform I was sure he'd once worn. I couldn't trace his plonking catchphrases to any of the usual mystical sources—Sufism, Kanalism, Zen—but it would be something militant, from one of the desert places; the dogs of war have hot dry breath. "You talk about entering in, but you are too respectful to do so," he continued. "You stick to our campfire at night. I love nature better; I go sleep with her."

No wonder Ariel had tried to whisk me off the planet without meeting this crew. An eccentric oldster, an academic know-it-all, a shirttail boy and his ineffectual father, a monk, a mystic warrior, and a misanthropic redhead. A good break for my patron Condé: they couldn't even coordinate table talk, much less a scientific inquiry.

"The commissioner is still waiting for a reply," Foyle finally broke in, irritated as usual. "We are not wholly dependent on the original survey, sir. My freighter can scan the planet from orbit. I have specialized equipment. Particle detectors, magnetic-resonance and gravity-flux analyzers, and so forth." When she mentioned her ship, she began to finger a fine gold chain around her neck. A pendant, enameled in swirls of aqua and turquoise, bobbed up to the throat of her gray jumpsuit, then retreated beneath it again.

"An impressive package," I said.

"Which would do us a lot more good in rotosynchronism, directly overhead," she said, after an unreadable glance at Ariel. "Unfortunately, the satellite construction crew has port authority here, and they've assigned my vessel a low circumpolar orbit. 'To keep it out of the way,' they claim, which is ridiculous. I think their security honchos prefer that it behave like a defense satellite—a prominent decoy, in case someone should attack the planet. The usual paranoid—"

Ariel stepped in, gentle but firm. "As a matter of fact, this is a time of real danger for the senator. I can't go into details, but if Security is playing it very safe, it's because I've told them to. You should know that, Foyle."

"Oh, you take responsibility," Foyle said. "But what do you *give*?"

Ariel turned her face to me and poured on the charm. "Sympathetic as I am to what our friends are doing here, I was not authorized to divert one munit's worth of construction equipment or worker time to this project. You know what building is like in the fringes, sir, on an uninhabited world. Machine-intensive, despite shipping charges that make you cut spare parts and backups to the bone. I have fewer than sixty workers, including those in orbit. Every one of them is a specialist, every man-hour counts. I help this dig when I can. I've kept their batteries in constant relay to the main camp; I've sent two of their vehicles through our motor pool for repairs; I've—"

"You're careful not to replace the radio, though," Foyle observed. "So you don't have to hear from us for a week at a time."

"And look at the Otis system!" Lagado said as if the words had been choking him.

Foyle looked thoughtful. "Yes, I think the commissioner would like to see the Otis system."

"The . . . Otis system," I repeated.

"I have to admit that I'd find another expert opinion helpful there," Wongama said.

"Time to adjourn to the site anyway," Hogg-Smythe decided. "I'm sure the commissioner can't wait to get at it."

Seen close-up, the Stone Huts looked less like card houses, but no more like anything else. The disproportionate thickness of the black slabs was more impressive, as was their matte finish, marred only by occasional patches of lichen and a few sequences of engraved characters. Although most of the walls were slanted, Wongama had assured me that this was due to the shifting ground, the uneven way the Huts had sunk and resurfaced over the millennia; the constituent slabs still joined at perfect right angles.

"I can't get over the *way* they join," I said.

"That's what 'alien' means," Foyle agreed. "The material itself is a ceramic smelted from local stone, stronger than any stone you'd find in nature. I don't know how much of the original survey report you've read yourself, sir—"

"Actually, there's been so little time," I said in a confidential tone. "Just taken over the post, and, uh . . ."

She looked unsurprised and almost sympathetic; she glanced over at the others to see if they'd heard. They were still rehashing the dispute they'd tried to draw me into as soon as our convoy of terrain buggies had reached the prairie floor. The acres under excavation were marked out with laser-reflector stakes into a grid pattern, only a few squares of which showed signs of actual digging. These "test pits" were connected with "test trenches" across grid lines, and the big debate was whether, in view of the negative results, the baseline had been ill-chosen. Quickly gathering from the faces of Foyle and Hogg-Smythe that one alignment of the grid would serve as well as another, I'd refused to take sides.

"Stronger than stone, you say?"

"Yes. We humans only discovered this form of ceramic sixty or seventy years ago. We know enough about it to be able to date these slabs, and to state that some of them have been exposed to great pressure and great heat since they were forged. They're not huts for living in, of course, though some of them may have been used as tool lockers or temporary radiation shelters. What they mainly are—incredibly—is sawhorses."

"What?"

"It's the only hypothesis we have, aside from Lagado's 'religious shrine' nonsense. The overall layout of the Huts, the pressure marks on their tops, and the patterns of heat stress all seem to indicate that the central ring of structures was used to prop up something huge and heavy while it was being worked on with high-energy tools. A spacecraft, or part of one, during an emergency stop."

"Who would do that sort of repair on a planetary surface?"

"Not humans, that's for sure. It's the same totally alien idea of practicality you noticed in the slab joins."

The huge slabs were not welded or riveted together, but fitted like antique woodworks.

"That's a dovetail, and the open-sided ones employ what is called a mortise-and-tenon joint," Foyle said. "The fit is so perfect it's unreal."

"And those characters inscribed near the join?"

"Probably alphabetic, rather than ideographs. Thus far, they're the only design motifs we've been able to give Senator Mehta's people. To decorate his palace, you know."

"No way of figuring out what they said, I suppose."

" 'This side up,' " replied Wongama, rejoining us. "Or 'Put tab A into slot B.' "

"Really?"

"Piet believes they're just reference marks for the robots that assembled the structures," Foyle explained. "Plausible enough. Unfortunately—"

"As Foyle will delight in telling you," Wongama interrupted, "my analysis of the construction code is contradicted by a few of the Huts, as though they'd been put together incorrectly. And of course we don't believe that."

"The true, religious nature of the glyphs has yet to be revealed," Lagado suddenly insisted at my side.

Time to change the subject and touch on the only point I felt genuine curiosity about. I gestured at the scores of brooding black fins, arches, and boxes, some of them jutting as high as thirty meters from the grassy plain. "You know, I can't help thinking how surprised a layman would be to hear that we archaeologists consider . . . all this . . . a minor, almost insignificant find."

"Yes, it's visually impressive, isn't it?" Hogg-Smythe said. "Like everything left behind by the so-called Titans . . ." As if her epaulet-festooned safari jacket weren't colorful enough, she was carrying a man-high crook for a walking stick. "I wonder if they were as lonely as we are? Are starfaring races so rare, so short-lived, that they never share the same time and place? Do they always give up, as so many of our species have, on interpreting the few epoch-old shards their predecessors have left behind?"

"Is there nothing at all here except the Huts themselves?" I asked.

"We've discovered artifacts," Foyle said guardedly. "But they aren't good news. Here, I'll show you."

She led me a hundred yards to a small field shelter, carefully pinning back both entrance flaps before we went in. "I try to keep it ventilated during the day," she said. "These celluloid solutions can be explosive."

She was referring to a glass tank on the table inside; it contained something brown in a clear fluid which emitted a pungent chemical smell. "It's a shovel handle," she explained. "Here's another." The pitted shaft of wood she handed me had a hard transparent coating. I hefted it. "I found that one a month ago, in wet clay three meters down."

Wongama's tall frame hovered outside the shelter entrance. He wrinkled his nose at the acetone smell. "Foyle is best at preserving ancient *methods* of archaeology."

I tried not to look baffled.

"I always travel with the old chemical preparations, just in case," Foyle explained. "Petroleum jelly for leather, ammonia for gold, and so forth. I've babied these handles. Kept them from drying out, moved them through eight stages of solution—water to alcohol, then xylene, and two days in acetone before I started adding the celluloid. And meanwhile, everyone kept telling me to wait for a crystal restoration, the Otis system would be fixed any day now. It wasn't, though, was it, Piet? If not for this field expedient, both specimens would have split and rotted away the moment they dried."

Wongama snorted and disappeared.

"Good job," I said. "But you called these artifacts bad news."

"The worst. Evidence of what every archaeologist fears most—a previous expedition. These are human tools, from about twelve hundred years ago, broken and discarded during a dig. If you hold the copper grip on this one up to the light, you can see a trademark . . . There. Roughly translated—"

" 'From the cooperative foundry at Holmscroft, Avalon,' " I read. " 'Labor intensive for real value. Manufactured 2480. Product—' I guess it would be 'design,' a number of words borrowed from Svenska and Deutsch—'Product design Guild-approved 2235 A.D.' Let's see. 2235 Oldstyle would be 290 in our calendar, early colonial period."

"You have a good eye for Ur-Linguish, Commissioner."

"You sound surprised."

She smiled, for once. "Sorry. The last sub-commissioner I dealt with didn't strike me as a real archaeologist."

"Indeed. Now, where is Avalon?"

"Was. It was one of the early colonies from Old Northern Europe that first opened up this fringe—died out since, hundreds of years ago. Perhaps their digging party was the one that contaminated this planet with Terran life; the timing's about right.

"And that's the reason why there are no small artifacts. The place has already been stripped. No excuse to give up yet, though. Those old-timers didn't have an Otis system. Now," she added with sarcasm, "if only *we* had one . . ."

We were back outdoors again, heading, I feared, for the mysterious but inevitable Otis system. The sun was not yet high, but had already burned the last of the dew off the wheatlike grass. The background insect noise had shifted from the mating exotica of the night into a workaday droning.

We rejoined the rest of the expedition where they stood, surrounding a much larger field shelter and the jumble of machinery it contained. Ariel was with them, looking anxious in the face of a no-win situation. Either she'd permitted amateurs to ruin the area, or she hadn't done enough to aid their efforts. Everyone was waiting to discover my attitude—including me.

The Otis system consisted of a number of boxy robots, quarter- to half-ton units, some with treads, some with ground-effect skirts, and even a few with legs. Diggers and loaders, I supposed. What appeared to be the master device was much larger, mounted on a half-track vehicle.

Lagado must have memorized the brochure that came with the system. "If we could only get it working," he forced out before anyone else might speak, "we could excavate the whole area to twenty-five meters' depth in less than a week. Vertical-face mode *or* level-stripping. Every cubic centimeter of dirt sifted. Every artifact preserved, boxed, and catalogued." And how long could Condé's barrow elude that kind of search, I wondered.

"We rented the system with a grant from my university," Wongama began.

"We all chipped in," Foyle said sharply.

"But there was no provision for repair."

"The whole system's down?" I asked. "Too bad. But sometimes there's nothing—"

"The peripheral units have no autonomy!" Hogg-Smythe said, shaking her finger in my face. "A terrible design! The central unit's down, and we can't run even the simpler slave units off a wristcomp."

"What a shame," I said. "But sometimes there's just nothing—"

"I've traced the trouble to one small module in the central unit," Foyle announced. "I'm sure that if I could just use the construction crew's diagnostic and coding equipment, I could clear it right up. But Citizen Arsenovich only gives me a song and dance about interactive feedback and taking no chances with the Mehta Corporation's property, blah blah blah. Perhaps if someone more diplomatic than I were to ask him"—she turned to face me—"he'd be more tractable."

"But there's no problem there!" Ariel said with relief. "When you asked us before, you wanted the whole system analyzed. If you've really isolated one small module, I'm sure Wu will have no objection. And since the commissioner will be here all this week to personally supervise the Otis at work, it's too good an opportunity to pass up. Pull the module and we'll take it back with us right away."

"Excellent!" Foyle said. Diplomatic relations had been restored. "The plain should dig quickly. I can't wait to get a crack at Ken's ridge—or even the marsh."

"You could stay and lay the groundwork." Ariel was all aid and comfort now. "I'll fly back and make sure Wu repairs the module."

"Better if it's done by someone familiar with an Otis," Foyle suggested. "I'll come."

"That's unnecessary," I said. "I'll be glad to take care of the module personally."

I beat down her objections with bland insistence. Ariel spoke for everyone else:

"I'm sure the commissioner knows what has to be done."

Foyle had bundled the module into a small box along with hard copies of the schematics and manual. I did not drop it out of the flitter at two thousand meters, but the temptation was strong.

As marsh, then forest, sped away beneath the two of us, Ariel plied me with endless questions about business opportunities and living conditions on other planets. I couldn't tell her much. I'd tended to stay on the fringes of the human sphere, away from the central worlds directly administered by the Consultancy; besides, I was distracted.

The Otis system raised questions in my mind. If such a thing existed anywhere, why should someone with Condé's resources tell me that there had been no fast way to excavate his barrow?

On another front, why should the one unit to conk out be the indispensable one? It could be sabotage: one of the archaeologists trying to keep the others from a find he intended to smuggle out for himself—possibly even Condé's barrow. That would almost put us on the same side. In any case, I would have to retain total control of the Otis module, run the diagnostics myself, and announce that it couldn't be fixed.

Ariel was flying the craft from Bunny's seat of the night before; she had the Standard F license you'd expect of a bright young executive. Sitting next to her, in front of the locked-out manual controls, I'd been trying to look as though I were used to being chauffeured. Neither of us was prepared when the most urgent of the warning panels' three alarms went off.

The flitter suddenly decelerated and lost a little altitude, though Ariel kept it in trim. "Power loss to the outer port blower," she told me. "No readout on why, so far. Had to shut it down smoothly—uneven torque can rip them apart. No problem, but—" We dipped again, and the change in impeller noise was obvious now. "That was the outer starboard," she reported coolly. "Same thing. Must be a general power-plant malfunction, because the radio went, too. But there's a battery backup, and I've put it on automatic distress."

"How bad is it?" I asked.

"We could fly all day on the inboard blowers," she said. "We probably will. But you'd better put down that box and fasten your seat belt." She punched through various diagnostic paths. "Without knowing why we're losing power, I can't say we won't lose more. And these birds aren't like airplanes; you can't keep them stable on one engine. If either wing goes, I'll have to cut the other. And if the tailfan goes, it's probably best to go ahead and cut them both. It won't glide well, but a few seconds without spin is all we need to eject.

"Don't get me wrong," she added. "I don't think it will come to that. We're only a few kilometers from base now, and—"

The alarm sounded again. The lights for both the port and tail blowers flashed red. Ariel had preset the shutdown; it was smooth.

Nothing is quieter than an aircraft when first you cut off all the engines. But then you hear the whisper of the wind.

"That's life," Ariel said, her voice tight but controlled. The emulator board continued to flicker with status lights, reporting on the automatic trim of our glide. Ariel's hand flipped up the small protective bubble over the ejector-seat button. Through the noseport I could see a break in the surging forest, but too far ahead.

"Ready?" Ariel said, and I grabbed her wrist before she could push the red button.

"Don't panic!" she ordered, struggling with me as I reached past her to hit two controls. The trim lights went out; the whole panel went dark. We stopped gliding and began to fall.

Chapter Seven

WITH SABOTAGE ALREADY on my mind, I'd instinctively ripped Ariel's hand away from the red button; it would have been too easy for someone to have booby-trapped the ejection seats. The rest was force of habit, if a hundred years out of date. I'd killed the Standard F dash in order to attempt a restart under good old manual control.

The tail of the flyer gave a sickening swing upward as we nose-dived into the trees. I had to release Ariel's wrist to trim the foils, but she believed in me or my uniform and didn't reach for the ejector again. I flipped the last toggle in the restart cycle and waited, waited, waited—some fraction of a second—the planet a spiked club swung at our faces.

But under direct control all five blowers caught. They registered full power—they'd never really lost it—and even though I knew, hauling back on the stick, that it was too late to avoid a crash, I had a measure of control now, and I could hope to make it survivable.

The nose pulled up sharply as we decelerated. We hit in a shallow dive rather than a plunge, and at first the thin treetops bent and parted beneath us, almost a safety net.

But then something wrenched us sideways with terrific force and an impeller sprayed green confetti across the noseport with a buzz-saw shriek that just as suddenly choked short. The opposite blower kicked upward, standing us on one wing even as we plowed ahead. I overcorrected. The craft bottomed and skipped, skipped and bottomed again randomly across the strange broken plain of treetops and upper branches. The rudder was gone and a second engine was smashed, while the whiplash and the whirling made real control impossible. All I could hope to do was hang on long enough to fire cushion-bursts at the last second, when we broke through—

—the cradle will fall,

And down will come Baby, cradle and—

"Wake up, sir!"

Crashing sounds became the lapping of liquid, onrushing leaves shrank to shining green pinpoints . . .

"Wha—?"

Distant darkness, starred with a thousand flashing lights, then a dark face, close, glistening with drops of sweat.

"You gotta wake up, sir, we're counting on you!"

It was Entzwame, the chief petty officer in charge of security; he reached down through myriad swirling colors and shook my bare shoulder. I was in a glass coffin. No, a suspend-sleep tank. Warm water rinsed off the suspend-gel and warm drafts of orange air dried me, but inside I was still cold, cold and blue to the bone.

I snatched at trailing mental wisps—which dream was this? The suspend-sleep tank had just sent me through one of my old outer-space fantasies: fighting the controls of a plunging shuttle with a beautiful girl at my side—infinitely preferable to real life on a navy ship. "I feel sick. Something wrong with the tank?" I asked. The words sounded as if I'd said them many times before, like an actor trapped in a long run. Trapped . . . "Did I miss a wake-up?"

"No! Please focus on me, sir. Here, sir. *Look* at me, you bastard, sir!"

"Larkspur? What the hell do you expect from *him*?" said a high-pitched voice, "He was half-crazy to begin with!"

Entzwame snarled. "Shut the fuck up!" Back to me: "Lieutenant Larkspur? You understand where you are, don't you?"

"His eyes aren't spinning too bad," someone said. "Just get the codes out of him, maybe."

I tried to sit up, but failed, while everything around me swam violently in shades of goose-shit green.

The captain's face loomed over Entzwame's shoulder. I was afraid he'd chew me out, but what he said in his Academyaccented baritone was, "And do you, in fact, know the muffin man?"

"Get him outta here," Entzwame whispered to one side.

"*The* muffin man. The muffin *man*. And do you know where he lives?" the captain went on. "I know, oh yes, I know where he lives." His professionally jovial face turned strange and sly. "I know where he is this very instant in time and space. But he's out of space. And he's out of time."

A hand on his shoulder. The high-pitched voice again. "Here you go, Cap'n, thatta boy—You sure do know your knots, don't you, sir?" And I recognized the speaker as he led the captain away—Fleischer, the cook. But we weren't in the galley, or in the sleep bay either. We were on the bridge. The bridge of the *Barbarossa*, its banks of instruments flashing randomly and its holo globe displaying some milky and impossible hallucination.

I pulled myself up against one side of the glass tank, shivering in my nakedness. "Why wheel me onto the bridge? Where's the O.O.D.? I feel whacked-out, Chief, did I miss a wake-up?"

"You gotta listen to me, Lieutenant," Entzwame pleaded. "The sleep tanks went bad. All of them. A few of us at least got wake-ups, but we couldn't get out and fix anything until just yesterday. And, Lieutenant, the officers didn't get *any* weekly wake-ups. None of you except—"

"Who's running the ship? How many weeks did I miss?"

"You gotta keep your grip now, Lieutenant, we're counting on you. You've been under for *four months*, sir."

"What? No." I shook my head, and regretted it as things came apart, then flowed back together. "No, Chief. Four months is too much. People go crazy. Just one month without a reality check and you lose it all, Entzwame, you lose . . . everything. Who has the conn? The captain's not—"

"He's gone, Lieutenant. They're all gone, Forrester, Ohara, Lumumba, they're all stark raving, we got most of them tied down, you're the last one to wake up and you gotta hold on."

I slumped back into the gel pad. Cold, colder.

"I know this dream," I said, trying to reassure him.

Entzwame shook me violently. "No!" he shouted. "No more dreams, sir! It's worse than I said."

"That's right, worse, I remember this one. Shipboard emergency, captain helpless, it's up to me. Fate of the ship, fate of the Alignment, fate of . . ." He didn't look reassured; I had to stop babbling. Straight face, straight spine, play it out. "You say it's worse than that?"

A big man, he yanked me up by the armpits, out of the tank. His face loomed before me, a reflection in smoked glass. "You're with me now, aren't you, sir?"

"What? . . ." So cold, fresh from the freezer, the drugs still in my blood . . . I had to take notes. I checked my breast pocket for a recorder and my nipple pinched me. Oh. Right.

A wizened white woman's face erupted into existence next to me. "The computer's sick, too," she said, all the tragedy of time in her voice.

"Gladys," Entzwame said tenderly. She winked a tear at me and disappeared.

"Look." He flew me in his strong, warm arms to the captain's board. The colored lights tried to blink in some pattern, but failed pathetically. I shook off Entzwame's hands and managed to lean upright—but the holo tank refused to play its part. What was that, oozing against the gridlines? An insane amoeba, a woman's passion, a coalescing galaxy? The scale had an error reading of plus or minus infinity, which was the length of my fingers as I reached for the function keys. Error calls marched up screens.

The skeleton crew had gathered around me in the requisite worshipful formation, though they kept flickering in and out, particularly Gladys—but that was only fair, she was a ranch hand from my uncle's farm on Wayback, and didn't belong there at all—and I was dutifully trying to feel my way into the savior-prince role. But it wasn't coming. Data, data, everywhere, and not a thought to think.

Entzwame finally fed me a cue line. "The universe has *shrunk*, sir. Nothing in it but us, and today—it's getting smaller, it's folding in toward us! That's what the captain said when he saw it."

"Well, he's hopeless, isn't he? Get hold of yourself," I said. It was ludicrous, but he took it from me; he wanted to hear it. "The computer's sick, that's all. We're not reading the real universe. Am I the only officer on his feet?"

Entzwame shook his head, and mine spun. "Lieutenant Helter got out of his tank before anybody, sir, I don't know why. He wasn't even in the wake-and-walk rotation, but he got out—"

"Should have woken us," I said.

"Shoulda let us out!" a parrot shrieked.

"Shut up!" Entzwame turned back to me. "Helter's not clear about when he got out, and the record's been blanked. He looks sane, he talks sane, but crazy things have happened and only he could have done 'em. He's fired the p-spacer at least once—"

"Okay, that's why we have a praeterspace drive, in case the survey goes sour. So he tried to take us home?"

"No, sir, he sent us into space, but without a target star."

"Can't have, oh God, we could be anywhere in the universe, then . . ."

"The universe has *shrunk*, sir!"

"Will you shut up with that, Chief? Good man." I swung back to recheck the screens, and—seeing its opportunity—the deck hit me very hard in the face.

Upright again. A large black hand caressed my face; a thumb pulled back my eyelid; a huge bloodshot eye peered into my brain. I almost fell into the shimmering chocolate pool, diving board quaking beneath my feet. But I shook off the hands again.

"Counting on you, sir."

"I remember the scene, thanks."

"Never mind the outside view, sir, it's crazy. Gladys, show the lieutenant the p-space bay." Small white hands flew over the keys.

It was like an Academy classroom exercise, emergency refitting. "That's the field-shaper ring," I said dutifully, "but the forward arc's been disassembled. The p-space generator's been retracted straight back across the cargo bay into the shuttle anterior, followed by the shaper—I know this one! Emergency two-man escape contingency for a wrecked ship—"

"But the fucking ship's *intact*!" Entzwame said. "Sir."

"Lieutenant Helter did this?"

"Yes!"

"By himself?"

"We've got the heavy-load waldo rails, sir," he pointed out, "from when this was a colony support cruiser. The computer helped. Computer's fine, sir, it's the *universe* that's—"

"Belay that. Get a grip," I told the man who was propping me up. "How does Helter explain this?"

"We can't get at him, sir. He's out there now, fitting out to leave us."

"Fucking officers!" shrieked the parrot.

A sudden moment of great clarity. That's why I was needed, why Larkspur must be good enough to play the hero. It wasn't that the crew was technically incapable—it was the chiefs who ran the ship, usually—but they had limited operational codes, passwords, computer privileges. Helter had locked them out of the cruiser's central shaft with an override code. An officer's code. But not, one suspected, a code of honor.

He floated in midair, an ill angel in blue-white, his irises bleached by the colored lighting, his prematurely silver hair adding to the albino effect. "I didn't have to let you in, brother. I've reset all the codes. But I'm taking the chance I can trust you." Helter licked his lips nervously as he settled to the deck.

I tried to reorient. There was no gravity to speak of, not even its centrifugal counterfeit, here in the nonrotating core of the ship. But as compensation for my loss of balance I'd acquired clothing, an engineer's overalls—with something heavy and comforting in one pocket, something pressed on me with a whispered word in the last moment before I'd stepped into the rotation-lock. And a holster, and a pistol. But—where was I again?

"I thought one or two officers might make it out of the tanks sane," Helter went on. "The book says one out of ten, after four months. Maybe your Kanalist training gave you an edge, or maybe your poetry. Oh yes, I know all about you. We're frat brothers."

It was the aft hold of the ship's shuttle, almost unrecognizable because of the emergency lighting and the crammed-in bulks of the praeterspace generator and field shaper, a copulation of infernal engines.

The shuttle's lights shifted to red—which meant something, something vital, but what?—and Helter's face looked demonic in them, his eyes suddenly darker. My heart thundered and stumbled.

I groped for his first name, and as I did so my right hand flew of its own accord to the pistol. But I steadied the laser-green aim dot true on the center of his breastbone before he could blink. Not bad, if the gun wasn't a hallucination.

"I'd like to believe in *your* sanity, too . . . Nick," I said, "but I need to know what you've done—and why you're doing it."

"Let's get one thing straight," he said. "I outrank you at the best of times, and unlike you did *not* recently get my brains scrambled. It's absolutely essential that you defer to my judgment. Everything is at stake."

"Including the crew. Looks like you're ditching us."

He adopted what he might have thought was a soothing voice. "I'm doing the right thing, brother. I'm dealing with extraordinary circumstances, and may need your help later. But this is bigger than the ship, bigger than the Alignment. We're talking about the fabric of the universe itself."

"Fate of the universe, yeah, I remember. You rigged the suspend-sleep tanks, didn't you? Why?"

He shook his head, but not in denial. "We're beyond that now, brother. Haven't you seen the sensor data on the bridge? Don't you realize what it means?"

"That you rigged that, too?" I suggested, in a parody of his humor-him-along voice. "To keep the ship from navigating while you went off to meet whoever you hope to meet?" A sudden inspiration, as I remembered the origin of this fantasy, Summerisle's hokey warning. "A fellow agent of the Few—is that it?"

He started violently, drifting off the deck. "You know of us? Then perhaps you know how we hijack ships—by entering praeterspace without a target star."

My hand shook, but the laser targeter continued to dance around the kill zone. "If you've done that, we could be anywhere in the universe now; our return coordinates may be no good from here; you may have marooned us—"

"No, no, no," he insisted, under apparent strain; he was waiting for something, something imminent—"that's just what they *tell* you, when ships disappear. This is the reality. We left space-time at a right angle, Larkspur—*we never went back in!*"

I would have laughed at him, but I didn't want to lose my tiny friction-hold on the deck, and with it my aim. "You *are* crazy, Nick. You can't take matter out of space-time, they're two sides of the same coin, we couldn't exist without a universe to—"

"You've *seen* that universe, you moron!" he snapped. "The bubble in the holo tank! A bubble universe, outside normal space-time, created by our emergence!" He continued to glance nervously around the hold and began to wheedle again. "Don't you want to help me, brother? No one knows what it's like to burst a bubble from the inside, how much of a shock—two of us at the helm will double the chance of keeping control. And you're a Kanalist, you can understand: discipline; the virtue of an élite; the necessity for . . . secrets?"

"You created the universe," I said slowly. "To park our ship in?"

"Yes! And every universe I create, I learn a little bit more. But this time . . . this time I had a revelation!"

I reminded myself not to look him in the eye, to keep my aim locked, as he raved on:

"I've added it all to the ship's log, all my observations and theories. But we can't just wait to be salvaged, we must break out now! If I'm right, the Few must be warned, we have to protect the integrity of the universe against *the bubbles*, Larkspur, the bubbles—"

Maniac, I was sure now, but too late, as he got what he'd been waiting for. As a soft beep sounded behind me, the emergency lights went into their green phase—a launch sequence!—and my green laser dot became invisible. The cradle holding the shuttle released with a jerk—

And my shot missed him easily. The ejection charge kicked in as I flailed for a handhold. Helter disappeared for a moment, then tackled me. My wrist exploded into an agony I had never known and the pistol disappeared. He dodged my kick with grace, seized a stanchion with both hands, and piston-kicked me through the interior hatch. I fended off a control panel with my good hand and my forehead.

He jackknifed in after me. He must have wanted to finish me off, but found it more imperative to grab a control seat. In the forward viewports, the smooth white hull of the *Barbarossa* was picked out by automatic spotlights. Then the shuttle flipped 180 degrees, swatting me against a bulkhead. I got a glimpse of something vast and sickeningly incomprehensible before us, then rebounded into the cabin just as the main engine fired.

Only in dreams can one fall like this. I hit an acceleration seat, inverted but otherwise perfectly, sacrum to head support, head to sacral support. The momentum of my legs flipped me around in a forward somersault. My balls tingled in relief at not being smashed. With a twist, I absorbed the impact against the bulkhead with my feet, my buttocks.

The only pain besides my wrist was where the heavy object in my pocket bit into me. My last gift from the crew, maybe just for luck, their best friend in a liberty port . . . I fished it out and played dead, sly as any savior-prince, holding it concealed in my hand, blade side open, thumb on the stud. Acceleration phase done, the shuttle hurtled on; the ship receded.

While Helter unstrapped, I just floated in midair, eyes half closed, mouth half open. He took a pry-bar from the tool locker, raised it to strike, drifted toward me purposefully. *Homicidal maniac*, I thought, and when he spun me around to get at my head I flicked the knife open and flicked his throat open and sprayed the green-lit cabin with jet-black blood . . .

Behind the computer's transparent access door, a brass-colored data disk I'd seen before—the *Barbarossa*'s log—spun and spun. To his twisted "observations and theories," Helter must have added a launch sequence for the shuttle. And it was locked in. I hammered heroically at the panel, trying not to look through the forward port. Behind me the praeterspace generator began its warmup, humming and clicking as it prepared to make its effort. And then a disembodied head appeared before me.

It was Entzwame's face, coldly afire. As if the Admiralty would have paid for full-hologram communications in an escape shuttle. But it was there; it screamed, and it cursed me.

"I can't get back!" I told him. "It's too late, I've gone too far. I wake up soon, I'm sorry, I always wake up here."

"Too fucking late? How can it be too late and too far, you bastard, sir, when we're outside time, and outside space? *We'll always be here*, no matter how many dreams you hide in, always fucking always, until you *bring us back in*! Always, always, al—" And then his white teeth and white eyes exploded into a trillion viewport stars, cross-sections of space-time sliced me through like an egg, the data disk popped free of the suddenly silent computer, and still I didn't wake up. I wanted to wake up, I cried and pleaded to wake up. But it's not clear I ever did.

I am alone. There is only the void now. Not a trace remains of the survey cruiser *Barbarossa*, the lost *Barbarossa*. My ship.

Chapter Eight

A PATTERING SOUND. I must not have blacked out for long at all, two or three seconds. How could the trauma dream strike so fast, with such impact? Was I finally cracking all the way? They were supposed to get less awful with time, but ever since I'd entered the Blue Swathe . . . I heard Ariel moan next to me.

Black mulch covered most of the noseport, leaving us in semidarkness. I remembered the muddy little clearing now, the way it had looked an instant before we nosed into it. With the engines shut off again, for good this time, there was no sound except that brief patter of branches we'd torn free—and then Ariel's inexpert curses, piping from beneath the forearms bent over her head in crash position. I was the first to throw up, but Ariel needed no further encouragement.

Ariel had left the stinking cabin, but I remained to take a last look at the emulator that had failed us. Stupidly, the system's diagnostics checked out fine—except for two gaps in the automatic log. One ten-minute period was missing from the hour before the flight, and another ended the record. Just the sort of cutting in and out you'd expect if the cybercell was dying. Perhaps it was only bad luck that the failure had extended to the warning systems, but I had a different theory.

As ancient as myself, the emulator still included a digital log buffer—even in my day something of a vestigial organ, but useful in cases like this as a partial backup log. Sure enough, at the receding end of the command train, almost pushed out of memory by the emulator's subsequent translation calls, I discovered a discrete set of human commands. A special program. It included a function to conceal its own interference by blanking out the main log; hence the missing ten minutes just before we'd taken off.

Judging by the program's mnemonic tags, someone had commanded the emulator to send false power-loss messages after a certain distance flown, trusting Ariel and me to dutifully carry out our own murder by shutting down the engines.

Presumably, a military skeleton coder—a sabotage model—had generated the code; a standard maintenance tool wouldn't be specialized enough to bypass all the safety routines, not in ten minutes. Was the saboteur too young to have encountered one of these old buffers? Or had he thought that the incriminating program would be pushed out of memory by crashtime? Or—

I checked the third possibility, and heard myself curse when I'd confirmed it. The saboteur had also manually disconnected the canopy release mechanism. If we'd fired the ejector seats, they would have smashed us into the ceiling and exploded. Everything within the cabin—the canopy, the computer, all evidence of the crime—would have been incinerated.

Artful.

There was no time to think about who had done it—only to

cover it up. I started by running the diagnostic commands a second and third time, thereby pushing the tail end of the sabotage program out of the buffer. I had no choice. A deliberate attempt to murder a sub-commissioner would have to be reported to the Column, and I couldn't do that.

Just before lifting the door of the cabin, I remembered to go back and take some things from the first-aid kit. The repairmen at the construction base would chalk up any equipment loss to the accident, though in fact Ariel and I had been unhurt. I tucked the items out of sight before descending to meet her.

She had thought to take the Otis module with her, worse luck. She also bore evidence, on the seat of her pants, of having slipped and sat down in a puddle earlier, and she pointed out the tricky ground now. "Careful, sir," she said. "Your poor uniform's been through enough."

"And the flitter? The damage looks worse from out here," I noted.

"There's a lot to salvage, though," she said. "More than if I'd let it go."

"Well, you'd told me how important your heavy equipment is to Construction. Also . . . if you've never ejected into trees, believe me, it's a last resort. I had to try the manuals first."

"Don't apologize! You were—" She laughed lightly and shook her head. "But now, sir, we must decide whether to walk, or to wait for the satellites to notice our distress call."

"The radio didn't survive the shock," I said. "Let's hike."

For some reason this prospect seemed to please her. "I have a bearing," she said. "There's a clear Earth-style magnetic north on Newcount, and my watch is set to it."

"You're the leader, then." My own wristcomp had been smashed to bits.

"Did you find out what made the emulator fail?" she asked.

"Its cybercell is completely dead." At least, it soon would be, for I'd isolated it from the system—as if to inspect it—and it would starve within minutes. "No way of knowing what killed it now, but considering how it lost control in phases, I suspect it was cyberbacteria of some kind. If you don't flush these old systems, sometimes—"

"Yes, I know. I can't tell you how sorry I am, sir. All our equipment has seen rough use. If only we'd had time to prepare for your visit—some advance notice." This was a delicate subject, but she had plenty of spunk. "Frankly, sir, I still don't see what's changed since the last sub-commissioner gave the dig his blessing. Of course, it's not for me to ask . . ."

"But it's a reasonable question," I said. Through an intervening stand of trees I saw a much larger meadow ahead of us. "I'm just a poor bureaucrat, and they don't always give me reasons either. But it may have something to do with the possibility of the title changing hands."

"What do you mean?"

"Well, if this Condé fellow does prove his claim to Newcount Two, any protected lands will have to be resurveyed."

"With all due respect, sir, the Column's sent you on a wild-goose chase. Sir Max Condé is a VIP, but he's also thoroughly crooked, and a bit mad. I know about his case, and it was thrown out of court a while back. He was furious about it. To tell you the truth, I think that he's the reason for our current security mania. Not that Senator Mehta would ever admit to being afraid of the Knuckle-Cracker."

"The Knuckle-Cracker?"

She laughed, but said quickly, "I hope Sir Max isn't a friend of yours, Commissioner. I shouldn't call him that, but we've picked it up from the senator. There's some story behind it. They spent a long time in each other's company once, and apparently Condé has this disgusting habit . . ."

"Well, don't worry. He's no friend of mine. And I'm glad for your sake if his claim is no good. But are you absolutely sure?"

She began to lay out the case in detail, and I stopped listening as soon as it became clear that she knew what she was talking about. So Condé had lied to me, about his rights to Newcount Two and God knew what else. I would have to interrogate Bunny, Shih Ho fighter or no; but I'd already known that.

Ariel had an informed grasp of Court of Claims procedures, and she was still showing it off. I didn't step on her enthusiasm. We had entered the larger meadow. Ariel tended to get ahead of me and then suddenly slow down, perhaps self-conscious about the rear view, her soaked slacks plastered to her skin. If she was right about the distance, the construction camp would be just beyond that last barrier of trees, a half-hour's hike. The exercise felt good despite the heat; a touch of whiplash was fading from the muscles of my neck.

The grass was greener here, with small flowers, coral and yellow and powder blue. Our passage triggered a flight of butterflies, and one of them, after circling me aimlessly for a few minutes, came to rest on the back of my outstretched hand. He was mainly orange, with black edges and markings, and without flexing the skin beneath him at all, I turned him at various angles into the breeze of our motion, watching his body go flat, the wings trimmed this way and that.

Give them credit: the life bombers stock a world with some sense of style. On Wayback, where I was born, where the sky burns like a hot iron and the grass is like steel wool and the scavenger birds never stop scanning, there are only well-camouflaged field moths. I'd seen my first butterfly on Nexus, standing in line to register at the university. One of these delicate painted fantasies had alit on a flower in the courtyard. And I'd thought, This is the place. Where even the moths are decadent and beautiful . . .

I must have slowed to a halt. I stood watching the butterfly, and Ariel stood watching me. "Look," I said, and held him closer to her face. I froze and after a moment said, "Fly." Without moving a muscle I concentrated on the feel of the insect against the back of my hand, blanked out everything else except that specific tactile sensation. Something physical but extremely subtle happens when you do that, a change in skin conductivity, perhaps. It's the basis of a number of "psychic" magic tricks, and—my usual luck in small matters—it was enough to make the butterfly take off on cue.

"How did you do that?" Ariel whispered.

"He was in the same daydream, so he heard me."

"What do butterflies dream of?" she asked.

We started walking again.

"He was dreaming that he was a poet named Chuang-tzu, somewhere in Old China, four thousand years ago," I said. "In this dream he is standing next to a canal, watching cherry blossoms fall into the water and drift away. He has a headache from drinking too much with former schoolfriends who have come to visit; they've boasted all night about their positions in the government, but he sees them only as pathetic and corrupt. And so, still thinking himself Chuang-tzu, the butterfly was wishing he could go back to bed, and dream of being in another world, another time, another body, with wings to fly. And then I woke him up, and all of it was true."

"You are a very strange man," Ariel said.

"Strange butterfly," I said. "Pensive and erudite. No doubt descended from a Monarch."

"Have butterflies ranks, too?"

"That's how the old species names ran, for some reason. Admirals, Emperors. This one resembled a Monarch—unless he was a Viceroy."

"What's the difference?"

"Spiritual," I said. "The Monarch was sour inside, like all autocrats. A defense against predators. The taste of a Monarch made birds sick, and they learned to recognize his wing markings and avoid him."

"And the Viceroy?"

"The Viceroy was lazier, sneakier—more civilized. Rather than abandon good taste, he simply evolved wing markings exactly like a Monarch's. So the birds avoided him, too."

"Then he wasn't really a Viceroy at all," said Ariel, "but a Pretender."

I laughed. "Just so."

"And which are you, Alun?" she asked.

Even words fail me, sometimes.

"Monarch or Viceroy?" she went on. "First you bite my head off at the spaceport, which I can't blame you for, because I *was* trying to hustle you offplanet before you could interfere with construction or anything. But once you've established who's boss, that's all forgotten. Now you stand around being terribly charming and informal and indifferent, doing magic tricks and talking to butterflies. You ask questions, but you don't listen to the answers, and generally act as if you're waiting to get back to a girl you've got stashed in your hotel room. But when an emergency comes up, you can pull on a third face and respond like a hero."

"Whoa!" I said. "Just a pilot who knows the manuals. You were a lot cooler when things looked worse."

"Well, where I come from," she said, smiling, "menfolk never back you up at all, so maybe I'm overimpressed."

"You really speak your mind, don't you?"

"And do you, ever? Maybe that's what I'm trying to figure out."

We'd already passed the advisable limits of talking about me. "And where *do* you come from?" I asked.

"A planet called Myrdal—from this neck of the Blue Swathe, actually. It's a beautiful little world, I guess. Everything well planned from the start. The population is small. Almost everything is automated. Everyone can devote his time to everyone else. I don't know. I've seen the starveling planets, and I know that Myrdal will always be a paradise compared to them, but there's something important missing all the same. I think there has to be more challenge to life, just enough of an edge to shape yourself against, you know?

"I wasn't the only one. On Myrdal nice girls have to be the responsible ones, the social managers who run the economy and the health services. Nice boys are supposed to keep the agro machines running and generally follow orders. But every generation, more and more of the men just opt out to play games. Black marketeering, mainly. Trading liquor or cigarettes or other forbidden things they smuggle in from offworld. The actual goods don't really matter that much, it's the game, it's the kick. The only other way they have to be somebody is to see how many of their responsibilities they can get out of. So the woman's role is to keep after them, nagging—or join their side, and wind up being used for laughs and thrown away. To hell with that.

"Thank God for the Column! I know lots of Freefolk complain about your military and the hard things that have to be done sometimes, but thank God for a system that outranks all the provincial governments. Someone has to keep the barriers down and the borders open. From the age of twelve one thing kept my spirit alive—the knowledge that someday I could go *someplace else*. Someplace where *I* could have the dirty fun of wheeling and dealing, and meet respectable men doing it, too. Someplace where men are given more constructive ways of proving themselves than by treating women like shit."

"And is the larger sphere all you thought it would be?" I asked.

"Still promising," she said, with a sidelong glance. "I've been lucky to get this far, this fast. It's been a lot of work. But to me commerce will always be a little illicit—sexy, even—and that keeps it fresh. A few more years on the senator's inner staff and I'll be able to afford Column citizenship."

"Is that so important?"

"If you want to go into interstellar business for yourself, yes, the right to use the Column's civil courts is essential. And the central worlds are the big casino; everything else is just playing jacks."

As the construction camp came into view, we walked harder and talked less. I wished I could share Ariel's optimism about the Column and the big reforms the Consultant had allegedly promised the party of Senator Mehta, one of his most prominent supporters. But, naturally, I took the historical view. The Consultant, whoever he was and wherever he came from, held a position analogous to a medieval king. He liked to dispense small but popular reforms—due process for debtors, scholarships for the deserving poor, more holidays for workers—because the love of the common people kept him the support of the regular navy, and held in check the great families that had founded the Column and controlled its bureaucracy and Shadow Tribunal. But he couldn't go too far. If he were really planning to extend universal suffrage and reform the court system, for instance—two rumors that had been flying about for years—the great families would take whatever risks necessary to put an end to his life. Besides, he couldn't afford to wound them that badly even if they'd let him; if the universal struggle was ever reduced to the Consultant versus the people, it might be too clear-cut for comfort.

But you couldn't expect Ariel, with her healthy-minded belief in hard work and meritorious service, to understand that sort of thinking. I compared her with much younger women I'd wooed at college dances, once upon a time—women who are all white-haired now, or long dead; Ariel would laugh at the styles we'd worn, the slang we'd spoken, the standards we'd upheld. Sometimes it is too overwhelming to know that I am one of those ghosts, and have no fit part to play in the here and now. I cannot raise a pen to compete with the monument they've made of me; and if you take away any poet's vocation, what's left is a bum: a shirker, a seducer, a sponge.

It's a morbid mood, a kind of burnout. Too much high living amid too many lowlifes over the past seven years, too many times hitting bottom between peak experiences meant to blot out the screaming dreams. But all those other ghosts keep kicking me out of the doldrums, keeping me honest. Liar, say the shades, fool. You're still alive. Your body and mind are only thirty-three, in excellent health, as you walk through green fields behind a gladsome girl with a perfect rear end. Ungrateful bastard, admit it: your blackest thoughts are only butterfly dreams.

Naturally, the spirit of honesty and intimacy and genuine affection that had sprung up between Ariel and me killed all chance of sex.

Perhaps wary of having opened up so far, she took the first opportunity to retreat into her work. After a bath and a brief supper, only the latter of which I shared, she took charge of the flitter's recovery and salvage. She spent the evening in conference with the construction bosses over the logistical problems created by the loss of the vehicle, and I was left to my own devices.

Fortunately, Construction Chief Arsenovich had no interest in the problem of the Otis module. I bullied him into at least showing me where the cybermaintenance apparatus was, in one of the prefab technical shacks. After running preliminary diagnostics on the module, I affected to let the matter go, and told Arsenovich to order a replacement from offplanet.

Next, I needed an excuse to work in the technical area overnight. I asked Arsenovich how the interior design people assigned to Mehta's palace intended to make their replicas of whatever artifacts the archaeologists turned up. He referred me to one of the decorators, who explained that they would create exact simulacra of any finds with a simula-kiln.

"A popular technology in the Blue Swathe," I said. "But I don't know much about it. I can't have any alien artifacts damaged."

"There's no question of that, Commissioner. The device is as simple to operate as a camera."

"Fine. Then teach it to me, and I'll operate it personally when the time comes."

He reluctantly complied. There were two quite different types of luminotrope glass, he explained, Alpha and Beta. The transparent—virtually invisible—kind, Alpha, could be produced quickly and easily, and in conveniently thin sheets, if desired. But the image of a physical object could only be produced at the center of a considerably larger volume of solid Beta type, and the process, he assured me grimly, was "*much* harder to explain, though simple in practice."

But I outlasted his lecture, perforce learning a craft I never intended to use, until he was finally willing to leave me alone in one of the prefabs with his precious machine, making "practice" simulacra of pebbles and twigs. I waited for the shift change and then returned to the cybermaintenance apparatus as though that were where I belonged. No one bothered me; the executives were all asleep.

It took me two hours to dope out. But I had the advantage of knowing exactly what I was looking for within the Otis master module, and I found it—trace evidence of exactly the same kind of reprogramming that had downed the flyer.

But why hadn't the saboteur used his skeleton coder to simply wipe the Otis cybercell clean? Conceivably because he or she had hoped to reset the Otis for private use, once everyone else had given up on it. That went along with the theory that one of them was working a valuable find in secret, with plans to smuggle it out for himself. Or herself. Foyle had technical know-how and equipment, as well as that—criminal?—record with the Shadow Tribunal. Her desire to have the module repaired could have been an act if she'd rigged the flitter, too; the crash would have destroyed any evidence of the module's reprogramming.

That was a pretty weak motive for murdering a Column official, though. I was either dealing with an awfully bloodthirsty smuggler, or with something bigger, as yet unseen.

The following day Arsenovich flew Ariel and me back to the Stone Hut site. As she'd promised the archaeologists the day before, she had cleared her schedule to stay at the dig for a week, and now she turned down the chief's offer of a radio, telling him to come get her if anything really big came up. From the grateful look he gave her I could see that she was not on vacation; keeping government officials occupied, and away from the workplace, is an important executive job.

Everyone expressed polite concern at my tale of the flitter accident, but no more; Bunny wandered off with a yawn. The archaeologists didn't take the news about the Otis module nearly as well.

"Foyle was sure it could be fixed," Helen Hogg-Smythe said. The cookhouse tent flapped in the morning breeze behind her.

"I still am," Foyle snapped. "May I have it back, please?"

I returned it with misgivings. Suddenly my afterthought of the night before didn't look so smart.

I had decided that since Condé had lied to me about his claim, he might have lied about the barrow, too. Perhaps I'd better take my own look at it, wherever it was. I knew where to search first: that balancing rock formation on the ridge. That meant I might need to run an Otis unit, even though the system had to remain down. Accordingly, I'd used the cybermaintenance apparatus to repair the module, but had set it to respond only to my password.

I hadn't foreseen that Foyle might go back to work on it. But she didn't trust me, I could see it in those green eyes. Did that mean she was the saboteur, who knew damn well that the module was repairable? An inherently suspicious bitch? Or a good judge of character?

"If you should think that you have repaired it," I said carefully, "please inform me before trying to operate any of the large units. I would have to inspect them first, for safety."

"Whose?" she asked, and disappeared. Her smile could have meant anything.

No one was happy with his sub-commissioner any more. "I suppose we'll have to make room for you in the men's tent, too, Commissioner," Wongama said gloomily.

Lagado began to sputter. "Perhaps your aide could bunk with Mishima, since he prefers the out-of-doors."

"What do you mean?" I asked.

"I mean he stepped out last night to wander into the hills. Woke us all up around three, trying to find his way back to the tent. Wouldn't apologize either, the—"

"That's all right, Dad," his son said quietly. The kid was too well-behaved for his own good; look at the summer vacation it had earned him.

"It may not be safe to wander at night, either," said Wongama. "The life bombers aren't supposed to have supplied any large predators, but there was a very suspicious disturbance near Foyle's tent one night. We tried to track whatever it was the next day, but lost it. Your aide should be warned."

"I have to consult with Velasquez anyway," I said. "I'll mention the matter to him."

I changed into what my protocol manual called a "field uniform," the tunic as white and sharp, but the boots and pants more practical. After a while I located Bunny up on the ridge. I was surprised at how thick the scrub trees were; the archaeologists—Mishima, mainly, according to what I'd heard—had made only a few paths through the underbrush. Bunny hadn't strayed far from them.

"Let's talk, Bunny," I said. "First things first. What the hell were you playing at, sending away our levy ship?"

"I've been expecting this," Bunny said. "You're supposed to be the soldier of fortune and I'm supposed to be the poor funk, but I guess it's the other way around, isn't it, playactor? You're the one who's too scared to stick."

"If that parts boat doesn't come on time—"

"Then you'll have to earn your money and play your role in front of Mehta for a few days. Be a man. If *I'm* not scared—"

"If you're not scared, there's something fishy about it. You've got something else going here, don't you, Bunny? You took a walk into the bush and met someone last night, didn't you?"

"You're dreaming." He pointedly turned his back on me, as was his style.

I raised my right fist and hit him lightly at the base of the neck. The hypodermic I'd stolen from the crashed flitter's first-aid kit injected him, a small compressed-air kick.

As he spun around I made the hypo disappear into the woods with a conjuror's throw-away sleight, and faced him in a reasonable facsimile of a martial-arts stance.

"Don't even know how to rabbit-punch," Bunny said with one of his more confident sneers. But his words were already beginning to slur. Emergency drugs are meant to work fast, and the closer to the brain you pump them the better.

Bunny shifted his body to feint a kick, and instead launched a high handblow that might have suckered me at its proper speed. As it was, it arrived so slowly I could come up with what might even have been a Shih Ho block for it. Bunny's face registered total incredulity as my arm straightened directly from the block into his face. I didn't hit him hard; I just wanted my fist to be the last thing he'd remember.

Chapter Nine

THIS WAS THE dark side of the ridge, shadowed by the morning sun, out of earshot of the people on the prairie, overlooking the dead lake and the marsh. At the highest point, partly visible from the rocky ledge where I sat, stood the balancing rock formation Condé had asked me to keep the archaeologists away from.

The ridge was a windbreak; the balancing rock's slenderness had presumably been shaped by the wind. But its string-of-pearls shape would be unusual anywhere, and I resolved to take a closer look at it as soon as I could.

I finished scanning upward and eastward to make sure we wouldn't be disturbed, then turned back to the marsh below. Slate-blue shrubbery and pale-green ground cover patched the landscape despite the alkaline water chemistry, and the plant life grew thicker the farther one got from the steep banks of the lake. The broad expanse of water looked shallow for the most part, but a large circular area of deep black hugged the ridge. I noticed that the hunting birds that skimmed the algae-covered ponds in the distance did not bother with the surface of the lake.

I heard a stirring below me. Just west of the boulder I was sitting on, the ledge dropped off steeply. Bunny Velasquez, rolling on his side as he regained consciousness, reached the point of no return and began to slide over the edge. He was brought up short—and shocked awake—by the strip of leather around his wrist.

He cried out and I said, sharply enough to penetrate, "Make no noise, Bunny, or I drop you."

I had removed his belt, made a small loop through the buckle, and fixed his hand in it. The other end was buckled to my own belt, which I was holding at arm's length. The reach of the whole lifeline was no more than two meters, but that was enough to make the difference between my sitting safely and his clinging prone to the slanting rock face.

The lake was a hundred meters below.

"What—what's it all about, Park?" Bunny asked, looking downward and then trying to find some purchase with his boots.

"The elegant thing about this friction loop," I said, "is that it's likely to go slack and slip off once you've hit the water. The belts will sink out of sight before they can contradict my story that you fell while climbing. Stop that scrambling, Bunny! If necessary, I can kick you in the head, and claim you bounced off the rocks before going in."

"But, but—my head—what happened?" Bunny dug the fingers of his free hand into a crevice.

"You picked a fight with me, remember?"

"I—yes, I hit you with the Cobra Opening, but, but—you were so *fast* . . ."

"Actually, I thought my Mongoose Riposte was a little rusty. Shih Ho is so out of date. But at least I stopped short of killing you. A mistake I can correct—unless you're prepared to tell me what I want to know."

"You're not going to—"

"Yesterday someone dropped *me* from two thousand meters. I am more angry than amused, Bunny. I want some answers.

"Turn your mind back to our flight here. Something out there in the marsh shows a signal flare whenever anyone flies over at night. Almost as though it's waiting for some particular passenger to signal back. You remember what happened when *we* saw that flare?''

''Park, I can't—''

''Better try, Bunny. Otherwise I know a quick way to make your whole life pass before your eyes.''

''All right, all right, the running lights went out.''

''More precisely, you turned them out. But why should there be anyone out there for you to signal? Why should Sir Max take the risk of putting more men in place, if he expects to have this planet turned over to him legally in a month or two? The answer, I found out yesterday, is that he's already lost his title challenge in court. So a crew has to empty his barrow for him right now, and their presence makes it even more important that you and I divert the archaeologists.

''That would explain why you're not worried about getting offplanet in time; the crew you went out to meet last night must be able to arrange its own transportation. But here's the puzzle. For some reason, I have not been clued in. In fact, I seem to be expendable. I don't understand that part, Bunny. Explain it to me. Now.''

Velasquez's boots scrabbled at the ledge again, and he slipped down a few inches. I leaned back to take more of his weight and saw ripples radiate across the dead lake from the pebbles he'd shaken loose, the splashing noises arriving a second later.

''You've got it all wrong!'' he said finally. ''It wasn't me on the flitter, it was her, the Foyle woman, she slapped my hand down as I reached for a map. It was deliberate, Park! I thought, like you, a signal.''

''Weak,'' I said. ''Do better.''

''So who could have been down there? Who camps on the ridge and admits to wandering around at night? Mishima, of course. And who could smuggle out whatever he found? Foyle, in her freighter. That's the only way to work a secret dig, you'd need at least two. Well, wouldn't you?''

''Keep talking. And quieter. She would see her partner every day, wouldn't she, Bunny? What would she need to signal him about at night?''

There were beads of sweat on his forehead, but he was looking up with more confidence now.

''About us, Park! We weren't supposed to come to the site at all, remember? The Foyle woman had been scheduled to put us off with a briefing at the hotel. She and Mishima could have arranged an emergency signal in case that fell through, a warning that she wasn't coming back alone, that he should cover up their dig and get back to camp. Come on, Park, let me up before we have an accident."

"Speaking of accidents—"

"What happened to the flitter, you mean? Well, it doesn't make any sense your way—does it? In your fairy tale, I have more reason than ever to want you around, in authority, to protect the secret dig. But, but remember, alien artifacts have to be turned over to the Commission for next to no compensation. So it's pothunters, smugglers, who would want you to have an accident, thinking you a real commissioner. Face it, it makes sense!"

"What were you doing up here last night, then?"

"Spying on Mishima, of course. And, and if anyone gimmicked the flitter, he's the one; he was hanging around it just before you left."

"And what did you find out?"

"Nothing, I got lost. That's why I came back this morning, I thought I'd go through his tent. That's what you should be doing!"

It was no good. I had to let him up before my hands grew too tired. Unfortunately, he hadn't told me anything new; the flitter saboteur had to have been around to screw up the Otis module weeks before, so I'd never really thought it was Bunny. But the accusation should have shaken *something* out of him; for instance—

"Why did Condé lie about his claim?" I demanded. "What's the good of our stalling the dig if he'll never get possession anyway?"

Bunny just shook his head, and whimpered when that made him slide another notch. "Where do you get your information? Mehta's people? What they don't know is, the fix is in. Sir Max will win on appeal."

I stood and hauled him up next to me. He lay at full length, gasping as though he'd just swum twenty laps. We stared each other in the eyes, each with his own reasons for self-disgust. Still, a terrorized Bunny was probably safer company.

"All right," I said. "I'm willing to check your story. Let's go search Mishima's tent. You play lookout."

Mishima pitched a neat camp and kept his personal effects tidy. "Personal" is the wrong word; it was all generic camping gear, except for a few books and his passport disk.

I was surprised he didn't carry the disk with him; if it was a phony, though, he might value it less. There were a few lines of Interlingua on the plastic case. MISHIMA KEN was indeed his name, reversed that way because HONSHU was his home planet. His coloring was about right, but wasn't he awfully big for a colonial descendant of Old Japan? No, I was thinking like a classicist; when I'm not a hundred years out of date, I'm more like two thousand.

The books were not without interest. A contemporary translation of the *Bhagavad Gita*, in appalling Alexandrines, and Xenophon's *Anabasis* in sturdy Ur-Linguish, probably the most recent rendering. Character clues? Also confirmation that he was a genuine student of the past, though arguably just faking it on literary knowledge, like me. He hadn't jumped into the archaeological end of the previous morning's discussion.

What I did not find was the skeleton coder. I figured that a cybersabotage tool would be no larger than a pistol, and probably smaller, for concealment. What had made Mishima's outfit look so much like a uniform? A tool belt, with pouches and holsters. As long as he wore that, he had little reason to leave the skeleton coder here.

I slipped out of the tent and—courtesy of Velasquez's keen sentry work—bumped into Ken Mishima.

Stiffened fingers stabbed at my eyes.

Mishima's instinctive attack was something very like the Cobra Opening so recently demonstrated for me in slow motion. The forearm block was still fresh in my mind, as quick as if practiced for years.

I heard a surprised grunt at the impact. But if Mishima hadn't pulled short his follow-up blow, I wouldn't have stood a chance. He was amazingly fast for a big man, and in perfect training.

He stepped back a pace and nodded once, as if to ratify a truce. Each of us rubbed a sore arm.

"My compliments on your proficiency," he said softly. "It would be embarrassing to blind a government official. I apologize—for not expecting you in my private tent. Nothing personal."

"Sorry I startled you," I answered. "My aide should have warned you I was waiting here. He was at the end of the path a moment ago . . ."

"Ah," Mishima said. After a moment he added, "He took off as I approached. Downhill toward camp. It may have been the noise."

"Noise?"

He cocked his head and stared into the middle distance. "It's not audible now. The Otis system. When she first started it up, it was quite loud."

"Foyle has it working?"

He nodded, expressionless.

"I have to go," I said. "We can talk another time."

He looked through the tent flap at his effects, then back at me. "I look forward to it."

As soon as I was out of Mishima's sight, I began to run. Downhill all the way, but I was still out of breath by the time I reached the larger camp.

I found only two of the archaeologists there, and no one else. Helen Hogg-Smythe was fidgeting behind the wheel of a terrain buggy while Friar Francisco slowly bore away its old battery. She waved her metal crook at me as he disappeared into the main storage tent.

"Hello, Commissioner! We were wondering where you'd got to. We'll give you a ride in a moment. You know how it is. Our batteries only run down once a week or so, but they pick the minute to do so with fiendish cunning. I must say, if your Citizen Velasquez hadn't taken the other four-seater in such a hurry—"

"And just where are we all going?" I said. The Green monk had reemerged with a replacement battery.

"Oh, I beg your pardon, you don't know. It's good news! Foyle has repaired the Otis system after all. Just like that! Though actually, you deserve most of the credit. She said your efforts had quite restored the unit's integrity. But—this is really rather humorous—it apparently also restored someone's old password system to working order." She laughed. "The perils of rental equipment! Well, cheer up, Commissioner—we're in business again."

"I specifically told her that even if she thought she'd fixed the unit, I—"

"There, there, Commissioner, don't worry. Foyle is quite a responsible person. She knows better than to start digging around the artifacts themselves without some sort of field test. And you know, she thought of the cleverest thing."

"Yes?" There was no point in flying off the handle. We weren't going anywhere until Friar Francisco had the new battery locked down.

"A riddle for you, Commissioner. What is Foyle going to

attempt to move? The perfect test. What is roughly the same size and composition as a Stone Hut, but much more delicate? More delicate, but also completely expendable, should the Otis mishandle it? Think, now."

For real-life riddles, just apply both Occam and Murphy—the simplest solution is the worst thing you can imagine.

"She's going to move the balancing rock formation."

"Got it, first try! And with such certainty, too. Isn't she clever? But she is impetuous. She won't wait all day for us, Friar Francisco!"

The monk was going about his task with the Zenlike deliberation of his order, spiritually at one with every lug nut. Without actually striking him, I managed to take over completely. Thirty seconds later the battery was connected and we were tearing up a new ridge path at devil-may-care speeds, Hogg-Smythe driving not as elderly people usually do, but as they logically should. I did not complain.

Everyone, even Mishima by now, was waiting for us on the crest of the ridge. It was a flattop just sharp-edged enough to be called a plateau, no more than thirty meters in diameter, with a path leading into dense scrubwood on the prairie side and an unobstructed view of the lake and marsh on the other. We pulled up next to the other large terrain buggy, near one edge. Most of the pedestrians stood nearby, also out of the way.

The balancing rock was a narrow concatenation of slabs and boulders—sandstone, schist, and quartz, orange and dun and dirty white. Its knife shape sliced fifteen meters into the big blue sky, and a high breeze whistled along the edges of the blade, above the thrum of engines and the snarl of human arguments.

We had arrived just in time. Foyle, her red hair a flickering blaze of contrast, was at the helm of the Otis system's half-track, using a control panel to coordinate the movements of the small slave units. A dozen of these swarmed about the column like black ants about to haul a twig. Those on treads dug and probed around its base. Others hovered on jets of air, and some had unfolded their legs into amazingly high stilts. As Hogg-Smythe set our parking brake, the stilts linked up to each other with lateral extensors and formed a lattice all the way around the rock, which now resembled a building under repair, surrounded by scaffolding. Flexible tentacles with rubberized palps at the ends reached out and wrapped around the circumference of the tower at a score of places, to ever so gently test and tighten . . .

But then Bunny, still arguing, climbed onto the hood of the half-track, interfering with Foyle's view, and the operation came to a halt. I rushed up to meet them, Ariel had been at Bunny's side until his ascent, tugging at his sleeve, but not clearly in opposition. She looked relieved to see me.

"I wish you'd waited," I told Foyle.

Those green eyes had an extra tilt when narrowed in anger. She was dressed for work, in heavy brown fabric. A huge backpack frame lay next to the driver's seat, bristling with the tools of her trade, even a padded locker for her chemicals. She had all the momentum of will and purpose; a little moral judo was called for.

"I suppose you want to stop me, too?" she said.

"Why?" I asked. "Isn't this what we're here for?"

Bunny made a noise as if he'd been stabbed.

I stepped up onto the half-track and stood next to Foyle as Velasquez said, "Commissioner, I don't think you realize the situation. This balancing rock formation isn't part of the archaeological site at all, but a feature of natural beauty that Senator Mehta is bound to want untouched. If this woman destroys it—seemingly under your supervision—the Commission could be held liable!"

Not bad at all, for impromptu. It wasn't lack of intelligence that made Bunny a fool. I wondered how much he knew about the secret we were supposed to protect here.

"I don't have any specific instructions about the rock," Ariel said. "But it is picturesque, and this is an area that the senator and his guests will visit. It's really up to you, Commissioner. If you think that this field test is necessary before work can begin on the dig proper, well, the excavation has top priority. And for all I know, Foyle can do just what she says she can, move the rock and put it back in place without damaging it."

"That's the whole point," Foyle insisted. "I can. And once I've proven that, we won't have to worry when we move more durable structures like the Huts."

"I appreciate your concern, Bunny. But I think you're underestimating Citizen Foyle." I turned to her and put an avuncular hand on her shoulder; she flinched with surprise, but accepted it, raising her chin at Bunny. "My aide is just thinking about how destructive an Otis can be in the hands of an inexperienced operator. And he's right. I'm sure we all remember the Phaiacian disaster. All those relics destroyed." No one said anything, but since I was looking at Foyle she felt obliged to nod her head.

I went on, as if to Bunny now, meeting his betrayed stare. "But we all learned from Phaiacia, Bunny! We know what they did wrong, we know the manipulations to avoid. Citizen Foyle, why don't you just point out the differences between your approach and the old method?"

"The old method?" she repeated.

"Or simply indicate the pronations we all stay away from, since Phaiacia."

"Well, of course, I don't remember the *specific* hangup they had at, um, Phaiacia, but—"

" 'Hangup' is a mild term," I said jovially, "for twenty dead and four bodies never recovered. But I'm sure you remember the basic configuration. Now, compare that with the, I must say, almost identical pattern you seem to be following here . . ."

"Actually," she admitted, "I'm not sure I ever heard of a planet called Phaiacia, but—"

I removed my hand from her shoulder. With wounded incredulity: *"Never even heard of . . ."*

Everyone stared at her until she flushed. "Oh, for God's sake!"

"Recall, Excellency," said Bunny, "that this is an *amateur* expedition."

"I owe you an apology, Bunny," I replied stiffly. "Still, we must do what we can . . ."

"Form an oversight committee to schedule everything in advance—" he suggested.

"Go over the manuals with all operators, establish a comprehensive training program—"

"Have to draw one up ourselves, but that shouldn't take more than three or four weeks—"

"And only another month to implement—"

"With me staying on after your departure, Excellency. To, uh—"

"Expedite things."

"Precisely."

"Shit!" Foyle slumped into the driver's seat. "Bureaucrats!" she added, and this exhausted her fund of obscenities. She punched buttons to recall the slave units.

Anger may have made her careless. The mechanical creatures fell back, but somewhere above us a tentacle slapped the rock as it retracted—not hard, but high up, where leverage was greatest.

With a high-pitched grating sound, the tower of stone slowly toppled over, falling straight toward the half-track.

Foyle and I, nervous types, made it off the vehicle in an instant. Ariel ran before us, looking backward. Bunny, facing the wrong way on the hood, was slow on the uptake and couldn't seem to move once he had turned. It didn't matter.

The tower came to a stop in midair, without a sound. It stood leaning over the half-track at an impossible forty-five-degree angle, and stayed that way. It held together, too; not a pebble had departed from the main mass.

Slowly, we gathered around the base of the formation, the other archaeologists joining us. We looked without speaking at the cleverness of the hinge, still invisible, the rock facings folded past each other. We felt a curious vibration through the soles of our boots, the whole ridge faintly trembling, and heard a sound rise and rise, like many voices, or the rush of great waters. It became a roar that filled the sky and drew us to one side of the plateau.

Something was happening. Something as big as the switch we'd thrown to make it happen.

As we watched, awed and silent, the entire lake below us disappeared. Emptied. Like bathwater down a drain.

Chapter Ten

AND STILL WE stared, and still we were silent.

What does one say about something as big as an earthquake, as eerie as an eclipse? Nothing that wouldn't have sounded tinny and all too mortal when the rush of water died away.

This, I knew as I watched the last cataract of brown water spiral into the immense pit, was Condé's "barrow." I was still stuck with my impersonation, but all other bets were off.

"Look! Look!"

Harry Lagado danced on the edge of empty air. Most of the lake had been shallow, and the greater part of the now-exposed basin was flat brown mud, still puddled here and there. The water had run out through a broad circular shaft close to the shore; it was at this huge well that Harry pointed. "Look! A dome!"

Slowly, more slowly than one might expect given the speed of the emptying, a bulbous shape emerged from depths beyond view. The dome, a spinning wet hemisphere of polyurethane appearance, was supported by a cylinder of equal circumference and increasingly revealed height—a blatantly obscene effect.

"Drills through the mud, and spins it off," Wongama said. "Can't say how many revolutions per second."

"Is it a missile, do you think?" asked Helen Hogg-Smythe. The resemblance to an ancient chemical-propulsion weapon was frightening—but then the illusion was dispelled.

The dome, having just passed the height of the former waterline, irised open and disappeared. The curved wedges that had composed it retracted, flexed, and plastered themselves to the outside of the cylinder, which was revealed to be a wide, hollow shaft. And now something like an elevator was rising within the shaft.

There was time to take a step back. Everyone appeared to be surprised at what was going on, though I noted that Bunny showed no fear. If Mishima or Foyle had secrets, this was not one of them, unless they were better actors than I had ever worked with.

"Very, uh, grandiose and impressive," Lagado said. "But notice, notice that technologically—"

"Pretty old-fashioned," Foyle agreed. "Yes. All mechanical, no force fields. Like a hollow asteroid base from colonial times."

"An artifact, in fact!" Hogg-Smythe said, and someone emitted an uncertain laugh.

Far below, the elevator deck stopped as soon as it cleared the lip of its shaft. "I put its area at about two hectares," Wongama said. The man had a mania for quantifying.

"We can't see *anything* from here," Harry complained.

"Just as well. They may not be able to see us, either," Foyle pointed out.

"Who says there is a 'they'?" Wongama objected. "Surely anyone running an underground station on this planet would have made contact with the senator's people by now. Unless they had reason to hide. In which case . . ."

"Why come up now?" I said.

"Exactly. And why come up empty? No. I think we will find that whatever it was, it's abandoned, running on automatic. The underground part can't be too big, or our orbital scanners—"

"Should have seen it anyway—underground!" Lagado insisted. "It's already too big to miss."

Friar Francisco had a deep, thoughtful voice. "This use of the balancing rock as a trigger for the opening. Why? Why not a little red button?"

"We know nothing," Hogg-Smythe said. "We have everything to learn."

The archaeologists, I realized, were in heaven.

For the first time we heard a mechanical noise, as the elevator desk swiveled briskly halfway off the shaft. It kissed the shore nearest the ridge and came to a stop with finality—a locking sound.

No one said anything. To suggest a closer investigation might have provoked someone to point out all the reasons to be careful and leave it alone—might have provoked the sub-commissioner to remind them that they were just amateurs, forbidden access to any new or important find. So no one said anything in front of me. They just went, and so did I.

Harry Lagado led the way, his father bleating unheard warnings from the rear. Most of the others were encumbered by pieces of equipment grabbed at random from the racks in the vehicles: Foyle was wearing her backpack, and Friar Francisco carried a tiny whisk broom and a trowel.

Helen Hogg-Smythe, hampered by a large coil of climbing rope—why?—tripped and stopped short, just in front of me, and I was nearly brained by the crook of her metal walking stick. After that I was more chivalrous and helped her over the rough spots.

"Rush and tear, tear and rush," she puffed—but as excited as any of them, like a young girl off to meet her lover.

"Don't, Harry! Wait!"

With the selective deafness of adolescence Harry dashed from the bank of the lake crater onto the elevator deck and ran toward one of the two small structures that broke its flat surface. But as the rest of us reached level ground and approached the bank he came halfway back, looking unsure of himself. By this time, though, his father was too short of breath to chew him out.

There he stood. The thing hadn't tipped over and dumped him down the shaft, or electrocuted him, or fried him like an egg. It was just an elevator. The rest of the party began to filter across.

Ariel hung back with me, as empty-handed, in a sky-blue jacket and overalls designed more for looks than for crawling around mechanical relics.

"What's that booth over there?" she asked, pointing at the larger and closer projection. It did look somewhat like a weatherproof telecom booth. Foyle was at its threshold.

"I think it may be a control turret," she called out.

I was reluctant to get onto the platform. Whoever had built the lift might have abandoned it, but—unlike the archaeologists—I had reason to believe that it had been found and used since. How deep did the elevator go, and what did Condé have stashed down there?

Even Helen Hogg-Smythe had decided to venture onto the deck, after tying herself to the climbing rope and securing the other end to a sturdy little tree on the shore. I gave a mental shrug and offered Ariel my arm. "Shall we?"

Friar Francisco stepped off just as we stepped on, murmuring something about going for a camera.

Our boots did not ring on the gray surface; the underlying metal bore the same slaty coating you see on colonial-era landing fields. And as we went farther and farther, I realized that the platform was large enough to accommodate spacecraft. I don't think in hectares, but it must have been a hundred and fifty meters across. No wonder the two little booths on its rim had gone unnoticed from the crest of the ridge.

I felt exposed. When Ken Mishima hailed me from the farther of the two booths, we headed in his direction. There was something off-center about the man, but I never doubted he'd be handy in an emergency.

This booth, set in far enough from the rim to avoid a dizzying view down the shaft, was more solid than the other, like a cannon barrel with a wheel-lock vault door open in its side and a large, tricky-looking valve on top.

"It's an airlock connector," Mishima said. "You can always tell a military design. No frills. Shaped only by need, like a soldier himself."

"Sure," I said, stiffening my neck against the g force of his turns of phrase. "But what does it connect to?"

"When the elevator is retracted, there must be a false lake floor that closes over it."

"Mimicking bedrock, to fool scanners," Lagado managed to put in.

"Certainly." Mishima nodded. "But individuals in diving equipment could be exfiltrated to the surface without emptying the lake and revealing the base."

"And at other times, when the planet was known to be secure," I said, "they could let the water out, and bring up this . . . cargo loader we're standing on. It's big enough to take a good-sized spacecraft down into hiding."

"A privateer, say, during one of the intercolonial wars," Mishima speculated. "Something reinforced for surface gravities because it couldn't afford to be spotted in orbit."

"I suppose . . ." Lagado said. "If the underground chambers don't extend beyond the radius of the lake, they might just escape scanner detection. And the holding tanks for the lakewater are perhaps concealed by the mass of the ridge."

"Were scanners less powerful in those days?" Ariel asked.

"No, by then human ingenuity had already peaked," Mishima said. "In our post-classical era, the war with nature is at a truce."

"Sure," I said. "Ruy, didn't you say that the clay strata here tend to confuse scanners?"

Lagado shook his head. "I don't say it. Some do."

"Wouldn't it be wonderful if there *is* a little more to it?" Helen Hogg-Smythe had just joined the conversation, her safety line coiled around one shoulder and trailing behind her. "Perhaps a small barracks down there, with some personal effects left behind? Even a trash basket could contain treasures. And for just a little while, perhaps a week, it's all ours!" She gave Ariel a playful nudge. "When you stranded us without a radio, you didn't anticipate anything like this."

"I wish you joy of it," Ariel said, smiling.

Hogg-Smythe's face fell. "But of course your defense satellites will spot it right away. They're always on the lookout for volcanoes and tidal waves and things of that sort, aren't they? When they notice this, they'll order a flitter sent immediately. You, Commissioner, will be obliged to report the find to your superiors. And that will be the end of our role."

"I'm not so sure," Ariel said. "Until the satellites are fully operational, I think they're concentrating on basic security—takeoffs, landings, and radio transmissions. They wouldn't ignore a forest fire, but this is less obvious. You may get your week here. Unless the commissioner wants us to load up a buggy with extra batteries and drive to the hotel. We could make it in a few days. Is it really so important to report it right away, Alun—sir? What will the Commission say if you don't?"

I knew what the Commission would say if I *did*—"Who the hell are you?"

Lagado surprised me with a way out. "Wait, wait, wait a minute! With all due respect, Commissioner, your jurisdiction is over *alien* artifacts. All we need to excavate *human*-built ruins is the permission of the planetary government, and the senator's representative is more or less that."

"Good point," I said.

"This installation may well be related to the Stone Huts," Mishima said, shaking his head. "We mustn't be ruled by ego desires."

His attitude seemed to surprise and irritate the others.

"No, no, it's obviously of human manufacture, colonial era," Wongama countered.

"I can prove it!" Helen Hogg-Smythe said. "Here, let me show you the other booth."

She led the way, perhaps too fast; by the time we arrived, she was panting. "Where is my stick?" she asked, and Lagado, spotting it back on shore, ordered Harry after it. Poised at the entrance to the booth, the boy looked torn, then ran. He jumped onto the bank just before Friar Francisco returned with his camera.

The walls of the booth were transparent and its gray dome was decorated with a rim of glassy black ornaments. Bunny was leaning against the outside, looking frustrated. He must have realized that he couldn't keep obstructing the investigation without revealing ulterior motives. For my part, I was resigned to the loss of Condé's money; I could only hope to arrange an early departure, before our cover was blown.

Inside the booth, Foyle and Mishima stood before what had to be a control panel. "See?" said Helen Hogg-Smythe. There was no data screen or instruction plaque, but the touchpoints were labeled in the alphanumerics of good old Ur-Linguish.

"Confirmed human," I said. "But please don't touch it. We don't want this thing to move just yet."

Wongama smiled tautly. "No, sir."

"I'm going to the far edge to look down the inner shaft," Foyle announced. I nodded, as if she'd been asking permission.

"I'll come with you," Ken Mishima said.

Ariel and I left the booth to Wongama and Lagado, who had already started an argument. Then Friar Francisco positioned us more shoreward, to provide scale for one of his pictures.

The midday sun washed into the slate-gray surface of the platform, and I could feel the heat through my boots. A rotten cabbage smell blew in from the marsh, along with puzzled birds that landed, pecked about, and took off again. I marveled at how quickly this mystery from an Arabian Nights cave was becoming just another abandoned military base.

Harry Lagado emerged from the tall grass on shore, waving Hogg-Smythe's staff. The old woman straightened and walked briskly across to meet him as he jumped back onto the platform.

"Alun," Ariel said, leaning close, "Was Lagado right? Or will the Column claim jurisdiction over this thing? I'm just worried about the red tape, if—"

The air filled with a deep whine. The deck shuddered and then pulled away from the bank. The rotation was surprisingly smooth and fast, the stop cushioned. The deck clicked back into place atop the shaft, isolated from the shore.

"Wongama!" I shouted.

"We didn't do it!"

"It's . . . it's all right," Helen Hogg-Smythe called out. She'd dropped the coil of safety line from her shoulder in time to keep the movement of the deck from tearing it off. It now extended without much slack to the small tree on shore; she started to untie the other end from her belt. "That's why I brought this. We'll just tie it to one of the booths and use it to get back across—"

A hidden klaxon began to sound from the larger booth.

I found myself running toward her. "Helen, hurry! Just take the belt off!"

She couldn't have heard me over the raving of the klaxon. She'd realized what could happen, but tugged uselessly at the knot, panicky. Harry dropped the metal crook and ran toward her, too.

The platform beneath our feet began to sink into its hole. Smoothly. Quickly. In effect, the circular shaft wall rose—pulling the safety line up and taut, swinging Hogg-Smythe like a pendulum. Harry managed to interpose his body and muffle the impact as the two of them crashed against the shaft wall. As I reached them the klaxon died and the platform came to a halt; we'd only dropped twenty meters or so. But it continued to get darker—and I realized that the mudguard dome was irising closed above us.

The two of them were still tugging at the knot. "Just the buckle!" I cried, but too late: one of the rising wedges of metal lifted the line, tugging Hogg-Smythe upward; her feet had left the surface. I threw Harry to one side and reached for the belt buckle, failed, and got a boot in the face.

But then, as the iris closed on the last of the sunlight, it also—with a loud snapping sound—severed the line. I caught the little woman as she fell, and she grabbed me around the neck as I staggered there. "Stupid, stupid," she moaned, and I shushed her.

"You okay, Harry?" I asked. He nodded, his face pale in the dim blue lights that had popped up around the rim of the platform. The others were coming toward us now, casting long blue shadows; they walked gingerly, as if the platform might give way beneath their feet. The klaxon spoke once more, and we all flinched.

The same dropping sensation again, but this time the shaft wall remained stationary relative to us; I almost thought I imagined the motion.

"The whole shaft's being lowered," Wongama said.

This descent didn't last more than twice as long as the previous one. Now we heard a great rumbling over our heads, and as the mudguard dome retracted again, we dimly saw our new ceiling—the lake's new floor: an enormous, girder-reinforced slab of layered stone. A moment later we were dazzled. Bright floodlights had been lit among the girders.

I put Helen Hogg-Smythe down. "Back to the control turret," I suggested, and we walked that way.

Lagado pointed at a hatch in the distant ceiling, directly above the smaller of our booths. "There's your airlock, Ken. If only we could get that far back up, and connect."

A new rumbling, a whoosh, and the roar of pumps.

"And if we had diving equipment," Mishima said.

"So stupid to tie myself like that," Helen Hogg-Smythe murmured. "What could I have been thinking of?"

"We all saw you do it, and no one thought twice," I said.

"Which is not to say it wasn't stupid," Bunny added.

"It's getting cold," Harry said.

"There are no doors in the shaft wall," Foyle pointed out.

"There ought to be, if people used to hide here for any length of time. There ought to be more."

The klaxon shouted agreement. The elevator began to descend again, within the shaft this time, the polished walls rising fast and faster.

Down and down, with no sign of stopping.

The floodlights turned themselves off once we'd receded from them. The rim lamps stayed on, however, dim and blue but permitting us to see stringcourses in the shaft wall shoot up at regular intervals. After arguing for a few minutes with Lagado over how far apart they were, Piet Wongama estimated our speed at forty k's an hour. We wouldn't go that fast for long.

We gathered around the control booth, except for Foyle and Wongama, who paced aimlessly nearer the rim. Ariel had backed up against me, and I put an arm around her waist. Helen Hogg-Smythe leaned heavily on her staff next to the Lagados; one of the tall boy's hands rested on her shoulder, the other on his father's. Lips moving without sound, Friar Francisco performed a devotion, while Bunny Velasquez slouched against the side of the booth, his head drawn in like a turtle's. Ken Mishima stood to one side as if waiting to receive—or give—orders. And everyone kept yawning. Not just from tension, but to pop our ears in instinctive response to the changing air pressure.

Wongama began to mutter about that. "Air pumps, or free flow to the outside shaft? . . . Free flow. You know, that may be why the lake is kept poisonous, the water-pumping problem would be bad enough without organic congestion . . ."

I noticed that Lagado was whispering, "Yes. No. Yes," as if keeping up with the argument.

Spinning their wheels. What was I reminded of? The *Barbarossa*, but never think about that, just know it's you, it's you they're waiting on.

". . . all these reservoir systems, must be tempting to use hydraulics," Wongama was telling himself, "but—"

"Piet!" I called out. Everyone jumped.

"Yes?" Wongama said.

"We're going to have to risk the controls. Just an elevator, can't be too dangerous. I want you to go through those touch-points, try them all, try combinations, any consistent system that occurs to you. Foyle?"

"Yes, sir?" A rare "sir" from her.

"I want you to keep a record of everything Piet tries, in case he loses his place or wants to take back some moves. If you get a good idea of your own, tell him, but don't argue.''

She took a step forward, then stopped, nervously fingering the pendant chain around her neck. ''I could use a watch,'' she said.

Helen Hogg-Smythe removed her wristcomp. ''Here, take mine.''

''Ken?'' I said next.

''Sir?''

''You know something about antique military hardware?''

''Yes, sir.''

''Why don't you observe, then? The abbreviations on the touchpoints may begin to make sense as Piet proceeds.''

He bowed his head, one sharp chop, and joined the others inside.

''There's not much more room in there,'' I said. ''We'll have to leave it to them.''

But the change in morale was striking. It was coming back to me, the feel for command. Commands themselves, that's all. It's nice if you also have special knowledge, experience, judgment. But if you don't, you can free those who do, clear away the distracting options, ask them by telling them. Once the initiative has been taken, it can be distributed.

''After all,'' Helen Hogg-Smythe said, ''we started this thing, somehow; we should be able to stop it.''

''I'm not so sure we did start it,'' Ariel said in a small but thoughtful voice. ''The platform didn't move until we were all on it. Friar, you went for your camera just as the commissioner and I stepped on. When you returned, Harry had gone for Helen's stick. But the very first moment all ten of us were finally on deck—that was when it returned to the shaft. And now this place is a secret again. No one will know where we've gone. No one will even miss us for a week.''

''What are you saying?'' asked Lagado. ''Someone . . . below, controlling us? Firstly, they'd have to have sensors up here—''

''How about these ugly ornaments on top of the booth?'' Ariel suggested.

I borrowed Hogg-Smythe's staff and tapped one of the black glass protrusions. It shattered, and Lagado picked up one of the pieces.

''A lens. Yes.'' He took a deep breath and spoke almost too rapidly to follow. ''But secondly, how could they be sure that we ten were all? They'd have no way of knowing there weren't others nearby. I think the platform is withdrawn automatically after a brief time, in order to protect the secret of its existence."

"Anything's possible," I said. "But I think it's worth killing all these cameras. If a machine is running them, it'll become less certain of us, and more careful. And if it's people, they'll have to come face us."

I had the others step back, smashed the rest of the lenses, and returned the staff to Hogg-Smythe.

The circular wall still streamed up beyond the rim, but suddenly there was a change, an extra push against our boots.

"Something!" Wongama called out from within the booth. I stuck my head in.

The touchpoints were lit from within. Wongama tapped one tentatively, and there was no additional change.

"That's it," he said. "We're locked in."

"Or locked out," said Foyle.

"Do you think so?" he asked her, the first uncertainty I'd ever seen from him.

And she was declining further into humanity, too, putting a hand on his arm. "No, I think you did right. That last series registered a command. And we're slowing down."

"When it stops, the panel will probably be free again," Wongama told me. "Then we should be able to find an 'up' option. It's a little more complicated than an elevator—there's a safety sequence you have to go through to get a response—but no serious security passwords."

"We're definitely slowing down." Lagado's voice.

Everyone moved outside. That's when the banshees attacked.

A half dozen high-pitched voices shrieked among us in the semidarkness. My companions shouted and flailed about desperately as brightly-lit fireflies followed the movements of their arms—shrieking and burning.

Helen Hogg-Smythe cried out and let her metal staff jump from her hand, and as it fell a weird blue ball of Saint Elmo's fire shot along its length and boiled away up the shaft. Harry Lagado had a hand in front of his face, and the glowing image of a naked girl, about twenty centimeters tall, stood on his knuckles, while on Friar Francisco's wrist was a blazing red spider of equal size—which vanished—as did the fireflies and the maniacal shrieking voices, gone as mysteriously as they had come, leaving us milling and shouting in confusion as we felt the weight of additional deceleration, slowing over a few hundred meters. I bent down and carefully touched the staff. No shock. I picked it up.

"My watch burned out," Ruy Lagado said.

"They all burned out." Mishima's voice was flat and impersonal.

"Look!" Harry pointed. A lit open space in the shaft wall was rising nearby, aligned with the control turret. A corridor became dimly visible beyond it. If we'd had a moment to think—but we didn't. The platform came to a definite halt.

And the hidden klaxon sounded again, too close, deafening. It was too much; inevitably, someone bolted, and the rest of us followed.

Perched in a heap within the revealed corridor, we watched our only transportation drop away. It stopped again a dozen meters down, rotated to bring the control booth around to another corridor opposite us, paused, blew its klaxon, and dropped again. Out of sight.

Ariel gave a little cry and jumped up. She'd seen a small control panel next to the doorway. One touchpoint, at the top and larger than the others, might have been a call button. She pushed it and looked down the shaft.

Instantly a metal door slid downward across the opening to meet the floor with a locking sound.

Ariel threw herself at the metal facing, pounding on it with her fists, shouting, "Piss on it, piss on it, *piss* on it!"

When she finally turned around, pale and shamefaced, she said only, "Well, that was silly."

"On the contrary," said Ken Mishima. "It's only good form, to use anger against fear. Both are then spent."

I had other things to worry about, but the man was getting me down. One phrasemaker is enough for any party.

"What . . . *happened* back there?" asked Helen Hogg-Smythe.

"Electromagnetic pulse," Wongama said in a tragic voice, cradling his watch as though the wrist itself were broken; some wristcomp users become totally dependent. "EMP. Caused by our movement through a powerful field, or perhaps by its internal pulsations. Took the form of a power overload. Lit up the wristwatch screens, set the speakers screaming, and burnt them out entirely."

"I even picked up a charge along my staff," Hogg-Smythe said. "But what were those images in the air? The spider, and so forth?"

"The watches again. Previously stored holograms forced through the projectors. Isn't that right, gentlemen?"

Friar Francisco nodded. Harry flushed.

"I guess that explains it," Hogg-Smythe agreed.

"And more," Wongama said. "We were wondering why this place had never been picked up on scanners. The veil of energy we just passed through could be the key." He looked down the empty, curving corridor. "Which in turn means that this complex . . . doesn't have to be particularly small."

"No more exploring!" Ariel said. "We've got to get the elevator back. We have a panel."

Wongama straightened up and looked at the small metal plate and its array of touchpoints. "Similar, but different," he said. "I don't like the look of that lower keypad. This is the logical place to require a password."

"I don't know anyone who's going to figure it out but you," I told him.

"At least we established the difference between prefixes and root codes . . ." He propped himself against the wall and leaned over the panel.

"What's back here, do you suppose?" Harry asked, farthest down the corridor. His father seized his arm.

"No more running ahead of us, Harry."—and in this sentence, mysteriously, it was decided that we would explore a little after all—"No more running without thinking. The commissioner is in charge."

"My legal authority is pretty tenuous here," I said. "But I'm willing to coordinate things as long as it's useful."

"That suits," Foyle said, and the only other permission I seemed to need—Mishima's nod—followed.

I told Wongama that we would just poke our noses around the corner, but that someone would stay within earshot. He nodded absently.

The corridor curved away to the left, featureless except for the ceiling lights, only one in five of them lit. The way was wide, but we took Mishima's advice and proceeded in single file.

"If the place is abandoned," Harry asked, "why the lights?"

"You leave self-maintaining installations running," Mishima answered, "to last longer. Especially a hiding place like this—just in case you might need it again sometime."

Within a hundred meters, the corridor straightened out and opened into a large, high-ceilinged chamber. It was almost spherical, with an impressive circle of statues or monuments filling the center of the sunken floor and a number of closed doors and access panels lining the sides.

"Looking bigger all the time," Ariel said.

"Yes, isn't it splendid?" said Helen Hogg-Smythe, but she sounded uncertain.

We were clearly standing in the room's main entrance. While most of the statues faced inward, toward each other, the foremost—a dart-shaped memorial stela—bore a plaque angled at our position. The farthest, a group of heroic figures, was spread across a base tall enough to raise it above the rest, into our view. The tall group did not quite block sight of a diorama or holographic representation set into the far wall, behind dusty glass: a fanciful landscape. But the stela had captured my attention.

The plaque bore two messages, the higher of which looked as if it had been carved long before the lower. I walked closer.

The higher message was inscribed in the quaint sans-serif style once called Modern, the same lines in three versions—Ur-Linguish, Deutsch, and Svenska:

HERE WE FIRST ENTERED THE PLACE OF THE TITANS,
I MAY 2470.
HERE WE FOUND SANCTUARY.

The lower message was in a more elaborate font, and translated only once, no Svenska:

WE DEPARTED ON I SEPTEMBER 3068.
TO THE TITANS WE LEAVE THE GRATITUDE
OF TWENTY-FIVE GENERATIONS.
TO ALL REFUGEES WE LEAVE THE PLACE ITSELF, AND A WARNING:
YOU MAY FIND YOURSELF HERE,
BUT DO NOT LOSE YOURSELF.

The exploration party drifted about in small groups. Ariel, who probably couldn't read Ur-Linguish, tagged along with me. I entered the main circle of statues.

There was nothing on the other side of the stela. The other pieces were mainly busts of stern-looking men and women, set on strangely shaped pedestals of blue glass. Dusty swivel chairs were bolted in front of several of them, which seemed odd.

The largest piece, the raised group study, was odder still. The towering figures, men and women in jumpsuits or coveralls, were molded in the heroic style and attitude of a familiar genre, "planting the flag." But that's not what they were doing.

They appeared to be stuffing a giant snake into a mail sack.

We had approached more closely to read the plaque on this monstrosity when Helen Hogg-Smythe appeared at the edge of the circle and said, too quietly, "I think you'd all better take a look at this."

We followed her to the rear of the chamber, the inset glass case, and the diorama behind it. The glass front was some ten meters wide and nearly as high, heavily streaked with dust. Behind it was a three-dimensional rendering of a strange cityscape. On either side of the model stretched serried rows of ugly black buildings, with the suggestion that they went on and on, a great metropolis, the architecture itself monotonous and overpowering, but happily broken up by a series of green little parks with lakes and copses. Many blocks were connected in midair by slender transparent tubes of what was presumably meant to be a transportation system. In the foreground, one could look downward; a little cemetery appeared nearby, with crosses and other human symbols just visible. Just past its fence loomed a peculiar black wall, tall and oddly shaped. From the sharp angle that came forward to meet the cemetery, it extended far back in a narrow V that divided most of the city, then finally turned broadside left and right to form the city limits. Beyond this barrier one saw only wilderness, forest and plains rolling all the way to where the horizon met a strange sky, dull gray with fine silver lines tracing through it.

The meticulousness and credibility of detail was amazing, but as Hogg-Smythe cleared a larger area of dust this became less surprising. Because it wasn't a diorama. It wasn't even a hologram.

It was a window.

Part Two

The Maze

Chapter Eleven

POSTCARDS FROM A dead city:

You are inside a magic cavern full of buildings and trees. But the cavern is too large to take in, the buildings appear fake or wrong, and the green clumps of trees look lost and unlikely—not oases, but mirages.

Cramped plazas. Stretched-out high-rises topped with crenellated fortress walls. Terraces with insane overhangs that provide no view at all. Block after block the same, and then a break in the pattern that is even uglier, a ziggurat of squat modules seemingly fitted together at random. All clean and shiny, except in one roofed mall, where worn-out maintenance robots lie under centimeters of uncollected dust like cattle bones in snow.

Most of the buildings are black, composed of the same ceramic slabs as the Stone Huts. There are no doors, only sliding panels to keep out the rain. And it should rain, for the ceiling—a silver-lined grid of luminous blue-gray panels, some blacked out—is kilometers above, and white clouds with oddly shadowed bellies can be seen, motionless, in the distance.

Titans. A good name for the architects of this huge place. Even here, within walking distance of the abandoned city's great elevator entrance, there are alien buildings that the human refugees of twelve hundred years ago never got around to colonizing. They are empty; the original inhabitants left nothing behind.

What were they like, these aliens? Their staircases, benches, and built-in shelves would seem to indicate a size and shape not unlike that of humans. But why then the vaulted ceilings—sometimes twenty meters high in rooms ten across? There are no paintings of them on the walls, no statues in the parks. No representational art at all. Where decorations are incised, here and there, they are cold, colorless, and abstract. Self-portraits of a different kind?

But then there are the parks, so delicate by contrast that from a distance you expect bonsai trees and pocket-mirror ponds, and are surprised to find them life-sized. Above you spiral the glass arteries of the transport system, and these, too, seem creations of a radically different sensibility.

Could the humans have added these features later? But the human districts dispel this idea. The familiar wood panels of the colonial style line the great black boxes. The simple work of regular folk; it looks lost here.

All ghost towns—all empty buildings—would rather you went away, but this city is something colder. Not malevolent, but devoid of the promise that sustains, like the eyes of a woman who loves another. There is nothing for you here, humans. A doorway to step into until the rain stops, some cold dark night when there's no place else to go. Nothing more.

I returned to the transport stop, careful of my feet on the transparent staircase up to the terminal. I'd sent Harry on ahead, to see if the others had left a message for us.

The transport system still worked. Its computers recognized that we were the only users, and routed us as if on private cars. The surviving maps of the system were of human origin, brass plates in Ur-Linguish, which most of our party could read; stops were color-coded to buttons on panels. Foyle had pointed out that these codes, too, would be human additions—the Titans didn't appear to have had much color sense.

At first the archaeologists had been hell-bent on exploring. They assumed that since the builders of the cavern city had been aliens, "my" Commission would take over the site. As amateurs, they had only one day to make discoveries of interstellar importance.

We had visited a number of subway stops together, the major intersections of the system. We soon determined the limits of the district once recolonized by humans, and realized how empty the rest was, no alien possessions left behind.

But then Friar Francisco, passing through to check on Piet's progress at the elevator door, discovered how to make the statues at the entrance talk. And when it became clear that they were programmed to relate the history of the city, the others were drawn back to listen. They were academics, after all—easily torn from fieldwork, when other people's notes lay ready to hand.

Not that I wasn't willing to rejoin them. Just a few hours of the vacant-eyed buildings, the looming false sky, had been more than enough. I'd embarked on this last foot tour mainly to keep restless young Harry from going alone, and to convince myself that the place was indeed deserted.

But any suspicion that Condé had a team of men hiding here, looting alien artifacts, had died when I'd grasped the size of the city. It was too much and too big; the only way to exploit the place was with all the privileges of recognized ownership, and surely Condé wouldn't jeopardize his chance to acquire that by scattering men about. I was his agent, and he hadn't trusted even me with the truth. There was no reason to expect others.

Harry met me at the entrance to the terminal, turned around, and called to someone inside. "Here he is!"

Ariel was waiting for us on the platform next to the accelerator tube. She'd agreed to be a runner for those of us who could read the language.

"They sent me for you," she said.

"Does that mean Piet's beaten the lock?"

She grimaced. "Well, he claims that's imminent. And the rest of them want to show you what they've learned."

Harry looked embarrassed for his father and the others. "They *are* discoverers," he said. "They deserve some credit."

"Of course they do," I told him as we entered a car. Ariel punched the controls that would move us two stations, past the large stop overlooking the humans' cemetery, to the main entrance. We watched through transparent panels as the city rolled beneath us.

"See what I meant before?" Harry said to me. "The little parks were all connected once, and they weren't blocked off from that wilderness behind the big wall, either. The city and the countryside were supposed to, to—" He'd speeded up and jammed, like his father, but he brought his hands together, fingers meshing, to—

"Interpenetrate each other?" Ariel asked.

"That's it," he said. "A word like that."

"And you think that's the way the Titans liked it, that it was the humans who blocked off the larger park for some reason," I said. He nodded.

"It's more than just a park," Ariel said. We looked at her. "But let them tell you—I'm not sure I believe it."

"All right," I told them. "Astonish me. How big is this place?"

"It's the heart, brain, and spine of the planet," Helen Hogg-Smythe said with great satisfaction. "It's tremendous!"

We'd made a circle within the ring of statues at the main entrance, some of us standing, some sitting. Friar Francisco had discovered why swivel chairs were bolted in front of the monuments. Their blue glass pedestals were actually library terminals, touch-activated, intended for the use of students. "It's a good thing that they have text screens for older children," the friar had noted. "*Spoken* Ur-Linguish would be beyond most of us."

"Start at the beginning," Harry begged. "Please."

"Just a moment first," I said. "Piet, shouldn't you be working on the elevator door?"

Wongama was bent over the largest terminal, at the base of the great sack-the-snake monument. He just waved one hand around his ear, as if I were a mosquito pestering him.

"That terminal is linked to the main public library bank," Friar Francisco explained. "Everything we need to know about the elevator exit will be there."

"Very well," I said. "From the beginning, then. The city was built and abandoned by aliens before any humans arrived on the scene; that I can see. Start with them."

"The aliens?" said Foyle. "Undoubtedly Titans. That name had already been coined when the humans who left this library arrived here. Titans were the first extinct spacefarers whose artifacts humankind ever ran across, and they got a poetic name—the forerunners of the gods. They must have been about human-sized, and very similar to us biochemically, requiring much the same atmosphere and so forth. They came to this planet about a million years ago. They never tried to live aboveground; what we regard as normal surface radiation was probably too much for them. Instead they dug in and took control of the planet."

"Took control?"

"I don't know how else to put it. This is the only city, but it has taproots that run deeper than you would believe, and farther, too."

"If you mean that it's geothermally powered, I think we all assumed—"

"That's just part of it," Foyle said. "And the power system is more sophisticated than that. For instance, it gave the Titans control over the planetary magnetic field—and don't ask me how. For all I know it has something to do with rechanneling convection currents in the molten core, it's that big."

"I remember you telling me something about a magnetic field surge a million years ago."

She nodded. "They engineered that. Apparently the Titans were more sensitive than humans to their electromagnetic environment. Some aspect of it, anyway. Perhaps they wanted to create a stronger Van Allen belt between themselves and this sun—who knows? Then there's the pulsing field at subsoil level, probably part of the stress-feedback system that maintains the cavern's integrity. Whatever else it does, it screws up any scanners above, concealing the whole colony."

"I told Piet, and I told you," Lagado put in. "Anomalous field, I said, but no, you said *clay strata*!"

"Fantastic," I said. "People have always been carving cities out of asteroids, but that's dead rock. This is the crust of a living planet, and the size of the dome is unbelievable. That wilderness beyond the city wall must extend six or seven kilometers."

"Go ahead," Bunny told Foyle. "Astonish him." And the other archaeologists smiled as she let me have it:

"Try six *thousand*."

It didn't seem to be a joke. But it was impossible, and I said so.

"Oh, rarely more than thirty or forty k across," Helen Hogg-Smythe explained. "A tunnel, rather than a dome. But a tunnel all the way up the spine of the major continent, ending at the north pole."

"Remember, I *told* you that the central mountain chain was recent, and weird." Foyle's eyes glittered. "But we rationalized that away, along with everything else. Commissioner, those great mountains were boiled up, or thrown up, or dug up only a million years ago, just to make space for the corridor beneath them. I think the Titans needed a baseline that long to obtain the sort of control their machines had—still have!—over fundamental planetary processes. Continental drift, volcanism, seismic waves. *It's all regulated*, the whole planet has been tamed to protect this city."

"Not just the city!" Lagado said. "The Hellway."

"The what?"

"The wilderness park," Foyle said. "Ruy is right, the park

is the main thing. This city at one end, some control structures at the other, and the park fills in the vast corridor between. The Hellway—that's what the human refugees called it later—was very important to the Titans, for reasons we can only guess at. It keeps the atmosphere down here going, of course, but it could be much smaller and still do that. It includes plants and animals that may have been native to the Titans' planet, but it's not just a nature preserve. According to these terminals, it also contains bizarre life-forms of the Titans' own creation, genetically engineered for . . . well, what might be entertainment value."

"*I* think it was a religious retreat," Lagado said.

Wongama broke the surface long enough to groan, but Hogg-Smythe said firmly, "Quite possible. Look at that hideous black city. Imagine the psychic relief of escaping from that into wild country. But, as Foyle says, there's no way of reading the Titans' minds now."

"They lived here for hundreds of thousands of years," Foyle continued. "Pretty amazing in itself, compared with human instability. But finally, about the time Neanderthal man died out on Old Earth, the aliens abandoned the colony. Total evacuation, every building emptied. But the park creatures were left, and the maintenance robots, and the engines that control the planet. Perhaps they intended to return someday. Perhaps they will. But that's all we know about the Titans."

"Wait a minute," I said. "What about the Stone Huts? Where do they fit in?"

"The Huts are a red herring," she replied. "The Titans didn't build them. But that's another chapter of the story."

And this was Helen Hogg-Smythe's to tell. She stood up to speak, but patted the terminal next to her first, as if to give it fair credit for the information.

"The human refugees who left these plaques and statues originally lived on Avalon," she said. "One of the first wave of colonies in the Blue Swathe, the so-called Arnheim group. The Arnheim colonies were financed and outfitted from Old Northern Europe, about fifteen hundred years ago. Their founders, British, German, Scandinavian, were social democrats who hoped to adapt their politics to high technology in ways that hadn't been tried on Earth. Each colony was a separate experiment, the same basic charter modified from planet to planet by majority vote.

"By and large, they were successful experiments, too. Stable, prosperous worlds like Myrdal, for instance . . . Weren't you born there, Ariel?"

Ariel nodded. "A little dull," she said. "But people have done a lot worse."

"Some of the Arnheim worlds departed from their charters over time," Hogg-Smythe went on. "Catharensis Five, for instance, is now a capitalist bazaar, wealthy but without a cultural character of its own. Others went the opposite way, turned insular and puritanical. That, we are told, is what happened to Avalon."

She smiled and patted the terminal again. "Bear in mind that we are hearing only one side of the story. The version that the descendants of refugees chose to tell their schoolchildren, centuries after the fact.

"Once upon a time, then, on Avalon. During the colony's first century, morale was high. But then it lost its way. The Distributors, the civil servants charged with minimizing class differences, became a hereditary ruling class in their own right. They couldn't publicly enjoy luxuries denied to others, but they could aggrandize themselves in another way, with power. They passed new regulations, zealously enforced, against everyone else's 'class crimes.'

"The petty-minded rules extended from wage controls and employment quotas down to tiny details of dress. High achievers in any field were handicapped like racehorses, and ostracized if they still managed to distinguish themselves. The only permissible competition for rank was in the civil service exams—for which the children of Distributors were secretly coached.

"After a few decades of this, many citizens came to believe that Avalon's social equality was not just a sham, but unnatural and wrong from the beginning. They formed the Meritocratic party in opposition to the Distributorship.

"The government branded these dissidents as 'Elitists' and outlawed their party. But as so often happens, the rebels defiantly adopted their enemies' label, and it became the banner of a more and more radical movement. Questioning every leveling principle in Avalon's charter, the Elitists attracted not only the disaffected found in any society, but the clever and the talented and the daring. The natural elite, in short. They came to be feared by their fellows, despite their idealistic goals."

"Idealistic?" Foyle said with surprising bitterness. "I suppose. If you're fond of cant. All their propaganda about pursuing excellence and realizing individual potential seems queasily familiar. The First Columnards were fond of the same catch-phrases—I guess *they* got them from the Kanalist lodges they subverted—but what do those ideals mean in practice? 'Let the better man rule, so long as it's me.' "

Bunny looked outraged; Lagado, for one, averted his eyes from my Column uniform. But Hogg-Smythe stuck to cases.

"I don't think you're being fair," she said. "You have to judge the, um, Elitists in the context of *their* history, not ours."

"Helen's right," Ariel said. Like Foyle, she seemed to be taking the discussion personally. "I haven't read this stuff, but—"

"You haven't lived among the 'Renaissance men' of our own era, either," Foyle said. "You haven't seen how much damage their ideals and high standards can do—even the best of them, intending the best."

Ariel, flushed, was beginning to stammer. "And you—you don't know what it's like to—to have a whole righteous planet, all the good people . . . tell you every day how evil you are, for just trying to be your best, to be yourself. None of you knows."

She was wrong about that—although I'd been on Foyle's side until Ariel's words struck a chord. Wayback. The old country. Much as she'd said, though not socialist. That would have been too la-di-da for salt-of-the-earth types like us. Cheat, steal, and sue for more grazing-land all your life, that's business, but don't pull the uppity on us when you get it, mate, we know where you came from, and did you see the fancy dress Ferguson's old lady was wearing in church? Already putting on airs, thinks her piss is perfume. And as for you, boy: *A lying smooth-tongued slacker like your Larkspur father, curse the day my sister ever fell for his so-called family name. Raised you like our own, but you're too good for us now, ain't you, with your book learning and your poofter card tricks and your snooty jokes. But proud as Satan and always in fights, I wish your respectable ancestors could see the poncing dribbet of a no-good their trust fund is sending to Nexus bloody Varsity* . . . A mouthful of sour milk from the past, and no choice but to swallow it.

Friar Francisco's voice was low and gentle. "Surely we don't have to refight the Elitist rebellion now?"

Foyle's tone conceded nothing. "Sorry to have interrupted, Helen. Do go on."

"It wasn't the usual sort of civil war," Hogg-Smythe said, frowning. "The Elitists didn't want to rule, they just wanted to emigrate. But Avalon couldn't afford to lose so many of its best scientists and engineers and managers—couldn't even afford to jail them. The rumor spread that the Distributors intended to 'reeducate' the Elitists' children—in fact, confiscate them and hold them hostage for their parents' good behavior. True or not, it turned the Elitists from a party into a conspiracy.

"It wasn't hard for them to make their break. Brains and will and audacity, they had. When the time came, they hijacked the finest vessels of Avalon's merchant spacefleet and scuttled the rest. A crime, their historians emphasize with glee, made possible only by the Distributorship's overcentralized economy. And so the Elitists—ten thousand strong—reached freedom.

"But freedom, if you'll forgive the observation, is not a place; you cannot settle there. The word was out. The other Arnheim worlds had heard nothing but evil of these people who called themselves Elitists, and in any event would be treaty-bound to extradite them back to Avalon. Other colonies were as yet few, and while this fringe is unusually rich in Terroid planets, the Elitists did not want to start a society from scratch. Then they ran across what we call Newcount Two.

"A somewhat Earthlike world, its intense magnetic field mysterious but harmless. A place, they had thought from a distance, that they could farm for a few decades until scout ships could find a more congenial society for them to join. Not an idle wish, in those days, when colonies were sprouting everywhere like mushrooms. Of course, Avalon would be searching for them in the meanwhile, for political reasons and to regain their stolen ships; but there was nothing the refugees could do about that.

"Once in orbit, however, they quickly spotted the entrance to the abandoned city of the Titans. It's the only entrance, except for a tiny outlet at the pole, but at that time it was not concealed or disguised; in fact, there was a large half-buried structure around it. When they discovered what was beneath it—and scannerproof, too—the Elitists knew they'd never find a better hiding place.

"A few of the city's park extensions could be converted to farming. And if decades had to be spent here, they could be spent profitably, learning the secrets of an advanced, exotic technology. The refugees put it to a vote, made the commitment, and moved in en masse.

"It was they who built the elevator and the lake reservoir. A big job, but they had the engineers, and as we have noted, the technology was a known quantity, common to asteroid bases of that era. When the elevator is retracted, nothing scannable is left aboveground. The balancing rock, for instance, triggers the lake door via simple mechanics, a pull cable threaded through ridge and bedrock; no electromagnetic signal is transmitted."

"But why build it so big?" I asked. "And why have any trigger at all, topside?"

"You're forgetting about the scout ships," Hogg-Smythe said. "They would be gone for years at a stretch, and there was no way to predict the exact times of their return. And you certainly wouldn't want them transmitting the fact of their arrival. No, the scouts needed their own door handle, something they could count on finding quickly, no matter what season of the year, no matter how many years had passed. Since it had to be prominent anyway, why not make a virtue of that?" She looked roguishly at Foyle. "After all, no one ever disturbs a balancing rock formation."

Foyle didn't quite smile. "I can imagine the system working while the Elitists were here to maintain it," she said. "I'm surprised to find the lake's pumps running so smoothly after six hundred years, though."

But I thought: maybe they hadn't been. Otherwise Condé would never have found the place. What had he told me? *The entrance was well disguised, once, and I restored that.* I wondered if his work crews had left anything behind. But it wasn't my worry, or wouldn't be much longer.

"I still don't see where the Stone Huts fit in," Ariel said.

"Well, once the Elitists had committed themselves to the planet, it began to seem less secure," Hogg-Smythe went on. "The magnetic anomaly might attract attention, and then a world this hospitable would be carefully searched. But when an Avalonian search party finally did reach Newcount Two, what did they in fact find? The Stone Huts. An ancient Titan landing site, clearly visible from orbit. Avalonian archaeologists—the ones who dropped those shovels Foyle dug up—soon established how small and short-lived the alien camp had been, no reason to spend much time on it. They also turned up a few technological artifacts planted by the Elitists, carefully chosen from the city's warehouses to support the scenario of an emergency repair stop. Do you see what else the artifacts seemed to prove? That the Elitists—technophiles—had never passed this way, since they would have picked any alien site clean if they had.

"In short, as Foyle said, the Huts are a red herring. The Elitists had used the Titans' own construction equipment to take apart the abandoned surface structure, to reassemble it into the mock 'sawhorses' we call Stone Huts, and to subject those to forces and stresses that fit the scenario—just in case the Avalonians analyzed them in depth."

"And the construction codes on the slabs?" Foyle asked. "The ones that didn't match up?"

"Additional 'evidence' that the sawhorses had been jury-rigged for emergency repairs," Hogg-Smythe explained.

"But why put the site so close to the real city entrance?" Ariel looked puzzled. "Wasn't that asking for trouble?"

"Tell me, Commissioner," Hogg-Smythe said, "since it's your hobby: don't magicians usually hide things in plain sight?"

"That's one way to do it, yes," I said. "In this case, I wouldn't have taken the risk."

Hogg-Smythe shrugged and nodded. "The plan was audacious, even arrogant. Elitist, in other words. But we should also note that it worked. And that ends a chapter in the story, I think. Besides, my mouth is dry."

She sat down.

"And thank you," I said. "But what happened to the Elitists? The plaque says they arrived twelve hundred years ago, and left six hundred years later—I realize the record stops there, but . . . any idea what happened to them?"

I was looking at Lagado as I said this, because he'd been twitching throughout Hogg-Smythe's speech as if he had additions to make, but when everyone turned to him he just sputtered helplessly. "I have yet to finalize my sociological conclusions," he said at last. "I'll defer to the friar."

"Well, first of all," Friar Francisco began, "they never did master the Titans' technology. Only bits and pieces. They could work the Titans' construction equipment, and even learned to use the devices that controlled the ecology and gene pool of the great park, or Hellway. But the Elitists could rarely grasp the underlying theory. And when they took the machines apart, they found almost nothing. Nothing comprehensible."

The Green monk pointed upward, at the heroic statue group. "This commemorates their greatest triumph. It meant to them what the first Moon landing must have meant to Old Earth. Just the beginning, they thought. But they never advanced beyond it."

I regarded the bizarre figures again. "Snake milking?" I asked.

The archaeologists laughed.

"That 'snake' is a cybernetic cable," Friar Francisco said.

"One element of the Titan control network that governs this planet's magnetic field from the north pole. Those humans in the memorial have just lifted the cable from the original Titan coupling, and are plugging it into another which they have built themselves. The Titans liked gigantism, that's evident; they didn't care how inefficient it was. This great control coupling was just a scaled-up version of the governor in one of the simple construction machines that the humans did understand. But it was still considered a great triumph."

"*What* was?" Ariel demanded. She sounded tired.

"I'm sorry. The Elitists' new coupling reduced the planetary magnetic field to Earthlike intensity again. Newcount Two's disguise was now complete. There was no field anomaly to attract unwelcome attention. But it meant much more than that to the Elitists. Forging their own destiny, holding fast to their own history, was of great importance to them. Those heroic figures are making this planet a little Earth, you see. They are restoring the Garden.

"But as decades passed, it became evident that the humans would not prevail after all, would never truly make this place their own. Their morale suffered.

"The scout ships still came and went. But new generations knew nothing except their own form of government . . . whatever that was—the details are obscured by slogans and shibboleths. Only a certifiable utopia would have tempted them to emigrate. At the same time, the dead city oppressed them, its unfathomable technology mocking the cleverness that had once set their forefathers apart.

"They desperately needed spiritual reaffirmation. And at last they found it. They created . . ." The friar paused, his lips pursed. "But it had to be more spontaneous than that, no matter what deliberate synthesis went into it, too . . . There *arose*, let us say, a cult. A mystery religion, with a mystery religion's emphasis on individual enlightenment. At the same time, though, an established church, not as wild and mystical as, say, the Orphism of the ancient Greeks. More like the Freemasonry of Enlightenment times, or the Kanalism of our own era. The ritual through which every boy and girl entered adulthood and citizenship. It seems to have bound Elitist society together again, restored some sense of shared purpose. And the actual rite of passage was another symbolic triumph of humanity over alienness."

"How so?" I asked.

"The humans used the only Titan machines they had mastered to shape the Titan park. They restructured it into a series of subenvironments, testing grounds for their children. The rite of passage was literally that: the young candidates for adulthood had to traverse the Hellway from the city to the pole, learning small secrets of life along the way."

"They'd hike six thousand k?" Ariel objected.

"Oh, no, there are means of transportation within the Hellway. I gather most candidates made the passage in a week or so."

"So they found some adventure and purpose in this gloomy place," Ariel said. "I think that's great."

"Why *Hell*way, though?" Harry asked.

"That's the exasperating thing about skimming a history," the friar said. "Details drop out. And translation is a problem, too. But in a mystery religion, you know, the candidate is often taken through a symbolic death and hell, only to be born again at the end of his journey."

"Furthermore," Foyle said darkly, "if your social goal is to bind people into a Folk, under the leadership of the hardy and the few, and you can't use the traditional method—wars of conquest—maybe you'd put them through another kind of hell instead."

"There are cults of fear and cults of joy," Friar Francisco said. "We have only the Elitists' own description, which is of course biased. Anyway, let's finish the story.

"After five centuries in the Titan city, their morale restored through religion, the Elitists were struck down with plague. A family of chameleonlike mutant viruses—the descriptions recall the dread immunosuppressant epidemics of late classical times. The Elitists would defeat one strain only to be faced, in the next generation, with another. Their population dwindled. By the time they finally wiped out the disease, too few of them were left to maintain their traditional way of life. They reexamined the reports of the scout ships, and decided that after six hundred years, one of the Arnheim worlds had become tolerant enough to accept them.

"Spiritually they were no longer the same Elitists who'd intended to trade the Titan technology for wealth, rank, and immortality. The years of struggling for life itself may have made them more rigid and steadfast in their religious belief; all they wanted to bring away from the planet now was their cult. Like all zealots, they thought they would transform the universe. They compiled what they called the White Codex—hundreds of years' worth of investigation into the Titan technology, distilled. This treasure they took. And they left behind these files on their history, brought up to date at the end, as a time capsule. And so they reentered the human sphere."

"They didn't, though," Foyle put in. "Maybe they didn't master the Titan technology, but from the hints they left behind we can be sure that what they did learn would have revolutionized some of our human sciences. Not to mention our knowledge of the Titans themselves. I say they didn't make it."

"An accident in space?" the friar suggested. "There's an even uglier possibility. The Elitists could not know, as we do, of other 'lost' colonies who have tried to rejoin the mainstream worlds with the aftermarks of exotic viruses in their genes. The Elitists may have been recognized, quarantined, and sterilized—or worse. That's how populations drop out of history. Their extreme religious views would have made it that much easier on their executioners' consciences.

"Maybe I'm wrong, maybe they foresaw that danger and infiltrated some world without proclaiming themselves. But I don't believe it; I can't see them accepting total assimilation and obscurity. If we have never heard of them, it can only be because they did not survive."

He looked around sadly. "This is their only immortality—a few tiny additions to something quite inhuman."

A long silence followed this speech. Finally, Ariel spoke. "I think I'll stick to building new cities. The old ones are too sad."

"I'm sorry for them, too," Foyle admitted. "For what their ideology brought them to."

Piet Wongama cleared his throat. "Their numbers must have been very small at the end, if that matters. They left virtually all their spacecraft behind. Valuable property. I'm sure they would have taken as many as they could crew."

"Ah, the quantifier resurfaces," I said, to polite laughter. "And how do you know this?"

He pointed at some cryptic flashing on the screen in front of him. "This indicates Level Null, the lowest floor of the Elitist's elevator complex, where scout ships and transports were off-loaded. The readout says that most of the hangars are still full."

"That's interesting."

"Level Null is where the elevator has been all this time, too," he went on. "I've figured out everything except what started us down in the first place; that's beyond me. But the elevator's stuck at the bottom. I'm afraid my confused button-pushing—and your smashing of the control-turret sensors, Commissioner—triggered a safety shutdown: one stop at every level and a power-off at the bottom until the command stack is cleared."

He smiled. "The good news is that we can clear it from that panel at the door. As I thought, security was never a big concern here, just safety checks. The sequences weren't meant to be confusing, and it wasn't too hard to look them up."

"Then, it's time to go," I said. There were murmurs of protest, but I quashed them. "I'll let you return after we've filed a report, and to hell with regulations. In fact, I'll commandeer the next boat to stop at Newcount and report the find personally—and I'll insist you be allowed continued access as discoverers. But the five or six hours we've already spent here without taking official action will count against me; let's not drag it out any longer."

This went over well, even raising a satirical smile from Bunny, who had been sunk in gloom all afternoon, probably trying to figure out how to pay his gambling debts once Condé heard of our failure. Hogg-Smythe hefted her staff, Foyle strapped her huge backpack on again, and Wongama led us back through the curving corridor to the elevator door.

With his wristwatch out of commission, Wongama had been reduced to rolling up his sleeve and writing control sequences on his forearm with a wax specimen marker of Friar Francisco's. But at least he'd gotten them right. When he hit the last touchpoint the whole panel lit up, and we could feel the vibration as the great platform rose to meet us from far below.

The door slid up and open. Wongama stepped backward in surprise.

A tall, hardfaced man was standing on the elevator, not far away. He wore simple clothes of Lincoln green and a soft hat with a feather in it, and he carried a wooden crossbow. "Here they are!" he called out to the score of similarly dressed men in the distance, shook his head at us, and said, "Decided to let us out of our bottle, did you?"

Smiling genially, he raised the crossbow to his chin, aimed in our direction, and fired.

Chapter Twelve

THE MAN ON the platform must have aimed to pick off Wongama at the panel—keeping the door open until his companions could join him. But Bunny Velasquez had darted forward as soon as the bowman appeared, oblivious to anything except his own convenience, saying to the men in green, "There you are—finally!" as he crossed the line of fire.

The crossbow bolt caught Bunny at the base of the throat. He collapsed backward in a grotesque limbo step, his spine severed. A single bright spurt of arterial blood fell with him and wrapped across his white tunic like a red sash when he hit the floor.

Now it was the bowman's turn to freeze, amid confused cries on all sides, as Wongama hit a few touchpoints on his panel and the door came down, cutting off the last few words of another man in green: *"—fucking moron, you've killed our contact!"*

Wongama and I stared at each other. Ariel was crouching next to Bunny's body, in my shadow, whispering, "OhGod-OhGodOhGod." Ken Mishima stood back, flattened almost casually against the wall. The others had retreated around the curve of the corridor; only Foyle was still in sight and unpanicked. A long moment.

Then lights danced on the panel and Wongama's face snapped back to it. He hit a few more points; they all lit up, then went dark. "They know how to use the panel in the control turret, anyway," he said.

"Can you keep them out?" I asked.

"They're blocked out for one full-dress safety check, that's all."

"How long—"

"Maybe ten minutes. Long enough to recycle the air in the basement hangars. But it's nonrepeatable, Commissioner. Anything more confusing will just set off an emergency shutdown like the one we caused before—and remember, that opens every door on the way to the bottom, starting with this one."

"Ten minutes, then," Foyle said. "Two to plan, eight more for a head start. To somewhere." Her voice didn't sound as cool as her words.

"Who *are* those people?" Ariel asked. "Why those outfits, bows and arrows . . ." Her voice still echoed the spell of the talking statues, the dead past, ghosts.

Foyle was quick to reply. "I recognize the green outfits," she said, in her commonsense voice. "Forest fatigues issued to the Iron Brotherhood—one of the bigger mercenaries' unions. They only kill on commission. Somebody must have hired them to guard this place, keep it secret."

Wongama could think fast, too. "If they really were bottled up when the elevator was shut down, then their headquarters must be Level Null. It's the best place to watch the elevator from, but it has no other exits. And if they are just guarding the shaft, that would explain why they know so little about the controls."

"They knew enough to bring us down here, when they saw us on the platform cameras," Foyle said.

"But not enough to disarm the balancing-rock trigger in the first place," Wongama pointed out. "Or free the platform, these past—what, five?—five hours. With luck, they may know even less about the city proper."

Helen Hogg-Smythe had returned, along with Harry Lagado. The others crept behind. "But why such primitive weapons?" she asked, and we all looked down on Bunny's body with a sudden awkwardness. The chance for a decent observance had passed, though; the few shudders were furtive and meaningless, as if customers had been fooled by a mannequin in a store: so human a shape, but not alive.

"Waste of time to guess," I told them. "We've got to clear out."

"Couldn't this just be . . . some sort of mistake?" Lagado said.

I looked at the ring of white faces; even Brother Francisco had lost color. "I don't think so," I said, starting back toward the city entrance, using words to drag them after me. "Only the target was a mistake. They called Velasquez their contact. That would explain his strange behavior, all right. Flashing a signal when we flew over the marsh, slipping out at night, trying to keep Foyle away from the balancing rock. He must have linked up with these people the first time he visited Newcount, months ago. So the mercenaries have conspired with a Column official to conceal the city, and now they've blundered and killed him. They've got a lot to cover up, and they wouldn't have pulled us down here on the elevator in the first place if they weren't willing to make us disappear. We have to stay out of their hands somehow."

We passed by the busts, and beneath the great bronze cable-couplers, which, like most patriotic statues, were placed too high to see well, to believe in, to take inspiration from. Then the ceramic city looked back from the picture window.

"Split up from here, and regroup elsewhere, that's basic," Foyle said briskly.

"I think we'd better follow one leader," Hogg-Smythe countered.

"It's a classic guerrilla retreat problem," Foyle said. "Unless you've managed a guerrilla campaign yourself, Commissioner, you should take it from me."

"I really must dig up that police record of yours someday." I looked to Mishima, sure he'd announce military expertise of his own, but his pensive face was unreadable. I asked Foyle what she'd suggest.

"Use the transport tubes. One car for each of us, and program them to keep hitting stops after the passenger gets out—false trails. Every car to hit every major station, where lines cross, leaving no clue to the one we actually regroup at."

"Which will be . . . the second farthest?" Wongama suggested.

"One of the closest," I said. "Something within walking distance of here, I think."

"Yes, the big shaft is the only practical exit to the surface," Foyle agreed. "No point in getting too far away from it. And the sooner we're off the transport, the better. In case they figure out how to shut it down."

"How about the cemetery, then?" Hogg-Smythe asked.

Foyle looked through the window dubiously. "I suppose it's not *too* close. And as a park stop, it would give us a clear view of the elevated tubes. Yes."

"Okay," I said, "do it. Piet will decide what buttons to push, Foyle will go to the cemetery first to find good cover and organize arrivals. Ken, someone has to leave last; it should be someone who knows how to take care of himself."

He nodded sharply. "Of course. But aren't you coming with us?"

Ariel, standing before the local elevator to the transport terminal, looked back at this, those bright blue eyes locked on my face.

"No," I said. "I have to stay behind. We're *not* guerrillas. We can't fight our way out, and we can't hide forever, without food or information. I'll conceal myself here, get behind them, and use the elevator to go for help. Piet, write down the clear-codes and the up-code for me."

"You won't get the chance," Foyle argued. "And even if you did, there's no radio on the surface—"

"Remember the recon satellites—I can start a brushfire or something to attract their attention. Even if I can't get back up, I'll be in a position to overhear the mercenaries when they come through, get a line on their plans; then I'll try to rejoin you. At least this way you'll be waiting *for* something."

"I have another suggestion," said Ken Mishima. "Talk with them. The Iron Brotherhood is a major labor union. It can't afford to murder Column officials."

"But it can make them disappear," Foyle snapped. "Especially in a semiautonomous zone like the Blue Swathe. Mercenaries play politics in the fringes all the time; I've seen them work. But yes, we probably should save you to bargain with, Commissioner, as a last resort. Ken or I should stay behind instead."

Ariel had returned to my side. She was not the only one who appeared to agree with Foyle's suggestion, or Mishima's. But both were predicated on the notion that I was a real Column official, and mercenaries hired by Condé would know I wasn't.

"The time has come to tell you the truth," I said. "As some of you may have suspected, I'm not a regular sub-commissioner of non-human artifacts."

Almost everyone nodded at that, which irked me, but I plowed ahead regardless: "I have a broader assignment than that. Certain political duties which I am not at liberty to discuss. But negotiations with these people are out of the question. Half our ten minutes are gone. I expect you all to start following orders."

And they began moving out. Piet handed me the elevator codes, on a scrap of paper from some notebook of Lagado's.

"But where will you hide?" Ariel asked.

"Don't worry, I know what I'm doing," I said—each new lie coming a little easier—and she stood on tiptoe to kiss me lightly on the lips. Foyle, the last to go, looked on with a crooked smile.

"I thought you were an agent of some sort. But no matter how good you are, without a weapon . . ."

"There's something in that backpack of yours that might help," I said. "Turn around and let me get at the chemicals."

She obliged me, but said, "I'm afraid you're mistaken. If you're thinking of the acids, they're too dilute."

But I removed one chunky vial and closed the padded box. "Just take care of our friends." We were alone now. "And don't be so sure they can't take care of you. There's plenty of brains and guts there."

"You can trust me," she said. "I wish I could say I . . . Oh, well. Luck."

Around the bend of the corridor, the lake-elevator door slid open with a slight hiss. A storm of footsteps pattered from the same direction, becoming more resonant as it burst upon the statue chamber.

Commands rang out, curt and rapid, but almost bored in tone. Someone reported from the picture window that cars could be seen moving through the transport tubes, and someone else acknowledged the fact without apparent interest. Ten minutes passed.

Then I heard two voices from the foreground, bass and tenor—and usually opposed to each other, so I labeled them Pro and Contra:

Pro: "Well, we had our chance to take them clean, and your corporal blew it. Doesn't matter, though."

Contra: "Stupid bastard walked into the line of fire."

Pro: "I said it doesn't matter. All we needed from Velasquez was the senator's arrival date, and he gave me that last night, in the woods. He was always supposed to be expendable afterwards. Like the other white suit."

Contra: "The other one is ours, too? Then why did he smash the platform cameras?"

Pro: "Condé never trusted him with the real story."

Contra: "Lucky him."

Pro: "Are you going to start up again? Wait."

Another flurry of orders: all the lake-platform stops to be guarded, best available weapons, shoot-on-sight protocols; and the local elevators in the statue chamber to be checked out, too, destinations determined, one man to stay behind and watch for enemy attempts to return. Then more footsteps, dying away.

I lay flat again. Some of the mercenaries would be crossing

the high waist of the spherical chamber, where the corridor joined it, and that was the only angle from which I might be seen. But my own restricted view, of little except the ceiling, reassured me that I had been right; the bronze figure group was just high enough to make a blind spot where I lay, atop the high marble base and between the two rows of heroic cable-couplers.

Another ten minutes, and then a quieter room. The crisp pacing of a single sentry in front of the side doors. And Pro and Contra again, their voices low.

Pro: "It would have been neater if we'd smeared them here, but there's still no problem."

Contra: "No problem? Our base is blown, and the senator is arriving months ahead of schedule. Condé's left us screwed."

Pro: "You're not thinking straight. The base isn't blown until those professors report back, and they never will. According to what Velasquez said last night, no one even expects to hear from them for a week or two. So the senator's arriving just in time, before anyone comes looking. Now listen. While you were trapped on Null, Juan flashed down confirmation to the forest watch. It's okay. He has all the codes and passwords for the orbital defenses, and he and Phil have wangled so much comm duty there'll be no trouble getting back to them; he says he can disable the message boats on two hours' notice. And I can't see the ground assault taking more than a few hours; then we can lift the spare construction shuttles into orbit and mop up there. So there'll be no problem about welcoming the senator a few days later with all the right codes. He won't suspect a thing."

Contra: "If some of the orbital guys shoot it out, the damage will be visible from space."

Pro: "So there's been an accident during construction. The senator won't turn back over that. And once we have him, our problems are half over. This is his retreat. No one will come disturb him. If necessary we can get him to write some messages out—we've got a couple pilots who can deliver them—and postpone any visits he's expecting. Only a month or two of covering up that way, and then we can hand the whole mess over to Condé's bunch to proceed with as planned; the client can make his own kill, and no one will even know the Brotherhood was involved."

Contra: "If Condé can deliver! If not—"

Pro: "If not, we still have two hundred troops stuck here without transportation. You carry on as if we have a choice,

Jacques, but Condé's our only way out. At least I'll be able to show the union a profit on the deal.''

Contra: ''We should have had a field representative come in the first time Condé changed the contract. 'Guard duty'!''

Pro: ''Look, if it makes you feel any better, I did try. It's on record that we sent back word. Now all we can do is our best. Like not shooting our own people in the fucking throat.''

Contra: ''Bows don't have scan sights and arrows don't have lock-ons. I always said we should break out the real weapons.''

Pro: ''For what? Eight months without resupply, and I'm supposed to risk taking fine-tuned A-rifles through that electromagnetic pulse?''

Contra: ''We could've shielded one crateload. And if we had, those civilians wouldn't be running around loose now.''

Pro: ''So? They've got no arms, no food, and no other exits to the surface. The platform is guarded. Let the professors starve or come crawling. They won't be missed, not in time.''

Contra: ''But suppose they are? Can't you at least move up the schedule?''

Pro: ''I just got the arrival date last night. The way I see it, I have one week to make a professional op out of it, and I'm going to use every minute. Even if the senator arrives early, we can take him on the ground the day after—hell, it might work better that way.''

Contra: ''And just suppose one of the satellites gets a warning first, four or five six days from now, some time when Juan or Phil isn't on comm duty to intercept it?''

Pro: ''You're like an old woman, you know that?''

Contra: ''Patch, patch, patch. Every new disaster, you put another patch in the master plan, but it would take just one hint of danger from this system, and that senator will arrive with a Column navy escort and six brigades of marines—the navy'll back the Consultant, if they get the chance. Just one of those archaeologists popping up anywhere on the surface and signaling a satellite, and we're screwed. And there *is* another way to reach the surface from here. It's in the post description.''

Pro: ''I know what you're talking about. But you can't be serious. You think those women and children are going to—''

Contra: ''Exploring places like this is their business. And after seeing Velasquez buy the farm, you think they don't know their lives depend on it? You're crazy if you don't let me try to round them up first.''

Pro: ''And you're crazy if you think I'll clock it as combat pay. But what the hell. I'm tired of having you in my ear. I'll let you have everyone who's on report, that's twenty guys, and the extra hunting equipment. And take Principato, too."

Contra: "I don't want him. I know everybody thinks he's hot shit—Sergeant Superman. But he can't control himself. Would have grabbed that redheaded piece right out of her tent, if I hadn'ta stopped him."

Pro: "Well, now he can have her, can't he? You motivate him, and he's like three extra guys. Not that we're undermanned anyway, I could take that construction camp with forty troops if I had to, so spend all the time you want . . . Look, it's your fantasy, not mine. I don't even see where you'd start."

Contra: "The post description has all the dope on the other exit to the surface. It's a roundabout route, I remember that . . ."

Pro: "All right, all right, let's check it out . . ."

It would have been the only thing I really needed to know. But now they walked away. The lake-elevator door hissed open and shut again a moment later.

I'd heard enough, however. There would be no sneaking or bargaining my way back to the surface. I'd be lucky if I could just rejoin the others. And how had I come to be that quintessential boob, the hero on the monument? Partly, it had been the fear of what Foyle or Mishima might find out about me in this position—and I'd been right about that—but mainly, inexcusably, it had been the costume and the limelight and the women looking on.

Below and off to the side, the sentry clopped back and forth.

I had one edge, the vial in my hand. Foyle was bright and tough, but like most people she saw only the labels of things—not the heavy glass, good for hitting with, or what was once called the "spirit" of the fluid inside. But I would need the advantage of surprise, too, and I'd have to work close up. As I pondered this, the sentry's footsteps changed course, suddenly louder, nearer.

I could tell he'd entered the ring of statues, but then I heard the creak of one of the swivel chairs and relaxed. Of course. What's guard duty without a place to sit? I slowly raised my head to look down at him. A slow peek is actually less likely to draw attention than a quick one—the quick and clever die young, but tortoises live two hundred years—and no problem, he was watching the side doors anyway, a cocked and loaded crossbow resting on his knee.

The merc was a man of average height, heavy but not flabby, powerful-looking. His head was bare, so bald that one of the green forest caps would have slipped right off it. His face was slack, but the small dark eyes looked sharp and observant.

I didn't care about those side doors, however. The local elevator I wanted stood elsewhere, to one side of the picture window, hidden from the guard's view behind the tall pedestal I was lying on. Unfortunately, I couldn't get down without giving myself away. I'd climbed up by way of footholds that were now well within his field of vision, and the blind side was a straight drop. But I had no choice, and no reason to wait.

I slowly wriggled between a pair of bronze feet, toward the side of the monument farthest from the guard and facing the elevator. By the time I'd got the length of my body clear, parallel to the top edge of the pedestal, the swivel chair creaked again, loudly. Had he heard something? Was he on his feet? There was nothing to do but make sure the cork on the vial was almost loose, roll sideways, snatch at the pedestal's edge just long enough to swing my feet down first, and then let go entirely. Free fall, and the floor coming up to hit me.

Chapter Thirteen

It was a five- or six-meter drop in stiff boots—but the knees bent just right, a half-bounce, and I didn't even have to shoulder-roll, just stand up. Lucky, because the guard came around the side of the monument with unbelievable speed for a man of his bulk. But he didn't know what to expect and I did; I took that split second to thumb the cork out of the vial and throw the contents in his face.

To Foyle it was just the cleanser she'd used on old gold, but imagine straight ammonia in your eyes and nose—

The bald merc gave a high-pitched incredulous noise, blinded and choking. His trigger finger tightened convulsively and the crossbow bolt whickered up to rebound off the ceiling. I ran five steps and hit the button next to the elevator, but the doors didn't open; the car was on some other level, and it had been a mistake not to reach in and bash him with the heavy vial when it might have been easy.

I was on him again in a second. He was blind, all right—he couldn't open his eyes to the burning air and hissed in pain when he tried—but he heard my approach, and the chunk of glass in my hand passed harmlessly over his head as he lurched forward to butt me hard in the stomach. I fell back half-stunned. He got in a good kick before losing contact with me, then snatched a bolt from his bandolier and loaded his weapon as if in the dark.

He was too good, too game, but I heard the cushioned clump of the elevator arriving, regained my feet, and reached the doors just as they opened. The interior was palely lit.

Another mercenary stood inside, staring at me, one hand on the button panel and the other cradling what I thought was called a "shotgun."

He was as surprised as I, his gunpowder antique aimed at the floor. He jerked back, the cocked weapon swinging up, as I sidestepped. And then a breeze moved past me with a noise like a scythe in tall grass and the shotgunner's upper body kicked backward, a crossbow bolt in his chest. I half jumped, half fell, and twisted back to see Baldy squinting after his shot—whether he'd had a glimpse of me framed in light, or had just gone by the sound of the doors, I'll never know.

There was an explosion within the elevator, the gunpowder weapon going off as it fell onto the tips of its barrels, and the discharge sent it cartwheeling through the air past me to clatter and skate across the floor. Baldy fell back several paces, his face screwed up against these incomprehensible noises as he reloaded his crossbow by feel. I dove across the tiles for the gun, scooped it up and rolled sideways into a passable one-knee infantry crouch, aimed, and pulled both triggers.

Nothing happened—I'd feared it, both barrels had fired—but I'd had my luck, and couldn't count on more. The fat man had a bolt ready for the slot but hadn't drawn yet, and I crossed the five meters between us in two bounds, gripping the gun like a bat by its twin barrels and swinging its stock at his head.

He saw or heard enough to bring the crossbow up to block. Our misused weapons met with the dull clunk of someone chopping firewood for the first time. Now we hacked at each other as if with broadswords, dancing in a tight circle, grunting and swearing as we struck. I had the advantage of clear sight, but the bow was lighter and handier than the heavy gun. I managed to deliver one blow to the face, smashing Baldy's nose sideways and opening a cut above one eye to leave him blinder than ever, but meanwhile—intentionally or not—he outmaneuvered me. Crouching and swinging from squarely in front of the still-open elevator, he'd cut off my line of retreat.

I lunged, overbalanced, and missed him clean. It brought me to my senses. I throttled my gasping, did a soft-shoe backward, and by so doing disappeared from Baldy's lightless world.

His features were already too twisted to register emotion, but I could see panic in the next few jerky swings of the half-smashed bow through empty air. His stance shifted nervously as he awaited attack from an unknown direction. I was still too fired up to pity the poor bastard, but I felt a flash of multifarious disgust, as if at a bearbaiting—and then the elevator doors began to close. Baldy whirled at the unexpected noise behind him and I stepped forward and clubbed the back of his head.

Rubbery neck muscles partially cushioned the blow, but he staggered into the elevator, the doors bouncing off him, and then dropped as though hamstrung, collapsing across the legs of the man he'd shot. I stepped in after him, snagging his feet off the doortrack with my own boot, and pushed the down button. Lying on his belly in a bright pool of his comrade's blood, Baldy began a noseless, back-of-the-throat snore. The other man was a corpse, already pale and waxy-looking in the elevator's milky light. But my own hand at the button panel looked just as fake and lifeless for a dim, cold, half-deaf moment before my senses caught up with events.

The doors opened, not onto street level, but one stop short of that, the transport station. Ken Mishima must have just pushed the up button on the other side of the portal. He jumped back, then froze, staring at me and the bloody bodies at my feet. "Get in here!" I snarled, and hauled at one of his arms; the big man was too stunned to resist. I pushed the down button again.

"I . . . Everyone else got away," he said, "but some men came through and I had to hide under the platform, and then I thought I might as well come back and give you some—" he hadn't stopped staring, as I busied myself straightening the lines of my uniform—"some help."

"You were going to just walk back in there?"

"I was sure you'd have wound up talking to them in the end. The Column always deals."

"Not much chance of that now. And we can forget sneaking past the guards; there are two hundred of them."

He knelt down between the bodies with an old soldier's unconcern for gore, and I had the sudden sick feeling he'd insist we finish off Baldy. But Mishima was only interested in collecting weapons. He looked up from the crossbow and shotgun with the most expression he'd ever shown me, spooked bafflement.

"They're both *smashed to junk,*" he said. "What did you— How did you—?"

The elevator doors crashed open onto a dead street.

"I had to use both hands," I said. "Let's go."

We jogged to the old human cemetery by way of the narrowest streets we could find, trying to stay out of sight of the elevated transport tubes in case the pursuit team should use them. Mishima was in excellent shape, despite a slight paunch, and he could talk while he ran.

"If you really are a Shadow Tribune, I have something to say."

"I never claimed to be one," I gasped, "but try me anyway. You're not really a historian, are you?"

"I didn't say that. I'm not saying anything if you won't trust me."

"With the information that I'm a Tribune? Would a real Shadowman admit to that?"

"Ah," he said, "I understand." As if that weren't enough to kill the conversation, he added, "Truth must ripen before it can be digested."

"Sure," I said.

The cemetery was a large wooded park at the boundary between city and wilderness; a black wall twenty meters high veed forward to meet it and curtained off all view to the north. Inside, the trees and grasses looked like variants on Terran strains—presumably Elitist imports—as did the birds and insects, the first animal life I'd seen in this underworld. As we passed through a second gate marked ELYSIUM, I realized how much larger and hillier the cemetery was than I had thought, and wondered if finding our comrades would be a problem. But then Harry Lagado hissed at us from behind a wild hedge. He said Foyle had placed him there as a lookout, then gave us directions to the hiding place.

The old paths had been overgrown hundreds of years before, but still made shadowy dents in the tall grass. Tombstones, too, were but half obscured, emerging from the waves of green like breakers. The Elitists had fashioned their memorials out of white marble, perhaps in contrast to the Titan ceramics they'd had to live with; the stones showed the wear of rain, but remained legible enough for the archaeologists to argue over. I heard Foyle's voice first; it led us to a grassy rise.

"Here's another one," she was saying. " 'Died in the Hellway still a boy, Juli 2886.' What sort of society engages in child sacrifice?"

"That's only two deaths attributed to the Hellway, a hundred years apart," Helen Hogg-Smythe replied patiently. "Maybe there are many more, but then again, maybe not. I'm finding it harder to read. Is it just me, or is the sky getting darker? Maybe it follows the surface's day and night."

"Look at all these adopted children, though," Foyle went on, undeterred. "Usually joining a family full-grown, after their rite of passage. Replacements for natural children lost in the Hellway?"

You'd have thought they'd keep their voices down, just on general principles, but no; and we would have had to shout to quiet them.

Hogg-Smythe's tone was a plea to change the subject. "I just had a thought. Why 'Elysium' and 'Persephone Walk'? Why did the Elitists switch from using Nordic names like 'Arnheim,' 'Avalon,' and so forth—after their forefathers' tradition—to names based on Greco-Roman mythology? Just part of their rebellion?"

"A reflection of their darkest fears," Foyle replied without hesitation. "The Elitists had turned their backs on traditional Eurosocialism. What would they be most afraid of becoming instead? What right-wing Terran political movement was deeply, viscerally tied to the old Nordic religions and lore? You're a classicist."

"The Nasties, you mean. Swastikas and all that."

"Nazis, I think it was. And much more vivid in civilized memory twelve hundred years ago. I think it's very significant that the Elitists should suddenly shy away from any Wagnerian cultural echoes. Their parent colony had a clearer conscience."

"Oh, but really, Foyle. If you're going to argue by opposites—"

"You should do it in whispers," I said as Mishima and I cleared the crown of the hill. "Real nasties are searching for you even now, children."

The six of them were sitting on a family group of tombstones, framed against the darkening sky, not quite a family group themselves—Ariel too blonde, Francisco too dark, Lagado too soft to be related to the others. But they looked at us with almost one reaction: pleasure at our survival quickly dampened as they realized that no one had reached the surface for help.

I briefly recounted how I'd eavesdropped and escaped.

"The news is not good," I said. "There are two hundred mercenaries. They'll keep the lake exit guarded. They're sending in a team to actively pursue us, too, but at least it's small, and doesn't know where to look. And they won't have field radios or modern weapons."

"Why not?" Ariel asked.

"They must have their combat equipment cached aboveground somewhere. They know what the electromagnetic pulse in the lake shaft would do to it, so they haven't gone to the trouble of bringing it down here, where they don't need it anyway. But it must be standard to bring a complement of sport-hunting weapons along on a contract like this, to a planet with forests that can supply fresh meat. Military A-rifles, with their radar scanners and smart bullets, might be picked up by the recon satellites, but not bows and arrows and gunpowder."

"That explains the green forest outfits, too," Foyle remarked. "But why risk surface hunting at all?"

"They can't have been resupplied in a long time," I said. "And they probably need the action. Morale is poor. Didn't you tell me about a disturbance in the bushes the other night? Well, a merc was stalking you, Foyle, until some others overpowered him." I let that sink in a moment. "But now they're expecting relief in a month or two. And that's more bad news—they're not just guarding an archaeological find. Their client wants Senator Mehta dead. They're going to assault the base camp just before he arrives, and lay a trap for him."

"But who would—" Ariel began.

"Their client is Sir Maximilien Condé," I said. "An old personal enemy of Mehta's, as you know. The Knuckle-Cracker."

"But how could he hope to get away with it?" she asked. "Senator Mehta is the most important man in the Blue Swathe! The great families don't like his party much, but everyone says that the Consultant is sympa—"

"Every powerful man has powerful enemies," Foyle said. "Isn't this Condé a high muckamuck, too, admiral in the militia navy or something?"

"Not any more," Ariel said impatiently. "Not unless the Senate investigation of defense contractors clears him. But I suppose he could still have allies in the militia; he's paid off enough officers there . . ."

"I got the impression that something bigger than just an assassination is planned," I told them. "What, I don't know, but the details don't really matter. One warning message to the senator can still stop it. But we'd have to be on the surface to deliver it. And I don't see how we can get there; the mercenaries have orders to shoot on sight."

"Speaking of which, Foyle," Mishima said, gesturing northward. "Is it sound guerrilla practice to place your back against a wall?"

It was true that the city wall towered above us. The far slope of the hill we stood on ran directly into the prow of the huge black V, where the junction was marked by a great crypt of white marble half smothered in wild hedge and creepers. No name appeared on its front, but an open archway invited further exploration.

Foyle pointed at the crypt. "When there's only one hole in that wall, Ken—yes, you want to be straddling the exit."

"We can escape to the wilderness through there?" I asked.

"Very likely," Hogg-Smythe said. "That's why I suggested this t-stop. And I wanted to see it for its own sake. That crypt is the entrance to the Hellway. The legendary portal through which every Elitist eighteen-year-old had to go. From there he or she would travel thousands of k's, have instructive adventures, and finally be affirmed as an adult and a citizen under the stars of the north pole."

"Why a crypt in a graveyard?" Ariel asked.

"The usual symbolism," Foyle said. "Entrance to the next world. Death before rebirth. That sort of thing. But the more I look at the cultural background, the less I think of the Hellway as a safe hideout."

Hogg-Smythe looked fed up at this. "They sent their own children through it—"

"But we're not sure why. Perhaps to justify the upper classes in their rank, by weeding out the weak and unfit. It could be a very dangerous place."

"I must agree with Helen, Foyle," said the friar. "We don't know enough about the Elitists to take such a dark view of them."

"Someone is coming!" Mishima snapped, looking down the other side of the hill. "Wait—it's just the boy."

"Probably wants relief," Foyle said. "He should have waited."

I had the feeling that I'd overlooked something important. "Helen, you said something about stars at the north pole. Is that where the other exit to the surface is?"

"I thought we'd told you that before," she replied. "Yes. But we'd have to traverse the entire Hellway to reach it, Commissioner, and where would we be once we had? The polar wastes. Now, if we had a radio . . ."

"I . . ." Foyle's voice was strange. She began again. "I didn't mention it before, but I have a way of communicating with my ship, if we did reach the surface. I could relay a message to the satellites. We could—"

"Hold on, this is important," I said. "The Hellway is the *only* way to reach that exit?"

"Yes, we *said* that."

"And that crypt is the only entrance to the Hellway?"

"That, too," Foyle said dryly.

"Then, we have to get the hell out of here. Condé must have used those library terminals, too. He wrote up a post description for his guards, and—" But I was far too late.

Harry Lagado came puffing up to us. "Men in the street. Couldn't tell if they were coming in or not. Sure they didn't see me."

"They didn't have to," I said. "Get down off those stones, people, aren't you listening?"

I crouched next to Mishima, and he pointed south. Birds were exploding from tree after tree. "Already close," he said. "And there may be flankers—yes, look there."

"No choice, then," I said. "Wild country is our only chance to lose them. Head for the crypt, everybody, the Hellway. Come on, run!"

They were slow at first, perhaps unbelieving, but then we heard thrashing sounds in nearby shrubbery, and someone shouting, "Isn't that them?"—and like the birds, we flew.

Chapter Fourteen

We had no choice. We pounded and puffed toward the crypt, praying we'd find the way through it. I pulled ahead, wanting to inspect the ground before the others arrived. Piet Wongama must have had the same idea; his long legs carried him past me and through the entrance.

"Overhead door, maybe," he panted when I staggered in. "But no controls." A glance proved him right. As the others entered, I surveyed the interior. We were in a dimly lit chamber that seemed limitless in horizontal extent, although the ceiling, a black and white checkerboard of meter-square panels, was low enough to touch. A few small bright lights gleamed in the distance. The floor was black and smooth, though faint lines sketched out tiles the same size as the ceiling panels.

As my eyes adjusted to the dim light, I was surprised by an insect drifting past me, head high. It was an oversized wasp of iridescent gold, trailed by colorful, insubstantial plumes; it shone like a queen of the air in the light from outside, then faded away into the dark interior. As the last of our people came in, Harry Lagado shepherding his father, I saw a half dozen more of the wasps following them, while a stream of others flew out, higher, through the crown of the arch.

The worn-out runners made despairing noises as they took in the situation. There was nothing for it but to run on toward the distant darkness where floor and ceiling met. Outside, brush crackled; the mercenaries were close behind us. We began another sprint, somehow. Not so hard for me, or Ariel, or Mishima, but Foyle had that backpack, Lagado his weight and clumsiness. Regardless, they all pounded on, pounded on.

Something almost brushed my head as I ran beneath it, a broad round papery mass attached to a dark square of the ceiling. It left only the faintest impression; later, I would see one more clearly. Onward, onward.

Behind us, the archway's overhead door came down.

The entrance had been the brightest source of light. The sound of footfalls faltered, then returned, as most of us looked back. My own glance to the rear showed that Ariel had lagged a little behind me, while the others were strung out widely. If I slowed in this darkness I would just get in their way. As I faced front again, my cheek brushed against one of the big bird-of-paradise insects. I swore and lurched to one side without stopping as it serenely floated off.

There was no way of knowing how far we'd penetrated the chamber when the few lights ahead of us went out. I came to a dead halt. The rattle of footsteps died away; voices called out in the utter darkness. Thinking of Ariel and perhaps of others too trusting for their own good, I shouted, "I'm here!"

A soft but somehow immense moan sounded all around me. "I'm here," I said again, but the sound of my voice had a different quality this time. Moments passed and the only reply was my own panting, and that, too, sounded less resonant, more closely echoed.

I reached out and touched a flat surface, hard and slick. Then my hands found two walls perpendicular to that one, and I could touch both at once. Worst of all, I now backed into a fourth. I was inside whatever it was, not outside.

I spun around in a momentary panic. It wasn't mere claustrophobia; I was a sunplunger, after all. It was the glassy feel of the walls, like a suspend-sleep tank, where you dream and dream and trust others to wake you up before you lose all sense of what's real and what's not . . .

Assumption: partitions had risen from the floor or descended from above, trapping me on a square tile the area of a ceiling panel. I braced my back against one wall, raised one leg and pushed out against the other side. Then I tried both legs, full strength. There was a slight, tantalizing give in either direction, and I was sure now that I dealt with thin partitions rather than solid walls. But subsequent kicking, hitting, and swearing proved that they were both unbreakable and somehow sound-absorbent. The corners met squarely, without gaps. I wondered how fast I'd use up my air.

Lights came on, revealing the walls to be transparent. I now realized that every panel in the chamber—floor and ceiling—could be lit like a lamp. The top and bottom of my cell glowed a bright, pure white, painful after the minutes in darkness. The panels adjacent were also lit, one block in every direction past the glass. Beyond that, the main chamber's floor and ceiling had gone totally nonreflective all around me, making my booth an island on a sea of blackness.

Not the only one, however. Every member of our party was immured in the same way, and as brightly lit. Museum displays. *Homo sapiens*, Early Column Era. Piet Wongama and Ken Mishima had been farther ahead in the direction of our flight, which oriented me. Ariel was nearly level with me to one side, the ever-surprising Helen Hogg-Smythe close behind. Harry Lagado was far to the rear, on a line with his father and what had to be Friar Francisco, while Foyle was a considerable distance off in her own direction, only that red head distinguishable between tiny planes of light.

Ariel waved and appeared to be shouting something as she pounded on a wall that was invisible to me. Not a sound could be heard. But it was good to see that I was not alone. Less dreamlike.

We had failed to realize that the Elitists' rite of passage was still a living custom, presided over by their old computers.

We were being treated as candidates for adulthood, and as such could not just stroll from the crypt to the countryside. The ancient ritual demanded disorienting mysteries first, like the blindfolded walk in Freemasonry or Kanalism's hour in the Black Chamber. I smiled back at Ariel and tried to suggest, with a shrug, that the situation wasn't dangerous.

But I'd assumed that the mercenaries were locked out. They weren't.

Reopening, the bright arch turned out to be farther than I had imagined—less illuminating—but all of us turned to face it. A few minutes later the mercenaries entered, moving in well-drilled pairs, sneaking along the edges, their weapons raised against the ambush I was glad we hadn't tried.

We saw the little silhouettes stop, point, and turn what had to be binoculars in our direction. Some went back out, only to return with others. Eventually, fifteen or so came toward us, well dispersed and hard to see. It took a long, long time. The point man, armed with a bow and arrow, had nearly reached the Lagados when the lights went out once more, all but a patch of ceiling panels around the glow of the archway.

Again the immense groan sounded. I touched a wall and it seemed to be resonating with the noise, but that was all. Then the rings of tiles and panels adjacent to my cell came back on, while the center blocks, my floor and ceiling, stayed off. This way I could see the crouching, baffled mercenaries more clearly than before, no ghosts of my own reflection in my way. I could see the other islands again, too, but relit in the new manner; with their central squares out, their cell walls were no longer transparent from my side, instead reflecting the surrounding panels.

Lights out again. It hadn't quite lost its surprise value. Because this time full darkness returned; the last off-on had been a diversion, covering the reclosing of the archway door.

Now the mercenaries were as lost in the dark as we, backstage at the mystery play.

After a long pause, cells began to light up again, one at a time. Some new displays had been added to the museum; the themes were "primitive weapons" and "military fatigues." Members of our party were reappearing, too. But there were no islands of adjacent blocks this time; only booth floors and ceilings were lit, and more dimly—no, it was just that the glass walls around them were less transparent, a blue-gray tint overlaid. I understood why the mercenaries kept turning around and around, but Ariel had seen her cell before; why was she—?

Then it was my turn, and I understood. The squares above and below me blazed to life, and with all the light coming from within the cell, the outside world was cut off.

My walls had become perfect mirrors, endlessly reflecting each other—four infinite corridors, with partial views of illusory corridors parallel and intersecting. A universal matrix of glass cells, and in each cell a Larkspur uniformed as a Parker, alternately facing me or turned away to face the next, and all of us spinning around, trying to take in the whole.

I stopped, cupped my hands into a tube around one eye, and pressed the tube against a wall. This created a small transparent window into the larger chamber, which was still blacked out; I could see the faint glow of the other cells. Assuming they were as brightly illuminated as my own, some trick of polarization—shifting laminations within the glass?—was being employed to trap most of the light inside each, maximizing the mirror effect.

I dropped my hand and reentered the illusory honeycomb of Larkspurs. The half-infinity of them facing me looked pretty glum, though the illimitable radiant planes above and below made our faces appear pink and unlined.

I hate floors that glow. Take away all shadows and you don't seem to be standing on anything. We Larkspurs would all have been floating in unrelieved whiteness except for the faint impression of lines where the image walls met, and a fadeoff of intensity in the middle distance, a foggy receding grayness.

I turned once more, to spooky effect. Precision-drill clones.

Wait a minute. What had happened? Why was only one subcommissioner facing me now, a vacant corridor behind him? I spun on my heel and put out a hand.

Empty air. This wall had slid up or down, out of sight, its edge flush with ceiling or floor. And before me stretched a long corridor—a real one. Evidently the computer controllers could raise or lower glass walls along any tile edge to make cells, rooms, or hallways at will.

They had lit the floor and ceiling panels down the length of the corridor, making mirrors of the sides and cutting off any view of the larger chamber. The hall ended in a tiny, distant silhouette—another person, or just another reflection. At least it was nice to see no Larkspurs in between. Perhaps there would be a side opening or two near the end. In fact, I realized, there could be many cross-corridors, so long as they were also lit; I wouldn't be able to tell an intersection from another mirror except at point-blank range. I put out a hand again as I stepped forward—the strange glass could be awfully clear, and I was beginning to calculate the pitfalls—but the way was indeed open. I knew not in what direction, but I walked.

Ranks of me marched an enfilade of corridors, sandwiched between glowing planes. True geometric planes, mind you—the infinite kind. The figure at the end of the corridor was indeed a reflection in another mirror, just half as far away as he appeared. There was a good stretch of imaginary corridor behind him, the infinite regress beyond that too small to see; he was therefore the sole Larkspur to march against the tide of them marching to my right and left.

But suddenly the tide broke. I stepped into a new square and only one Larkspur followed me, on the right. So the left was a real corridor and—I reached out a hand confidently and stubbed all the fingers—there was a real piece of clear glass in my way. I swore at it. As I'd feared, unpolarized panes, when lit on both sides, were virtually invisible.

The next cross-corridor, however, was not only lit but open. I took the right turn, saw a head-on reflection a few tiles away, but was given another turn before that dead end. Left, into a long stretch indeed, with a side view of Friar Francisco at the end of it. I called out, but he walked off to the right and disappeared, and when I chased him I ran head-on into another clear pane.

Then my corridor was blacked out.

This was indeed a looking-glass world: you saw much more clearly in the dark. The unlit side of a glass wall was not a mirror; I was still enclosed, but now the panes were transparent. I could once again see the great ebony-tiled chamber around me. Not far away, a mercenary in fatigues was walking along a path of lit tiles parallel to the course I'd been walking a moment before. From this side of the glass, polarization made his corridor appear dimmer than mine had been, but there was no other indication that anything separated us. He couldn't see me, though—only his own reflection, the same view I saw in the wall beyond him, an infinite regress of mercenaries without a single Larkspur in it.

Other corridors, some with right angle turns in them, could be seen in the other directions, one far away. I could see into them all—Hello, Helen!—but no one could see me. Still, it was an illusion to think I stood outside the picture. There might be many clear layers between us; I might be in a one-block cell again, for all I knew. More looking-glass logic: when I could see the most, I was most likely to run into a wall. Then I heard the great moaning from the upper air again. The maze walls were being reconfigured for me. Perhaps.

Let there be light, said the god in the machine—and there were mirrors.

I walked down the shiny new corridor, looking to right and left. Hello, boys.

Down a short length, turning right and facing myself, another right, another walk, left and a long stretch, right for longer still, a choice of right or left or straight—choose left to avoid doubling back. And on and on. I would lose the soul of an artist soon; I was getting sick of my own reflection.

I knew something about mazes. When I was in school and steeped in Kanalism, looking forward to that final walk among symbolic scenes that caps one's initiation—the Shining Fare, our version of the stations of the cross—I had read up on the lore of the famous labyrinths of antiquity, the tricks for solving them.

But of course, if people keep moving the walls, there's no strategy at all, and no point. It's all a sham, a wait for the computers running the game to call quits, turn on the lights, drop the walls—

And leave your party at the mercy of enemies who outnumber you two to one. So, just in case there *is* an exit, you walk, without knowing what it will look like, as in life. And when random choices are required of you, you make them, as in life . . .

I had been walking all day, one place or another, and by my reckoning it was now late evening; nor had I slept much the night before, working on the Otis cyberdiagnostics. I was too tired to think well, but I forced myself to memorize a long sequence of turns and the number of blocks between them. Perhaps ten minutes' worth. Then I retraced my route to see if it matched.

It didn't.

I experienced something like relief. Proof that it was a sham puzzle. Permission not to think.

Ibid. From the Latin: "In the same place."

I turned a corner, and my outstretched hand hit glass. I expected to see my own face and instead found Ruy Lagado standing in a lit corridor perpendicular to mine. The glass between us was invisible—no reflection, no dimming of his side.

Lagado seemed overjoyed to see me, and I welcomed the change myself. He tried to semaphore in some code I didn't recognize. He couldn't understand my spacer hand signs either. Not that we had anything to communicate, it was just a basic human urge.

His fat face lit up, and he dug into the pocket of his jacket, coming up with a small notebook and a marker. He began to print something out, clumsily and slowly. Waiting for him to finish, I noticed that the infinite repetition behind him was not of three cells—his, mine, and the empty one at my heels—but six. So there were another three empty blocks between his back and the mirror.

And as I watched, a mercenary appeared in one of them, eerily, walking through what had seemed to be a mirror in its side. He turned and saw us. He had somehow lost his hunting piece, if any, but he had a knife, and was unafraid of civilian numbers. He charged.

Shouting, I pounded on the glass that would protect me, trying to warn Lagado. The partition gave a little, it vibrated in that mysterious way that absorbed sound, and the little sociologist heard nothing, two handspans away from me, head bent over his notebook, as the merc charged—

Into a clear glass wall just behind Lagado. Bounced off, fell flat. I was too relieved to laugh. Jumping to his feet again, the enraged soldier tried to kick his way through.

Lagado didn't hear this either. He looked up, beaming, and showed me what he had printed out: THEY MOVE THE WALLS VERY MISLEADING I THINK.

I nodded politely and pointed over his shoulder, tapping the glass. He didn't get it, reaching up to tap it, too. So I pointed back over *my* shoulder and moved sideways. I saw him peer past me, past the empty cell behind me, into the reflections beyond that: my back; his front; and behind him, *Who the hell?* He spun around, but as he did the adjacent corridor must have been blacked out, because the mercenary disappeared—just Lagado and me again, and more of us—and as Lagado turned back to face me with a "How did you do that?" expression on his face, my hall was blacked out, too, and I could see him jump when he found only a mirror in front of him.

Walking away in the dark, I couldn't help but think about working this into a stage illusion.

Ibid. Every now and then another type of mirror stood slantwise across a block, creating a new type of illusion: the corridor would appear to continue forward, when it was actually taking a right-angle turn. I had to be very close before I could see the faint diagonal lines on floor and ceiling that warned me I was actually looking around a corner.

I saw a wasp that way. The plumed giant, as long as a finger and silvery in the white light, flew in jerking zigzags back and forth. The angry curve of its abdomen brought back a sudden, vivid image from childhood: a barbed fishhook going into the ball of my thumb. I didn't take that turn.

Ibid. A mercenary walked through one of the seeming side-mirrors far ahead—no, wait a minute—one reflection of me was in the way. He was really behind me, farther in that direction than I had come myself . . .

I spun around. He wasn't close, but he'd get closer; that reflection of me had marked a dead end in the direction away from him.

Slowly, enjoying himself, he nocked an arrow behind his huge metal recurve bow. It probably had a forty-kilo throw, but he paced closer. Wanted to see if he could drive it all the way through me, I thought, then realized that an arrow isn't a bullet. He was minimizing the chance I'd dodge.

I walked toward him.

I had passed other intersections on this corridor. I had to reach one of them, sidestep before he fired, and meanwhile . . .

I talked sense to him: "You don't want to mess with a Column official, buddy. Besides, you guys are as lost as we are now, we could help each other, my friends have information you need"—that sort of thing.

Only I didn't make a sound, just moved my lips.

For a moment I feared he didn't get it, or would risk one of his few arrows anyway. But then he swore, lowered the bow, and started forward slowly, groping ahead with one hand for a pane of invisible glass. I remembered to look relieved when he spoke, as though realizing I couldn't hear him. And I tried to look nonchalant about continuing to narrow what was in fact the empty gap between us . . .

But then I stepped forward another block and the reflections on my right flank didn't follow. Eureka! I wanted to make the dodge to the right quick and unexpected, maximizing the chance he'd lose track of which intersection I'd taken. Suppressing the childish urge to shout an insult now, I bolted to the side—

To smash my kneecap and my old bum wrist, and bounce off invisible glass. The lateral corridor was closed, and I had involuntarily cried out. The bowman heard me, not twenty meters away; I saw him grin.

Yes, he was lost, yes, he was frustrated, yes, his orders didn't make much sense anymore, but so what? At least he had permission to kill someone. At least he was still the big man, the man I'd run into under dozens of faces over the years, one more personification of power reduced to lowest terms. I could feel sweat sprouting on my back as the bow came up, and dropped to my knees when I thought he would fire. No good; he caught himself. Adjusted his aim. Let fly.

I had a split-second's impression of a blur coming toward me, but even as I flinched, another arrow seemed to emerge from a side corridor between us and strike his at a right angle, tip to tip, destroying it utterly—to land, broken and spent, not far from my feet! For an instant the bowman and I stared at each other stupidly; then I jumped up and forward, looking for the next intersection, laughing at my luck.

He'd been around a corner all the time, a diagonal mirror waiting to smash his arrow! I don't know if he figured it out, but he did come running, to be momentarily twinned as he made the turn, his face working furiously. But by then I'd already heard the sound of my deliverance, that immense moaning, and for the first time I saw a wall move, the edge of it anyway, a sheet of impenetrable glass rising between him and me.

The bowman saw it, too, came up to it kicking and swearing like a schoolboy—but now I didn't hear a thing.

He raved on. It was so stupid. What had he been deprived of? How could he work up so much fury over it? I'd only been terrified before; now, I was irked.

I stepped close to the glass between us, adopted a perplexed and almost pitying expression, and pointed contemptuously down the new lateral corridor that had opened to my left. He swore some more, soundlessly. I shook my head, sneered, and jabbed my finger to the left again.

He hadn't calmed down, exactly, his face still crimson, but he was tracking again. Why didn't I just make my escape? What the hell could I possibly be trying to show him? He couldn't see anything. Not yet.

One hand on the sheathed knife he obviously didn't need, he stepped to the side of the frame on my right in order to get the best possible angle on the corridor opposite. I joined him, a half step away from the glass, as if to get out of the way. Still unable to see anything, he pressed his face close to the glass, closer, almost touching—

And I elbowed the flexible partition with the full weight of my body, sending him staggering back with a bloody nose.

Oh, I howled. A master of subtle comedy. I had to lean against the Larkspur next to me, I was laughing so hard, while Bloody Nose threw himself against the wall again and again like a madman. I demonstrated the obscene hand-gestures of various planets for him and walked away, still laughing.

You had to be there.

Soon I slowed to a stroll. Hurrying, you might smash your face. Especially when your corridor was blacked out. Slow down and observe the lit-up hallways around you, so near and yet so far.

Hello. I looked through clear glass. A new feature, displayed in an odd little loopway.

A papery mass hung from one ceiling panel, and giant wasps-of-paradise circled it in the erratic manner I'd noticed earlier. It was a hive, all right, surprisingly small; I was fascinated by the way the wasps' "plumes" rolled up into nothing at all just before they entered their nest. But they swarmed out as fast as they went in. And busy bees are not always happy bees.

I had a thought. The other hive I'd seen was near the entrance, back when it was open. There'd been no walls, then, and few lights. And that had been the norm for—how long? Centuries, perhaps. The burning white panel above their hive was bound to disturb and threaten the wasps. I was glad of the glass between us.

Especially when my own corridor lit up again, and they could see me. One flew near and instinct made me step back, unable to see the protective glass I knew was there. And now, beyond the hive, Bloody Nose appeared, another arrow nocked in his bow. He could see me, but couldn't know if he had a genuinely clear shot. He was still furious, still brainless, and now enraged to discover another concealed corner as he entered the loop.

Perhaps he came from a world without stinging insects. He swatted the first few down with unconcern, reached out to confirm that there was glass between us, worked his mouth disgustedly, and turned back into the swarm.

I was close enough to see a barb enter the back of his neck. This was news to him, all right, but he still didn't run; he swung his bow and knocked a half-dozen wasps out of the air.

I could see how it was going to be, and winced for his resemblance to a human being. I still hated and feared him, but didn't want to watch.

And couldn't look away.

He swatted out again, the metal bow gleaming like a sword. And swatted out again, as more and more of them dove in to sting. And bounced off the walls, too pained and panicked now to find the one that was really a corridor. And swatted out yet again.

It had its own rhythm and inevitability, a ballet on the theme of human stupidity and violence. I could almost hear the thrum of the huge wasps, the contrapuntal whistle of the bowstring through the air.

His face was contorted beyond any mere emotions as the stingers sent their poison into him. His mouth twitched spastically; the long muscles of his arms and legs jerked without intention now, and sent the bow scything through the hive itself. It broke open, and the full swarm boiled out, the long plumes unfurling like lancers' pennons as the wasps circled and struck, circled and struck.

When I lost sight of Bloody Nose he was just flopping about. It had been enough to break the spell. It had been too much. My corridor was blacked out again, but I blundered away at high speed, fending off with both hands, full of guilt for having ever wished anyone dead. And for knowing, as I slowed, exhausted, that I would do it again, soon enough. I drifted along, massaging my left wrist; the old break never set right, and impact always makes it ache.

But what was this? Who were these foxfire wraiths—what was their role in the mystery play? Embodiments of conscience? Ghosts of Christmas Yet To Be?

Foyle and Helen Hogg-Smythe were sitting in adjacent cells, faintly illuminated in blue. They waved, urging me toward them.

The space between us was a black unknown, but I tried it and found an opening. I reached a block adjacent to them and the wall between us slid away as another rose in place behind me, two more faint blue panels turning on to link my cell with theirs.

A wave of weakness came over me. I didn't actually hit the floor, but that was because they were supporting me; I hadn't seen them do it, but they had taken my arms. They held me up. They let me gently down.

Chapter Fifteen

MY WRIST STILL hurt. Someone had given me a ball of gel to squeeze for therapy. It squished out between my fingers and around my thumb as I grasped it, then returned to a sphere when I relaxed my hand. Squeeze—a little pain shooting from my palm up my arm to near the elbow, wrist tendons becoming defined. Relax—a shiny amber ball, heavy, warm in my palm. This was an important activity. In and out of shape, that's the healing process.

I sensed feminine warmth, and heard a woman's voice. "Are you back with us? Do you know where you are?"

For some reason, I didn't want to open my eyes. And I realized, with a thrill of panic, that I had no answer to the question.

"Do you know *who* you are?"

Overwhelming relief. But even as I gave the answer, I began to remember that I shouldn't.

"Evan Larkspur?"

The sad laughter of several people. I opened my eyes and saw a simple hospital room. Whitewashed adobe walls, wooden furniture, institutional attempts at homey decoration. Stage center, the square and suddenly familiar shape of my doctor; two male interns or nurses stood attentively behind her. She was a stocky woman with iron-gray hair, brown eyes, deeply tanned and freckled skin. A strong jaw, short lips. She smiled kindly, as if forgiving an infidelity with total understanding. "I had hoped we'd seen the last of these lapses."

"It's coming back to me now," I said. "But what's so funny?"

One of the interns pointed at the cheap reproduction bust on the nightstand: a brooding, effeminate face in plastic. "Sorry. It's a standard joke, that's all. The guy in the asylum who thinks he's Larkspur, or the Consultant. I didn't mean to laugh." Sitting up now, I could see the mirror behind the bust. "Doesn't look much like you, does it? We should take it out of here. You read the name off it and give it back to us every time."

"Every time?" I said. "How many times have I lost my memory?"

My doctor answered carefully. "You've never remembered anything coherent from before the crash. But there've been five of these other lapses, where you forget everything you've learned since. They always pass, Freeman Notwan. More quickly every time."

"Yes, I'm . . . I'm almost with you now." Horror and disgust accompanied the memories. The human race was divided into Freemen and Citizens now, and ruled by my Nexus classmates grown old, the worst enemies I could possibly have; "Larkspur" was a tin household god. "Notwan" had been something to offer the doctors instead, a variant on Odysseus's old dodge in Polyphemos's cave. They knew it was a lie, thought I was an itinerant smuggler, but didn't care. They were kindly people, but nothing good would have come from telling them the truth. Had it been dumb luck, or a protective mechanism, that had brought my memory back in phases?

She nodded sadly. A warm, flower-scented breeze entered the room through open windows. She signaled for the others to leave us alone.

"Aptitude tests tell us you are a competent space-pilot and a profound scholar of language and literature. Do you remember anything about your formative years this time?"

I shook my head. But in fact I squeezed and relaxed, squeezed and relaxed: the dun plains of Wayback, sun beating down; a night-moth snuffing the candle I read by; a line of kisses up Domina's white inner thigh; Summerisle solemnly warning me of vast conspiracies and secrets too horrible for mankind. All real, if anything in the universe was real. Training in the navy, boring but real. The edge of a suspend-sleep tank against my hand as I entered it, the cutting edge, the dividing place. After that, nothing real . . . Hiding in a harem. Sailing a windjammer in a storm. Fighting hijackers and cosmic disaster in space, just as Summerisle had foretold . . . I felt a wave of revulsion for the last dream, its sickening mock-heroics.

"You had a great interest in astrophysics," she said. "Do you remember that?"

"Astrophysics?" This was new.

"We gave you access to the library. I'd call it a layman's interest, nothing too technical."

What was she—? Oh, yes. Bubble universes. A hundred years had passed, but in all the new accumulation of knowledge, no mention of Helter's "bubble universes." Image of a bubble. Fragile. A dreamworld. But if it popped, what would I find?

"We think you were a smuggler," she said. "We see a lot of them here on Far End; we're at the limit of Column control, and most of us like it that way." She smiled to reassure me. "And it would explain why you would be traveling space with substandard equipment."

"I thought nothing survived the crash."

"Your vessel sank in the sea, true. But a crash doesn't speak well for its spaceworthiness, does it? And there's no doubt in my mind that you're also suffering from a suspend-sleep malfunction. At first, to be frank, we thought you irremediably psychotic. But now that you accept the unreality of the trauma dreams, the only problem is concussion amnesia. It's a loss, but you can start over. There are people who value good pilots here. And let's say they can supply you with a serviceable ID."

"I remember you telling me that before," I said. "I'm with it, now, thanks. I think it's best I leave soon."

Something kept her in the room—perhaps had kept her from discharging me before—something personal, I thought. "Are you sure there's nothing else we can help you with? I think you remember more now. You're certainly more guarded. But you don't seem happier."

"What would it mean," I asked slowly, "if I couldn't suppress one of the dreams?" Image of a bubble. "If it's full of details that are no good, if it's physically impossible, but still seems as real as the solid memories. Why would I hold on to this one, when I've let more attractive ones go?"

She didn't probe. She just looked thoughtful. "There is also psychological amnesia. The dream could have just enough truth in it to be an effective mask for something you don't *want* to remember. The usual reason is a sense of guilt or shame."

I didn't have anything more to say, and soon she turned to go. A bubble. A mask. Why should I be the only one to survive? An officer *could* use his codes to commandeer the escape shuttle, might not want to share air and supplies with twenty others . . . Just the sort of thing you'd expect from an artistic type who'd only fantasized himself the stuff of naval heroes. And it was true, what she'd said. I still didn't want to believe it, to burst the *bubble*—a sly, guilty clue from the unconscious?

I'd rather think that *everything* was a mask. Couldn't that be true? Couldn't a lowlife smuggler prefer to imagine himself the legendary Larkspur? The asylums, I reminded myself, are full of them, and I'd had plenty of time and enough access to the library to build up the story, and think my memory was returning "in phases." I didn't *look* like him, apparently. Why torture myself with guilt for his Lord Jim act, when there was no shred of evidence that I really was—

"If you're going to go," she said, turning back, "don't forget your keepsake. If it still means nothing to you, it may at least be worth some money." She opened the nightstand and handed me a small brass disk. "An antique like that."

I reached for it with my left hand. Squeezed it, released it. Squeezed it, released it. They probably didn't use data disks anymore, I thought—wouldn't recognize the coding on the case. As she closed the door, I felt the tears begin to come, as I bore down harder and harder, despite the pain, on the log of the survey cruiser *Barbarossa*, the lost *Barbarossa*. My ship.

When the crying became sobbing, they came and shook me. I tried to be quiet, I knew I must be quiet.

They were shaking me again. "Please wake up, Commissioner, you sound miserable, please." I had to open my eyes. I was lying on the hard tiled floor, my head in Helen Hogg-

Smythe's lap. Foyle, who had been looking down at us with concern in her face, straightened up and turned her back.

"Feel better now?" Hogg-Smythe asked. I rolled over and blinked at the huge dark chamber. I could see that everyone had been segregated into dim blue groups of three like ours, most of them far away.

"That time I flew you . . ." Foyle said. "Tell me, do you always have such bad dreams?"

"Only when I sleep."

"And who was 'Barbara'?" Hogg-Smythe wondered. "Or should I ask?"

" 'Barbara'? . . . No, that would be my *barber*," I said. "My last session with him was particularly traumatic."

I stood up. There was nowhere to walk, but I stretched my legs.

"This would be the barber who dyed black roots onto your gray hairs?" Foyle asked.

"What? Oh, the silver streaks. Ridiculous fashion, isn't it? But all the rage in the central worlds."

"First I've heard of it."

"Spend a lot of time at official receptions, do you?"

"Do you? Do Shadow Tribunes?"

"So contentious, Foyle," Hogg-Smythe said. "No one would think you were so worried about him a—"

A green-eyed glare cut this short.

"I've never claimed to be a Shadowman," I said. "Just a bureaucrat with a few extra political duties. They issue us a cloak and dagger sometimes, in the fringes, but we don't wear them well . . . Sorry I conked out on you two. I didn't get any sleep last night, and all this walking—"

"Yes, we saw you," Hogg-Smythe interrupted. "You went about so purposefully, but the mirrors toyed with you. Why didn't you just—"

"Stop and *reflect*?"

She laughed and shook her head. "Dear Commissioner."

"Oh, he's quick enough." Foyle turned her back again.

We looked across the black sea at the other blue islands.

"How long has it been this way?" I asked. "Everyone celled up, I mean."

"Not long," Foyle said. "But you were out for hours and hours first. I had a long nap, too, then took the watch until you woke up Helen with your twitching and talking."

"She's not quite this rude to anyone but you," Hogg-Smythe said apologetically.

"How many hours?"

"The wristcomps burned out, remember? But it's been a while. The mercenaries just wouldn't quit walking. I don't know, it feels like four or five in the morning now, don't you think, Helen?"

"I have no opinion."

"Has anything interesting happened?"

"There was a loud voice," Hogg-Smythe said. "In Ur-Linguish, we think, but with a heavy accent. Our best guess is that it said 'Why so long, why so many decades?' But it didn't respond to replies."

"Anything else?"

"One of the mercenaries appeared to be unconscious," Foyle offered. "Some robots, like dogs with hands, dragged him over to share a cell with Ken and Ariel. I thought those two would have the sense to tie him up with his clothes, but they didn't."

"Where? I don't see them."

"That was the last thing. Some of the cells have sunk into the floor, out of sight. Should be our turn soon."

"Well, don't worry. That 'unconscious' merc was probably dead; I saw one stung by giant wasps. Did anyone else get trapped with the enemy?"

"Piet and the Lagados found each other; that made three, which seems to be the magic number. The friar got caught with two soldiers, but they were just talking peaceably as they sank out of sight. They'll probably want to check back with their superiors before killing a holy man. Funny little scruple—There goes another group." She pointed.

I followed the line of her finger and saw a distant three-block cell of mercenaries slowly sink into the floor. The blue light winked out and they were gone.

"So where do we go from here?" I asked.

"Helen, you read more about that than I did."

"Apparently pilgrims must still go through the whole rite of passage," Hogg-Smythe said. "Even though our group must be confusing the computers. It would be too much of a coincidence for this to be the right time of year for a Hellway run. But perhaps they're fitting us in now because we're six hundred years overdue."

"Assuming we do get the standard treatment, what can we expect?"

"Oh, dear. Remember, I only had time to skim it. We've been divided into initial teams of three. Now, each team will be sent through the Hellway's own closed-circuit transport system to a different place in the wilderness.

"There are scores of these subenvironments. Testing grounds, all quite different. Their secrets were well kept from generation to generation. Even if your parents and grandparents broke the taboo against preparing you for the Hellway's surprises, the odds were you wouldn't face the same tests. Naturally, those library terminals didn't reveal much either.

"But the ground rules are simple. Once we exit into a testing ground, our goal is simply to reach the next t-stop. If the path isn't obvious, the way will be north—I think we're issued equipment if necessary, including a direction finder."

"That's it? We hike to the next stop?"

"And solve any problems we face on the way. Learn a lesson, have an unusual experience . . ."

"Survive an ordeal," Foyle suggested.

"I'm afraid it *is* all rather vague," Hogg-Smythe admitted. "The library files we read were intended for children who already knew the moral purpose of the Hellway, whatever that was.

"Anyway, when we've finished our test or adventure, the new transport terminal breaks up our team; each of us is sent to a new place far ahead, with new partners. Which suggests that each subtrek is supposed to last about the same length of time—one or two days. Teams of three or four are preferred, but if one team gets hung up somewhere, it may be given additional reinforcements. And there was a whole section on the *social* makeup of teams that was hard to follow. 'A desirable mix of classes.' "

"Of course," Foyle said. "Masters need servants."

"That's only your hunch, we've no evidence. But to continue: the average number of subtreks for each candidate was three, depending on how quickly he got through them. Five or six days total, and then a ceremony of affirmation at the north pole."

"Five days would be soon enough to warn the construction base against the mercenaries, if we could contact a satellite as soon as we emerged," I said. "The merc commander was going to take a week to plan his operation."

"We all have at least two chances of being teamed up with mercs before then, however," Foyle pointed out.

"But will the mercenaries understand what is going on? Will

they know enough to go north? To cover ground at all?" Hogg-Smythe asked.

"Maybe not," I said. "And if we *are* eventually teamed with some of them, they may be willing to keep us alive as translators. But let's hope it doesn't come to that."

"Amen," said Helen Hogg-Smythe—as we sank through the floor.

Our walls had become perfect reflectors again. "I hope to God I never see another mirror in my life," Foyle said. Actually, she looked pretty good in them; disaster suited her. I helped Hogg-Smythe to her feet.

One panel slid down. What was revealed was not a corridor but a transport-tube car, different in design from those of the Titan city system. We sat down and it began to move, with a moderate but constant acceleration; we probably reached a high velocity, but there were no windows to judge by.

A robot voice began to address us in confidential tones. The women groaned as the Ur-Linguish words came faster. "It's not fair," Foyle complained. "We actually can read the language, but no one speaks it."

"Silence!" I snapped; she looked at my face as I cocked an ear to the speaker, and evidently put off killing me. I cast her, Hogg-Smythe, and everything else out of my mind, sinking back into the consciousness of a seventeen-year-old student in the second largest library in the galaxy as he pored over ancient texts everyone else had forgotten—at first just burning for a way to distinguish himself, to outshine Domina Wintergrin's snob boyfriends and catch her attention, but later motivated by a purer love for the secret world he'd discovered in them . . .

I could never have translated the old poetry—understood stress and elision, assonance and resonance, true rhyme and false—without learning to read it aloud first, practicing until I'd sounded like one of the old recordings. Whether I could still wrap my tongue around Ur-Linguish's consonants or not, I could certainly hope to follow it by ear. Only the dialect was in my way. The occasional borrowings from Deutsch I could guess at—I'd worked through Voss's Homer once—but the accent seemed to show the Svenska influence. I couldn't be sure; old recordings of "Scottish" and "Swedish" accents, as different as chalk and cheese to our ancestors, sound much the same to us.

"I think it's asking us—no, it's telling us that we haven't supplied our, our 'clans and home parishes.' " I barely noticed that our capsule had begun its deceleration phase as I continued to translate. "This will make the . . . 'partnering' difficult. Now he's reviewing other things you said, Helen. Other things. The water is safe to drink most places . . . unless we are issued canteens in the, uh, anteroom, in which case stick with that water. But the plants and animals are never nutritious, sometimes poisonous. The, uh, stored food is all—gone away?—gone *bad*, of course, but computers can synthesize enough for such a small group of, uh, seekers. Ration your food issues in a . . . no, lost that bit . . . If extra equipment is offered, you will need it . . . There are, uh, *gefahre*—dangers, but if you fail to find the correct, uh, waterways?—that's not right—and disgrace—damage?—yourselves—remember the watchers, who will . . . do something to you."

The deceleration became more pronounced.

"At the beginning of a test, always look for a . . . guidepost? and its . . . motto, maybe. And remember that you are on the path—against? Over? Through? One of those goddamn German prepositions that could mean anything—on the path somehow related to mastery. The path to *over*mastery? Something like that."

"Something like that," Foyle repeated, grim-faced.

"By 'German' you mean Deutsch, don't you?" Hogg-Smythe asked with admiration. "You even *think* in Ur-Linguish, Commissioner."

The car came to a stop.

A last sentence. Solemn tones.

"We are being given a few minutes to compose our thoughts before our first . . . yeah, I think 'test' is right. And a sign to contemplate."

A luminous form began to coalesce in the air above the closed door, a hologram animated to take shape slowly.

"I wish I'd got the exact words, because I think it was important," I said. " 'Go forth under the sign of overmastery to come.' "

We watched until the floating symbol became clear. Foyle was the first to understand it.

And she swore. And she turned pale.

"I told you so!" she said. "I told you what sort of people they were. 'In this sign, conquer!' Wasn't that it, Commissioner? So this is where their *ideals* led them."

Hogg-Smythe peered up at the hologram.

The sign of overmastery was the image of a bundle of birch

rods tied together with a red strap. Protruding from the top was the head of an axe.

"How you carry on, Foyle," she said. "Hardly the swastika you would have predicted."

Foyle gave a bitter laugh. "It's too perfect. The Roman equivalent! Denying the truth about themselves to the bitter end."

"The axe is a common symbol across many cultures," Hogg-Smythe insisted. "The first human tool. Clearer of forests. The shape of a peace pipe. I believe the Old Rite Kanalists even used it as a symbol of liberty. The Green Church—"

"You're thinking of the labrys, Helen," I said—again, not me speaking, but that same seventeen-year-old boy, something of a pedant. "The *double* axe was a prehistoric European holy sign, and yes, religious groups still make much of it.

"But the emblem before us is something else, an ancient Roman symbol for the *imperium*, the power of the state. Ultimately, the power to punish. The single-blade axe is for beheading criminals and prisoners of war, the birch rods and strap are for whipping slaves and children. Bundled together, they are called the fasces.

"Mussolini revived the symbol two thousand years later, to represent his own party. The Fascists.

"I'm afraid Foyle is right. Be prepared for anything. When people like this say they'll 'test' you—you can't afford to fail."

A moment later the door opened, but the fasces did not go away. Beneath the whips, and under the axe, we walked out to face the Hellway.

Chapter Sixteen

I LOOKED THROUGH an arch of stone at a vast prairie and a swatch of blue sky that might almost be that of the surface, only a little dimmer. We continued to hang back in what the robot voice had called an anteroom, a cave connecting the transport with the prairie. Provision racks lined the stone walls to either side of the exit.

We discovered food in plastic containers. Three backpacks had been laid out; Helen and I donned two, but Foyle just went through the contents of the third, adding a few bits of camping gear—matches, a roll of toilet paper—to the rig she already wore.

"I see nine canteens," Hogg-Smythe said. "Now, didn't the voice say something about that?"

"Yes," I replied. "If water is provided here, we take it, and shouldn't drink anything we find outdoors—not this leg of the trip."

"Besides, we were told to take everything," Foyle pointed out. "But what do you make of all this cord?"

A dozen coils of fine black cord lay side by side, ready to pack. Picking up the first one, I exposed a small plaque, which advertised the line's lightness, amazing tensile strength, and convenience.

"Supercord," I said. "Useful stuff, I guess, and lighter to carry than rope. But why should we need so much?"

"We could make quite a large fishnet with it, I suppose," Hogg-Smythe suggested as we each packed our share. "But we're not supposed to eat the fish!"

We stepped into the artificial daylight. The t-station proved to be the only major outcropping, with flat land all around. A few paces from the exit, a fin of granite jutted waist-high from the beige grass. A weathered metal plaque was bolted to its face.

It bore a bas-relief executed in the same style as the heroic bronze cable-couplers I'd hidden between in the statue chamber. Here some Roman demigod on the order of Hercules wrestled a large bag sewn from skins, with stylized puffs of air escaping from the seams. No relation whatsoever to the heading just below:

ENDURANCE OR INGENUITY

There followed some directions in smaller type, not so cryptic:

WEATHERVANES WILL POINT YOU NORTH.
CROSS THE WATER VIA BRIDGES, DO NOT WADE.
THERE ARE GEFAHRE TO THE WEST, DO NOT BE DIVERTED THAT WAY.
THE HORNVIEH ARE HARMLESS.

"They seem to be looking after our safety," Hogg-Smythe pointed out to Foyle.

"We don't know what we've supposed to 'endure' yet," Foyle observed. "Or how mobile the 'dangers to the west' are. But meanwhile—that must be north." She pointed at the weather-vane on an openwork metal tower a few hundred meters away. With the t-station and a southern breeze at our backs, the single arrow pointed away, and the long grass bowed before us as we began our hike.

Hour after hour, we plodded the flat grassland. The prairie was interrupted only by occasional muddy water holes. Although the sky grew lighter for a while—a series of panels flaring white in slow succession, to simulate the progress of morning—it never got as bright or warm as on the true surface of Newcount Two.

Unreal, unreal. The illusion kept flickering out, every time I raised my eyes. On any horizon the sky looked a genuine blue, but directly overhead the ceiling was closer, less tinted and blurred by the atmosphere, and we could see the tracery of square panels in a grayer, darker circle. And that remained true no matter how far we walked; the ceiling's underbelly seemed to be gliding like a manta ray to exactly match our pace.

Something else was looming over the landscape, too, shadowing it in other ways. But I couldn't quite tell what. Aside from the sky, it was a plausible enough scene. The grass had a dusty-sweet smell and insects crawled through it. We saw a few animals like rabbits with raccoon arms, and once we flushed a covey of heavy flightless birds, who gave a series of haunting low whistles in the first moment of panic. But we heard no other animal noise, I finally realized—that was part of the strangeness, no sound but the wind in the tall grass. And no storm clouds to account for the heavy feeling of expectation in the air.

I wondered if the others felt it, too.

Despite her heavy pack, Foyle tended to get ahead of Hogg-Smythe and me. Then she'd stop and survey the horizon through field glasses as we caught up. "She is quick, isn't she?" Hogg-Smythe said once. "I hope I'm not holding you up. I do walk fifteen k a day, usually."

"That's, that's all right," I panted. "Just as well to pace yourself." We reached Foyle. "See anything interesting yet?"

"You can make out the top of the next weathervane," she said. "Notice that the wind is always from the south. Don't ask me why . . . Nothing new to the west except those shapes in the distance. Not animals, I think. And too many of them to be the watchers."

"Watchers?" said Hogg-Smythe.

Foyle's eyes were slits. "Maybe you've forgotten, Helen, but I haven't. The voice said that 'watchers' would do something to us if we failed our test. Monitor robots, presumably. But I don't expect great numbers of them."

She looked back at the distant, motionless shapes. "Through the binoculars they might be topiary bushes. But we can't take a closer look. That would mean diverting to the west, and we've been warned against that."

We kept trudging north.

Nothing broke the monotony for an hour, although Foyle continued to note new mystery bushes in the distance, northwest as well as due west now. And then an irregular rank of slender trees rose across the horizon dead ahead; in less than two hours, we would overtake them.

Meanwhile, we discovered the confetti.

There'd always been a sprinkling of them, but too few to attract interest: large colored petals, sometimes blowing free in the wind, but usually clinging on grass blades. But we saw no trees or flowers that could have shed them, and in time realized that they were creatures in their own right, like insects. Most of the time they were passive—motionless flecks of white, pale blue, or pink. But every now and then, as the constant breeze stirred the stalks, a few of them would rise up and fly around.

At first, an old butterfly aficionado, I was interested in them, and extended a hand to one. It landed and plastered itself flat against my skin. The "confetto," as Foyle called it, was an oval strip as long as my forefinger and thinner than paper. It flew by folding itself to create various airfoils, flapping them as wings or gliding on the wind. It had no other visible features, no head or limbs. Whatever sensors it had must have been microscopic.

Where it had landed on the back of my hand, it clung, as if by static electricity. I felt that sort of tingling, but also an unpleasant coolness. I scraped up one edge with a fingernail and the confetto seemed to resist for a second, then curled up into a little tube and dropped off, to unfold and catch the wind and glide off again.

"I don't like these butterflies, somehow," Helen Hogg-Smythe said after a similar experience. "They should be fun and interesting, but they're not *alive* enough."

"Barely alive at all," Foyle said. "Adapted to this low-energy environment." She waved one hand at the dim sky. "They rarely expend energy, just collect it."

"Living off light, you think?" Hogg-Smythe sounded dubious.

"That, or pollens in the air, or something else as ubiquitous. You can see they don't search for food like regular butterflies would."

"Call them moths," I suggested. Foyle looked at me askance. "I'd rate them lower if I could, but I consider moth the bottom rank." I scratched my hand where the thing had landed; it was red and irritated.

"Confetti-moths, then," Helen said.

A handful would collect on our clothing as we moved through the waves of grass, but on rest breaks we'd scrape them off. Sometimes, when a lull in the wind was followed by a strong puff, we'd see large clusters of confetti-moths rise and swirl aimlessly for a few minutes here and there in the distance. But not in a live way. More like the dust devils you see in the blind alleys of cities, dwarf tornadoes of wastepaper and detritus . . .

We reached the trees. They turned out to mark the edge of a waterway, a straight line not quite perpendicular to our course. The water was some twenty meters across, but we couldn't guess the depth; it was nearly opaque with algae. We followed the bank east to a nearby stone bridge, inspecting a few of the slender trees on the way.

Feather trees, we would call them. Their wine-purple foliage reminded us more of feathers than of leaves, veining off the branches with no stretches of bare twig, stirring almost noiselessly in the breeze. Even the black bark was soft, with a rubbery feel. Foyle proved we could climb them for a better view, but found nothing new to see.

The sideless stone bridge was solid enough to last for another thousand years. Halfway across it, Helen Hogg-Smythe pointed out one of the raccoon-rabbits on the bank we were approaching.

First the creature drank, in an odd, craning way. Then it cleaned itself. Using its unrabbitlike arms rather than step into the river, it washed a confetti-moth from its back with a thimble-fistful of water.

Suddenly, it caught sight of us. Instead of bolting into the grass at its back, it shuddered as if cornered, with no way out. Then something rippled in the water nearby, and at this the creature forced itself to retreat—creeping, not running, into some reeds.

"What extraordinary behavior," Helen said. "That disturbance in the water—I wonder . . . Perhaps there's more than one reason why they gave us canteens."

And soon, looking straight down, we saw the eels.

They were three meters long each, and as thick around as my arm, a darker green than the water they snaked through. Their heads were hideous, the mouths a mass of complicated prongs and suckers, the eyes like those of humans, but larger. They moved freely up- and down-stream in great numbers, leaving transient trails of clear water behind them—evidently straining out algae wherever they went.

"Would they have eaten that rabbit, do you think?" Helen asked. "Look at that fat one! It's huge compared to the others—but it doesn't look like it's swallowed something. Its skin is all loose and bloated."

"Shedding?" I said. "Or pregnant? Look how many follow it, like they're protecting it."

"I *don't* think they could eat rabbits," Helen said quickly, reversing herself before Foyle could do it. "Those strainer mouths of theirs wouldn't permit it. But the rabbit feared them. Are they electric eels?"

"Probably not," Foyle told her. "Electric fish tend to be blind—they sense prey with their electromagnetic field instead of their eyes."

"You've studied electric fish?"

Foyle looked uncomfortable. "Not exactly. Before my husband died, we lived on Vesper."

"The nature preserve?"

"It was then, yes. We helped manage the place. Roger and I were fire wardens, but the zoologists were always showing us the more exotic animals."

"What a lovely life that must have been!" Hogg-Smythe exclaimed. "I remember when everyone in academia was trying to join one of the research teams there. But the place was turned over to colonists after all, wasn't it?"

"After a period of resistance," Foyle said. "Yes."

Her tone slammed that door.

But I had other things to think about. The rabbitoid had finally let me see what was shadowing the whole landscape. It wasn't just the artificial sky—it was fear. It was quiet terror.

Not just of the eels in the water, but of something on land.

Why should a rabbit be afraid of running into the grass? And the cries of the flightless birds fit, too: just occasional low warning calls, no showing off, no song. Even the passive, mindless confetti-moths showed those occasional bursts of swirling panic, when irregularities in the breeze made it seem as though something were pushing through the thick sward near them. Some predator.

I told the others my suspicions, but somehow they didn't sound like much out loud. I suggested we avoid the taller grass, but we'd been doing that anyway. Foyle seemed amused at my apprehension. "You've never spent much time in wilderness, have you, Commissioner?" asked the ex-warden of Vesper—and I couldn't say what I might have, about Wayback, the planet where Evan Larkspur was born. But I did notice the women sticking a little closer together after that.

On a bridge over the third waterway we had to cross, Foyle said, "It's really all just one river, isn't it?"

"I think you're right," I replied. "This time it flows east to west again. Or rather—"

"Northeast to southwest. Less of an angle than that, but an angle."

"Right. One river, flowing south, that crisscrosses back and forth in front of us."

"I wonder why they cut it that way. The bends must be tricky."

"Cut it?"

"Robots probably have to dredge it periodically, to keep the part we see so neat and geometrical." She looked sharply at Helen and me. "Remember that this is all artificial, and a test. Think of everything the landscape provides us with as either a problem or as part of a solution."

"I'll try," I told her earnestly. She snorted and pulled ahead of us again.

Hogg-Smythe leaned in my direction, speaking quietly. "She gets on my nerves, too. But she's probably right."

Though we held our course, the mysterious bushes Foyle had noticed appeared closer and closer, some due north now. We would get to see them after all.

Lagging behind together, Hogg-Smythe and I engaged in nervous small talk. She complimented me on my Ur-Linguish translation again, and I mentioned how strange the robot's Avalonian dialect had been.

"I can understand borrowing from Deutsch, but you don't expect to see an old basic word like 'danger' supplanted by something as foreign as 'gefahren.' "

"Oh, but the Avalonian tongue was quite artificial, Commissioner," she explained. "Deutsch and Svenska words were officially adopted on some sort of proportional system, for political reasons. The master plan didn't take, of course—synthetic languages never do—but it left its marks. Since you have some Deutsch, be on the lookout for bilingual puns; I gathered that those were common."

"Great. I always thought my life would depend on a pun someday."

"What do you think about this fasces symbol, Commissioner? Do you share Foyle's dark opinion?"

"I didn't do the background reading you two did. But that did appear to be a character out of Roman mythology back on the plaque. And if we assume that the religious change which bound the Elitists together again was a harder attitude, a harsher discipline—then yes, maybe their cult was a harking-back to Ancient Rome. Stoic, class-ridden, militarist. 'Come back with your shield, my son, or on it.' That's the parental spirit we have to be scared of."

"Why hark back to Old Earth?"

"That's standard for secret societies, to pretend that they've preserved the folk wisdom of one of the earliest cultures. Ancient Egypt for the Rosicrucians and Freemasons, Minoan Crete for the Kanalists, and . . . uh, matriarchal prehistory for the Green Church, I guess. Rome is only slightly younger. Hell, they're all the same age now that Old Earth's uninhabitable."

"But that was my point," Hogg-Smythe said. "There's been a blurring and borrowing across many traditions."

"It may look that way," I answered. "The fasces is like an inverted ankh, the double axe like a Christian cross. But the differences are significant. The double axe comes from an earlier time than the fasces, but a more mature civilization. The Cretans' days of sacrificing children to the state were far in their past; their royal axe was tall, thin, stylized—a ritual weapon, from a land of traders and artisans, not slavers and soldiers."

She gave me a sidelong glance. "You seem to know a good deal of Kanalist lore, Commissioner. Are you an initiate? I know many government officials are. Reformed Rite, of course."

"Once upon a time—" I began.

"Look!" Foyle cried out. Our heads snapped in the direction she pointed. Upward.

It was unmistakeably a balloon—a large one, judging by its position on the horizon. An inverted teardrop shape of pale green, it had been launched somewhere to our north. With the wind at our back faster than we could walk, it soon sank out of sight in the same direction.

"But we'll overtake the place it launched from," Foyle pointed out. "Perhaps that's the next form of transportation we'll get."

We saw another balloon within an hour. This one had popped up from somewhere in the west, and we had a long time to observe it before it, too, would disappear in the north.

I hated to watch it go, with the endless march ahead of us. And—I still thought—with something malign waiting for us in the tall grass.

"It does seem to be carrying passengers," Hogg-Smythe said. "Or cargo, anyway. Can either of you make that out?"

I borrowed her field glasses; Foyle was using her own. But we both found the mass at the bottom of the balloon too shapeless to evaluate.

"Seems to have found an equilibrium altitude, anyway," Foyle noted. "That's interesting."

"Isn't that normal?" Hogg-Smythe asked.

"In a real sky, yes. But we're inside a container—I wouldn't expect as much of an air-pressure gradient. I'm no physicist, though. And of course, we don't know how the atmosphere is managed here. This steady breeze, for instance. No reason for it to arise naturally. I wonder if it's manufactured."

"To accommodate the balloons!"

"Why not, Helen? Why not?"

By then we'd reached the bushes. But "bush" turned out to be the wrong word. Foyle thought they might be some sort of cactus, but none she'd ever seen.

Imagine a hard, sausage-shaped gourd with two, four, or six thick roots raising it off the ground, like stilts. As if even these plants were scared of something that crawled in the grass. Some of the gourds were smaller than my head, others over two meters long and half as wide. Scaly-skinned, they ranged in color from orange and yellow and green to dark brown, and came in a number of bizarre shapes.

Only the young, colorful ones were still rounded; they were

like kegs on wooden legs, and as we proceeded northward, we saw strange-looking birds tap them with needle-shaped beaks. The browner, older-looking gourds had collapsed inward until opposite sides touched and merged, becoming warped planes, like parachutes or sails. But not thin enough for balloon material, I noted—very strong, almost petrified, though there was a slight leathery give when I tried to bend one of the four-rooted ones.

Weird, twisted. A garden for Hieronymus Bosch. I could tell that the others shared my vague repulsion. But then we were in clear prairie again, and finally saw the hornvieh—Deutsch/Avalonian for "cattle."

The herd creatures were big enough to have been alarming if the plaque hadn't told us they were harmless: shaggy brown mammaloids as high as my shoulder, each carrying a thousand kilos on its six cowlike legs. We decided to call them "hex-oxen," and later just "hexen"; Foyle's more correct "hexungulates" didn't seem worth the effort.

We soon left the first herd behind. They never stopped grazing except to groom the confetti-moths off each other, and slowly. Ludicrously so.

"They might be natives of the Titans' world," Foyle said. "This artificial Titan sky seems to be low in ultraviolet light. Titanworlders might tend to be more energy-conservative than we. Like the confetti-moths. Hence the slowness."

But the hexen's other peculiarities were hard to understand. The second herd we passed, like the first, was grouped around a mudhole. Another hint that the river was somehow dangerous? And it was odd that the creatures didn't space themselves out at random, as grazers usually do, but instead worked in a circle, outward. Maybe they just didn't want to get too far from their mudhole. Or did the grazed-flat circle itself represent some kind of safety?

I wondered if the eels were electrified after all. And amphibious, too, slithering invisibly through the grass and—

But that was stupid. Their mouths were strainers for algae, and they had as much food as they could want right where they were. The eels were not the predators. We soon found out what the eels were.

Foyle had said "Balloon!" when it was still just a dark mass behind a clump of feather trees on the horizon. When its green roundness became apparent, Foyle and I took some of the weight from Helen Hogg-Smythe's pack and we proceeded at double-time.

But when we reached the river, there was nothing to do but watch and marvel.

The balloon was an eel. One of the bloated ones. It rested in a pool at the center of an island composed of hundreds of normal eels, in the middle of the river. Most of its body was inside the envelope of balloon skin, out of sight. The neck emerged near the bottom of that envelope and looped through the water back up to the head, which was clamped into a thick valved pad of skin on the outside.

A dozen other eels were doubled over this meter of neck, their tails in their mouths and each of them linked in turn to dozens of others, the whole mass of the eel island anchoring the huge balloon in place. But there was always at least one detached eel with a different mission, its head engaged, half-submerged, in some operation with the balloon-bearer's.

"They're inflating it," Foyle said. "You were right all along, Helen. They generate electricity, but in a more localized way than Terran eels. Those prongs on their heads are electrodes."

"Are you trying to tell me—" I said.

"It's the only explanation. Electrolysis! They're breaking down water into hydrogen and oxygen. See that darker sphere inside the balloon? I think that's the oxygen; every now and then one of the free eels clamps on to that side patch and the inner bladder gets smaller. Get it? The balloon retains the lighter-than-air hydrogen, and the inflator sucks the pure oxygen to supercharge its metabolism. I wondered why they put away so much algae. They need the fuel; it takes a hell of a lot of energy to do what they're doing."

"But why are they doing it?" Hogg-Smythe asked.

Foyle shrugged. "For the ride, I guess. Let's say these are the feeding grounds, and the breeding grounds are elsewhere, someplace that can only be reached by air, by balloon. The pool where they land is the source of this river; after breeding, they flow back here to feed. Some simple cycle like that. It's bad enough to ask 'Why?' of evolution, but these things could never have evolved, especially not in an energy-poor environment—no, they were genetically engineered. One of the 'entertainment' species we read about, created by Titan biotechnology."

"The envelope can't get much larger," Hogg-Smythe observed. "Not with trees on either side of the river. It'll brush the branches anyway; lucky they're so soft."

"Luck has nothing to do with anything here," Foyle said.

A few minutes later, the balloon eel gave the signal for departure. A short hissing whistle came from its head and inflator eels stopped approaching. Anchor eels at the edge of the island released their tails and squirmed loose.

The mass became smaller and smaller, but there were still hundreds of kilos of dripping passenger eels hanging on when it became light enough, and, with a ripe unhurried suddenness like an apple dropping from its branch, the balloon lifted free of the water. Clear of the windbreak trees, it rapidly gained speed and drifted away to the north.

"Lovely. But just entertainment," Hogg-Smythe said wistfully. "I guess walking's safer, anyway." Foyle agreed like a stoic.

I didn't.

At dusk the temperature dropped and the wind became gustier, more erratic. The high grass swayed and broke apart. The birds huddled and emitted hushed whistles. Panic flights of larger and larger moth swarms could be seen here and there in the distance.

My nerves were screaming, the more so as the others did not feel what I felt, the imminence of attack. They were calmly discussing whether it was time to make camp yet, on this bridge, as I scanned both sides of the river for danger.

One bit of unusual activity stood out. A nearby herd of hexen had been mowing what looked like a dead straight corridor parallel to the river. But now they retreated back to their starting circle for the night, not quickly, but perhaps as quickly as they could.

I'd already put the glasses down, had turned to talk to Foyle, when it happened. The three of us heard an achingly loud, inhuman cry and spun to see the last of the retreating cattle lurch out of formation. He was coming straight toward the river and us, his movement through the ungrazed sward stirring up great clouds of white moths, his lung-bursting bellows testifying that something had hold of him. Something big.

I felt the women shrink back, and Helen Hogg-Smythe's hand gripped my shoulder from behind, drew me down to crouch with them past the crown of the bridge. But I couldn't bring my head all the way down. I ripped the glasses away from Foyle; I had to see, I had to know.

I swore under my breath—Foyle the one tugging now, only

to rise next to me and look as the hex-ox stopped screaming. We were staring right at it, not fifty meters away; it was being tortured and killed in a cloud of panicky moths, a few other hexen coming to its aid while the others lumbered back to safety, lowing piteously; and yet I could not see the predator.

Until something fell into place behind my eyes, like watching the foreground become the background in Schaelus's sculpture. I handed the glasses back to Foyle without using them, didn't need them anymore.

The predators had been in plain sight all along, all day, responsive to every movement in the area that might mean prey. And now they had their victim, fluttering down upon him in a great white storm—none of the blue or pink ones participating, just the white confetti-moths, flying in and plastering themselves to the beast from south, east, west, even north, as they beat their mock wings against the wind. Tens of thousands of them; we'd never realized how many lay quiescent in the taller grass.

The hex-ox wasn't running anymore, nor crying out. It didn't seem able to. Its six legs had splayed and straightened in a stiff and unnatural way that balanced its body securely off the ground, maximizing the area the moths could reach. One of the other hexen made a few feeble attempts to lick off the steadily thickening coating of white while the other tried to nudge the victim forward, toward the river; they seemed exempt from the blizzard attack, but soon gave up and lumbered off with sad moos.

Now the hex-ox was finished. In another few seconds the moths had covered its eyes, nose, mouth, and every square centimeter of skin, layer atop layer, like papier-mâché on a piñata.

After a minute all motion had ceased. The hex-ox no longer resembled an animal, but could now be recognized as something else—a scaly gourd on six long stalks.

We huddled together on the lowest of the stone steps, the breeze cold against our backs.

After what seemed like a long time, Foyle said quietly, "And the ones with four roots were rabbits. And the ones with two were birds . . ."

Night was falling fast, colors fading; the last shadows of hundreds of piñata gourds lengthened across the plain. It was just possible to make out the blue and pink and white flecks of confetti floating passively on the waves of grass, in every direction, as far as the eye could see.

Chapter Seventeen

"LET ME RECAP," Foyle said.

"Fine, if you'll leave it alone after that," Helen Hogg-Smythe replied.

We'd camped on the bridge, where few moths clung, though we would have to move out among them, somehow, in the morning. Foyle had collected enough hex-ox chips during the day for a fire. It was welcome; the stones we sat on were cold. The sluggish river swept below us quietly, except for the occasional splash of an eel breaking the surface.

Foyle sighed and nodded. "Very well . . . The moths would seem to be native Titanworld creatures, from the original version of the park before the humans came. Adapted to the Titan sky, energy conservers. Most of the time passive, either wrapped around grassblades or permitting themselves to drift in the wind. If there's a disturbance in the grass or air nearby, the closest individuals settle on the source—a big puff of air creates a big swirl of searchers—but judging by our experience neither case necessarily triggers a mass attack."

"Some threshold number," I suggested.

She nodded again. "Only when they sense they've already got 'a good start' on a capture do they emit some signal—a pheromone, perhaps—that prompts a whole cloud of them to fly in, even against the wind. They didn't even settle on the hexen that tried to help. Because of the energy cost, or because they begin to change to paste as soon as they hit, they have to go for the maximum chance of making a capture, a single target."

"Notice that they come in three colors," Hogg-Smythe pointed out, "but only cooperate with their own."

"Agreed," I said. "All the piñata gourds we've seen were one solid color—yellowed, so that we didn't recognize the original white, blue, or pink. Maybe that's another reason why we didn't see mass attacks happening all the time. Maybe there has to be a chance predominance of one color first . . ."

Foyle sighed. "Maybe. An evolutionary device to make them more selective. After all, this is the climax of their life cycle.

"The commissioner has suggested that they pass some substance into the skin." I found myself once again scratching the back of my hand, where I'd let the moth light. "In the massive dose it may act on the nervous system, to spread and straighten the limbs of the victim. This makes coating the victim easier, and stabilizes it on what will eventually become its 'roots.'

"Because the piñata—victim plus coating—turns into a plant-like thing. The moths, scales, whatever you want to call them, differentiate into new functional forms. Maybe the roots obtain water and acids to help digest the animal inside. Somehow, this vampirism must lead to the birth of new moths. Maybe they breed inside the piñata as it hollows out, or maybe those birds which feed on the piñatas carry their seed somewhere . . . And maybe you're right, Helen—this isn't getting us anywhere.

"I see a single ray of light: their essential passivity. We may just keep lucking through them."

"I believe we're immune, not lucky," Helen Hogg-Smythe said firmly. "As you say, the hexen and the vampire moths probably evolved together, on the original planet of the Titans. They complement each other—the cattle move so slowly that they rarely attract moth attention. We move quickly, but must be biochemically incompatible, the wrong taste or smell to be their proper food."

"They usually land on our clothes," I mentioned. "No flesh taste there—another thing in our favor."

"We can't be sure organic fabric is indigestible," Foyle said, shaking her head, "or that the moths will know it is. They stick to it, we know that. And if enough stick . . . I'll grant you that their skin toxin doesn't figure to paralyze us, coming from a different biochemistry, but it could still poison us. And—"

"But look at the social logic of the situation, Foyle," Hogg-Smythe interrupted. "People do send their children to survival camps, and even to boot camps, but not to death camps. I refuse to believe that the Elitists meant this to be a plain of death."

"I'm not suggesting it would kill everyone. But I do think it's intended to winnow out—"

"The old and weak, is that it?" Hogg-Smythe rapped out.

Foyle continued in a more gentle voice. "The Hellway was meant for eighteen-year-olds, Helen. Future centurions. For all I know, it was the immature who got killed, the ones too thoughtless to keep scraping the moths off."

"What do you think, Commissioner?" Hogg-Smythe asked.

"We don't have to share all of Foyle's assumptions to be pretty damn scared of these things," I said. "They're all around us now, but remember—when we started, we saw gourds nowhere except in the west. This could be the big western danger we were supposed to avoid. Maybe the moth territory has drifted northeast over the last six hundred years, across what used to be a safe path for pilgrims."

"Why should the maintenance robots permit that?" Foyle asked. "But if that theory will keep you two wary tomorrow, that's all I ask. Shall we table the discussion?"

Hogg-Smythe and I agreed.

The Hellway sky was even stranger by night than by day. It still pretended to be real in some ways. There were "stars," for instance, and the ceilinged zenith had faded to the same black as everything else. But waves of color would come and go among the clouds. Spotlights would stab down toward random targets on the ground. A silent and invisible agency went skywriting in luminous green haze, and left a large, eyelike shape glowing over one horizon.

We watched for a long time in silence. As the fire burned lower, we wrapped up in the strong, warm blankets we'd found in our backpacks.

"Should try to sleep soon," Foyle suggested. "Won't be too hard, after all that walking."

"But first," Hogg-Smythe said, "you were going to tell me more about Kanalism—from the inside, Commissioner."

"Was I?"

"I hope you will. The subject fascinates me. They say eighteen out of twenty-two signers of the Free Compact were lodge members—and the whole Federal Alignment sprang from that."

"It's true," I acknowledged. "Most schoolbooks relegate that to a footnote, though. Like the Masonic symbols in the Great Seal of the old United States of North America. History isn't supposed to be made by secret societies—they don't leave enough paper behind for the historians."

"But then, a hundred years ago," Hogg-Smythe said impatiently, "the fraternity quite openly lobbied for the First Column's new constitution. And now I understand that Kanalist membership is almost a prerequisite for a high position in the Column."

"You have to realize," I said uncomfortably. "That's Reform Kanalism.

"Under the Old Rite, the emphasis was definitely on individual fulfillment. We—they adopted a royal symbol, but not out of identification with the state. Rather, out of the feeling that we are *all* potentially kings and queens. An appeal to talent and heroism, rather than fear and duty like the fasces. An appeal strong enough to have had a liberating influence on civilization for centuries."

Hogg-Smythe pursed her lips. Her next question was a little seditious, but I hadn't disguised my sympathies much; in a semi-autonomous fringe like the Blue Swathe an official could afford to show a little nonconformity. "What . . . went wrong?" she asked.

I shook my head. Then Foyle answered.

"They sold out." She spoke as if with personal bitterness, though the Federal Alignment had crumbled a century before. "What always goes wrong? You can bring out the best in people, but once they're the best, they expect to rule.

"The Nexus University chapter was the key—the oldest, most influential chapter. The only institution that spoke simultaneously to the schools, the young, the rich, and the powerful. Within Kanalism they called it a reform movement, so as to label whoever didn't go along a reactionary. But the truth is, most went along with a will."

She paused, eyeing my Column uniform a moment, then went on contemptuously. "The Shadow Tribunal itself was invented at Nexus U., over sherry and biscuits. And no one raised any resistance except a doggerel song:

Alignment dead without a mourner,
We all line up to watch the fight:
Right and Left in the same corner,
Against what's left of the Old Rite."

"You seem to know a great deal about it," Hogg-Smythe said. "Are *you* . . . ?"

Foyle shook her head, dark red hair breaking in waves. "But my late husband was a student of Kanalism. He was under the illusion it was worthwhile."

"Real Kanalism was," I said. "It was—"

"What's real is what *is*," Foyle insisted. "What most Kanalists choose to do. It's inevitable. In real life, Christians will either become a Holy Roman Empire—or let another cult do it and throw them to the lions."

She stood and gestured with both hands. "The proof's all around us. Think of the Elitists on Avalon, Helen—chafing under dictatorship, galvanized by a threat to their children. And when they got a chance to start their own world, what did they build? *This.*"

The wind rippled her campfire shadow on the moth-flecked grass.

"A torture test to determine which of their children was fit enough to rule the state, the losers to perish. And even here, 'a desirable mix of classes,' so that the contending future masters would have future servants along to do the heavy lifting. This was where their ideals led, and it only took them a few hundred years to arrive. Their soul had already died here, before the plague killed their bodies.

"As for the Kanalists, they kept their virtue just about as long, the typical few hundred years, and that's all. That's all it ever takes, that's reality. The rest, the Old Rite, is just beautiful, outworn, sentimental rubbish. Like a Larkspur play."

I didn't argue with her. It was too late in the day.

I'd been dreading my dreams on that nightmare plain. But I had none, and woke oddly refreshed. Something was happening, down where the black currents allow only occasional messages to reach the surface. I accepted the gift without questioning it.

We started out early, through morning mists that would have seemed pretty and cheerful the previous day. But all was gray and sinister as we sidled past the moths we'd waded through without a thought before. It was funny, but no one laughed.

The dew had no sooner steamed off than a heavy overcast moved in. A general grayness hung on. I could see it in the sky, the grass, and Hogg-Smythe's face; she looked her age for the first time, walking with a slight hunch, leaning more heavily on her staff when she had to pause. At least Foyle and I had talked her out of her backpack, and had split the most necessary items of her gear between us.

We were deep in balloon country now; in the first few hours we saw a dozen in flight, and passed one being inflated. Piñata gourds became more common again, the brown, six-legged variety indistinguishable at a distance from the hexen they once had been.

We stopped at each stone bridge to scrape off the moths that had collected on us. It seemed harder to do than it had the day before. One would curl up and drop from your arm, then open into a falling-leaf flutter that brought it into sticky contact with your leg. Bending down to remove it, you made your back available to the ones shaken from a comrade's hair.

I found it hard to see the white variety against my uniform, and always left a few blues and pinks behind, too, in case there was anything to my color-imbalance hypothesis. So magic begins, in the hope that some intentional act, however unproven, is better protection than doing nothing.

But Hogg-Smythe's outfit was the real problem, all those safari-style pleats and epaulets and pocket flaps, dozens of crannies for the moths to work themselves into. And they seemed to like her skin more than mine or Foyle's; she was constantly brushing them off her face, until Foyle improvised a scarf for her. But I think that's what started the argument, Foyle's insistence on tying it herself. I'd pulled ahead for once, and didn't hear all of it, but Hogg-Smythe apparently felt patronized by the tall beauty who leaned over her and brushed her off and complained about her choice of clothing.

I went back to break it up and noticed that Hogg-Smythe's voice was a little slurred. I wondered what the cumulative effect of the moths' skin toxin might be on us, with our Terran biochemistry. But the old woman's mind seemed clear enough. "I resent being treated like a child, Commissioner," she complained. "Why have I been singled out?"

"Let's all calm down," I said. "It's going to be a long day. Right now, let's just walk. The next river crossing's not far; we'll do another cleanup at the bridge. Foyle, why don't you move ahead and set the pace? We'll string out a little bit to make less of a disturbance as we pass. Helen can keep an eye on your back, and I'll bring up the rear."

There were two red spots of anger on the redhead's cheeks, but she looked sorry, too. "Yes, all right," she said. "Here, better let us give your backpack a scrape first, then." I turned to let them brush me down, and then we set off again.

We walked and walked, passing another weathervane tower. My uniform boots weren't made for hiking: hurt, two, three, four. Sometimes I heard the low whistles of some prairie birds in the distance. It was exactly the same sound as yesterday, but how much more frightened it seemed, now that I was sure.

The wind had become dangerous, stronger, with the sort of uneven puffs we'd seen agitate the moths the day before. It pushed away the overcast without a hint of rain. Things had shadows again. But hold on, two, three. Stop. That's no shadow on the back of your calf, it's a lining of blue—shit! feel it?—all the way up the back of the leg.

I peeled moths off in strips like old wallpaper, and as I bent over to do it saw how many white ones lay in plain sight across my front and clawed them off, too, shuddering. More of them than ever before, but they dropped fast enough, some fluttering down but none flying up, and when I had them under control I was glad I hadn't cried out and made the women double back.

But when I looked ahead again I could see nothing of Helen Hogg-Smythe. Just a whirling cloud of pink confetti.

I shouted frantically for Foyle to turn as I shrugged off my heavy pack and ran. We reached her at the same time, began swatting and swiping. The wiry little woman was already more than half-covered, and new arrivals from tens of meters away had begun to meld glutinously with the first wave.

They came down on us like a blizzard, with the same snow-tingle of coldness when they bounced off hands or face. Few stuck to me or Foyle—she'd been right, the attractant was a pheromone, a powerful dead-grass stink emanating from the first wave of landers—but we were still hampered by them, half-blinded and half-deafened by the leafy pasting. Hogg-Smythe had gone limp under the onslaught, not stiff-legged at least. But our scraping efforts were pathetic, like bailing out the ocean. Helen was going under.

Ocean, water. The raccoon-rabbit washing itself. I remembered what the hex-ox had done the day before, when he'd found himself in this deadly hail.

I bent down and slung Hogg-Smythe across my shoulders, shouted "Water!" and took two lurching steps toward the nearest mudhole.

No good. I could see the cattle had retreated into a tight ring around it, a solid mass of flesh, insulated from the moth-grass by their grazed circle. Like yesterday's ox, I would have to risk the river—so I changed course with a wrench, pulling the moths with me toward the dimly seen bank.

Foyle jogged alongside, flailing through the swarm that followed us, screaming something about eels. But I had a single thought in my head now, and held onto it like a talisman.

I felt the top-heaviness of my load with every shock against my knees and feet, but once I attained some speed the run became easier, the imbalance working for me, as if I were falling and falling and falling, but forward. Once or twice I pulled ahead of the hungry cloud, only to have the next patch of long grass I entered explode into pink shrapnel beneath my feet.

But here was a feather tree, sure sign of water, and Foyle suddenly darted before me, a flash of red hair as she jumped in first—a diversion for the eels?—and I was over the edge, toppling onto my face.

Green water crashed past me, loud then quiet, and cold.

Up on my feet, sputtering, just waist-deep—that was a break—I found Foyle at my side, her hair now a long brown slick, and we pulled Hogg-Smythe's head out of the water. I don't know what magic I'd expected; finished piñatas appeared rainproof. But at least new moths had stopped following, and now I had an instant to think, *Cut off their air! Cut off the scent!*

I felt across the pink oatmeal mask of Helen's face for her nose, gripped it closed with one hand as I brought the other up beneath her chin, and forced her whole body underwater, straddling it to keep the legs down.

Foyle waded around us, peppering me with coolheaded questions to which I gave the reasoned reply, "Shut *up*, God damn you!"—and she did shut up. We stood there in clean air, watching dirty water flow over the pink mummy that had been our friend.

At first nothing happened. I'd held my own breath in sympathy, and just when I couldn't do it any longer, the coating began to break up and dissolve.

I saw the first eel then, swimming a handsbreadth away from my downthrust arms; it took a long time to wriggle past, but there was nothing I could do but remain in place. Then it was gone, and Hogg-Smythe was clean, and Foyle helped me lift her onto the steep bank, safe.

But as I tried to climb out myself I tripped, because something heavy had tangled in my legs. Something long and thick and slimy. And even as the body writhed clear of me, the head darted back vengefully, its electrode prongs clamping onto my thigh.

Contact.

Lightning strikes the world-tree, burns the world-tree, becomes the world-tree, one of its secret roots trying to tear my leg out of its socket. I heave back at the roots of the world, every muscle rigid, as the sky strobes to black a thousand times in half a second, but the fiery whiteness is still too bright for all that, burning its way down every nerve ending until existence itself will flicker out, out—

Out of it, collapsing sideways against the bank. Blues and greens were coming back into the picture, but there was still a flickering above me. It was the eel. Foyle must have pulled it off me by the tail, and now she was stuck with it, whirling it as fast as she could in a lariat circle to keep it from coiling back at her. It was a heavy beast, and I heard her little grunts of effort as she spun around, until a final swing sent it flying out over the river. Even before the splash, she yanked me halfway up and then left me to crawl the rest of the way as she dropped beside Helen Hogg-Smythe to provide artificial respiration, and that was okay, crawling up through the mud was all I really wanted to do at the moment, besides closing my eyes . . .

I spat grass out of my mouth and rolled onto my side. "Thank God," Foyle said, kneeling next to Helen not far away. "That's both of you breathing. Are you burnt?"

"I don't think so," I said after feeling my leg. "The pants probably helped." I stretched, trying to feel my way back into the mainstream of time. "Is Helen really all right?"

Hogg-Smythe sat up, coughed, and reassured me herself, then lay back heavily. For a few minutes there was nothing but the sound of our panting.

"So much for our immunity," Foyle said at last. "So much for the overland route."

"I'm not crazy about the swimming, either," I said. "I had an idea, once, about using one of the big piñatas to make a boat, but—"

"But everything's arranged to make a boat worthless," Foyle said. "The current runs the wrong way, and the zigzag course would keep us from making real progress until our food ran out. No. The land and water routes are out.

"You know what that leaves. Don't you?"

Chapter Eighteen

FOYLE THREW THE stone at me as hard as she could.

This time it got all the way across the river, passing just to one side of the squirming island of eels and the huge green globe they were inflating. It landed at my feet on the bank, and I picked it up and untied the end of the fine Elitist supercord that stretched back to her. Pulling the cord taut, I tied it to a shoulder-high branch of the tree behind me.

So much for the static line, the last connection we had to make. I waved, and a few minutes later, after crossing a bridge some fifty meters downstream, Foyle rejoined us. I untied another cord, the tension line, farther down the bank, and she helped me draw it in more tightly, despite an elastic resistance; then she tied it off again. " 'Night' will fall soon," she said. "For a time there, I was afraid we'd be too late. We might have had to cover some distance before we found another eel-mass so close to a bridge."

"And the trees," Helen Hogg-Smythe said a little faintly from where she sat in the grass nearby; her strength seemed to come and go since the moth attack. "Trees facing each other like this."

She gestured at our theater of operations, the straight lines of cord on either side of the eel-mass, connecting feather trees on opposite banks. A puff of breeze set them to whispering, and we all flinched, inspecting ourselves for moths.

"Oh, the eels always mass between trees," Foyle said when this latest false alarm had passed. "They need the windbreak during inflation. And our needs are considered, too."

"You really think we're *meant* to do this, don't you?" I asked.

"Whether it's safe or not, yes. Look at how all the details jibe. The lightness of the line, for instance—we couldn't have made those throws with rope."

"No argument. 'Ingenuity or Endurance,' the guidepost said.

We've certainly had all the hiking we can endure. And this is pretty ingenious, if I say so myself."

"Funny," she said. "I remembered it as being *my* plan."

"I thought up the gondola," I pointed out.

"True."

The breeze ruffled the feather trees; the river current chuckled around the eel-mass. We waited. And soon the central eel gave a whistle to announce that it was fully inflated, the bottom of its envelope touching our lowest cords on either side. Anchor eels began to drop off, and the balloon began to rise. But then it stopped.

Feathery branches high above on either side of the river, laced together crisscrosswise like a corset, gently held the green globe down. That had been the hard part, the tension line—climbing up to loop it around a branch, throwing the free end across, and climbing down to catch the return throw, again and again. It had taken hours. But the snare worked; we'd captured the balloon.

To the eels it could only seem as though there was still too much weight for the balloon to lift. Slowly, more and more of them dropped off.

"A little too low for our purposes," Foyle suggested. We untied the end of the tension line and, leaning landward against the resistance of the bent branches, allowed a little more slack before tying off again. The bottom of the eel-balloon was now two meters above the water, but as soon as it came to a halt more eels would have to do their duty.

We waited. No matter how cleverly they'd been engineered, the Hellway animals couldn't think. Instead, they followed rules. *If the balloon won't rise, it's still too heavy. Drop off and swim on.* The last few hangers-on seemed reluctant, but in the end they all left, looking for new masses, and the water beneath the balloon ran clear.

We helped Helen Hogg-Smythe into the gondola, which was already loaded with our belongings. Once it had been a hex-ox, grazing the prairie. Then the vampire moths had changed it into a piñata gourd. The gourd had emptied, died, and dried out, the solid six-footed shape flattening and hardening and bowing upward. It had been easy to uproot, and had passed our tests of strength. Now, upside down in the edge of the water, it was a double-layered bowl with six straight handles, its bottom two meters in diameter—not too tight a fit for the three of us, especially while Foyle and I were standing. Between handles, the sides curled a meter higher than the bottom, but it was not a natural boat; we would have to be careful not to capsize it.

I grabbed at the static line, Foyle the tension line, and we hauled our craft out between them, toward the center of the river. We stopped when we were directly under the balloon mouth and secured ourselves in place between the tree lines with temporary cords to the gondola's legs.

I inspected the balloon-eel's head, which was intricately clamped into a valved protuberance on the lower envelope wall. The eyes were closed, and I began to wonder whether the creature was still conscious, or even alive. No knowing. From where I stood I could have reached the juncture of monstrous sphincter muscles where the inflated part of the body ended and the neck began. A darker mass, the rest of the body proper, could be dimly seen curled up within the semitransparent envelope. The neck's bend, from the bottom of the balloon to where the head clamped on, formed a loop nearly a meter long. Now Helen Hogg-Smythe handed up the saddle we'd made for it.

It was one of the blankets we'd been supplied, folded over and crudely sewn into a pillow. Braided lengths of cord ran in and out of slits in the top layer. I slipped the saddle between the eel's neck and the balloon and connected the edges that flopped over. Then we tied the ends of the braided cord, eighteen in all, to holes drilled at intervals in the gondola's legs, trying to maintain an even strain throughout. Finally we disconnected the temporary restraining cords and held the gondola against the current by hand instead. We looked at one another without speaking, unable to think of anything undone, but seeming to share a sense that it had been too easy. Time to go.

Foyle cut the tension cord and we both sat down next to Hogg-Smythe, quickly, as the feathered limbs twenty meters above us sprang away from each other and the gondola lurched out of the water. There was a moment of suspense as the tension line snagged somewhere among the branches, a few of which still blocked the balloon's ascent. Three overeducated voices said, "I was afraid of this!" at different speeds, and then a puff of wind shook the trees, the line ran free again, and we were aloft.

The eel was still alive.

We'd only shot up the first fifty meters, still ascending, and already something had gone wrong. We barely had time to react to it—a strange creaking noise as the whole envelope above us visibly expanded against the decreasing air pressure—and then the eel vented hydrogen through one of its head valves to keep itself from bursting. At least that was how we reconstructed it, shaken, after the deafening whistle stopped.

"Real balloons have to do that too," Foyle assured us. "I forgot."

Soon the balloon reached an equilibrium height, something like the same hundred-odd meters we'd seen the other eels attain, despite our being a lighter-than-usual load. "So he adjusted his gas pressure to our weight," Foyle observed. "Another indication that we were meant to fly him, I think."

Ballooning is magical. You have a sudden appreciation for the phrase "Our spirits rose." The world rolls by, but the best part is that you haven't really left it—you stand in the open air, hearing the same sounds and smelling the same smells you'd experience if you were walking among the trees and grass below. There is no wind in your face or ears; you are one with the wind, and belong wherever you go.

The great green envelope above our heads added to the illusion of naturalness by blotting out the ceilinged part of the sky. And as we watched our round shadow float across dun prairie and shiny water and violet treetops, the afternoon passed into a plausible imitation of cloudy sunset in the west. Hogg-Smythe dozed, reclining in the bottom of our basket. Foyle and I more often stood, leaning against the support lines and taking in the view. We didn't talk much, though we felt obliged to estimate our speed—only six or seven k an hour—and to wonder how the flight would end.

"I don't doubt that this thing is bioprogrammed to land at a chosen spot somewhere in the north," Foyle said. "But just for the sake of argument, suppose we saw our next t-station somewhere below instead? We can always go up by throwing out ballast, but how could we go down? We can't release any hydrogen."

"There's always a knife."

"Sometimes you *astonish* me, Commissioner." She shook her head. "You can puncture a fabric balloon safely, but this one's made of skin—elastic. Don't children play with rubber balloons where you come from? Haven't you ever stuck a pin in one?"

"Without popping it, yes," I said. "It's an old magic trick. You put a piece of adhesive tape onto the balloon first, and drive the pin through that; the hole stays small. In our case, we have cloth, and flour and water to mix into paste. We could make a papier-mâché 'tape' if we had to, and prick through it with a knife. I'm not pushing the idea, mind you, but you did ask."

"Sorry."

"For what? Astonishment is no insult—to a magician."

"But you claim to be so many things, Commissioner. Civil servant, archaeologist, confidential agent, and magician, too. It's hard to keep track."

"Ever hear the phrase 'Renaissance man'?"

Her smile, which had been mocking but not unfriendly, disappeared in an instant. "Not recently," she said in a flat voice, and turned to face the view.

Artificial twilight blurred the outlines below. But after darkness fell, bright and unblinking 'stars' appeared, and a few distant clouds lit themselves up from within, silvery, like huge moons. Helen Hogg-Smythe awoke from her ominously heavy sleep with a faint gasping sound, and we found we could see well enough to have our dinner.

Evidently refreshed, the old woman leaned out between leg-posts to examine the changed landscape. As she remarked, the beams of silver light had a remarkable sharpness, bringing out the separate edge of every tree-leaf.

"You make it sound like a beautiful world," Foyle said with her new dead voice. "And you know better."

"That was then, and this is now, Foyle," Helen answered gently. "This is a wonderful experience, and your own idea. Enjoy it while it lasts. What do you think, Commissioner? To take flight by hitching a dead cow to an electric eel—it's like something out of *Cyrano de Bergerac*!"

Foyle's voice again, from over her shoulder, gravely:

> *"I might construct a steel grasshopper-craft,*
> *Its hind legs triggered by explosives aft,*
> *And so, in fumes of nitre, by jumps and jars,*
> *Attain the bluegrass pastures of the stars."*

When she turned, the strange mood appeared to have passed. She smiled when Hogg-Smythe said delightedly, "Committed to memory! This, from a young woman who badmouths the classics."

"Trick memory, no effort," Foyle replied. "And I hate to break it to you, but that's the Larkspur translation."

"Oh, but it's not that Larkspur's so *bad*, you know," Hogg-Smythe said. "A good minor poet, with a gift for satire. It's just that your generation has spoiled him for me. Like doting parents who make Junior recite his party piece every damned night."

Foyle laughed. "I know what you mean." I did, too, actually. "I think that's why I like *Cyrano* the best. His third play, a straight translation—the only one he did. Not so presumptuous as 'adapting' Shakespeare et al."

"Quite so," Helen said firmly—and with good cheer, more alive than at any time since she'd been attacked.

"The other plays have their moments, though," Foyle went on. "I thought so once, anyway. My husband and I used to read them together. Roger was fascinated by Larkspur. Before we married—when he was still my Lit professor—he wrote a book on the legend of the Eighth Play, the one the Reform Kanalists are supposed to have suppressed."

"Oh yes," Hogg-Smythe said. "Because Larkspur was an Old Rite Kanalist, or something?"

"Yes, that's the legend," she replied. "And Roger had joined one of the underground Old Rite lodges, as a young man, just to emulate his hero."

I couldn't help interrupting her. "Underground . . . Old Rite lodges?"

"Oh, they exist." She shrugged. "More of them, on more planets, than the authorities would like to believe. Or maybe the Column just doesn't care. It's not like the Old Rite constitutes an effective resistance. They just argue doctrine with each other, and wait for the Master of Masters to descend on them with the True Ring from Crete, and sweep the pretenders from the chapter houses—et cetera."

She was watching my face. I must not have concealed my emotions very well. "Anyway," she said, "Roger eventually concluded that Larkspur had never actually been initiated himself. The Kanalist lore in *The Enchanted Isle*, he found, is full of inaccuracies."

"The hell you say!"

"You sound so outraged, Commissioner. But then, as a Column official, you must belong to the Reform version of the order, don't you? That's one of the most interesting things about Larkspur, the way every party claims him for their own.

"Reform Kanalism *was* invented by Larkspur's classmates at Nexus University. And he knew the key figures in the cabal—Lucan Kostain, Domina Wintergrin, Alexei Von Bülow . . . but somehow, reading about the period, I can't imagine he really fitted in with a wolf pack like that.

"Of course, he wasn't the fiery radical that the underground likes to believe in, either. More the clever but gauche provincial, the sort of boy who'd do card tricks at parties. Oh, pardon me, Commissioner, I forgot . . . He admired the ideal Kanalism celebrated in his plays, but he never risked the disillusionment of actually joining the society."

"You're sure of that?" I said.

"Roger was," she replied. "You might read his book, *As Strange A Maze*. It's about the final act of Larkspur's *Enchanted Isle*."

"I've never seen that one," Hogg-Smythe admitted.

"*The Enchanted Isle* is an adaptation of *The Tempest*," Foyle explained, "but it's also the Kanalist *Magic Flute*, full of references to the lore and customs of the society. Their Labyrinth, for instance."

"A ritual maze?" Hogg-Smythe seemed fascinated with all things Kanalist.

Foyle shrugged and grimaced while she went on, as if describing the disgusting symptoms of a disease she'd once had. "You know these mystery cults. At some point they like to lead their initiates through a symbolic maze of some kind. We've already been through the Elitist version of that, I guess, with the mirrors. Well, the Kanalists put theirs at the end of the ceremony. It's allegedly based on the labyrinth of Knossos, in Minoan Crete. That's nonsense, archeologically, of course. But anyway.

"The walls of this Labyrinth were decorated with various scenes from Greek mythology. A cram course in early Western culture, with special emphasis on the Kanalist saints: Odysseus, Daedalus—the crafty people who follow their own course through life. But there was only one winding way to the staircase exit at the center of the Labyrinth. Kanalists called it the Shining Fare.

"The story is that Larkspur somehow broke into the Labyrinth a week before his play was to be performed." As she spoke, an electric flicker of images passed before me: Domina naked in the Black Chamber. The mosaic of Odysseus about to fire through the axes. The dead-end wall etched with gold letters that said:

YOU HAVE CHOSEN THE RIGHT PASSAGE
HERE ENDS THE SHINING FARE

and then the staircase leading out. But there was none of the trauma sickness to it, and I could still follow what Foyle was saying:

"He mapped and memorized the correct path, which even Masters weren't supposed to do, and wrote it into his play, in code."

"Some sort of mnemonic?"

Foyle nodded. "It's become one of those tiresome Baconian Cipher controversies. Anyone can play, since people can't even agree on the details of the Old Rite maze design. Only the underground lodges know the pattern, and they're still outlawed, technically, for anti-Column activities.

"But Roger risked a treason charge to publish his thesis. He was the only scholar in his field with authentic Old Rite experience; he was able to point out the places where Larkspur had faked the details. The mnemonic map of the Shining Fare, for instance. It's not quite right."

The last straw.

"Possibly your, uh, teacher is the one who got his details wrong," I suggested. "Lots of them. For instance, the *Cyrano* translation wasn't Larkspur's third play, but his first—a student exercise he revised after his first two successes."

"I've heard that theory, too," Foyle said, yawning, "but the bulk of critical opinion is—"

"*Critics!* Don't tell me about—"

"Commissioner, please," Helen Hogg-Smythe said, "don't work yourself up so. It's hardly important. Only Larkspur, after all."

"Quite right," Foyle agreed. I took a deep breath and let it go.

We swept on through the night. The luminous clouds turned different colors. A meteor shower was simulated to the east. Helen Hogg-Smythe went back to sleep. Her breathing turned so stertorous that Foyle knelt by her side to make sure she was all right.

When she stood again, we spoke in whispers. "I just don't know what to think," she said. "If the moth toxins were going to kill her, it probably would have happened by now. Our omniphylaxis treatments were renewed just a few days before you arrived on the planet. Maybe that's saved her, but then again, maybe it's only delayed the crisis."

"She has a strong constitution."

"For her age, you mean." She swore softly to herself, a lament. "She's been so many places, seen and done so much.

Married six times. Survived the Siege of Pfennigbricht. Sang professional opera as a girl. And a hundred other things I would have liked to hear about, could have learned from. But no, not me. I wouldn't let her get too close. Too threatening to my precious independence."

"A professional teacher. Like your husband."

She didn't look at me. "Yes. Roger was a full professor, with degrees in six disciplines. And a fencer and a horseman and a painter. A *Renaissance man*, you see. He had an ideal of what humans could be. 'Whole-souled,' like Larkspur heroes. He didn't know if he would ever achieve it, but he was sure that I could. He . . . created me. He was . . ." She let it trail off, and shook her head.

"What happened to him?"

I didn't think at first that she would answer, but then the words came, flat, impersonal. "We were quite a little community of demigods, back on the Vesper Preserve. We looked to Roger for leadership. His ideals got everyone killed, in the end. Him, too. Everyone but me."

Now she did face me. "That's why I was so sure Helen was wrong about the Elitists. I knew. The idealistic stage never lasts long. Your group seizes power, or the group in power snuffs yours out, and that's all. Just as we will be snuffed out, if we can't rise to every Hellway challenge like true Hitler Youths."

"I can't say I disagree."

"Of course you don't. You keep in with every camp, don't you? I know your kind. You joined the Column government to get it off your back, but not to change it. And now you're safe to nod at my seditious views, because you're in no danger of acting on them. I don't know why I should blame you; we all have to get by somehow. But you seem to be a man of parts, Commissioner. You could have been—"

She broke off suddenly, and pointed over my head. I turned and looked.

The eel had opened an eye.

The larger-than-human pupil rolled slowly right and left, passing over us incuriously to take in the ground on either side. A strange sound began to issue from the head, rhythmic and bellows-like. Bulges moved through the series of sphincter muscles in its neck, rippling the saddlecloth.

We watched for a few minutes in silence. "I think we're going down, slightly," she said. "But he's not releasing hydrogen, is he?"

"The next time one of those clouds is shining behind him, look through the envelope. Look at that interior bladder, the one that stored the oxygen before. He's compressing air from the outside into it, to make us heavier—without giving up any hydrogen."

"So he can go back up again later, by letting the ballast air go," Foyle said. "All right. But why change altitude, except to land?"

"Look at our shadow," I answered. "Isn't our line of flight a little more easterly now? We must get a slightly different direction of wind down here. Beautiful! He's using the different wind layers to trim his course. I'll bet anything he drops us within five meters of his target when the time comes."

Foyle objected. "Beautiful? There's no reason for complex wind patterns down here. They're being manufactured somewhere, just for the eel. He's not choosing a course, he's following a program. And so are we. This big phony stage set has reduced us to characters in a play."

"Helen was right about you," I told her. "You've got to learn to live in the moment. If we don't have many left, all the more reason."

"Spoken like an Old Rite Kanalist," she said bitterly. "Past and future are an illusion. We can be reborn at will. And of course, we are free. As free as the programmed wind."

She sat down, curled up next to Hogg-Smythe, and closed her eyes. It occurred to me that if she was a character in a play, I—as her husband's inspiration—was her true author. An uncomfortable thought, like the fact that Helen Hogg-Smythe and I were once the same age. Didn't I sleep with an opera singer once, in college?

I sat at their feet and kept track of the eel's maneuvers, the patient eye, the rippling throat, the changing view below. I knew I would never see such a thing again.

The evening's talk swirled through my head, plays and college days and ideals and reputation. I had to distract myself from Foyle's main thesis: the idea that the Kanalism I'd spent my youth on had never been better than the Elitist crypto-fascism, or the real Fascism before that—her un-Kanalist idea that we are just trapped in history's repetitive pattern, and cannot follow our own golden thread. Despite everything, I still wanted to believe otherwise—still wanted to believe in myself, for one thing. And as the night wore on, I realized I was spinning out a play. A new idea, *Cyrano On the Moon*.

We take off from act three of the original. Cyrano has just left Roxane and Christian alone and, being a playwright himself, can see where the story will go from there. And so, in the middle of his conversation with De Guiche, he suddenly breaks off. Instead of just talking about going to the Moon, he actually goes—a flight of poetry—and that's our play. On the Moon, it turns out, long noses are especially prized. Moon maidens throw themselves at his feet. Men copy the cut of his clothes. His poetry and plays are praised, not for their own virtues, but as part of the cult of personality centered upon him. And Cyrano can't take it. He returns to the original play, accepting his fate in order to reclaim his soul, as a hero must. Only a character in a play, but what a character!

I grew more and more excited as I toyed with it. The perfect vehicle for a hit-and-run treatment of fame, fashion, the literary life—or at least one literary life. And a reunion with an old friend.

But who was I kidding? I hadn't written a line for years. Sometimes I forgot that Larkspur was dead.

Foyle and I said little to each other throughout the following day, aside from her noting that the grass appeared greener now, and my speculating that the color was simply unadulterated by undertints of white, blue, pink—that we'd passed beyond moth country.

By midafternoon we could see where we were meant to land. There was no doubt about it, because the balloon ahead of us was making its descent. And as Foyle had guessed, we were aimed at the eels' breeding ground, the source of the river.

The prairie ended in a steep ridge that extended east and west a great distance; greener, hillier country continued to the north. Dead ahead, the ridge was crowned with a grassy plateau. There was a large pool—or small lake—in the plateau, apparently spring- or pump-fed, because it spilled over into a waterfall of some forty meters' height and the river extended from that.

The spillway started as a sheer drop, but appeared to be a rounded slide where it met the prairie at the bottom, and there wasn't as much white water and mist as if there had been rocks. No doubt the compact bodies of the eels could survive this way of returning to the river.

Foyle and I watched through field glasses as the balloon ahead of us made an odd little dip and bob at the last second but splashed down successfully, just past the south bank of the source waters. The heavy mass of passenger eels anchored it in a slow drift across the pool until it managed to deflate; then all subsided into the water, which was already half-green with their squirming relations.

"Ten minutes and we'll be among them," Foyle said. "Every one of them electrically charged. Maybe we'll wish we'd settled for the moths."

"No, look," I said. "See that bunker on the far side? I think that's our transport station. You were right the first time. We were meant to make this trip, and survive."

"The gondola will capsize," Foyle pointed out. "You or I could take our chances swimming, but . . ."

She didn't have to say it. For the past hour, we'd been unable to rouse Helen Hogg-Smythe. And yet her breathing was strong and regular now; we weren't about to write her off.

When you approach something from the air, its aspect doesn't change much from minute to minute, but remains at toy scale. Until you cross a certain threshold, and then with every second your destination grows not only larger as you watch, but more real. Less escapable.

"There's another way," I said. "Look at that north bank, beyond the pool. See the way it ripples? That's tall grass, maybe soft, and the slope looks gentle."

"So? It's not where our eel is going."

"No. He'll go for the pinpoint landing at the south end of the pool, to cover himself against the northward drag while the balloon deflates. But suppose we drop ballast just before he makes it."

"We'll go back up, fast," she said. "But I'm sure he'd compensate to bring us down again."

"Oh, I'm counting on that. But venting the extra gas would have to take several seconds, during which you'd fly north. There's a good chance you'd clear the pool entirely, and hit the bank instead."

"At five or ten k an hour," Foyle said. But she was considering it.

"A nasty jolt, and you'd have to roll out—and roll Helen out—awfully fast to avoid being dragged. It wouldn't be a picnic, but it wouldn't be a swim through electric eels, either. And it demands nothing of Helen."

"That's true. And we don't know. She may come out of this sleep later, if she gets the chance; she came out of it last night . . . How much ballast do you think we should drop?"

"Me. Or you."

She looked sharply at me. "That's unnecessary. That backpack of mine is pretty heavy. Jettisoning even a little weight probably has a big effect."

I shook my head. "You saw how fast that last balloon deflated. That's how fast this eel will be able to compensate. We have to make it hard on him. And another thing. The grass landing will be less risky if there's less mass in the basket, fewer arms and legs in the way, fewer bodies to get out."

We'd begun to go down as fast as we went north, causing a sickening feeling in the pit of the stomach.

"You believe the Hellway's a gantlet, a test to destruction," I said, "and maybe you're right. But I think a transport stop waiting at the side of the pool means that it's swimmable. That may even be the safer way, so I offer you your choice."

She shook her head, pale and grave. "I think you're asking for the worst of it. But I couldn't leave Helen behind. That makes it fair, doesn't it, if I take responsibility for her?"

"More than fair. Brace yourself, then. Plan your moves." I took off my boots, put them inside one of the waterproof-looking provision bags, and tied that onto my belt. We already had blankets around Helen; Foyle quickly wrapped them in enough cord to make a handier bundle of her.

While she found her own stance, I stood and swung one foot around the outside of a gondola leg, gripping the post with both hands, my toes pointing inward and my back to the empty air. We could hear the rush and roar of the waterfall now; we'd pass over it in a moment and splash down seconds later. When we'd been higher there had been little sense of motion, but now the landscape flew by, dizzying.

"You're ready to hold her down now?" I asked. "When I jump, the basket will jerk up and try to throw you out."

"I'm not stupid!" Foyle snapped, but looked immediately contrite. And then the words tumbled out. "I'm sorry, I'm sorry about some of the things I've said to you, I don't trust most people, and you're so strange—but not, I think, such a bad man. Just not a very credible commissioner."

"Everyone's a critic," I said, which was as good an exit line as any, only just then everything went to hell.

Chapter Nineteen

THE EEL VENTED hydrogen with a steam-whistle sound and we plummeted, a dozen meters short of clearing the falls. Still driving forward, too, we would smash into the wall of water within seconds, and when you're braced for one scare it's no help against another; my hands were frozen to the gondola leg, my mind a swirl of mist and air.

And then we entered the updraft which neither Foyle nor I had foreseen. For when the wind from the south hit the ridge it could go nowhere but up, and our eel-pilot had factored it in.

Within a few meters of the falls we rode up as sharply as on a roller coaster. The eel shrieked out gas to bring us back down again as we crossed the edge of the grassy plateau. We clung to posts to avoid being tossed out by the whiplash, Foyle's long legs holding Helen's inert body down. And then the rich smells of grass and silt rose around us, along with another wave of turbulence, dark water suddenly everywhere below, hundreds of eels in view and the gondola about to join them—and I had to live up to Foyle's good opinion, didn't I?

I let go. With one loud snap, the black lake swallowed me whole. I descended in a white shroud of bubbles, unable to see, hear, or think. But then I slowed, hung suspended, and after what seemed like a long time began to rise again.

I'd made a simple plan in advance—a dead man's float. The initial splash might alarm the eels, but I would do nothing further to threaten them.

The water was warm and buoyant. My chest felt tight as my ascent gathered momentum . . . the no-color past my eyelids grew lighter and lighter . . . and then, with a gasp, I broke the surface.

Floating on my back, I saw the balloon descending again, as planned, but from higher than I'd thought possible—and making faster time northward. I could do nothing but curse as it overshot the grassy bank and the rise beyond, too, before dipping out of sight. Unknown territory.

Coils of eel kept splashing into view near me, and I felt an occasional rubbery impact, but managed not to respond. Soon I lifted my head for another look around.

I was drifting toward a hole in the scenery—the waterfall. From this vantage I could see a mesh fence across the mouth of the falls, and it looked strong enough to bear my weight.

I was still considering the possibilities when the eels discovered me.

The first one went around and around my right leg like a whip at half-speed; the second snaked up my left arm to coil at the shoulder. One of them—I couldn't see which as I craned my neck for air—threw an additional loop around my waist. The eels were as thick as a strong man's arms, and could have crushed me if they had meant to; instead they slowly writhed to some other purpose, a spiraling squirm I could feel through my clothes. I waited, as paralyzed as if the voltage had already hit me.

Now the shift in weight sent my body in a slow half-roll onto my side. I could still breathe, but took a mouthful of water and tried not to cough as I spat it out, nothing to annoy the passengers. The living cables tightened a little, but at least this kept me rolling, full-circle onto my back again. Now I could bend my neck and look down the length of my body, and see enough of the way the eels were intertwined to understand.

I was not being attacked, and as long as I didn't stir an eel up, as I had the day before, I needn't be electrocuted. The eels had something better to do; I was just a handy platform. Anyone who's ever tried to make love in a swimming pool will understand.

The sound of the falls grew steadily louder, the twinings of the eels more rhythmic and powerful. I could only stare up at the artificial sky, thinking that at least no one would say, "He died as he lived . . ."

The slow tendency to drift became a definite current, and I could see the water swirling on either side. Slowly, slowly, and just in time, I bent my free arm over my head—to take the impact when I hit the wire mesh of the falls' restraining fence. The current spun my body around against the barrier lengthwise, and now the whipped-up white froth at the spillway threatened to choke me.

The eels gave each other—and me—a few last fond squeezes, and slithered off. I grabbed at the mesh with both hands and yanked myself vertical, head out of the white spume. Gasping for air, I blinked the water out of my eyes and took in the vast prairie spread out below.

I wasn't home free yet, pinned against the fence wire by the onrushing rapids; more heavy green eels washed against me, three-meter lengths writhing over my shoulders, throwing brief anchor holds around my neck or outstretched arms. But ultimately they always sought the open spaces in the fence and the long slide back to their feeding grounds. Meanwhile I kept every movement slow. The wires cut into my hands at first, and I made no progress until my feet found holds, too, but with every centimeter I reclaimed from the current the load seemed lighter, and soon I had hauled my dripping body above the waterline, into cold air.

I made the long traverse along the top of the fence to shore without much trouble, watching swirls of white water and the occasional dark eel rush over the edge beneath my sidestepping feet. I had plenty of time to admire the falls, rainbows in the mist at its foot, and to notice a staircase running up alongside it from the prairie floor. *Ingenuity or endurance.* Meaning that the Elitists had honestly expected some of their children to 'endure' a two- or three-day hike through vampire moths, and reach that staircase on foot? Unbelievable.

I had to cross some slippery rocks from the end of the fence to the bank, and did slip once, but my clothes couldn't get any wetter than they were. I stopped to strip and wring them out, and—seeing no moths—rolled myself dry in the long grass before putting them on. I unbagged my boots and wore them, but carried my uniform tunic in one hand so that the breeze could finish drying shirt and pants as I hiked—though it was beginning to get dark, and colder.

Beyond the rise was a country of green rolling hills that threw back echoes as I called after Foyle and Helen Hogg-Smythe. No sight of them, no reply. No knowing how much farther they would be blown. A wave of familiar self-loathing swept over me, survivor's guilt, *Barbarossa* sickness. Despite my best intentions to save them, I was the one who'd bailed out safe.

But if Hogg-Smythe had remembered the Hellway rite correctly, the next t-station would have separated our party anyway. Meanwhile, someone still had to beat the mercs to the pole, or none of us would survive in the long run. I returned to the eel pool while I could still see and followed its edge until I found the t-station, a low, moss-covered bunker.

At my approach the door slid open to reveal a narrow horizontal space like a torpedo tube. A robot voice ordered me to lie in it, and I did. Blackness. Motion. Time and distance passing, but how much?

The Hellway transport let me out onto a rocky mountainside. A belt with food packets and a canteen popped into the torpedo as soon as I got out. I grabbed the belt, opened and ate one of its doughy meals, and strapped it on like a bandolier. The door closed, and the lights went out.

The underworld's night sky stretched above me, playing its mysterious games. An intense beam of silver illuminated a circle of landscape five minutes' walk away—apparently for my benefit. It was the sort of favor the heroes at Troy had received from Olympus, and as I made my way down the steep slope I considered the various horrible fates of those heroes. With friends like gods, you don't need enemies.

My exit point had been an otherwise inaccessible place, a pocket among jagged heights. The only pass down into flat country appeared to have been filled by a rockslide; sharp-edged boulders protruded from a mass of dirt and gravel like the spines of a stegosaurus. But closer inspection showed an alternate route, a circular tunnel slanting beneath the rubble through solid rock. As soon as I reached it, the light from above went out. Subtle.

The tunnel was dimly lit by a lamp at one end, where an elevator stood open. The lower tunnel wall was discolored, and I wondered if maintenance robots had just recently cleared out six centuries of washed-down dirt. I stepped inside the elevator. It took me an unknowable distance downward and let me out again on the opposite side of the shaft; although underground, I still faced what had been the downhill direction.

I found myself in a new corridor, horizontal this time, but still circular in cross-section, between two and three meters in diameter. The tunnel ran through living rock, the wall surface as smooth as if cut by running water—or a particle beam. The light source was a narrow strip set flush to the stone, centered above me and running in a continuous line the length of the tunnel. Two ranks of small metal loops ran parallel, four or five centimeters to either side of the strip; they looked like hangers for something, but they were bare.

After a short walk the tunnel ended in what appeared to be a door, an iris of interlocked metal leaves. At the top of the door rim, a push button jutted from an ornately sculpted plate. The bas-relief depicted a baffled ant emerging from the spiral corridors of a snail shell. I knew how it felt. Beneath the picture, in Ur-Linguish, was the legend THE ONLY WAY OUT IS THROUGH.

I pressed the button and the door irised open to a bare shoulder's width. I crawled through it awkwardly, rolling to the floor on the other side.

The tunnel continued before me, but this stretch was sheathed in leafy vines, a green lining broken only by a narrow margin of stone on either side of the light strip. The light burned hotter here, too bright with UV to stare at for long. Instead of running across the strip, the greenery doubled back through the loops I'd noticed before.

The woody vines branched and tangled beneath broad leaves that overlapped each other in competition for the light. Though there was a faint smell of wet earth, I could not see any; lower down, the vines interweaved to form a dense brown mat or cushion several centimeters above where the true stone floor would be. It would be like walking on a mattress.

It was all too neat and pat, like the eel airline. If the vine was so strong and vital, what kept it from choking the center of the tunnel? Was I going to run into plant-clipping robots? I decided to back out for the time being, perhaps wait for teammates to arrive. But when I turned to go, the door shut in my face. No button. No options.

The tunnel curved gradually to the left. I followed it, bouncing from side to side as well as forward, sometimes having to grab at leathery green leaves or the underlying vines for balance.

The entrance receded around a bend behind me, and the tunnel split into a Y. The left tine quickly branched three ways, and the way I chose led me around a curve into a dead end.

It was another maze.

I retraced my steps and kept going. It was almost like walking in low gravity, and thinking of it that way, I soon found a special flex of leg and foot that propelled me forward without too much dangerous upward bounce—a kind of lope. I'd just hit my stride, my head held high for balance, when I came to a sharp bend, brought my feet together on the downstep to make the turn, and crashed through the mat into empty space.

I dropped more than three meters, then hit another vine mat like a trampoline and bounced. My head narrowly cleared the edge of the hole I'd fallen through, bobbing briefly back into the vertical connector—a glimpse of circular light-strips lining it—before I dropped again.

This time, I bent my knees sharply when I hit the lower mat to kill the bounce. I was in a vine-walled tunnel, just like the one above. A frame of glowing light-strip outlined the hole overhead, less than a meter wide. The hole one floor above evidently lacked such a frame, and the vine mat had covered it—but only thinly, because of the connector's hot interior strips.

After a few practice hops I managed to bounce high enough to catch hold of the top of the connector and drag myself back up through the broken mat to my original level. I got dirt on my fingers doing it, and concluded that there was some soil between stone and mat.

It took another hour to finish exploring the upper section, but I saw it all. The tunnels weren't as confusing as the mirror maze had been, with its reflections and identical angles and computers changing the walls. Here, for one thing, I could tear away patches of leaves to mark where I'd been.

At one intersection where I did this, I uncovered a small opening in the stone, with a mesh grill in front of it—to keep out the vines? The wall immediately below the grill was streaked as if by muddy water. Part of the nutrient system, perhaps? Too small for an exit.

I doubled back to the door a few times, but it stayed closed, no surprise there. I found no connectors upward, and only two downward; I noticed the new one's covering mat had been broken by someone else, the torn places white and fresh. Returning to the other hole, I dropped through it again, more deftly this time, and began to explore the next level.

At first it seemed more extensive, but I mastered its twists and forks in less time. Practice. In addition to four connectors downward, I found two new ways up, into top-floor sections separate from the one I'd entered by; the three combined might have equaled the area of the lower level.

But one of them I was reluctant to explore. Here the vines had not been deterred, but had invaded the connector; its interior light-strips and what I could see of the tunnel above glowed a dull and somehow disquieting red.

I decided to leave the red section be, and come back to it if I had no luck elsewhere. I dropped down another level, explored a sub-section, then bounced back up and crossed over to another.

I couldn't decide whether there was just one type of vine or several. In two sub-sections the leaves were noticeably smaller and softer, but greener and more healthy-looking. In some tunnels these smaller leaves glistened with what I took to be exuded sap—clear, sweet-smelling, almost a gel—and elsewhere this gave way to a dull white dustiness that might have been the same stuff dried up.

Several times I heard a rustling in the vines, but cautious poking among the leaves revealed only harmless-looking insects. Then I rounded a corner into an explosion of barks and squeaks. I jumped back and caught a glimpse of curious, intelligent eyes behind a sleek snout.

A rat, and a big one. There was a furious flurry of leaves, and it disappeared beneath the vine mat.

Within a few hours I'd established the probable limits of the top three floors, though I'd stayed out of all the red-lit sections I'd found. And I knew there were more floors below, each following the same basic pattern—a simple one, despite the curving mazes within.

Interior walls ignored, the floors were oblongs of the same size, each shifted forward relative to the one above it, like an enormous staircase going down.

I was satisfied. Helen Hogg-Smythe had implied that within the Hellway, the correct direction of travel would usually be clear-cut. Forward and downward, for instance—the logical way to descend the mountainside I'd seen on the surface, and I could take the guideplate hint to mean that the only way *out* was to go *through* all the levels.

But not yet. I was exhausted. I didn't know which muscles the flexible terrain had stressed more—the small ones normally unused, or the major groups I'd used in unaccustomed ways. They all screamed, from toes to shoulders. Meanwhile, against the scrim of my mind, the leafy green walls, brown mat floor, and eye-searing yellow strips played on and on, forking and doubling back and hitting dead ends. And the mental jumble was echoed by the mad verses I'd composed to keep track of section after section—mnemonic lists of twists and branches, turns and choices, right versus left, e.g.:

WhiLe RoyaLs feaR the faLse RepoRts
Of Reds who scRibbLe LibeLs,
DisLoyaL LawyeRs RuLe the couRts,
And LiaRs sweaR on bibLes.

Dozens of those. When tongue twisters aren't spoken aloud, they spin the brain instead. I had to sleep, and see if my strategy for the maze sounded as good when I awoke.

The vine mat was comfortable enough, once I returned to the top level—the only one where I'd heard no rustle of rats. I fell asleep in minutes.

I found myself on a hillside, next to a ruined house. I recognized the setting immediately: Nightmare Number Five. As usual, I knew perfectly well that I was dreaming. But there was something different this time as well. I felt no heavy freight of dread and guilt; if anything, I enjoyed the breeze.

The old beggar woman came, and we talked of the ruins, as always. I was visiting my old Master Summerisle's home, two years after reemerging into history. It was the only way to learn what had happened to him in the century since I'd left. In Nightmare Number Five I always find out that, like me, he hadn't aged much. Just five or six years—then they'd executed him as a subversive, torched his home, and defaced every name from his family crypt.

I ask her about the holes in the ground, and she tells me the local legend about the soldiers who came and spent a year digging and searching for the Vice Book—or Book of Sin, as the name had come down to her.

"But they never found it," she says. "Because he would never use such a thing. He was a good witch, everyone said that. They say they'll build a statue in Summerisle's memory now, because the Consultant has 'rehabilitated' him. And that may be. The Consultant always likes to be kinder than his Column, when it doesn't cost much." She realizes what she has said, and cringes. "But he *has* made things better," she adds anxiously. "When I was a girl, the tax farmers could hang a man's children and laugh at him in court. But not since the Consultant came."

And I make the inevitable comparison. On one hand, the Consultant, tossing a few crumbs to the populace to earn the support of their children in the navy. On the other, a genuinely good man. Summerisle, who had spent seventeen years in a tent, tutoring a colony that had reverted to savagery. Summerisle, who had entered a burning university building three times to rescue smoke victims who did not have—as he explained it—his mastery of breath control. My valiant, wise, and sometimes laughable adopted father, whom I had abandoned when he needed me most. As I'd abandoned Kanalism, the Alignment, and, of course, the *Barbarossa*.

Then the orgy of guilt begins. I tell the old woman about the *Barbarossa*, about the data log that should explain what sort of disaster overtook the ship. But decoding computers always return the same answer: the log is whole, and in navy format, but has been subjected to some method of "global distortion" to keep it from being read. And who could have done this but me, in that blacked-out stretch of time in the lifeboat? But, I explain to her, *I haven't destroyed the evidence,* only the disk; I've kept the data itself on my person, in an artificial fingerbone. Having long since abandoned my fruitless search for scientific mention of the "bubble universes" that would make my *Barbarossa* dream more possible, my *Barbarossa* crime less likely, I would face the truth, no matter how shameful, if only I could *remember* it . . .

But suddenly, this time through Nightmare Number Five, I dropped all that. There was no nightmare. I looked around at the ruins, the hillside, the old woman, and knew them all for two-dimensional props. All my grief and guilt seemed phony and assumed. Self-important, too—to believe that I'd had the power to save the Alignment, for instance.

It had been growing in me ever since entering the Hellway, the power to let the nightmares go. Somehow I'd picked up the golden thread again. Maybe I'd taken the easy way out when I left Nexus, but now I was back on the winding way through. I was exactly where I was supposed to be, in the Hellway's leaf-gutter, hiding from rats, with someone shaking me awake. Not happy, exactly, but on the right path.

"Alun!" An expression of urgency gave way to relief on Ariel's face. "Alun!"

"Hullo," I said.

"I was scared when I saw you lying like that."

I took a firmer grip on reality and sat up. Ariel knelt before me wearing a provision belt like mine, her blue hiking outfit sadly wrinkled. Our friar of the Green Church, his olive robe as drab as ever, made the sign of the tree behind her. "Blessed is the seed," he said. "Blessed is the fruit of the vine." I resisted the temptation to lie down again.

"Better me than a merc," I said as Ariel helped me up. "And just as glad to see you two. When did you arrive?"

"A while before you, I guess," she said. "It was just luck we decided to recheck the upper tiers for exits this morning. Maybe we shouldn't have followed the ripped leaves, but we figured it might be better to meet whoever was ripping them face-on. We're trapped together in any case. But are you alone?"

I gave them a brief account of my first Hellway test—what had happened to Helen Hogg-Smythe, and the last I'd seen of her and Foyle.

"That's bad, about Helen," Ariel said. "I have a lot of faith in Foyle, she's strong and smart, but it's bad news all the same. You might keep it from Harry; Helen was like a grandmother to him."

"So Harry Lagado is with you. And the others?"

"Harry's father and Wongama? Harry started out with them, and says they had no trouble with their first passage. Not really, anyway. Sounds like Ruy and Piet argued a lot."

"Well, it's good to keep up the old customs in a new country. So let's see—I guess the computers split them up afterwards, and sent Harry here. What about you? Weren't you and Ken Mishima partnered with a dead merc back in the mirror maze—the bee-stung guy?"

She made a face. "Not for long; the computers finally got straightened out and sent robots to take the body away, before putting us in a t-car. Their voice seemed to be asking lots of questions about the dead man, but we couldn't understand much.

"We're going to have to be careful with them," she added. "That's one thing that *has* changed since colonial times. These old-style computers may seem as smart, within their domains, but they don't have the overall grasp of ours. I'll bet the Hellway was meant to function under human supervision. Right now, parts of it are running perfectly, but without a clue that others are out of order."

"I can believe that," I agreed. "But you were saying?"

"Oh, well, finally Mishima and I reached the Hellway. Between the two of us, thanks to the statue-chamber briefing, we were able to figure out how to proceed."

"What was your first test?"

"No big deal. We had to walk a ledge, that's all. The transport let us out on one end of a tall, narrow wall along a lakeshore, and we had to walk the top of it to the next stop. It was a long walk, and it got dark, and sometimes it got very narrow and very high, and at one point it crossed the water, and you could feel waves crashing against it . . . I mean, it was scary, but as long as you didn't *get* scared and lose your head, it wasn't really that dangerous."

She winced and took a breath. "Except one bit where it had crumbled away. That was tricky climbing—and Mishima didn't come back for me, either; it was the sound of the waves, he couldn't hear me. But I got back up okay. And I don't think that the gap was part of the test, I think it was just out of repair. Let's face it, six hundred years."

"I don't know, Ariel. Foyle thinks the dangers are intentional, and she may be right. What did the guidepost say? That could be a clue."

"Guidepost? There wasn't anything like that. Except—at the very beginning, there was this old-fashioned metal bootscraper. And there were four raised Oldstyle letters along the rung—you know, right where you'd wipe your feet. I don't know the language, but the letters were *f*, *e*, *a*, and *r*."

"Interesting," I said. "Friar, I didn't mean to be rude. You must have a story to tell, too. Last I heard, you were partnered with two of the enemy."

Friar Francisco looked deeply uncomfortable. "It was all very sad," he said. "They were brutal, ignorant souls, who didn't understand where we were or what was happening to us. None of us could follow the computer's speech, but I revealed a little of what I had learned from my reading. I made them think we would have to journey for weeks, and so they agreed to let me live—as their guide, cook, and servant. They said they would ask their commanders, later, if they could spare my life. But I had no illusions about that.

"In fact, our test was simply to move down a certain stretch of river. I think we were intended to tame and ride some deerlike creatures who visited the banks for water, but my companions scared them off. They were good woodsmen, though; they cut down some trees and made a handy little raft.

"At this point I prepared dinner. I knew, of course, that the Titan flora and fauna were incompatible with our digestive systems, and could even be dangerous. But some Terran life-forms were included when the Elitists reshaped this park, and I was able to locate some harmless roughage. I pretended it would be a healthy meal. I think the mercenaries suspected something, because they made sure we all ate the same plants, and waited until I'd gone first . . . They died a few minutes later."

"What? Didn't you eat the same meal?"

"Yes," the friar said gloomily, opening one of the pouch pockets of his robe to show me a number of plastic vials, "but I didn't poison mine.

"My order's drugs are medicinal, of course, but when necessary . . ." his voice trailed off a bit. "Poison's traditionally a woman's weapon, therefore sacred to the Triple Goddess, and permitted by her under the Dispenser's Dispensation.'' He looked up earnestly. ''I was not without mercy, you understand. I gave the mercenaries the sacrament of abortion; they will get another chance to be human beings, the next time they're incarnated.''

''And who can ask for more?'' I said. ''Meanwhile, we'll have their guns to use. Or are they crossbows?''

He looked even more uncomfortable.

''You did bring them with you?''

Ariel rolled her eyes. ''Says he's not allowed to carry weapons made of iron or steel,'' she murmured.

''I know it seems silly to someone not of my faith,'' he began.

''No, no, of course not,'' I said, not quite felling him to the ground with a sympathetic clap on the shoulder. ''To hell with it. Weapons haven't done the mercs any good. We'll get more use out of your biology and zoology, and my Ur-Linguish. And with luck, we can finish our second test quickly.''

I explained my strategy for finding the exit.

''I'm afraid we haven't been as systematic,'' Friar Francisco said. ''Spot checking, and trying to understand the ecology. But . . . yes, I've seen nothing to conflict with your analysis. Ariel?''

''I think it's worth a shot,'' she said. ''We can always come back and try every tunnel on every floor, but there are so many of them—it stands to reason we're supposed to rule some out.'' She turned back to me. ''Were any of the sections you explored red? Red lights?''

''Yes. Or no—I didn't explore those.''

''We haven't been in one either,'' she said, ''just peeked.''

''Have you seen a pseudo-gastropod?'' Friar Francisco asked. ''They would rarely come this high.''

''Would I know if I'd seen one?''

''Count on it.'' Ariel grimaced.

''Then I haven't. I've seen some insects and a rat, though.''

''Indeed?'' Friar Francisco stuck his head out from his cowl, his eyebrows migrating to his bare crown. ''A Terran-derived rat?''

''I don't know, Friar. A ratlike animal.''

The Green monk began to drift down the tunnel, poking among the vines. ''Rats,'' he muttered—almost a curse.

''Maybe we should inspect one of the red areas before going ahead with my plan,'' I suggested. ''Maybe that scary red light is the only thing we have to go 'through' to get 'out.' As simple as facing our fear—which used to be spelled *f, e, a, r,* by the way. See what I mean?"

"Hmm," Ariel said. "The main thing is, let's *do* something, and not just talk about it. What do you say, Friar Francisco? A red section first?"

"All right," Friar Francisco agreed. "Though I don't think there's anything special about the red sections. I've the notion that they're—"

"Help!"

The cry was faint. I was only sure I'd heard it because the others looked toward the hole, too.

"That sounds like Harry," Ariel said. I was the first to drop through the connector. On the new level, a shout gave me the direction. Soon Ariel and Friar Francisco loped close behind me.

The corridor branched. Ariel and I took one side, the friar another. Our tunnel straightened out, and suddenly I had to jump over a hole to keep from falling through, while Ariel barely stopped short.

Another high-pitched shout came through the narrow portal between us. It sounded lost. "Over here, Harry!" we called.

"It's *coming*!" came his voice. "Can't believe . . . fast!" I heard the squeegee noise of yielding vine-mat below, and a dull hard impact—I knew the sound, had made it myself when bad bounces sent me into the ceiling. Before I could drop down and offer help, the teenager appeared in view, holding his head and white with terror.

He glanced behind him. "Still coming!"

Friar Francisco appeared at the end of our tunnel and approached Ariel's kneeling figure, his dark brown face worried but stern. "Don't panic, they're harmless," he called down.

"*What* are?" I asked—the kid was hysterical; there was no sound of anything approaching him—but Ariel, more practical, just told him to jump up.

Harry wasn't quite tracking. As he reached up a hand instead, I saw more than one bruise on his forehead. By lying across the hole, I could just reach him, but his hand was sweaty with fear and I couldn't get enough grip to lift with.

"It's not stopping!" he cried, looking back, and the friar said something I couldn't catch.

The bright strips lining the connector were blinding me. "Just jump up and down," I said. "Like a trampoline."

I reared back on my knees to give him room. After a few spastic twitches, he tried the mat, but missed his footing on the first bounce. He fell over, his foot caught between vines. Struggling ineffectually, he closed his eyes to whatever he thought was approaching.

Francisco was saying only "Silly, silly, silly," and I had braced my hands and lifted my bent legs forward, intending to elbow-jam down slowly since I couldn't jump without stomping the boy, when Ariel gave a little cry and pushed me back.

Purple afterimages from the light-strips swam in front of my eyes. I couldn't make sense of what I was seeing, hadn't expected there to be anything to see. But at the bottom of the connector, something white and glistening flowed over Harry Lagado as he screamed desperately. Then his shrieks were cut off and the mass kept coming, engulfing and then building on top of him, higher and higher, semitransparent but containing cloudy orange shapes that soon eclipsed the boy's image. A wave of sickly sweet odor filled my nostrils. I had a momentary impression of a thin jet of white jelly coming up the connector, a red eye the size of a golf ball at its tip—and my head jerked back. Ariel faced me across the hole, silently mouthing, *No.*

And when I looked down again, there was nothing left. Just the mat, covered with that clear gel I'd thought of as "sap" when I'd seen it on leaves—the trail of slime a garden slug might leave, if it were the size of a hippo.

Chapter Twenty

"OH GOD," SAID Ariel. "Oh God, it swallowed him whole."

"A slug?" I said, still blinking. *"A giant slug?"*

"Of course not!" Friar Francisco snapped—at both of us, apparently. He gathered the skirts of his robe in one hand and without further warning vanished down the hole.

Confidence is contagious. So is stupidity. Another moment

found me standing behind the Green monk in the lower tunnel, watching the creature retreat.

"I trust Harry had the sense to hold his breath," he said.

What the friar had called a pseudo-gastropod looked even more grotesque and impossible when seen whole. A glistening pale sack about man-high, it slopped outward to brush the lower tunnel on either side, like a rubber balloon full of gelatin, air bubbles, and candy-colored guts. Now ten meters down the tunnel, leaving uneven swatches of clear slime on floor and walls behind it, the creature moved like nothing I'd ever seen. The outer skin appeared to go up and over, as if the animal were rolling, but the inner structures didn't follow as fast, nor did the overall shape rotate, always tapering toward the top. And when it looked back at us, nothing turned; instead, its two long eyestalks seemed to skate across its rippling upper surface.

The large blood-red eyes waved randomly, and then the stalks bore them away again. The creature slowed, shuddered, and heaved, expelling a mummy-shaped turd of slime—which drew erect, developed legs and arms, and began to paw at the gunk all over its face, crying with humiliation and spitting schoolboy curses.

"Harry?" Ariel had descended unnoticed behind us.

The boy did not seem to be hurt. Even the coating of slime could have been worse, its faint fruity smell almost pleasant. Harry wiped gobs of the gunk from himself and flung them about, and we fell back to give him room.

Friar Francisco tutted at my side. "We'll have to wipe you down with dry leaves," he said when Harry gave up in disgust.

"We thought they were so slow." Harry's voice was shrill but steadying. "Even when it got interested in me, I wasn't afraid because I could just walk away from it. But when it made me run, I started hitting the ceiling and everything got cloudy and scary . . ."

The slug stopped and gave its impression of turning around, a topological mystery in aspic. Then it raised what would have to be called its head. A long vertical slit puckered into existence, then gaped in a rude yawn, and the creature stuck its tongue out at us. The organ uncoiled to the length of a man's arm and revealed a toothed, raspy surface. We fell back even further. The creature seemed to taste the air, then licked at the leafy wall. The tongue, not unlike an elephant's prehensile trunk, coiled back into the maw with a large swatch of leaves; the creature began to munch.

"I knew it!" Friar Francisco pushed forward for a closer view. "They feed on the vines. And look! It's rasping off the larger, tougher leaves. Younger shoots will now get the benefit of the light."

"Why didn't Harry get chewed up, too?" Ariel asked as the creature continued its noisy grazing.

"It never swallowed him," the monk replied. "Not only is Harry too large, he's an animal, and the pseudo-gastropods are vegetarian. Everything has its own nature; you must learn to trust that."

"It didn't eat me, Ariel," Harry said. "It sort of made a tube around me. Then it coated me with gunk and squeezed me through, somehow."

"Peristaltic contractions," the friar explained. "Harry doesn't belong in the creature's simplified world, so it went around him—all the way around. The pseudo-gastropod feeds on vines. It must contribute food to them in turn—its lubricant slime or its feces or both. Essentially a closed ecosystem, driven by the light-strips." He paused thoughtfully. "It can't be quite that simple, of course. The insects probably play middleman in various ways."

"And are there many of these slugs?" I asked.

"From what we saw yesterday, I doubt there are more than a dozen or two. They can flow up or down the vertical shafts, but downward must be easier. The upper floors will be fertilized less often, and I don't know why they aren't worse off for it."

I told him about the grill I'd seen; the news pleased him.

"I knew the system couldn't be entirely closed. So water and nutrients do come in, and the slug-poor upper floors strain out what they need before allowing it to trickle down. It all balances out."

"Where do the rats fit in?" I wondered.

"They don't belong here," he said dogmatically. I reminded myself that this was his true field. "Too busy, too destructive. They don't belong here at all."

"Neither do we," Ariel said. The slug had started drifting in our direction again.

"Their size is intimidating," the friar admitted. "Let's move back upstairs and dry Harry off."

The leaves with which we scrubbed Harry proved to be slightly less absorbent than vinyl. But wherever we scraped the slime thin it soon dried into fine white powder, easily dusted off.

"How can a slug that big live?" I asked. "Not to mention haul itself around."

"I do wish you'd stop calling it that," Friar Francisco said. "It's not a slug. More likely inspired by the jellyfish and not naturally evolved at all. It's been genetically engineered for sheer improbability, like those mock eels you told us about. And it's not one creature, but a colony of many, like a Portuguese man-of-war."

"How much of this did you read the other day, and how much are you guessing?"

Now I'd offended him. "There wasn't time to read up on specific life-forms," he said. "But I don't have to *guess* anything. Eel, slug, caterpillar, snake—each moves in a characteristic way that reveals its inner structure. The peculiar flowing forward you just saw is unique to Gyal-wa colonies."

"Gyal-wa?"

"That's what we would call them, after their inventor. Gyal-wa was one of the first great genetic engineers of classical times. The colonies he created were tiny things, designed to clean out occluded coronary arteries. But the Titans must have invented them independently, along with tools for composing them on a grand scale—their usual style."

"What do you mean by a 'colony'?" Ariel wanted to know.

"Just that. A collection of independent creatures. Billions of unicellular animals organized into 'binders'—spongy accretions of hairlike proteins. A Gyal-wa binder is built and maintained by cells which live in its interstices and control its flex and consistency with their secretions. Along the outer skin, the binders are of course knit tightly together; within, a more fluid structure facilitates the ablative transport of nutrients.

"Eyes, tongue, digestive organs—these are all quasi-independent creatures, composed of more specialized binders. They can travel wherever they have to without forcing the whole colony to shift its weight by turning around.

"This conserves energy—one of the reasons why it can be so huge, Commissioner. And it's not nearly as massive as you think. Some of those large internal organs must be pneumatophores—gas pockets, like those which cause jellyfish to float."

"But everything has to work together, too," Ariel said. "Without a common brain?"

The friar shrugged. "Have you ever seen a school of fish, or birds in formation? Plenty of coordination—though little sense of purpose."

"Then why did it follow Harry?" she asked, and added, her voice carefully controlled, "Why is it following *us*?"

She pointed at the hole near the end of our tunnel. A narrow column of pinkish white jelly was rising from the connector. It grew taller and thinner until it fell over, and then the mass below began tranferring up and across its L-shape in little waves.

"Wonderful, isn't it?" the friar asked.

"Nifty," Ariel said. "But why do they follow us around?"

"They must feel or hear the vibration in the vines and think we're other pseudo-gasts," the friar said. "But when they catch up with us, we're not, and they don't know what to do with us."

"Are they looking for mates?" I asked, thinking of the eels.

"Doubtful," the friar said. "With Gyal-was you keep everything very simple. Constituent cells reproduce, even organs may, but the colony itself does not. The same twelve or twenty have roamed this place for a thousand years. They don't breed, they just live forever." He smiled mischievously. "Like monastic orders."

"Why do they look for each other, then?" I asked.

"They may struggle for territory . . . Also like monastic orders, I'm sorry to say." He beamed at a new thought. "And that would keep them patrolling actively, which is better for the vines." I understood why Ariel was treating this gentle soul with such irritation. He was in heaven, enjoying himself too much to help us leave.

So I tried to make my question sound like a challenge. "What are they *for*?"

"I beg your pardon?"

"They're not natural animals; they were engineered for a purpose. The eels were for air travel. What are the slugs for?"

"They're not . . . slugs," he said, but his pensive tone indicated that I might have set the hook.

Ariel was watching the slug accumulate with an expression of distaste, and tall Harry had moved behind her, trying to look indifferent.

"Harry's ready," she said. "Now let's go."

The entry shaft of the red section glowed dully at my feet, the color of hot coals. I looked across at the others and Friar Francisco nodded at me as if he thought I needed reassurance.

Maybe I did. I finished clearing away the last of the creepers we'd torn out of the connector; they might have been climbable if they hadn't taken up so much room.

"That mat looks too thin for a jump down," I said.

The Green monk silently pointed to the forgotten coil of supercord tucked into my belt, saved from my last testing ground. I took it out, doubled and redoubled it to the necessary length, which would also make the fine wire less painful to hold, and tied one end to the nearest ceiling loop. Amazing what people expect of a man in uniform—even more so what he finds himself agreeing to do. I climbed down into the crimson unknown. My knees and elbows occasionally bumped the connector's interior strips, but they proved as cool as rubies.

There were no surprises at the bottom. It was another vine tunnel, the only difference being that the connector frame and overhead strip had dimmed to red; the vines were accordingly less healthy, kinked and coarse-barked, with far fewer leaves. They hung in dull gray tangles against the slick black rock and its blood-colored reflections. A child's dream of hell.

"It's only the lights," I called up to the others, and they joined me.

"God!" Ariel said after looking about. "This place is awful."

"Death on low heat," I agreed.

"On the contrary," Friar Francisco said. "Just autumn or winter, a phase of necessary dormancy, like human sleep. Artifical ecosystems often retain the seasonal cycles of the genome they were modified from. A good engineer obeys the trace of Mother Goddess that remains in his creations."

"Then why is it 'winter' in some places, but not in others?" Ariel asked.

"I know!" Harry said. "You can't shut *everything* down. The pseudos wouldn't like that."

"That's my guess," the friar agreed. "A staggered schedule. Every section dims occasionally, but never too many at one time."

On we walked. The red tunnel's vine mat, though still well-knit, lacked resilience. Without so many leaves to absorb sound, our voices returned in hollow metallic echoes that killed conversation. Instead we listened to the soft pitter-patter of unseen rats.

We found dead ends to several tunnels, doubling back when

necessary. We made slow progress, but no one suggested splitting up.

"I still say this red looks like emergency lighting," Ariel said. "Or even a warning."

"Feces!" blurted the friar.

"I beg your—"

"Excuse me for interrupting," he said, reaching into one of his capacious robe pockets, "but I see some pseudo-gast feces I should collect." He pulled out a sample box and a plastic bag, kneeling down next to a large dark cake on the mat.

"Do you absolutely have to?" she asked. "Is it sanitary?"

He delivered his "Silly, silly, silly" litany, using a folded leaf like a pair of tongs, and added, "We didn't even know slugs would visit red sections until now. As for their dung, you saw what I collected yesterday. Inoffensive as creamed peas, with a few white stems thrown in. It's only the red light that makes this look brown."

"Okay okay, let's not dwell on it," Ariel said, walking away with her face to the wall. A few paces later she stopped short. "Do you think your flashlight still works?" she asked.

From another pocket the Green monk produced a metal cylinder the size of a large cigar and handed it to Harry. "Give her this, please," he said. "I don't know, Ariel. It was even worse this morning. I bought it new for this trip, but that electromagnetic pulse has done something to it."

I saw what he meant when she turned it on. The beam flickered from bright to dim to nothing at all. A few blows from the heel of her palm revived it for the moment.

"Well, what do you make of this?" she said, a note of triumph in her voice.

The friar dropped what he was doing and joined the rest of us.

Where Ariel played the flash we saw a narrow vertical crack in the tunnel wall. It extended all the way to the light-strip. A few tendrils of vine had dug into the hairline of exposed dirt.

"A break," she announced. "So these are in fact emergency red lights, to warn us of unsafe tunnel walls."

"Oh, I doubt that," the friar said. "If the Titan cavern complex can maintain its integrity for a million years—"

"But Titans didn't plan the Hellway," Ariel pointed out. "Humans improvised it with Titan construction equipment. We don't know what earth tremors—"

"Your fear of the unknown comes from a secular education,"

the friar interrupted. "Stop and think. Do we have any reason to believe that similar cracks aren't a feature of the white-light tunnels, too, hidden behind the leaves? They could be like the gaps in a concrete sidewalk, protection against temperature change. Or they could be extra anchor points for the vine, to make sure it hugs the wall as intended. Without trust, how can we even turn a new corner?—or use the exit door if we find it?"

"But—"

"Look out!" Harry cried. Our gaze jerked to where he pointed.

Intestines floating in midair. Just another slug, I realized an instant later—if anything, smaller than the first one I'd seen, but transformed in the red light to something more ghostly and ghastly, its outer skin almost invisible, its interior structures pale and prominent by contrast. Ariel shot the flashlight in its direction, and it flared white, more opaque. It seemed as startled by the change as we were, retreating down the tunnel. The beam flickered, the creature seeming to cycle large-small-large-small in its strobe. Was it an optical illusion, or did the light also make it flinch? The slug backed around a turn and disappeared.

The friar had fumbled out a wax marker and a book of sample labels—the only way he could take notes, I realized, with his wristcomp gone. "Am I right in thinking it was less than full-size?" he asked us. "And that it showed photosensitivity?" We muttered replies, still a little spooked.

"Why is it here in winter?" he muttered. "Smaller than the others—bullied into undesirable territory, hmm?" He took back the flashlight and sat down to write, legs folded yogically. He soon put the flickering torch aside, holding the tiny squares of paper close to his eyes.

"Let's hurry and finish here," Ariel said. She sounded fed up. "Have we exhausted the network in this direction?"

I consulted my mental maps. Right and left, and null for special choices, this time a sequence of couplets, ending

ReNted LoveR, moRNiNg afteR—
RumpLed LiNe(n), RibaLd LaughteR.

"We haven't done the left-branch-first variations yet," I said, and we left the friar behind.

It was no go. The way out was not through a red zone.

"Creepy place anyway," Harry said as we rejoined the monk.

He kicked at a gnarled trunk of vine, and half a dozen rats scurried away. Even Friar Francisco started.

"Rats," he said.

We reverted to my original plan. Although we couldn't always rule out side tunnels without some inspection, we managed within a few hours to find the descending forward path through another dozen floors. Slug sightings became more frequent. So did red sections, all of them showing hairline cracks.

And finally we hit bottom—a floor that broke the pattern. It was longer and wider than the others, and all of its sections connected. This made for a much more complicated and convoluted maze, in which even the backward-starting tunnels might snake around to hit the front perimeter—which I hoped would be close to the mountain face. Most of the tunnels were red, which tired both eyes and brain.

There were no more holes downward, aside from some small drainage grates—a good sign. But we couldn't find an exit, either. The main problem was the five or six roaming slugs that blocked path after path. Retreating from them and doubling back later, we sometimes lost track of which turns we'd already covered, and argued over which ones still had to be checked.

It felt like late morning. We had returned to a key intersection, not far from a short red tunnel that was my best guess for the exitway. It was blocked by a particularly sluggish slug. We sat down to eat and think; perhaps the slug would move on while we waited.

"I may be wrong about everything," I said. "Those slugs aren't just keeping us from the ends of tunnels, they may be keeping us from the down-holes to even more floors."

"No," Friar Francisco said. "Everything seems to indicate that you were right from the beginning. And you, too, Ariel."

She looked up in surprise, silent behind a mouthful of synthetic food.

"I've reconsidered," the Green Monk went on. "Your hypothesis about red tunnel walls serves to explain where the rats come from. That's the other thing I expect to find, somewhere on this floor, on the same side as the exit. A red tunnel crack large enough to admit rats from the surface."

"Why are you so sure they don't belong here?" I asked.

"Rats are tunnelers and killers, altering the environment on the macro level. A Gyal-wa environment has to be simple, simple, simple. With hypertrophied specimens like this, even more so."

"Because Gyal-was don't reproduce?" I hazarded. "They can't evolve to deal with changes in the environment?"

"No, they evolve too well," the friar replied. "The billions of individuals that make up the colony run through many generations in a day, and their interrelationships are meant to be flexible and accommodating. An adaptive mutation can run through the whole colony like wildfire.

"We've already seen that smaller Gyal-was, bullied into the poorer feeding grounds of red tunnels, have become afraid of white light. Why? Where there is no brain, there can be no thought. Instead, an adaptive mutation tends to protect outer-skin cells from being killed in intercolonial conflicts over white-lit feeding grounds. A small example, but it demonstrates the point. The only way to keep the Gyal-wa you intended and designed, the one that will do what it's supposed to do, decade after decade, is to insulate it from all environmental change."

"But what are they supposed to do?" I asked. "They're just getting in our way."

"That's not deliberate," the friar said. "You see, there's so much more energy cost to climbing up as opposed to flowing down, they naturally congregate—"

His mouth hung open, and it was a moment before he continued. "*Naturally!* You asked me what the Gyal-was are *for*, Commissioner. They're precisely for getting in our way! That's the test, to realize that. The only way out is to go through one of them, just as Harry went through one before."

"Oh hell, I hope not," Ariel said. "And I wish I'd finished eating before you mentioned it."

"I don't want to—go through that again," Harry objected.

"It may not even be safe," I said. "As you say, Friar, they have no brain. They have no way of knowing not to squeeze our ribs a little too hard, or hold onto us too long. Harry may just have been lucky."

"But not if this is the *intended* way to reach the exit door," said the friar, beaming. "I am perfectly willing to test the hypothesis myself. After all, we put our trust in the transport tubes—and isn't a mechanical system more likely to break down then a life system? I have faith, if you do not. Be truthful—isn't your real objection just silly squeamishness?"

"Common sense says we should eliminate the less risky options first," Ariel said firmly. "For instance, you just gave me an idea. Let's see how much the red-tunnelers dislike light. Let's use the flashlight on this guy around the corner, see if we can prod him out of our way."

"There's a thought," I said.

"Punitive rather than cooperative," the Green monk said. "But I suppose we could try it. More positively, I could try to lure the colony out with a branch of big ripe leaves from one of the white sections."

"Better and better," I said.

"But 'The only way out is through.' " He smiled. "You'll see. If necessary, I'll do it without you."

"First the flashlight," Ariel insisted. Friar Francisco shrugged good-naturedly and went through his pockets.

But as it turned out, he didn't have it. "I must have left it in that first red section," he said. "When the colony distracted us."

"That was the only red section on the fourth level, with access from Three," I said. "We can be there and back in under half an hour; the vertical path is short. And finding the flashlight won't take long if we all fan out."

"I'll stay here and try to coax the colony out instead," the friar suggested. "I don't approve of this aggressive approach."

Ariel and I looked at each other. "All right," I agreed, "but wait for us before trying anything else."

He shrugged and smiled.

"Maybe we should have pressed him," Ariel said to me from the lip of the red zone after we'd retrieved the flashlight.

"That would have made it into a challenge. Now he doesn't have to prove anything. And you can be sure the prospect of being engulfed will seem scarier when he's all alone."

"It scared me enough when we were all together," she said.

Harry was the last to climb back up the connector into white light. He'd been hampered by something in his hand. "What have you got there?" Ariel asked.

"The friar's sample bag. I found it near the flashlight."

"Oh great," she said. "We certainly couldn't leave *that* behind."

"But we're scientists!"

"And we leave no turd unstowed," I added. This got the reception it deserved.

"But he'll want this," the boy continued. "See, he thought

it was green, like the samples from white tunnels, but it really is brown."

Ariel was quicker on the uptake than I. *"What?"* she grabbed his wrist as though it were the plastic bag's handle, holding it where she could see it. "What are those white things in it?"

"The friar said stems," Harry replied. "Undigested. They do look funny, though." He shook the bag a little, and the white fragments shifted in the dry flaky dung. A larger piece came to the top, a delicate elongated structure with hollow eye sockets and sharp teeth. A skull.

"Rat bones!" Ariel said.

"Well, we always hear more rats in the red tunnels," Harry pointed out. "They like dark places."

"Which is lucky for the red-tunnel slugs," she said. "They don't get many leaves to eat. Don't you see it? They've adapted. Red-tunnel slugs eat meat."

Harry's eyes grew big and round. He choked a few times, like his father, but got out two words: *"Friar Francisco!"*

We couldn't run in a pack, not on those mats, and the connectors would have strung us out anyway. I reached the bottom floor first, at the cost of two head bashes against the ceiling, and reached the suspected exit tunnel a few seconds before the others.

I took in the scene at a glance. The friar and the slug were much farther toward the end of the red tunnel than before; the Gyal-wa must have retreated before the unfamiliar two-legged creature. It was now possible to see, past its wildly waving eyestalks, the shape of a door.

An untouched bunch of large green leaves lay discarded. The friar had removed his robe and balled it up under one arm, perhaps to protect it from slime. He looked as if he'd been standing in the same tentative posture for long minutes, unsure—a sturdy brown figure in pale green shorts, less than a meter from the agitated slug.

He looked backward at my approach, balanced on the edge of a decision. The others puffed into place behind me.

Perhaps I said the right thing, put the danger across in just the right words to pull him back in time. Perhaps Ariel's formula was just as good, or Harry's.

But we all shouted at once and he didn't understand. He saw only our panic, and called back something at the same time, nothing but the words "silly" and "trust" distinguishable. And he stepped forward.

The slug reared back, grew broader and taller. But it did not flow over him. Instead the vertical mouth slashed open, the "head" rose, and we heard a gassy moan of . . . anticipation? It took only a second. The wood-rasp tongue whipped out and smoothly, deliberately, licked the flesh from Friar Francisco's belly and chest. The friar screamed as he fell backward, and there were other screams in my ears when the slug dropped on him with the finality of a bootheel crushing a bug. It mounded forward, a ton or more of cloudy jelly in the hellish red light, the mouth parts swimming down to where they were needed.

And Harry ducked under my arm to run toward it. His usual coltishness was almost spastic now, terror fighting with rage for control, and he must have snatched the flashlight from Ariel, because he held it in front of him like a spear, screaming, "Get . . . *off*! Get . . . *back*!"

And as the flickering white light jabbed into it, the slug did back off. A glance at the disjointed scraps of the friar showed it was too late. But Harry—stiff-legged with hysteria—continued to force the slug back, meter by meter.

Ariel and I rushed forward to grab the boy. But now the thin mat beneath our feet began to boil and erupt with fist-sized gray bodies.

Streams of rats flushed toward us. They must have been piling up in the rear of the tunnel, trying to avoid the advancing slug; but now, as Harry forced the Gyal-wa to the very doorway, they were cornered and had to tear their way out under and around it. Even as the slug continued to retreat, its tongue whipped from side to side to catch or kill fleeing rodents. And as I reflexively hopped back and forth to avoid the hurtling gray shapes, I realized what was about to happen. The slug, too, would be cornered, its front-rank cells unable to get cooperation backward; their only other escape from the light would be to roll down and under, and then—

It happened. The whole colony began to flow back toward us, fast, the eyestalks bobbing up and down, riding the wave. Ariel got the flashlight back; I jerked Harry around by one arm; he seemed to snap out of it—and then the three of us ran for our lives.

At least the thinner mats of the red tunnels were easier to travel. We slammed into an intersection we recognized, but the shortest path toward a safe, white-lit corridor was blocked by another red-tunnel slug, slowly drifting toward the vibrations of our passage. The two other tunnels facing us were unknowns, but as Gyal-was closed on us from opposite directions Ariel made the choice. We pounded after her. She'd followed the fleeing rats, but I didn't know why. Our new tunnel angled back into the direction we thought of as "forward" and came to an end. But not the usual dead end.

Logic had led Ariel to what the friar had predicted, the rats' own crack in the wall. And the actual gap in the stone surface looked wide enough for us, too. The bad news was that it was choked black with earth and vines. The rat exodus found its own tiny pathways to freedom—but now it was our turn to be cornered.

We moved to face the slug that had pursued us. Which one? No matter. It slowed to a near stop ten meters away.

"Why doesn't it finish us?" Ariel gasped.

We stood there panting.

"No brain," I said finally. "Or at least not much. No purpose, no memory. Just impulses, tendencies. That doesn't mean it'll go away. It'll probably come after our noise and movement sooner or later."

"Let's try this." She shone the flashlight at it, and it slowly retreated.

"Easy!" I said. "Little doses. If you start the whole thing rolling, a little beam has no effect. That's what happened back there." She let the colony come to a stop a few meters farther away. It remained where it was, pulsing, and began to probe the undermat with its tongue.

I found to my surprise that Ariel was smiling. "It's okay now, Harry, Alun. Now we can dig our way out. See how thick the vines are, going into that crack? We must be close to the light of the surface, or they wouldn't be that healthy. And the rats will have tunnels along the same line, which should loosen the dirt some. Harry, you keep the first slug-watch with the flashlight, and remember what the commissioner said if you have to push it off. He and I will be digging."

I turned to face the meter-wide crack of earth and tugged on one of the thick vines that led into it. "Solid as a rock," I said. "And without tools—"

"They *are* tools," she said, pushing me aside. She jerked a vine back and forth until it was looser, then began to move it in circles, as if coring an apple. Loose dirt was screwed out, and the hole widened.

All of the vines could be worked that way, and she was right about the rat holes, too; when we broke into them, we could scoop out kilos of earth with our bare hands.

In the next three or four hours, I learned what it was like to work construction under Ariel Nimitz. It was hard labor at top speed, and I was the drillhead. As rocks and dirt accumulated around my feet she shifted them to the sides of the tunnel, out of our way. She threw a few of the sharper rocks at the slug, too, but they sank out of sight in the Gyal-wa's mass; the creature seemed more agitated than hurt, and she had to give up on that idea.

By the time I was too tired to continue, we'd created standing room for more than a meter past the crack. A boulder blocked the way forward, but I had made some progress above it, following the course of vines and ratways. I'd whittled through a few of the thicker vines with my belt buckle to make more space, only to find their far ends still as firmly anchored—the surface as far away—as ever. But I didn't have enough vitality left to challenge Ariel's inhuman optimism.

Finally she rotated us. She'd been waiting for me to make squatting room for her on top of the boulder, from which she could go higher. Now Harry would clear dirt away while I rested on guard, and they'd switch places when his extra height was needed. I listened to her almost without comprehension as she cheerfully told Harry how small cave-ins would "play right into our hands!"

Harry handed me the flashlight, whispering that it was nearly dead. The slug had shown a definite tendency to drift toward us except when pushed back; to husband the power of the failing lamp, Harry had let the creature settle only five meters away.

The diggers made soft noises behind me. The slug pulsed hypnotically as I gazed at the shapeless forms that swam inside it. I did avoid meeting its eyes. But I noted that the friar had been right about many things. For instance, the "head" of the creature was largely shaped by big interior flotation bubbles. Pneumatophores, he'd called them. I wondered what sort of gas the colony manufactured to fill them. Hydrogen again? No, what did grazers usually produce?—methane, maybe.

Another half-hour passed. I tried to understand the shifts that took place when I was forced to use the light, tried to intimidate the creature more efficiently. But the flash was failing. It was a disposable, unfixable unit, power source unknown. All I could do was screw off and discard the transparent guard up front and inspect the little acorn-shaped bulb.

The filament looked wrong, spotted with black. I found the bulb would wiggle slightly from side to side. The first few times I did this, it brightened and I was able to push the slug off a few meters. Then it just made things worse. The filament still glowed and sparked, but cast no beam.

The Gyal-wa slid forward, stopped, pulsed, and slid forward a little more. But I didn't see any point in calling to the others, creating more attractive vibrations. I faintly heard Harry's voice saying that he could see the sky, a pinhole at the very top of their tunnel, and I lived for a moment in the torture of hope, but then I heard Ariel's cheerful reply that yes, a few more hours and we might be free.

Everything had come clear. I was at peace. The slug was moving forward steadily now, beginning to build upward, too, beneath the ruby ceiling strip. Something sharp would be nice to have at the end, but I didn't want to ask Harry and Ariel for my belt buckle back, didn't want them watching this. I reached into a pants pocket with my left hand and ripped out the lining, wearing it like a glove. The slug had reared up two meters tall now, only a meter away, and I could see the vertical puckering where the mouth hole would appear, the tongue assembly swimming into place in front of the huge cluster of pneumatophores. I took a last glance at the flashlight's exposed acorn bulb; just a blue flicker was left along the filament, but I was almost happy. I knew what I had to do, and that was a first for Slugland.

The great mouth was opening, a hole within a cloud, like the eye of a hurricane . . . The friar had been right about many things. The way out, for instance—not his fault the rules had been changed. And as the slug came down on me like a red wave, I thought, Hell, the only way out is still *through*.

Chapter Twenty-one

I bent my knees, angling to fit inside the descending maw. The slug's grass-whip tongue snaked toward my face and I deflected it with the hand I'd gloved—*Not quite yet!*—the toothed muscle scratchily coiling around my arm, carefully tasting and testing the stiff, dirty uniform jacket. And it had to be now, before it flexed to rip my arm off, warm jelly pouring all over me, *now.*

I sprang erect, driving up and through the mouth, deep inside the slug with the flashlight in my extended right arm, the sharp little bulb aimed at the largest of the gas pockets. The pneumatophore had a protective outer layer, rubbery, resistant—that was inevitable—but I went up on my toes to force bulb and air through the last centimeter. The slug wrapped my body in a clammy embrace, but the bulb broke through even as it broke apart, one *chink!* one tiny blue spark along the filament—

And for just an instant the spark flared into a big ball of blue flame.

The methane explosion died almost immediately, just one tubercular cough, but the backlash nearly tore my head from my shoulders. The slug's long tongue spun free, its limp trailing end slicing into my neck and ear. A gelatin undertow yanked my feet out from under me. Thrown against one side of the tunnel by what felt like a high-pressure hosing of slime, I heard Ariel's scream.

She shook me back to consciousness where I lay; she was calling for someone named Alun, over and over. I threw an arm over her bent knees and pulled my head up to see. The slug had retreated down the tunnel. It couldn't be dead; it wasn't alive, only its trillions of cells were. But it had lost some or all of its pneumatophores, and lay puddled, unable to summon any height.

Ariel wiped slime from my face with her sleeve. The sticky-sweet smell everywhere made me want to vomit.

"If it got that far, it can come back," I said. My voice sounded strange.

"Not all the way," she said. "Didn't you hear us? Look. Look."

I had to roll over to see what she was pointing at, the opening we'd dug into the crack. The hole to the surface, high above, was still quite small, and we were hours away from getting out. But the light came in. Bright light, white light, flooding the excavation with safety. Ariel helped me crawl into it.

It was dusk by the time the last of us wriggled up onto the surface of the Hellway. We looked like creatures made of mud, and the surroundings suited us. We were near the bottom of a narrow mountain pass, its sides a jumble of slag and trash rock and a few scanty bushes. That's why rats would risk the slug tunnels, I would think later—for vines to eat; but now I only wanted to find the t-station.

We realized, but never said aloud, that we might not be able to get at the station from here. There was no reason why the exit door we'd sought down there had to reach the surface; it might connect directly with a t-tube. But I wasn't surprised when, after a short walk, we found a closed door into the mountainside, and a t-booth facing it. The only way out is through. A direct connection would just be more *through*; *out* means within sight of the sky. So I told myself, in a cavern six kilometers below the surface of Newcount Two.

The transport tube opened at the push of a button. The travel capsule inside was narrow and transparent. Two people might share it, in great discomfort, but a stern computer voice warned in Ur-Linguish that it would go nowhere if so loaded.

We had to split up. Harry and I sent Ariel on first; she kissed us each good-bye as warmly as our filthy faces would allow. Then I groped for some manly reassurances to feed the kid as we waited for his capsule to arrive. He beat me to it with a wan smile: "Can't get much worse, can it, sir?" And then he was gone.

My turn.

Each new transport car in the Hellway seemed to be of a different design. This one, the fastest yet, shot through tubes as transparent as itself. After a brief plunge beneath the mountain range, it took me along a stomach-churning U-bend upward and ascended with increasing speed high above a barren, broken plain.

Higher, higher, until there was a sickening reversal of perspective: the ground below blurred into skylike haze, while the underworld's ceiling became all too clear, its gray tiles looming well-defined and larger, larger. I was going to smash into it.

And I did, the tube extending into darkness and another lateral bend. After a longer horizontal trip I reemerged into light, and took a terrifying fall into the depths of a large lake. Then darkness and sideways travel again. The car slowed to a halt and the entry panel reopened. I stepped out unsteadily into a small featureless chamber lined with blood-red velvet. Doors closed behind me. The floor pushed against my feet, and I knew I was in an elevator, but at least its pace was bearable.

It opened at the top of a lighthouse.

Or so I would always think of it. In fact there was no lamp. But it was a circular tower jutting out of a sea, not far from a rocky coast, and the top floor was the right shape, all windows. A singsong robot voice emanating from hidden speakers informed me that I would be "in limbo" for a day or two, until I could be suitably teamed with another "seeker." I tried to talk back to it, explaining that I wasn't really a candidate for adulthood but a castaway in need of help, but the thing couldn't deal with me. Limbo.

But it made sense. We pilgrims were supposed to be regrouped after each trial, but no one could be sure how long the separate adventures would take. Furthermore, the controllers might prefer certain team-ups over others. To make their game come out even, then, they would occasionally have to take a card out of play for a round or two—an ace, a joker, or just a lucky knave.

It was a circular one-room apartment with a table and chair on one side and a crude pallet bed on the other. There were no other furnishings. In the center of the circle stood the elevator and a small bathroom, back to back. I stepped inside the latter.

The fixtures looked ancient, but the plain yellow soap smelled new and the single coarse towel appeared freshly washed. I enjoyed a long shower, scrubbing the shallow cuts on my neck and ear until they bled again; I wanted scabs without dirt in them. The cabinet over the toilet turned out to contain a bandage kit as well as some primitive shaving equipment, which I also used.

When I emerged, music was playing, and one spot on the wall glowed a gentle green, as if it were a touchpoint. I pressed it and the music ended—didn't turn off, but segued cleanly into a logical-seeming coda. A new piece in the same style began when I touched the point again. There was no way to change the selection or volume, but it was good stuff—a small chamber group improvising around melodies with the flavor of folk songs—and I let it play.

Tens of hours to spend and nothing to do. Music, but no book to read. Still wrapped in the towel, I washed my clothes in the shower, killing as much time as I could by carefully rubbing in the soap, rinsing, wringing out, and doing it again. I tried in particular to restore the whiteness of the uniform jacket—in memory of the way Ariel had once looked at it, perhaps. Then I opened some windows, and on their hinged metal braces I hung the clothes to dry.

The moment the full sound of the sea came in, the music changed. The strings that would have been half-drowned vanished, and the same tune continued, without dropping a beat, in a version for solo piano. Maybe I imagined it, but the computer improvisor even seemed to be taking some multiple of the wave period for its tempo.

I lay down on the bed and opened my eyes a seeming second later to find the clothes nearly dry and my arms and legs stiff and sore. I walked out the kinks, around and around the compass of the room, and dressed when the air got cooler.

An hour or two later the elevator door opened, revealing a hot meal on a wooden tray. I lifted it onto the table and sat down to eat. The plate, silverware, and wineglass looked old but sturdy. A china mug held strong coffee, its saucer inverted on top to keep it hot. The food was plain but hearty: fresh bread, a meat like veal with some sort of cheese sauce, peas and potatoes on the side. If it was all synthetic, it was skillfully done, especially the coffee. The wine smelled all right, but I saved it for later. And what was that other smell in the room? Wood resin, lacquer? I reinspected table and chair and realized that they had been freshly manufactured for me. Of course—the original furniture might well have gone rotten in six hundred years.

Another restless walk, yawning all the time, feeling the sea air heal me. Another nap with the same wonderful sharp edges, no sense of consciousness held hostage, just a replenishing of spirit.

Dusk fell, and mermaids swam up onto the nearby rocks to sing. Actually, the creatures resembled hairy seals with birdlike beaks, but their voices were eerily human in timbre, like a boy's choir. I decided they were calling back to the piano, and soon the piano began to phrase its tunes around them. Just a few would sing at a time, the rest grooming the seaweed out of each other's fur with their strangely twisted beaks. I watched them until it was too dark to see, and later heard them slip into the water and swim away.

I paced the tower circle into the night, watching the underworld sky go through its puzzling repertoire, simulations of stars, rainbow cascades, the occasional spotlight stab at something out of sight. And the crest of every wave below me burned a witchy blue-green with the phosphors of tiny surface creatures, on a sea as full of life as any found in nature.

In time I sat at the table, and a concealed spotlight in the dome above immediately illuminated its surface. I ran my fingers up and down the clean fresh grain, feeling as I hadn't in a long, long time. I suddenly knew, beyond question, that the average candidate for adulthood had carried a journal and a pen, and that this writing desk would not have been wasted on those earnest boys and girls in the key week of their lives.

But I had no pen, and what I felt—the light lifting of my fingers, the soft breath on the back of my neck—was just a tease, the Muse's revenge for having forsaken her so long. Besides, I had no subject—the Hellway was already living poetry, an epic series of "objective correlatives" for official Elitist virtues.

I sipped my spotlit glass of wine and considered. In one way the Elitists had the later Kanalists beat all hollow. They'd built the ultimate initiation maze. Not just symbolic of the world, but a world in itself, with still more worlds inside it, and a wealth of living creatures tailored to each.

Foyle had also reviewed the big picture, looking down from our eel-balloon. She had found the Hellway monstrous, not just in consequence, but in conception. To her—as to most—*artificial* is simply the opposite of *natural*, while randomness and ragged edges, however unsatisfying, are the only freedom we can hope for. But that's wrong. Unless humankind and its works don't belong in the world at all, subatomic particles and sonnets must be equally natural, part of one continuum linking freedom and order.

Foyle had said that the Hellway trapped us like characters in a play—but this prospect doesn't scare anyone who's actually written a play. We know how much independent life and will even those paper humans can acquire, enough to alter the story line unless other characters maintain it; we know that the framework of plot does not imprison, but provides a stage.

My own part, I acknowledged to the fire-capped sea, was one of comic relief in a historical tragedy, slated to catch a yard of steel in the guts, like Mercutio, before my line of chatter diverts too much attention from the leads. In the past I'd allowed myself to be written into a number of cheap thrillers; I would not turn down the honor of a subplot in the Elitists' epic cycle. It was full of horrors, of course, like every epic, but not to be rejected for that—unless we were to reject the larger world for the same reason, as philosophers and winos do. No, better to embrace the whole, and duck the bullets.

I finished the Elitists' wine and saluted their craft. But I reserved judgment on their society. They had forged something awe-inspiring for posterity; but if it was true that they'd meant half their posterity to die in it, just to keep up standards, then to hell with them.

And so to bed. Guilty over the luxury of clean sheets, I forced myself to think about Hogg-Smythe's face as she tried not to be a straggler in the land of vampire moths; of Friar Francisco, killed by trust; of the good chance that Ariel had been partnered with mercenary rapists this time around. But the punishment didn't take. Some gentle spirit of the air continued to ward off the suspend-sleep nightmares.

I am sitting at a plain wooden desk, in a tiny university room, an hour before dawn. I have just finished *The Enchanted Isle*. It will never be perfect, but it will never be better. Revisions will come, and may be cruel, but they will not touch these last five pages. For I have not written them, they have written me instead; they have drawn me out of myself and above my intentions; they have set down, in letters of blood and gold, what I must realize and become. I am like a child half-awake on Christmas morning, as yet unable to name the particular thing that elates me, but sublimely certain that it is all I could want, and unstoppable, because the whole world is being carried into it with me . . .

So many things won't matter any more, once this celebration of the Kanalist mysteries is played before my schoolmates. For once you know that you were born a king, that this world is your forest and its creatures your deer, all else falls into proportion. You will not want to be warlord or warden or hoarder now, nor ward heeler, nor whore. The only politics not utterly beneath you is *noblesse oblige*, the helping hand to those who have not yet remembered that they are your peers.

I've done my part there. I have crept through a maze of errors to discover that the golden Kanalist thread is still in place. We took the right steps all along, and said the right words, and nothing remains except to remember that they mean just what they say and are true: the secret of Everyman's noble birth is that it lies outside history, and can be reexperienced at will, like memory itself, like a work of art. The mystery has written itself out, and I will have it played on a stage, and all who see and hear will laugh and cry and marvel, saying, "*I remember now,* he's got it down exactly. The old story and the only one. My own, and my lover's, too . . ."

I woke up with tears on my face, feeling magnificent. I recalled everything without embarrassment. Not one fact of history or memory from my past could keep me from believing that I had once done great things, that I belonged at the top of the tower, shedding a little light—and that I should be happy. If this were the only elitism, no harm, I thought, wishing I could have presented my plays to the builders of the tower in time to make a difference. Maybe they, in their earliest stage, had been the ones I could have reached.

Sometime early in the morning the robot functionary told me to report to the elevator. I descended to a small briefing chamber, where I found Ken Mishima. He started to say something, but so did the robot, and Mishima had the brains to stay quiet while I tried to absorb our instructions. I didn't like what I heard.

"Did you get it?" he asked when it was over. His work clothes were dirtier than before, but he looked in good shape, and for some reason glad to see me. "It's good to see another fighting man," he added. These mystic warriors go through life like owls, dangerous in the dark, but blind all day. "Are we to supply ourselves for the next test?"

He gestured at an equipment rack before us.

"Yes and no," I said. "Strictly speaking, it's not a test. It's a rescue. Some of our companions have strayed into a 'nonfunctional area,' unless I got it all wrong. We've got to lead them out."

"Our . . . companions," Mishima said.

"Exactly. Whether they're really friend or foe isn't clear.

And I don't know what sort of trouble they're in. But we're being sent after them."

No food had been issued on the equipment rack, from which we inferred that our mission shouldn't take long. Along with lengths of rope, there were lanterns; I couldn't help but think how much I could have used them in Slugland. We were also issued plastic pullovers to fit our boots, with traction bottoms for climbing, and from a shelf marked "Optional" Mishima took some strap-on cleats he called crampons; he seemed to admire the compact way they could be made to fold up, because he put them in one of his utility belt pouches.

I took a good look at that belt. It was my first real chance to inspect all the mysterious devices he kept holstered on it, since he'd had it on him when I searched his tent.

He caught the direction of my gaze and straightened up cautiously, then gestured at the rest of the gear. "There are no pitons or hammers or carabiners, though," he said. "So serious mountain-climbing is out." I was relieved to hear it, though he seemed indifferent to any challenge.

Finally I considered the extra coil of supercord I'd saved from moth country. It was too fine for proper climbing, strong enough but hard to grip. Still, it had come in useful in Slugland, and I was loath to give it up; I tucked the coil under my broad uniform belt along the spine, out of the way for now.

Soon a door opened to one side of the equipment rack and we lugged our ropes into the revealed transport car. A two-seater.

"I don't know how many people we're going to meet," I said as the transport began to move; this time there were no windows at all to distract us. "The computers prefer teams larger than two. So far I've seen Foyle, Hogg-Smythe, the Lagado boy, Ariel Nimitz, and Friar Francisco."

I paused. "Ariel told me she had a little trouble when she was partnered with you. Something about the wall crumbling away beneath her, and you not going back to help. I hope you'll keep your ears open when you're with me." Mishima made no comment, so I returned to my account. "The friar is dead, I'm afraid, and Hogg-Smythe was in bad shape the last time I saw her. But I've been lucky not to have been linked up with mercenaries."

"I was half-lucky," Mishima said. "Ruy Lagado and I were teamed with two of them, but something bigger went wrong just as our transport was being docked with theirs. It didn't seem like a deliberate test, more like an accident. We crashed into them, the whole terminal ripped apart—and then seawater poured in from above! Lagado and I made it to the surface without harm, but the mercenaries were wearing heavy equipment, gunpowder weapons and ammo. We found one of them drowned, later—his gun ruined—and the other never turned up."

"I'm glad Ruy had you to look after him. Not really an outdoorsman, I imagine."

"Oh, but what could I do with him?" Mishima said lightly. "We had to cross cold, treacherous, broken ground. A fjord, with a fierce tidal bore—I suppose you'd still call them tides in this place . . . Eventually I lost him. But anyone who carries that much fat bears a death wish as well. It will be tough on his son, but that's life."

" '*That's . . . life?*' Spend much time memorizing that one, or is it original with you?"

The car was still accelerating strongly; judging by the feel—in comparison with, say, flitters—the cumulative speed might have reached a thousand or more k an hour.

"It is curious that I should actually take your needling personally," Mishima finally said with his usual poker face. "Some part of me must feel that you are not . . . negligible—not just the arrogant fop you appear, but a spirit of power, mysteriously disguised."

"One never knows," I said. "Even Lagado might have surprised you. Given the chance."

"I didn't realize that Shadow Tribunes had such a deep respect for life," he replied. "I know, I know: you don't claim to be one."

We passed the next few hours in silence.

We emerged at the lower end of a long, narrow valley lined with rocks and loose dirt.

"Which way do we go?" Mishima asked.

"North," I said. "There's a t-stop at the other end of the valley, from which we're supposed to leave one at a time."

"Yes," he said impatiently, "but which path do we take?" The two paths both showed footprints; one led up to and along the ridge to our left, the other mirrored it on the right.

The valley was so narrow it hardly made a difference. "You take east and I'll take west, for starters," I said. "One of us can always cut across later."

Mishima objected to dividing our party, but agreed we should scout both paths. Soon we stood on opposite lips of the rift. On the other side of my ridge the ground fell off sharply, leading to a vast desert. I could see a sandstorm in the distant west. I shouted a description across to Mishima. "What about your side?"

He refused to shout, but at length joined me, saying, "Rain forest over there." Together we began to trudge north along the west ridge, surveying the gullied valley below as we passed.

It was a strange backstage area between two of the Hellway's sub-environments, without a theme of its own, littered with outsized junk: the skeletons of huge, unidentifiable beasts; amorphous lumps of melted plastics and ceramics, often as big as houses; great pipes and cables snaking from one ridgeside into the other, sometimes broken in the middle and leaking steam, rusty fluid, or tangles of wires; and occasionally, motionless among the debris, a lost or broken earthmoving robot. The Skid Row of the Gods.

"Those we are to 'rescue,' " Mishima said. "Did you get any impression of what shape they'd be in? Is combat likely?"

"They're in trouble, that's all I know. We still have to go this way, even if we choose to pass them by."

After a few hours we came to a point where the ridge became so spiny with broken slabs of rock that it was impossible to continue, and the path led back down into the valley. Across the way, the other ridgepath did the same. Not without trepidation, we bowed to the inevitable and continued along the valley floor. The sides became gradually higher and steeper.

We had a nasty moment—an earth tremor, accompanied by heavy subterranean rumblings. We gave each other one terrified glance, trying to keep our feet and waiting for a rockslide to bury us, before it passed. Soon after, we arrived at our destination.

It looked like part of an immense concrete building, jammed sideways into the valley to stop it up, and so weathered with centuries, so bare of detail, that its chambers looked almost like caves in a natural cliffside. Jutting out of the honeycombed structure at every height up to the summit, some fifty meters above us, were pipes and tubes of various materials, big enough to walk into without stooping. If you were crazy.

What was it, exactly? Perhaps a section of basement from one of the more elaborate Hellway environments. Perhaps its pipes and tubes and passageways had once provided power and ventilation and drainage for a place like Slugland. But it had been torn up and dumped here, and now it was just an obstacle.

"Can we climb over it?" I asked—shouting, because a second tremor had begun to rumble under us. At that moment something black came hurtling down the side of the structure, and I had just taken a step backward to avoid it when Mishima reached out and yanked me into one of the wall caves instead.

What I'd dodged was just the shadow; the thing itself hit the area of dirt I'd been moving toward. And as we peered out from the cave I saw that it hadn't been a falling rock.

It was a long thin dart, with a needle nose of steel.

Chapter Twenty-two

MISHIMA'S HAND FELL from my arm.

"Well, thank you, Ken," I said.

"You're welcome. One must learn to separate real dangers from . . . shadows." I shrugged this off and looked out from the darkness of the cave. The dart stood straight up and down in the rocky ground, a slender shaft with a conical plastic tail.

"A blowgun dart," Mishima said. "Probably poisoned. Certainly shot from above."

"Poxy fucking bitch!"

We whirled at the hate-filled whisper, bumping shoulders. As far as we could make out, our chamber was empty. Mishima found his lantern first, and played it inward. Our hiding place was small, its other exits blocked with earth. But one of the smaller metal pipes, as big around as a pumpkin, hung down from the ceiling to end jaggedly a half meter above our heads. With my own lantern, I took a closer look while Mishima faced the cave entrance *en garde*. The voice had to have come from the pipe. I listened intently.

Silence. Then a soft hoot was followed by an eerie sustained moaning that could only be wind blowing across the mouth of some other pipe connected to this one.

But the prolonged scraping that came next was something else again. Metal distinctly rang on stone. Someone grunted heavily.

"Shit, shit, fucking bloody shit!"—almost a confidential voice in my ear.

"Hello?" I said loudly. Even Mishima jumped when echoes came back: *Hello? Hello? . . . Hello?* But that last one was somebody else's voice.

Nothing to do but continue. "Are you the one who fired on us?"

Silence. Then, "Go away."

I looked to Mishima. He turned from the entrance and joined me in the rear of the chamber. With a slight lift of his chin, he encouraged me to speak again.

"Go where?" I asked.

"Go away! Find the next transport!"

"We're not going to let you take another shot at us." My eyes met Mishima's; we were trapped.

"Fuck you, then."

" 'Steel rusts at dawn,' " Mishima said, his voice sharp. Another one of his wooden—

" 'Blades gleam in firelight.' " The answer from the tube was prompt, automatic. Trained.

" 'Thunder whispers . . .' "

" 'Lightning sings.' "

"If green is thirty-five . . ."

"Yellow is seventy-two."

"And the sum, in blue, is ten-C," Mishima concluded, evidently at the end of the identification sequence. "I am Colonel Mishima, a brother of the executive grievance committee, here on union business."

He once more locked eyes with me in the bobbing lamplight—a new introduction, and a cautious opening of negotiations. My mind raced back to what I'd overheard in the statue chamber, the Iron Brotherhood mercenaries talking shop—*We should've called in a field representative. . . . I did try.*

This could get tricky.

Mishima continued to address the unknown soldier. "What is your name and rating?"

"Principato. Sergeant. Sir."

"Well, Brother Principato. We have much to say to one another, and other codes to exchange. I am in the company of an agent of the Column government. We are here to prevent—error."

Of course. As long as Mishima continued to believe me a

Shadow Tribune . . . But did the merc at the other end of the tube know my original role in Condé's bloody farce?

"Do you understand?" Mishima prompted him.

"Don't know." The disembodied voice sounded guarded. A distant wind groaned through the pipe.

"Is there anyone else there with you, Brother Principato?" Mishima asked.

"No." Less hesitation this time.

"No teammates?"

"All killed, sir. Got me talking to myself."

"I want you to come down here."

"I cannot leave my position at present, sir."

"Why? What is your position?"

"I'm about forty meters above you in a small cave."

"What is to prevent you from coming down here?" Mishima spoke the language of command so fluently that it came as a surprise when the enlisted man did not answer immediately.

". . . Sir, do you have a shot of neuroblock antidote on you?"

"Certainly." Mishima patted his holstered utility belt. "Don't you?" And a touch of the lash: *"Answer my question."*

"Sir, I have fallen on one of these bitch-whore poison darts. I've got a puncture wound in my left thigh and even though I cleaned it out, you know how it works—even a little bit gets you the slow way, paralysis. I can feel it starting, sir. I don't want to risk the climb, but I could let a monofilament down for you to tie the hypo to. Then I can come down when I'm better."

"And *your* antidote kit?"

"I lost some of my stuff down a shaft."

The sound of his voice had continued to fade in and out, as if he were moving. Curious. "How deep inside the wall are you?" I asked.

Mishima raised one eyebrow at me, and called up, "The speaker is nominally a Commissioner Parker. You will address him as 'sir.' "

"Yes, sir. Sir, I am about five meters in."

Mishima leaned toward me as if to confide something, but I held a finger to my lips and shook my head. Even a whisper might be caught by the pipe.

He nodded and pointed to himself, then upward.

I flipped a finger at myself, at him, and back to myself, then pointed up.

He nodded again. "We'll both come up to you, Brother Principato."

"Well . . . can you use a ninja line, sir?"

"The gear we have is good enough for this piece of cheese. Show yourself at your cave mouth, and hang a cloth out to guide us."

"Yes, sir."

Mishima risked the open air first, but we both stayed half in, half out. There was a long delay. Then from the pipe came the echoes of Principato dragging himself along his floor, forty meters above us. It was another minute or more before a carrot-topped head poked out cautiously, halfway up the "piece of cheese." Trying to estimate the difficulties of the climb, I just barely caught sight of the rapid sequence of hand signs Mishima flashed the merc. They meant nothing to me, but at least there was no reply.

The climb was strenuous but not difficult, going from chamber lip to chamber lip and sometimes using one of the great pipe outlets to step up on. We were lucky that the next earth tremor caught us in stable positions; it was the worst yet, but after it passed, there was nothing to do but continue climbing.

The mouth of Principato's "cave" was larger than I'd expected. The smooth walls were pierced at various heights by pipes and toward the rear by a dozen square exits large enough to crawl through. A faint, stagnant breeze hooted and whined through the openings, but could not dispel a sulfurous stench and dampness. The merc was nowhere to be seen.

"Smells like a geyser," I said. "I think this whole valley is coming apart. Maybe that's why we were sent."

"Principato!" Mishima called out.

"I'm back here," the mercenary replied from the shadows. I was acutely aware of being silhouetted against the entrance.

"Show yourself."

"I can't, sir. My arm is paralyzed now, and both legs." Metal rang on the hard surface. "I'm over here. In front of you and to your left."

The mercenary was sitting up in a corner, supporting himself with his right arm. He was tall, muscular, and held himself with unconscious arrogance. At the moment he was sweating rivulets, and in contrast with his bright red hair and forest-green outfit, the pallor of his skin stood out sickeningly. It was obvious that his poisoning story was not a ruse.

One leg of his outfit was partially blackened with blood. I also noticed that his name, stenciled across his breast pocket, was somehow familiar to me. Why, though?

Around him lay a jumble of gear: backpack, gas ministove, reel of filament, and a long metal tube with a shoulder brace and telescopic sight.

Mishima nudged the blowgun with his boot and made a disgusted face. "Joke weapon," he said. "Hobby of yours?"

"I hunt for the unit," the wounded merc said grudgingly. "Sir."

Another tremor shook us hard, and didn't pass quickly enough.

"Do these quakes happen all the time?" I asked.

"No. They started a couple hours ago."

"How long have you been here?"

"Since just before dawn."

" 'Sir,' " Mishima said.

"Sir."

Even deathly ill, and outranked, Principato had something. This was the winner of every footrace, the school boxing champion, the toughest guy in his unit; you could sense it immediately. Not a sport, though. Just a lover of the crushing victory, looking us over for signs of weakness.

Mishima knelt—cautiously—by the mercenary's side. "Maybe you can tell us this, brother. What, precisely, is going on with your unit? What is the Newcount Two operation as explained to you?"

Principato barked a laugh as Mishima hit his good arm with the injection of antidote.

"As explained to me, sir? Well, as explained to me, we were supposed to ride shotgun on a shipment of goods, from factory to warehouse, and Newcount Two wasn't in it at all."

An unusually shrill moan from one of the pipes made him start violently. He looked at us with haunted eyes.

"Hold it," I said. "I want to take this from the top." I turned to Mishima. "Colonel, the Brotherhood's client was Sir Maximilien Condé?"

"Yes. It was a strange contract from the beginning, but it looked like easy money," Mishima said. "This Condé is an important government contractor. Up until recently, he was also a reserve admiral in the Blue Swathe's militia navy, and used government troops as security forces in his business.

"Just before he lost his rank, he had put together a large consignment of goods for the Column government. It was ready to ship. But without militia guards he was afraid—or so he told us—that traitors within his corporation, encouraged by his political reverses, would try to hijack it. So he wanted to rent combat troops to station on every vessel, preventing an inside job. Unusual duty for ground fighters, but he offered good money. We gave him eight platoons of commandos.

"Half the shipment went through, and half our brothers returned for reassignment. As for the rest—Condé said that the order had been cut back, and that he needed to extend the contract on the other four platoons to guard the overshipment until he'd disposed of it. Again, the pay was good. But there was something fishy about it, especially as the months dragged on . . . So the shipment was diverted here," he asked Principato, "and you were reassigned to guard the lake entrance?"

"That's what they told us," the merc said. "We been stuck down this hole for months—'cept to go hunting. Our major said the extension option had been invoked 'automatically,' so we're all, like, volunteers. Usual bullshit, but up till then, no hassle.

"Then this construction company arrives, with enough equipment to build a city, and starts parking recon satellites in orbit. Turns out we're trespassers, have to keep under cover. The client sneaks in with a dinky little boat-shuttle. Two hundred of us stuck here, and he only hauls out two lieutenants. A month later, we hear from them. The client has connections with the local militia navy, see, and he's faked up some militia records for our two lieutenants that put them at the head of the line when the construction company starts recruiting for experienced communications officers. So now our lieutenants are running the defense satellite radios, and we can talk to them on a tight beam from the forest without the construction guys catching on. And o' course, they're in a position to keep any messages from getting outsystem, if necessary.

"That was the good news, see—but the client had no fucking intention of pulling us out. He was setting us up to run an op! By this time, everybody's screaming to Lieutenant Schultz—he's the site steward—to get us a field rep and renegotiate our contract. He talks the major into making the looeys in orbit send back word to the union, somehow."

"The injection should take effect almost immediately," Mishima said, feeling the soldier's pulse. "You'll be able to get around fine at first, but the puncture wound will stiffen up this leg later—but go ahead. They sent back word about what?"

"About what's going on. Sir. See, the client's asking us to keep on guarding this cavern, says it doesn't matter about the construction crew topside, says *they're* the trespassers, and that the militia navy is going to kick them out in a few months. But at the same time, he sets the major to drawing contingency plans for a seize-and-hold op against them. And we *knew* there was something wrong with that—the looeys tell us some senator owns this planet.

"The whole thing's crazy. Like the government's fighting *itself*. We wanted the union to get the straight dope. But we never got a reply."

Mishima glanced at me and explained to us both. "The dispatch that reached the Brotherhood had passed through various hands, and miscoding had ruined much of it.

"We knew that the original contract had been extended, and that our men were under cover in disputed territory. We knew the name of the planet, and even the general area of the hiding place. What we didn't know was a safe way to make contact—without going through the client. And the client's judgment was just the thing in question; we had to go behind his back and talk directly to our men in the field. I was chosen. The executive grievance committee has given me a blank check to . . . rectify whatever mistakes have been made."

And suppose their client *had* involved them in a politically dangerous contract? Wouldn't Mishima want to eliminate any civilian witnesses to that fact? This put a new light on Lagado's death, and for that matter on the incident Ariel had mentioned . . . But there was no point in making an issue of that now.

"How did you infiltrate Senator Mehta's team of archaeologists?" I asked.

"That was easy. A database search of passport clearances for the Blue Swathe turned up the real 'Mishima Ken' while he was still en route. He was in fact a geologist the senator had met at a party, another amateur at archaeology, but we forged a new letter of introduction that made him out to be a military historian, since I have published a few papers in that field. The real Mishima took ill, missed his travel connection, and was replaced by me in quarantine."

"Is he better now?"

"In an existential sense . . . I was in a tricky position, however. I had to accomplish my mission and leave before the senator—who would know me for a fraud—arrived on a visit. And I had to somehow cripple the archaeological effort, which was searching the same general area where I knew the brothers were hiding. This, despite the fact that Condé might well infiltrate his own agent into the dig, someone at slightly crossed purposes to me . . . I don't think I can convey all the complexities of the situation."

"I grasp it, somehow," I said. "So you searched the woods for Brotherhood scouts and hunters—who'd be doing their best to avoid all contact—and meanwhile sabotaged the archaeologists' Otis system to slow down their own search."

"Yes."

"Then I arrived, with Velasquez."

"Yes. As we know now, Velasquez was Condé's agent. Back in the statue chamber, you said something about his signaling to men in the marsh?"

"I believe that's what he did," I said.

Mishima looked to Principato.

The mercenary had been sitting quietly, his head cocked, listening to the sound of the wind in the pipes with the intense but opaque look I'd once seen on the face of an old actor in the early stages of delirium tremens—when he was seeing or hearing things, but wouldn't admit it yet. It was the first break in his winner's composure; I thought it strange. Hadn't he heard that same noise for hours?

But he'd also followed the conversation. "I don't know those details, sir. I was with the outside hunters until . . . most of the time."

Until, until . . . until he was put under detention, maybe. I'd placed the name now; Pro and Contra in the statue chamber had mentioned Principato briefly, one of them had called him Sergeant Superman . . . Yes, he was the one who'd been planning to snatch Foyle. So he'd been on report, isolated from operational details—which meant I didn't have to worry about his giving away my connection with Condé.

"Exasperating," Mishima said. "I *saw* the signal flare that night, but by the time I'd picked my way through the marsh, the brothers were gone."

"So you guessed that one of the new arrivals belonged to Condé," I said. "Is that why you sabotaged my flitter?"

Mishima didn't turn a hair. "Ah, it *was* sabotage, then! I wondered why Velasquez looked so suspicious when I surprised him coming out of the craft that morning. And now that we know he was Condé's man, it makes sense that he would try to kill you. You were about to fix the Otis system, and help the archaeologists find the hideaway; in the event of your death, he could claim certain powers as your deputy, maybe shut down the dig entirely. Let me guess—was it he who accused me?"

"Yes," I admitted. I could hardly correct the false assumptions in his story.

"But I would have been crazy to kill you," Mishima went on reasonably. "If you'd been bribed to act as my client's agent, well, we still had hopes that Condé's contract was a legal one; I wasn't going to shut it down otherwise. If you were a genuine official, an assassination would just make political trouble for my Brotherhood, the sort of thing I'd been sent here to head off. And if you weren't genuine—what else could you be except a Shadow Tribune? Only an imbecile or a lunatic wears Column whites without permission, but the Tribunal can do what it wants. Killing a Tribune would be even more political than killing a commissioner."

"If you were so anxious to stay on the good side of the Consultancy," I said, "why didn't you identify yourself in the statue chamber, as soon as the shooting started?"

"I would have," he replied. "You'd searched my tent earlier, so naturally I thought you were on to me. Then, after Velasquez was killed, you announced your mysterious political duties and told me not to leave until the others had gone. I thought you were simply getting the civilian witnesses out of the way. As you may recall, I headed back to the statue chamber—to represent the union in the frank discussion I was sure you intended us all to have. It was quite a shock to discover that you'd arranged something else. Open war, shoot on sight, and the brothers likely to kill me before I'd get a chance to identify myself.

"Then, in the graveyard, you revealed that my brothers here were out of control, mixed up in some plot to assassinate a senator. I decided to match your discretion. If you ever did admit your membership in the Tribunal, I'd come clean, too, and offer my assistance. But if you were something else—say, a genuine sub-commissioner of alien antiquities, swimming way over his head and pretending to more knowledge and authority than he had"—he shrugged apologetically—"then revealing myself to you would only limit my options. I decided to keep traveling with you; I'd protect you and the civilians—build good will—until I saw a chance to talk with my brothers. Before I could negotiate amnesty or reparations, I had to know what we were guilty of."

"And you haven't had a chance before now?" I asked.

"Think about it!" he said. "You heard that identification routine, how complicated it is. It was never intended to be used on a battlefield. If it weren't for our 'speaking tube,' I'd have had my head blown off before I could say the first line."

He took a deep breath. "But now here we are, everything out in the open." He turned to Principato. "Just what are you guarding on this planet, soldier?"

"Deepspace war machines," I told him before Principato could reply. "Planet-killers, that sort of thing."

Mishima looked back at me.

"Don't pretend you haven't guessed," I said. "Condé is a *defense* contractor, currently under investigation. And way back in the statue chamber, when Piet Wongama gave us that computer report on Level Null—where your brothers were—he mentioned that nearly all the spacecraft hangars down there were occupied. He assumed they were full of ancient Elitist ships, but you and I know differently now."

Mishima was silent.

"Condé discovered this city long ago, and realized what a great scannerproof storage bay it would be." I turned to Principato. "When you brought the arms shipment down the lake elevator," I asked, "was there already a stockpile here?"

The merc nodded. "A regular navy. One of the things that made us nervous."

"So Condé's been illegally manufacturing extra war machines, and diverting them here, for years," I said. "Maybe he honestly did think it was his planet—certainly he didn't expect Senator Mehta to move in at just this crucial time, when the Senate investigation had forced him to transfer the last illegal load from his factories."

"But if the arms are illegal, what's all this talk about the militia navy coming in to support Condé's claim?" Mishima asked.

"I think you've figured that out, too. There isn't anyone to sell major war machines to, except the Column's Consultancy. So he plans to use them himself. A coup. Apparently he believes that enough key militia navy officers are still loyal to their old admiral, and will back him. 'The navy will support the Consultant, if they get the chance,' that's what your brothers said in the statue chamber, but the great families who created the Column aren't crazy about the Consultant's populist reforms, and they can back Condé with big money. He'd have the advantage of surprise, too, striking from the Blue Swathe—a semiautonomous fringe whose Senator Mehta is one of the Consultant's liberal allies.'' I put some nicely modulated outrage into the big finish: ''This is high treason.''

''But if the upper managers of the Column don't want a Consultant anymore,'' Mishima said, ''what does Condé get out of it?''

I shrugged. ''The Blue Swathe, maybe. In a way, returning it to the Column. 'I have wiped away the Swathe's democratic Sodality,' he can tell them, 'but if you acknowledge me as your satrap, I will give you more direct control over the Swathe than you ever had before.' That sort of takeover is an old story in the fringes, isn't it? Especially in fringes like the Blue Swathe, where too many of the old Federalist liberties still prevail. That's why you've been playing your cards so close to your chest. You thought Condé just might pull it off, in which case, why shouldn't your union collect a fat fee for helping out?''

He said nothing, and I realized I'd better keep talking, and make it good. ''But the plan is doomed to fail. His arms stockpile has been discovered, months before the planned revolt within the militia. He can't move it without revealing himself to the senator's people. His only chance is to take the entire planet when the senator is himself present, and stall events for a month or two with forged messages from the senator. That was the plan I heard being improvised when I eavesdropped in the statue chamber. It's an act of desperation, and it's based on the idea that the Consultant is not yet aware of Condé's activities.''

''But isn't that the case—except for you?'' Mishima asked.

''That would be a very dangerous thing for you to believe, Colonel M— You're still calling yourself Mishima?''

He shrugged. ''Names are just tokens.''

''So are you; so am I,'' I said. ''Tokens in a chess game that the Consultant has already played out in his head.'' I made my own mental moves, at top speed. ''Look, I know everything that's passed between Condé and Mehta since they were in the Column's new navy together, almost a hundred years ago. Every detail, down to the way Condé cracks his knuckles and Mehta clears his nose—I know why and where their feud began. I have been briefed on Conpdé's resources, allies, and probable timetable. The fact that I was sent here to work through the archaeological dig should tell you that I already knew where to look for his base. Because Condé *is* a new navy veteran, and a popular militia admiral, I was supposed to handle the matter discreetly, gather evidence for a secret trial. But if I disappear, if I do not file my regular report this weekend, a preemptive military strike has been planned; the units are already in place.

"The Consultant *and* a majority of the great families have chosen to stand by their senator, libertarian though he may be. Anyone on the wrong side of the street when the parade goes by is going to get run over, and elephants will shit on him. Do I make myself clear?"

"Commissioner," Mishima said, raising both hands in a placating gesture, "the Iron Brotherhood's part in this fiasco is nothing but an appalling mistake. Our field commander has exercised unbelievably bad judgment—if he hasn't simply been suborned. Clearly, Condé has deceived the union. You know we would never do anything to jeopardize our charter or destabilize the peace of the Consultancy. We are a service business, not a criminal gang."

My gorge rose; I thought of all the human beings the Iron Brotherhood had burned, shot, pulped, chopped, and vaporized for money. They'd be calling themselves "population processors" in a minute. "So?"

Mishima put his hand over his heart. "I hereby declare Condé's contract void."

He and Principato smiled at me blandly, with the eternal innocence of soldiers and cops everywhere. The wind hooted.

"That will hardly satisfy the Consultancy," I said. "And if the senator is assassinated, the Brotherhood will be held criminally responsible."

"All right," Mishima said, trying another hand gesture: openness and candor. "Let me offer a deal. I'll shut down this op, and turn its command over to you. Once in communication with my home office, I'll arrange for the Brotherhood's spies to help the Consultancy run down any other conspirators or caches of matériel—gratis. All the Brotherhood would ask in exchange is immunity from any criminal charges, damages, and civil liability arising from this affair."

"I can't make promises for the Column," I said—by this time oblivious to the truth of it—"but work it out for yourself. I'm the only chance you have of obtaining leniency, and if I am killed, or fall into Condé's hands—you lose it."

Mishima nodded and knelt next to his comrade. I walked about, stretching my legs. The humidity and stench remained oppressive.

"I've got to work my way up the chain of command to your chiefs," Mishima told Principato. "That old initiation code is too unwieldy. Give me any operational passwords you know. What field protocols have been assigned?''

"What? I mean, none, sir."

"None?'' Mishima stood up.

"No, sir. There's no official operation yet. We didn't need any passwords in the elevator shaft, and op codes won't be assigned until the day before we hit the construction camp."

"You got by well enough with him,'' I said to Mishima.

"A lucky break, I told you—talking through the pipe. An operational password is short and sharp, one syllable that says live or die.'' Mishima walked over to where I stood, halfway toward the rear of the cave. "Commissioner, I'll do anything to show the union's good faith. Or continue to, I should say—I've already saved your life once.'' He lowered his voice. "I wouldn't stop at killing my own brothers, if necessary, to shut down this operation or protect you.''

"Not just me, the civilians, too,'' I insisted. "They're under my protection, and I'm deputizing you.''

He shrugged. "It is all one.'' He held out his hand. I took it and we shook. Principato was already up and testing his leg.

"Now let's get the hell out of here,'' Mishima said. "Principato, the way out is north, over the top of this rockpile. We've rescued you as assigned, and I don't want to stay long enough to find out what from.''

Right on cue, the quake struck. It was the same loud rumbling, the same sense of being helpless in a huge, trembling hand—but this time it lasted a whole minute, and the floor tilted a few inches beneath us. The others bobbed and balanced, but I lost my footing and crashed into a wall three meters away, next to a large pipe opening.

I'll never forget the look on Principato's face when he saw where I was. The rumbling died away. A strange mewling came from the pipe, and Principato hunched his shoulders at the sound; on reflex I turned and flashed my light inside.

The pipe slanted steeply downward. *I lost some of my stuff down a shaft,* he'd said. This shaft had a faint light at the end of it, and in between, fewer than twenty meters away, lay a half-naked young woman, bound and gagged. It was Ariel. She'd been screaming for a long, long time.

Chapter Twenty-three

I DIDN'T HAVE time to shout her name, or react at all. I heard a shout behind me and then Mishima tackled me from the side. As I twisted out from under him, I had a glimpse of Principato escaping through the main entrance with the blowgun in one hand; he was limping, but not much.

Mishima got to his feet as I did. Dark blood dripped from his left arm. "Son of a bitch threw a star at you," he said, gesturing to a flat metal object on the floor. I picked it up and gave it to him. It was a wheel of razor-sharp knife blades with a hole in the middle, about ten centimeters across.

"Not poisoned, anyway," he said, after examining it. "What was it about?"

"He has Ariel Nimitz stashed down that pipe," I said as I helped him out of his jacket. The gash on his upper arm was superficial, though bloody. I was more concerned with Ariel, but I owed him one; if that thing had hit me in the head . . .

"Ah, that explains it. Brotherhood contracts always guarantee against rapine, and we enforce that with summary execution." He handed me a pressure bandage from his utility belt and I ripped open its envelope. "Constantly causes this sort of blowup. Stupid regulation anyway. Instead of worrying about venereal disease, we should be glad to spread martial genes. But when the brothers in public relations come up with one of their marketing ploys . . ."

I stopped listening, since it would only have led to wrapping the bandage around his throat. He paused, but showed no other reaction, when I squeezed the skin flap into its proper position, sprayed sealant on the wound, and later pulled the bandage tight; and talking or silent, he kept watch on the main exit.

"That's it," I said. "I'll go get her."

A faint drumming under our feet signaled the beginning of the next temblor.

"This place'll be coming down around our ears soon," Mishima said. "You owe it to the Consultancy to—"

"Keep going? Take a look. The pipe is facing north, and there's light at the other end. We can beat Principato to the t-stop."

He did look, but shook his head. "It's not tactical," he said. "We'd be rats in a trap. Principato can't go fast with that leg; I'll follow him and take him out."

"With your arm?" I asked, but perhaps he couldn't hear me over the rising tide of noise; he took off for the exit, and I returned to Ariel's pipe.

It was big enough to walk into, though I had to duck my head and keep my knees bent. It was corrugated, which should have given me traction, but a heavy streak of dirt along the bottom had been turned to slippery mud by the steam rising at the pipe's far end. I could just straddle the slick, fighting the steep downward slope with every step, and now the metal skin of the pipe began to squeal and vibrate as the quake returned in earnest.

By the time I reached Ariel, she'd managed to squirm into the best position for freeing her hands, her back to me. Her jacket was missing and she was naked to the waist; the white fabric that gagged her appeared to be a shredded remnant of her blouse. I knelt next to her and gingerly sawed at her bonds with the camper's knife I'd been issued in Mothland, afraid of cutting her.

The temblor wasn't dying down, it was increasing in force; so much dust was shaken free that it was hard to breathe. When I finally got her hands free and the gag off, I tried to ask Ariel how she was, many questions in one. She couldn't hear me over the noise, just turned with a gutsy smile. She was too practical to shield her breasts from sight—she had to brace her arms against the pipe wall—but I could see the self-consciousness in the way she held herself, one feather-touch against my heart, before the flashlight flew free of my hand, the earthquake reached its crescendo, and we were shaken out of the pipe like ants from a boot.

It was terrifying to shoot fifty or a hundred meters on our rear ends, a slide greased by mud, speeding faster every second—but it was also painless. When we rolled out onto the valley floor north of the concrete honeycomb, safe and sound, we both whooped with relief. Ariel was up first, and helped me to my feet, saying my name over and over and laughing. But this was cut short by a tremendous metallic creak from directly above us, where a huge culvert pipe crossed the valley. It was a crack in this pipe, and not a geyser, that had filled the valley with steam, all but obscuring the t-stop to our north. And as the earthquake continued to rumble beneath us, that crack kept tearing wider, and the agonizing sound alone would have sent us running.

We'd covered no more than a hundred paces when a final shriek of tortured metal was followed by an explosion, and we looked back to see a cataract of boiling water pour from the now-split culvert pipe. Perhaps the rain-forest air was going to be a little dryer tomorrow; meanwhile, a scalding river raced toward us. We ran headlong.

The vanguard of the flood must have been cooled by the ground it covered, though it was still as warm as a bath when it hit our legs from behind, nearly bowling us over. It was already hip-deep when we reached the transport-tube opening, but the door stood open just the same. The t-capsule inside was one of the smaller ones, and the same robot voice we'd heard at the Slugland exit announced that only one of us could leave at a time.

"No!" Ariel said fiercely. "We could both fit if we tried. They're not splitting us up again."

The robot couldn't have understood her modern Interlingua, but it repeated its message when we tried to squeeze in together. "Choose your order of departure now," it added insistently, pushing us back with the door buffer. "The water will get hotter."

I translated, fast. "That's a fact, too, it's beginning to steam. Sorry, Ariel, but maybe we'd better—"

She suddenly dodged behind me, then reached around in a tight hug to thwart my attempt to turn and face her, a parody on her seminudity. "No," she said behind my shoulder. "*It won't let us boil,* you'll see." She pushed me forward to jam the entryway again. The robot repeated its warning, Ariel her desire.

Inanimate object, meet the irresistible force. In the absence of a medieval philosopher, I decided to rely on my own specialty, and lie.

"We *can't* separate," I told the machine in Ur-Linguish. "Our, uh, climbing rope is tangled. We have to leave together."

There was no immediate response. Had it failed to understand me? Or was it testing what I'd said against its sensors' image of us?

"Tell it we're boiling," Ariel prompted below my ear, and I translated with real feeling, for the water was perceptibly hotter every second. "This isn't a test," I went on, "it's a rescue. Are you going to let us die?"

We never received a verbal reply, but the buffer snapped back and let us through. A moment later we were inside, packed tightly in water, like shrimp. And the capsule began to move.

It was a long, long trip.

The computer controllers flushed out the water, and for the rest of the journey hot air blasted through the top and bottom vents of the capsule. A robot voice informed us that we should remove our clothes and hold them out to facilitate drying. Actually, it addressed us in the singular—had probably already forgotten that there were two of us, with no room in which to maneuver.

I did manage to get my uniform jacket and pullover shirt off, and held them in either hand. We would have had a hard time getting out of our soaked pairs of pants, though, jammed together so tightly our legs couldn't bend, and we didn't try. So we swayed there in the hot breeze, stripped to the waist and constantly shifting against each other to accommodate the g forces as the capsule followed one of those fast, crazy-curve routes the Hellway designers loved so.

At one moment Ariel might be on top of me, chin hooked over my shoulder, her damp hair a sweet smell in my nostrils, forearms braced between her breasts and my chest; then we might nosedive, her ankles clamped around the backs of my knees, each of us reaching up with both arms to protect our heads, eye to eye and breath to breath; and with any luck at all I'd be on top again before she got her hands down.

A tantalizing mixture of sensations, but to tell the truth, a little too strong. Even when my Column-inscribed silver fly-buttons threatened to pop, I was never far from throwing up—and Ariel looked, if anything, less sure of herself.

We desperately needed a distraction from our distractions, and so, during the horizontal stretches, God help me, we talked. That's when I filled her in on Mishima's real status, and heard the first part of her story.

After Slugland, while I'd been held in limbo, Ariel had arrived in a wild country of rolling hills and steep gorges. She'd been captured immediately. The merc who got the drop on her was past middle age, and wounded, his ribs self-taped. He wanted no more of Ariel than to use her as a pack animal for his gear.

She slowly gathered from his rambling talk that he'd originally arrived with one comrade, and that they'd found tracks indicating that a third person had arrived some hours before them. They'd made the mistake of following the tracks, straight into a tree-fall mantrap that had wounded the older merc and killed his companion.

"They tend to underestimate us, you see," Ariel said. "They think we're a few old professors and their students."

Whoever had set the trap—Mishima hadn't mentioned it. Could it have been Piet Wongama?—had long since found the transport out of the area. The surviving merc had gone back to the entry tube, hoping an exit car would show up there. "That's the other thing: they have only a vague notion of what's going on, or how this place works." But Ariel's arrival had demonstrated that the transport only ran one way.

So they set out on the trek north together, Ariel and her captor. Although he was wary of her, and made her work hard, the merc shared the food and did not abuse her. His bandages made him clumsy, and while the local test wasn't difficult—something about a swinging rope bridge; she didn't go into details—he slipped, and fell to his death.

The next t-station capsule took her to the desert I'd seen in the west. Without a translator, she couldn't make any sense of the travel instructions she was given. Afraid of getting lost in the featureless west, she headed for the high ridge, and found the valley beyond. Unfortunately, Principato and another merc arrived from the rain-forest side soon after.

"Captured again," she said, with a smile that surprised me. The two mercs had quarreled over her. Principato didn't want to share. There was a fight. Principato knocked the other merc unconscious, tucked him into one of the wrecked machines for some reason, and took Ariel along with him.

"Maybe he hit that guy too hard," I said. "We didn't see any signs of life when we passed by later."

"Why did the controllers send so many of us to the same place?" Ariel wondered. "You and Ken made five."

"None of you were supposed to be in the valley," I said. "It's off-limits, for reasons that are now obvious—even robots seem to have a hard time there. Ken and I were only sent to bring the rest of you out . . . It's strange. I didn't think about it at the time, but since when did the controllers start worrying about our safety? That doesn't fit."

"Doesn't it?" Ariel asked. And, somehow ignoring the imperative double nudge of two highly placed nipples, I told her everything Foyle and Helen and I had discussed about the ultimate purpose of the Hellway. I wanted to get back to Ariel's own story, but instead she questioned me closely about the meaning of the Elitist fasces, the contrast with more humane cults like Old Rite Kanalism, Foyle's disillusioned attitude—a host of things I wouldn't have thought important to her. But it killed time. And then we arrived.

"Are we? We are! We're on the surface!" Ariel said at the first sight of a lighter, bluer sky than anything we'd seen in the underworld. Standing outside, she stretched her arms and spun like a pinwheel—a sight to file for future reference.

I pulled myself out after her and got a confused impression of a darkly shadowed bower of leaves with bright sky peeking through it everywhere. "How can that be?"

"I've been hoping for this," Ariel said. "Remember, you said three tests or so per person, and we've each had that. We've graduated."

"But there are only two exits from the Hellway," I objected. "The crypt we came in by, and somewhere near the north pole." I stood and tested the mossy, leaf-encrusted ground with my feet. The branches around us swayed in an unmistakable sea breeze, and I could hear gulls and other birds not far away. "Isn't the pole cold, a wasteland?"

"Well, yes," Ariel admitted. "And what are we *inside*, exactly?"

It was true, we were semienclosed. Although the sky was visible through the leaves on all sides, there was a framework ceiling high above us, covered with vines. And as I looked closer, I saw a similarity between that underside and the surface we were standing on—both reinforced with some sort of metal mesh, as well as tight-packed dirt and tenacious vegetation.

"I don't know," I said. "We'll have to explore." I reached back down for my dried clothes; once I'd retrieved them, the t-tube closed for good. I offered Ariel the jacket, but she wouldn't hear of it. "Not your *uniform*," she said with that peculiar intonation she always used for the word. She wore my shirt instead, and then helped straighten the jacket on me, like a tailor, with two careful tugs at its silly epaulets. Shining with her usual optimism, she headed off toward the nearest clearing, and as usual I followed her lead.

In order to get to the "clearing," we had to go down a flight of stairs, composed of the same planes of metal-reinforced dirt we'd been standing on, to another level. The lattice structure of our environment became more apparent as our eyes adjusted to the rain-forest contrast of light and dark. At one point I stopped just short of walking into one of the vertical metal shafts, as thick as a big tree trunk, that bound it all together. And later, when the breeze was particularly strong, every branch and vine around us swaying, we felt the ground sway a little, too. "Could it be we're in a tree house?" Ariel asked. Then we reached the opening we'd been looking for—a square of uncovered ground that fell off in a dead straight line, like the edge of the world—and saw that it was true.

We were up a tree. Over a kilometer up.

Of course, I could only guess the distance at the time. But our view of an ocean flecked with a few little islands in the distance was an airship view, higher than any tree could draw its sap. The greenery extended all the way down to water level, though; we peered over the edge to confirm that. And it extended upward, too, in the same spiral of overlapping squares, though not very far.

"Not one tree," I said. "A vertical stack of arbors. Vines and trees starting fresh on every floor, but everything blending together. Water must be pumped up. The birds and animals don't even know what altitude they're at."

"Arboria," Ariel said in a small wistful voice. "But not on the surface of the planet."

"No, you would have known if there were anything this tall on the surface. And I'll bet there have to be cables to the ceiling to help hold this thing up."

"It doesn't look like the ceiling, though."

"No. For some reason, they've made a more realistic sky here. Something the humans put in, instead of the Titans. Maybe that's good. Maybe that means you were basically right. We're near the end of the rite of passage, and they've given us an Old Earth kind of sky to graduate under. But where do we go from here?"

"Up," Ariel said without hesitation.

"Okay. But why?"

"Down," she explained, as if to a child, "is too far."

"Fair one," I said, "you are a born leader."

Now that we had an overview, it wasn't so hard to trace the structure upward; it was something like a vast spiral staircase, with more human-sized stairs or ladders to connect the giant steps. We took the climb with as much zest as if our cramped lie-down in the transport tube had been eight hours of sleep. The freshness and vitality of Arboria were contagious.

The sea air tasted delicious, and we walked through contrasts of sunlike light and green coolness. Scented fruits and wildflowers bobbed at the outer edges of the platforms. An endless variety of birds nested in the dark places and flew through the arbors at every angle, adding their songs to the rush of leaves and distant lap of waves. It was an enchanted land, a god's reward for surviving the desert.

This had to be the terminus, all right, the heart of the Elitist dream. What was it poor Brother Francisco had said, at the beginning, in the briefing chamber? He'd been talking about that heroic statue group, the six bronze Elitists recoupling a Titan cable in order to alter Newcount Two's magnetic field to Earth-like proportions—but he might have been talking about this, the inmost bower of the maze in which the refugees had planned to find themselves again: *Making this planet a little Earth, you see; restoring the Garden.*

More evidence. On every other level we passed transport outlets, as if this had been the final gathering place of Hellway survivors in the old days, when hundreds had gone through the tests at a time.

I took less interest in the other machines we saw half-buried in vines and creepers: outfeeds that bubbled black with dirt to replace the stuff that sifted away with each breeze; an unobtrusive gardener robot, with no ears to hear questions; lanternlike shapes raised up on little pedestals, purpose unknown, evidently kept clear of vegetation by the robots. The spur of fear was gone. I didn't really care how this environment worked, if it wasn't a test and a trap.

"I think I see the top ahead of me," Ariel said. "Just a few more turns now. And there's something there."

But I had stopped when the aerial shape fluttered down and hit me. *Moth!* I thought, and nearly smashed it from my forearm. Then I recognized an old friend, just in time.

It was an Earth-style butterfly, with the same near-Monarch markings as the one Ariel and I had seen on the surface. I called back to Ariel and showed her, and continued to marvel at the thing after it had flown away.

So it wasn't the life bombers who'd had the good taste to put that species on this planet. It was the Elitists, nee Avalonians, who had preserved it all the way from Old Earth—who'd had to have it with them even in exile, those first few months when they considered farming the planet's surface. My kind of people, I thought, not for the first time—and how could the same people have loosed the vampire moths on their own children? Would we ever understand this place, now that we were so close to leaving it?

For so we seemed to be. The transport station at the very top was different from any we'd seen before; it was the first one large enough for more than a few people, a huge vine-covered cabin as broad as one square of the arbor lattice, perhaps twenty-five meters across. The largest exit—hence the last? But we weren't quite out of these woods yet. The door wouldn't open.

The usual befuddled computer voice spoke with me when I pushed the single button next to the door. Ariel pressed close behind me; I could feel her body warmth, and the tickle of breath on my ear. By this time my Ur-Linguish skills were almost up to speed, and I was pretty sure of what I reported back to Ariel: "This is the place, all right. Not the finish line itself—but a place where the finishers assemble before going on to the graduation ceremonies. We're the first ones to arrive. And we're officially in limbo for at least eighteen hours."

"Meaning?"

"Meaning no one will interrupt us—or arrive, I mean, for eighteen hours. We can take it easy."

"Idyll in Arboria," she said with that same wistful inflection. "Where do we sleep . . . and eat, and so forth?"

"Back down the stairs. I'll show you."

We stopped at the first pedestal we came to. "The lantern thing on top is what we cook on, and camp around," I explained. I found the button to press, low on the stone base of the dais. It opened up to reveal bundled blankets and, next to them, cans of food and the hardware to prepare it.

"It's like being castaways on an island, isn't it?" Ariel asked dreamily a little later, as we sat on stools disguised as stumps, ate, and watched artificial dusk fall amid the tidal sound of the leaves.

Discomfort is the first thing to fade from memory; with every moment, our transport-tube trip seemed more like an unbelievably wasted opportunity. I was currently recalling Ariel's flesh tones, so white behind the pink that here and there the dawn blue of veins showed through. Knowing that every concealed centimeter was now pressed to my own borrowed shirt, my second skin . . . But eat your dinner, Evan. Build up your strength, as she finishes her story at last. About Principato, remember:

"Well, I knew what would happen when we finally settled in. But I'd thought—he was so arrogant and sure of himself about everything that I thought he'd expect me to want it. To at least talk to me first. But he just didn't bother. Smiled, made little jokes; to himself, really. I tried to get around him one way and another and he *heard* me; he just didn't listen. And after he'd torn my blouse off, and tied me up in a way that would, you know, make things easier for him, and taken off his bandolier, and undone his belt—he stopped, as though something were wrong, as though it were spoiled for him before he started. And you know what?"

"Uh, what?" I was a little startled at the cheerful and matter-of-fact way she was relating all this potentially traumatic stuff—and at the greed with which she ate, too, perfect white teeth gleaming in the lanternlight. Now she paused and considered her words. Her face was screwed up thoughtfully in the way that kept reminding me of a child. But there was nothing unripe or lacking there. What was it I felt, aside from affectionate lust? Something like the revelation I'd once had watching a housecat, and recognizing in it the essential tiger, something stripped down and polished to survive infinitely more keenly than a dodger and dreamer like me. Oh, I'm a survivor, too—going on a hundred-and-something every year now—but of a different and lesser order. The Sneakiae. I love life; but life loved Ariel, and that is all the difference in the world.

"I think I know what it was," she went on finally. "He wanted to have his rape, but not with someone watching. He'd finally noticed there was *someone else in the room*, me, and that was no good. He had to knock me out first. Bashed me on the side of the head. Is the bruise bad, by the way?"

I assured her it wasn't, and she tore into another meatcake, resuming with her mouth full. "I didn't quite black out, but I faked it. Don't know how that would have helped me, though, if we hadn't heard the voices then. God, that was creepy, the echoes and whispers coming from all those pipes. But I didn't let on, kept my eyes closed. Thought I recognized Mishima's voice, wasn't sure about yours. But I hoped, I prayed. And while he took his blowgun and went to take a shot at you, I managed to work my hands half-loose from behind my back and get at one of the spare darts from the bandolier he'd taken off. Hid it behind me. And when the son of a bitch came back for his bandolier, I stabbed him with it."

She shook her head ruefully and wiped a few crumbs away from her mouth. "But I had to keep my eyes shut until the last second, you know—and it's *hard* to just stick someone, too, no matter how much they deserve it; I'd never done anything like that before. So he was able to deflect it, some, and I only got him in the leg.

"He belted me harder that time, and when I came to, he'd already retied and gagged me. He was just finishing his talk with you."

"When did he move you into the shaft, though?" I asked. "I guess he had plenty of time while Mishima and I were climbing, but the poison—"

"He didn't take any chances on getting paralyzed too soon. Alun, he had me stowed down there before he even gave you two the signal to climb. My weight didn't bother him at all on the way down; he did the round trip in, I don't know, two minutes."

I shook my head and swore.

"Oh, he was something, all right," she said. "Something out of a nightmare. I can't tell you how I felt, trapped down there, nothing to keep me company but earthquakes. Then I started to hear bits of conversation, all distorted and echoed. And one voice sounded like yours, but I knew that it was just wishful thinking when I started calling out to you." She paused, a long moment with weight to it. "Just a silly fantasy out of a kid's book, you know, hero in Column whites coming to the rescue. But then the voice was louder. And there you were. And . . . and here we are." She put her plate aside, and I did the same—I know a cue when I hear it. She crossed over to where I sat, and very simply pulled the shirt over her head.

I reached for her waist where she stood and drew her close, my lips pressed, in that position, against her pale, taut belly. I could feel a distant tom-tom heartbeat, hers or mine, and tasted lightly salted girlflesh. There was a brief moment of civil war—north or south?—but two things had preyed on my mind all that long teasing t-trip, and I nuzzled upward to attend to them. A few full but pointed moments later and I had to stand up, too, long enough for Ariel to drink off a deep kiss and unbutton my jacket.

She slipped her hands under it then, but when I started to shrug it all the way off, she pulled her lips from mine. "Please," she said. Her eyes were shining with the strongest kind of fantasy, the kid's-book kind, and her voice already had the perfect confidence of a lover, of one who can ask anything: "Please, Alun, leave it on." Even as one hand dropped to undo my belt, the other came up and out to secure that jacket, fingers twining passionately in a crisp white epaulet. "Wear it the first time, anyway . . ."

And a man in uniform doesn't argue with orders.

Chapter Twenty-four

WHEN IT FIRST drifted into view, around "dawn," the butterfly seemed uninterested. But at the first sight of Ariel he hitched up short, in midair—and then lit on her shoulder, stunned, wings out flat. Taking us in.

I was trying to make sense of it myself, newly wakened after a night of little sleep. Somehow we'd managed, in a night of urgent and endless entwining, to weave our bodies into an outward-sloping wall of vines just past the edge of an arbor, I not quite on my back and Ariel sprawled across me. There was nothing beneath our green mesh mattress except a straight drop of over a kilometer, ending in the gray underworld sea.

The butterfly on Ariel's shoulder remained flat and stunned. My girl even *slept* greedily, not a muscle moving. What in God's name, the Monarch must have been thinking, had these two wingless, naked, incredibly fragile humans thought they were doing, to put themselves in such a situation?

Seemed like a good idea at the time. It had been darker then, of course—and busier—and we'd both been feeling rather immortal. Extrication would be a delicate business. As always.

But now Ariel has raised her head and blinked those cornflower eyes at the Monarch on her shoulder, and the wings remain poised, their poetic owner captivated. I see it now, her wondering half-drowned look and slow smile, the aimless drift of fine blonde hair in the sea breeze that swings us, the cloud color of her shoulder at first light, and the Monarch's wings like sunrise against it. I feel her against me, the fingers clutched to my shoulders, the warmth here and the moistness there. And smell the scents and hear the sounds, too.

Please. Let me recall it all, just as clearly, when I am very old.

Problem: if the arbor was an assembly point, then mercenaries would be arriving alongside our own people. There wasn't much we could do about that; there were too many entrance tubes to guard, even if we had weapons. We could only take cover, as near as possible to the locked exit door.

But first I took one more crack at interrogating the computer there, and the more I learned, the less likely it seemed that we had to hide. Only as the eighteen hours' grace period came to its estimated close did Ariel succeed in dragging me away to play it safe.

We cut it close. Scant minutes after we'd carefully worked our way into the secret center of a large bush, we heard someone approach—not by the tread, for the eternal rustling masked such sounds, but by the sudden agitation of the birds.

It might be Harry, or Piet Wongama. Or Mishima, if he'd survived the quake. But we feared it would be none of them, and it wasn't.

It was Foyle.

If we hadn't called her name as we broke cover, she might have accidentally fired the big crossbow she'd picked up somewhere, but seeing Ariel, she lowered it with a shaky smile.

We saw she'd also made a spear for herself—a polished straight branch with a hunting knife's blade whipped into its split tip. Her clothing showed similar Robinson Crusoe touches: she'd converted one of the heavy blankets from Mothland into a surcoat over the harness of her old backpack, and had replaced her stiff boots with mocassins made from something small, furry, and luckless.

Lowering the bow, she looked doubly glad to see us—both for who we were, and for who we might have been but weren't.

"Another safe team-up. Luck of the draw?" she said after less coherent greetings had been exchanged.

We told her what little we knew about that. First Ariel filled her in on the death toll in Slugland and the Valley Backstage, and then I relayed what I'd just learned from the computer.

"Up until now, the computers' goal has been to keep mixing and matching the pilgrims, to team each individual with as many others as possible," I said. "But this final phase is different. Sort of a celebration of the comradely ties we're supposed to have made earlier. At this assembly point—and at another Arboria like it, the door said, just over the eastern horizon—pilgrims are to be reunited with all their earlier partners to form a larger team. There will be two of these reunion teams, of roughly equal size. And our Hellway trip will end with a race between them, across the sea to the surface exit at the north pole."

Foyle looked puzzled. "And in Elitist times—"

"The scheduling was more complicated, lots more people, but the basic idea was the same. In fact, our small numbers have made us harder, not easier, for the computers to deal with. The door computer kept asking me about the deaths along the way, but couldn't understand my answers. They were outside its experience."

"Alun, you act like this is all good news," Ariel said.

"It is, once you hear the numbers. There are only fifteen pilgrims still in the game, that's what it told me. And for this final ocean race, they're to be divided as evenly as possible. Well, work it out. Seven or eight on a team. Which four or five will be sent to join us at this Arboria? The people who've been teamed with us in the past. That includes all our original party!"

"We've been with plenty of mercenaries, too."

"But how many of them *survived* being teamed with one of us? It's a pretty grisly record, when you think about it. Father Francisco poisoned his two, you survived one who'd already lost a comrade, Principato probably killed another and may be dead himself, Mishima and Lagado saw a few drowned . . . Our knowledge of the language has been worth a hell of a lot more than their military training. So it's mainly our friends who are coming here to join us, and if Mishima survived, there'll only be one or two mercenaries in addition. We'll outnumber them here."

"There'll still be an all-merc group over the horizon, then," Foyle said. "Racing us to the pole, which is right where we don't want them."

"But however this race works—the door won't give the details yet—the mercs are going to be at a disadvantage," I said. "Because without one of us to interpret what's going on for them, how will they know where to go, or how? I'd say that for the first time the odds are definitely in our favor. At least, if—"

"If Mishima and Harry and Piet Wongama are still alive," Foyle broke in. "If it's not just twelve mercenaries and us three."

"It can't be," Ariel said. "Not if the mercs have lost as many as we think."

"I've done my bit there, at any rate," Foyle said matter-of-factly. "And as long as I'm still armed and ready, maybe there's time for me to eat. Show me how; I'm famished."

"I'm still surprised to see you alive, Commissioner," she said, tucking into her second sandwich. "From the air, that pool you jumped into looked solid with eels."

Despite grime and exposure and makeshift clothing, Foyle was still sharp as a knife. She'd already let me know, with the cock of an eyebrow and a certain smile, that she could guess my new relationship with Ariel. Imagination, or bad conscience, made me read a warning in that expression as well: *Don't use her badly; she's my friend.* And she was always looking for more information, more control of events.

"The eels didn't bother me, though," I told her, and gave a few details. ". . . In fact, something occurred to me later. It could be that the eels were programmed to lose their power to shock during the mating period—it makes sense, for their own sake. So the worst thing I experienced in the pool was seeing how badly my plan had screwed up for you and Helen."

"We took a calculated risk," Foyle said, shaking her head. "Yours worse than ours. But the landing was bad, all right. We overshot the lake so high and so far, the balloon eel didn't even try to redrop. We kept bobbing up and down as we drifted—I guess all it could think to do was try to find an altitude where the wind would blow us back south. But of course there wasn't one. Its control became worse and worse, and after a few hours we crashed into the side of a hill."

"That's when Helen . . . ?"

"Died? Yes. One way or another. The watchers came for her while I was knocked out."

"Watchers?" Ariel asked.

"The robots that must referee this game," I told her.

Foyle nodded. "The tracks I found the next morning were robotic. They'd left behind extra food and water for me, having determined, I guess, that I was still fit enough to hike back to the pool. But they must have decided that Helen couldn't. She'd failed the test, and she was gone. I like to think she was still unconscious when they passed judgment on her."

Ariel opened her mouth, then paused as if thinking better of what she'd meant to say. "And you found the pool again?"

"It wasn't so hard. Walking against the wind kept me going south to the ridge, and the plateau was visible for some distance."

Apparently the controllers counted her hike back as a second test, since she'd only been one more place since then.

She'd been able to tell, inspecting the soft ground around her entry tube, that she was the first to arrive there. Since her new partners might be mercenaries, she laid a path into the forest that ended in a trap, and sprang it when she saw their uniforms.

So it was she who wounded one merc and killed his companion, whose crossbow she had subsequently recovered. Of course, she'd had no way of knowing that this would cause Ariel to be sent in as a reinforcement for the man killed, leading to more trouble later.

While she finished her meal, I digested her story. Neat work, to contrive a falling-tree mantrap in a few hours. One of those guerrilla skills she'd picked up . . . where? On the Vesper Preserve, I guessed, when the government tried to open that wildlife sanctuary to colonists—and when, if I was right, her husband's Kanalist ideals had started the war of resistance that had killed him. Yes. If the Column government had hired the Iron Brotherhood to take Vesper for them, that would explain where she'd dealt with mercs before, and why she showed cold pleasure at having to kill some of them now.

An adequate theory, and the few questions it left unanswered—such as how a former rebel against the Column had obtained amnesty—were none of my business. But she was certainly a fascinating woman, in her dangerous way.

And she'd been digesting our stories, too.

"I'm trying to fit this final race business into the overall picture," she said. "I guess it makes sense. Another Hitler Youth Camp activity, building team spirit for a soldier people."

I nodded.

"The question is," she went on, "whether the ordeals are over. Or will sharks attack the boats we race in—that sort of thing?"

And now Ariel spoke up, as if she'd been holding something back for a long time. She looked better than ever that morning, once more in my shirt. There was a certain glow about her that

I could take credit for, having polished all her surfaces the night before. But she'd stopped smiling, and looked ready for any argument she might start.

"I'm not sure I understand this theory you two have about the Hellway, its purpose and all," she said. "Or maybe it's just that I don't believe it. Foyle, why would you think the Elitists would subject their children to . . . ordeals, as you call them?"

Foyle patiently explained the political significance of the "sign of mastery" we'd encountered at the entrance to the Hellway. "Somewhere along the line," she said, "the Elitists must have become fascists, just the way the Kanalists of a hundred years ago became the first Columnards." At this Ariel glanced at me, but I let the "seditious" statement slide; I'd already established that Commissioner Parker was a tolerant character. "I don't pretend to understand the full fascist mentality, but clearly the Hellway exists to weed out the less hardy elements of a master race."

"But that's not clear to me at all," Ariel argued. "Maybe I'm the one who's wearing blinders here, but to me it's just the other way around. It's clear to me that the Hellway *isn't* supposed to kill people."

"How can you—"

"Look, the place is *broken*. You'll concede that much, won't you? It's been without human supervision for hundreds of years, and the robots haven't been able to keep it properly maintained."

"Yes, but—"

"And isn't it always the *broken* parts that kill people? Let's just take it piece by piece. The only danger in my first test came from a wall that had crumbled away with age. And it was tunnel damage that caused those slugs to adapt into meat-eaters."

"Yes, but what about *our* first test?" Foyle said—almost furious for some reason. "The moths, the electric eels?"

Ariel just looked at me, and sure enough, I found myself supporting her. "Remember, the plaque there did warn us about a danger to the west, Foyle. I said it even then—judging by the piñata gourds, it looked as though the moth territory might have drifted across the pilgrim path from the west. The robots should have prevented that, over the centuries, but since the system *is* partly broken—"

"And the eels?"

"We were warned against them, too, really—we were given canteens so that we wouldn't go into the river for water. But we needed the eel-balloon to make the trip in one day, by air, instead of enduring a dull march of three days or more. 'Endurance or ingenuity,' remember? And I *did* see a staircase next to the waterfall at the end of that test, for pilgrims who had made the whole distance on foot. I remember thinking, How could anyone have reached that staircase, given the moths?''

''Whereas, if the moths weren't supposed to be there . . .'' Ariel said.

''But we *were* supposed to ride an eel-balloon,'' Foyle said. ''And remember, we used a piñata gourd for a gondola, and those gourds were created by moths.''

''We didn't need that, though,'' I countered. ''With the supercord and those heavy blankets, there were plenty of other ways we could have harnessed ourselves to the balloon. The gondola was convenient for us because Helen was so weak then—a problem that wouldn't have come up if we'd all been eighteen years old, and if there had been no moths.''

''And the pool of electric eels at the end of the flight?'' Foyle said.

''You and I assumed that the pool was deadly. So we made arrangements that caused the balloon to crash. If we'd allowed the balloon to make the landing that it was supposed to make, though—you would have found out, as I did, that mating eels are harmless. Helen might have drowned, but again, she wasn't meant to be there, in that condition. As it was—she may have died in the crash. We don't know that the robots killed her.''

''You're buying it, aren't you?'' Foyle asked me. ''You're rationalizing everything.''

Ariel shook her head. ''There are no inconsistencies to rationalize. The other deaths have occurred because we and the mercs are at war, another hazard that clearly wasn't built into this place. Notice, the robots keep asking us why so many of us are dying. And they kept sending reinforcements into the Valley Backstage when it looked like we were having trouble with it. I mean, it all fits. Am I the one who's being dumb about this? Tell me where I'm wrong.''

Foyle no longer looked so angry. ''I . . . don't know,'' she said. ''Back at the beginning, at the Elitist cemetery, reading the notices on the family plots, we noticed that a lot of rich families seemed to have adopted children of Hellway age—as if they'd lost their own. And we definitely found some funeral markers for children who'd died in the Hellway.''

''Very few, though,'' Ariel pointed out. ''There were bound

to be a few. This place was meant to be an adventure, to take people to the edge of danger; that's why it's turned so bad without maintenance. But no matter where you grow up, no matter how humane the planet is, the rite of passage involves risk. On my home world, you knew you were an adult when they gave you your license to drive—and every year, a few of us crashed and died."

Foyle didn't say "Good point"—so I did.

"Understand, I'm not arguing with you about the Elitists' politics," Ariel said. "You two are the archaeologists; you know the symbols and the implications, not me.

"Oh, I admit, when Helen and the friar laid out the history for us, back in the statue chamber, I did identify with the Elitists a little bit. Their rebellion against the Avalonians seemed to me a lot like my own rebellion against the place I was born—another overdeveloped welfare state, founded by much the same people. And I liked to think that the Elitists were all like me, just individuals looking for room to be themselves in. It would be nice to think that you could build a whole society around that sort of person—the way old-timers talk about the Federal Alignment."

Ariel paused thoughtfully. "And I'd still like to believe it. I could see a society like that using the Hellway, unbroken, to give its children a special self-confidence. Where I come from, you just graduated into adulthood; it must make a difference to feel you *earned* it. And that you earned it with friends, that you can cooperate with all sorts of people even in tight groups. Your young individualists would need that lesson, or else you'd just get an every-man-for-himself society.

"But I admit it, Foyle. Fascists would have just as much use for self-confident kids with good teamwork skills. Who wouldn't? The politics behind the Hellway could come from almost any direction. But the one thing I don't see is the parents killing off their children in bunches, for no reason. There's no evidence."

Foyle looked subdued. "No argument," she admitted finally.

"It's strange," I said. "There really is no argument. You have everything on your side, Ariel, but I never saw it either. Foyle was sure the Elitists had to be monsters, and something inside me was sure she had to be right. Fatalistic, I guess."

"I can't explain it." Foyle gave a crooked smile. "Even now, I *want* to think you're wrong, Ariel. I want the Elitists painted the blackest black—a people who died out six hundred years ago. Why the hell do I care? What's it to me?"

"I . . . have a notion," Ariel began. "I'd like to run it past you, just out of curiosity, but it is a little personal." And I realized that they *had* been friends of some sort, for weeks before I met them, and that Ariel might know more about Foyle's past than I did. "I don't want to offend you . . ."

"Go ahead," Foyle told her. "I can stand it."

"Well," Ariel said, "is it possible that you have some personal identification in this matter, too? Every time you—and Alun, too, for some reason—every time you talk about the Elitists, you always wind up talking about the Kanalists instead. One group dead and gone, the other alive and powerful; there's no special similarity I can see. I mean, history's full of secret societies and religions and political movements. Is Kanalism so important to you that *everything* has to be compared to it?"

"Kanalism *isn't* alive," I protested. "Not the real thing."

"Only the Old Rite lodges—" Foyle said simultaneously.

Ariel smiled as if she'd won a point but wanted to be a good sport about it. "The Kanalists reformed—or sold out—and the Alignment became the Column. And that's the great tragedy of this century, isn't it? I mean, to someone who really believed in Federalism, who identified with the Old Rite?"

"It was Roger—my husband who really loved it." There was something hurt and broken in Foyle's voice, though her face remained the same. And Ariel knelt next to her.

"Not just him," Ariel went on. "Even—even our commissioner here feels the attraction of those old ideals; it's obvious every time he talks about them. Now to me, government is something you work around, that's all. Old people tell me that the Alignment was a better place, and maybe so. Still, it's a hundred years gone. But for some reason you two care. You're archaeologists, historians; for you the past *is* alive, and—and beautiful, I guess. You see yourselves living like Kanalist heroes in a free republic—"

"But it's just a dream," Foyle said dully. "There never was such a time or place. Not for long. If you listen to the pretty lies, and try to make them come true, as my Roger did, they'll just kill you. That's the way it's always been."

"Is it?" Ariel asked. "Or isn't it just less painful to think so? Less of a tragedy, anyway. If a people somewhere die fighting for freedom, well, you can tell yourself that they would only have become tyrants in their own turn. If that *always* happens, you never have to feel sorry for the Elitists, or the Alignment, or—"

"Or Roger. Or myself, you mean," Foyle finished for her. An astonishing thing had happened, in this place where the ground shook with every scented breeze: Foyle had begun to cry. "Sold out by others before I was born, you see. Poor thing." She swore. "It's so *sick*, and I always knew that. But I didn't know that it could keep me from seeing straight."

"God, you're hard on yourself," Ariel said. "You lost your husband, you lost a whole world you loved. Don't you have a *right* to be sorry? What are you supposed to be, superhuman?"

Foyle laughed through her tears. "Yes! It's the only way I do keep the faith. Oh, don't try to understand me, girl—or that handsome sellout behind you, either. I don't know why, but he's another one like me. He doesn't know if he's ten times better than everyone else, or a hundred times worse. It's the Kanalist disease: hypertrophy of the free will. We hold ourselves responsible for everything we do—and everything we don't do, too. So this one wears the uniform of a state he doesn't believe in, probably does more good than harm, but hates himself all the same. Like me, like every true Kanalist, he knows he *could* have been something great instead—a rebel, an artist, an explorer. Something. Another Evan Larkspur."

Birds sang, and the leaves shushed them. Foyle wept on Ariel's shoulder, and Ariel searched my face for God knows what.

But I turned away and left. That's what I'm famous for, if you think about it.

Chapter Twenty-five

SOON OTHERS CAME. We tried to play king of the mountain, get the drop on each new arrival, but it wasn't possible.

We'd been hoping for Harry Lagado to show up. He did, and ran into someone we were past hoping for, a few leafy levels beneath us, before we could find and "ambush" them. So we missed a family reunion—Harry's father, Ruy, had survived, despite the report Mishima had given me of their test together.

Ariel and I hadn't seen Harry since Slugland, which seemed

like weeks before. Forty-eight hours! Now, after more essential information had been exchanged, he told us that his next stop had been a sub-world of snowy highlands—a ski run, in fact. The test—considering the sheltered nature of former Elitist life—was probably just figuring out how to ski. The mercs who'd arrived before him had left tracks in the snow, making it easy to trail cautiously behind. He'd brought both his ski poles on to Arboria for possible use as weapons.

His father's story was more complicated. Although he did not accuse Ken Mishima of having abandoned him back in the land of fjords, he certainly couldn't explain how they'd become separated. Wandering a rocky shore, he had survived something like a tidal wave to eventually meet up with referee robots. They'd failed to understand his attempts to communicate, but had sent him to an even more luxurious-sounding limbo than mine, and twenty-four hours of rest.

It was good to see them together, the skinny boy hovering protectively over his dad, as usual. They felt like family to me, too; the whole archaeological party did. Oddballs and misfits, with nearsighted enthusiasms and a sleepwalker's talent for survival—no wonder they considered me their natural leader. Was it another argument against the Elitist fascism theory that the Hellway tended to favor our kind but killed the professional hard guys right and left?

But no, we'd taken losses, too, and now I felt them more keenly. I hadn't registered the fact of Helen Hogg-Smythe's death before—it had seemed somehow impossible that she would not be with us when we reached the center of the riddle. The Hellway had belonged to her, because she'd accepted it; she'd still found it beautiful, even after the moth attack. We were not beyond needing her special comprehension, but the world had slipped from her embrace.

And what about Piet Wongama, first-rate problem solver and fair sprinter? He belonged on the team if anyone did, but had been lost from view since he'd shared his first test with the Lagados. That meant two team-ups with mercs. Would we see him again, alive?

Yes and no.

We heard one sharp scream above the birdcalls. Amazingly, Foyle let me have the crossbow, since she was the only one who'd practiced with her spear, and we descended several levels—a party of five, four armed. Tendrils grabbed at our ankles, branches slashed at our heads, fans of foliage baffled our eyes. And yet we were only seconds too late.

The little clearing was neatly square, with a supply pedestal standing in the middle like an enlarged chess pawn and two transport tubes facing each other from opposite edges. The dead bodies broke the symmetry like litter.

The merc's head had been bashed in. A bloody shillelagh lay not far away, and Piet Wongama lay just beyond that—skinny limbs splayed but not relaxed, like a junked marionette's, his freckled face twisted in a final expression of anger and pain. There was blood on his back, but the knife that had killed him was elsewhere, in the fist of the one man still standing.

Ken Mishima.

Mishima's poker face served him well. His only reply to our hostile stares was:

"I was too late."

Foyle and Harry were moving in on his flanks, poised to lunge with spear and ski pole. But he seemed more concerned with the crossbow bolt I had aimed at him.

"Too late to get rid of the knife?" I asked.

He knew what I was getting at, but shook his head.

"I arrived through that tube," he said, gesturing. "They had come before me. They were struggling. Piet's stick fell when the knife struck home. I picked up the stick and used it—but I was too late. Perhaps I should have attacked the trooper barehanded instead, but I know Brotherhood training; we teach the knife well."

" 'We'?" Harry said, his voice high and strained.

That, at least, shook him. He started to ask me something—"You haven't told them?" perhaps—but shut his mouth again as Ariel breathlessly filled the kid in from the sidelines.

"He's supposed to be on our side now, though?" Harry asked.

"We have an agreement," Mishima said to me. "And I've held to it. I've killed one of my own brothers in defense of your party. What more can you ask of me?"

"I understood your story the first time," I said. "But I think there's plenty more to ask . . . If the rest of you don't mind, I'd like to conduct this interrogation in private."

They left us alone. I was amazed at the trust they placed in my integrity and prowess at arms. The only genuine superiority

I had over Mishima, of course, was that my cover story had stood up better.

Mishima had not gone pale; he was not sweating; his eyes were not searching for some means of attack. But I could feel the hairs on my arms stirring as if the air around him were charged, and pulling the crossbow trigger would have felt like pulling the ripcord on a parachute.

"I know you too well to think you'd do anything rash now," he said.

"Do you?"

"I admit I underestimated you at first. Your technique is flawless—the master who appears a dilettante. Even when I caught you going through my tent at camp and you blocked my Cobra Opening so naturally, I thought it a lucky move. But I have been the fool. No one could have survived so many perils on mere luck."

"It's hard for anyone to survive around you, it seems."

Deftly misinterpreting, he shrugged and gestured, not at Wongama's body, but at the merc's. "We made a deal. I agreed to protect the civilians, even at this cost."

"Wongama was a big man, fit and smart. He got this far despite your brothers. Suppose you arrived just after *he* used the stick."

"I did not kill him, the trooper did," he said. "Examine the knife. You will find it standard Brotherhood issue."

"But so are you, Colonel. That doesn't prove anything. I have to judge your protective skills by what I've seen—and I haven't seen much. You ditched me back in the valley."

"I took a ninja star meant for you, and kept Principato pinned down long enough for you to escape. You know I did my duty, you just want me to feel guilty. You play a deep game. But don't you still need me on your team?"

"Are you worth more to me than Wongama?"

"In combat—"

"In combat I need men I can trust. Lagado has also survived. He shares my low opinion of your protection."

"I was teamed with him before you and I made our deal. It was nothing personal; if I had needed him, I would have looked after him. Please, do not underestimate me as I did him, and you. You need me."

"Maybe. There's no way to know, now, how Wongama survived the team-ups he must have had with your brothers. He may have had to give them information. And the better the brothers understand what's going on, the more likely we are to encounter them at the pole." I told him what little I knew about the coming race across the sea. "It's a golden opportunity for us to leave them all behind, but it's also their best chance to catch us all in one spot. If we do meet them, what can you do for us? Can you order them to leave us alone?"

He considered it, but finally had to shake his head. "I have no op codes, no password. The recognition routine I used with Principato is just a convenience for nonemergency situations. It's not secure; we could have tortured it out of one of them by now, and they'll know that." I may have looked unconvinced, because he went on. "Principato wouldn't have played along with it himself, except that he needed the antidote I was carrying. I could lie to you and tell you they'll obey me—but there's no chance. You need me to help kill them. There's no other way."

"There will be seven or eight of them."

He shrugged. "Four for you, four for me."

"Maybe we should offer them odds, to make it interesting."

I'm not sure I'd ever seen him smile before. "A master's joke. But you don't fool me anymore. At the very beginning, you took out two of them in an elevator, unarmed. That's you. And as for them, the confusion at the command level has been reflected in their performance; they've fumbled everything. We have a chance. The Foyle woman will be a help. But you need me."

I fixed his eyes with mine. "I require at least three scalps from you. That buys your life. A fourth clears your Brotherhood's record with the Column. Is that absolutely clear?"

He didn't put his hand over his heart this time. But the way he looked at me, as if at a master, would have been reassuring—if there'd been a master anywhere near.

I stepped forward, to the edge of the world. And fell off. . . . Wings again, and falling, with the usual slight variations—Nightmare Number 1.1, perhaps. Again a lecture, again an escape on Daedalus/DaVinci wings that isn't an escape at all, not really above the maze, merely lost at a higher level. And falling again, falling, falling toward a metallic watery glitter. And now, with more realism than usual, I hear low moans from the leading edges of my wings, warning that my dive is too steep, that I am about to lose control. But this time the magic is on my side—I have but to straighten my hand backward, nothing up my sleeve, and the dive flattens. I roll out at a slight angle into level flight.

And here's the part that takes faith. Here's the part I, like you, must resolutely pretend to believe, because otherwise the play fails both actor and audience:

This time, it is not a dream.

I'd never even thought to wonder why we'd all been sent to the *top* of Arboria—how a race across the sea to the north pole could proceed from there. But the race was by air. We'd been given wings.

Mishima's bloody arrival had completed our "reunion team." Accordingly, the door to the imitation cabin in the topmost arbor had finally opened for us, revealing an equipment room and a small holo theater. A computer referee briefed us on our flying gear and the rules of the race we would fly against the merc team. With me to translate the Ur-Linguish, we would have an advantage over the mercs, though unfortunately many of the holograms were self-explanatory.

After the briefing and my translations, the only hard part was the actual moment of jump-off. The wings would not unfurl until their wearer was already in midair. Meanwhile they rode my shoulders, intricately folded back and forth across the small but supercharged electric motor whose blower pointed up and down my spine. To add to the feeling that I might fall like a stone, my legs were shackled, locked into metal braces extending from a rigid plastic corselet. My whole lower body was under the rig's computer control, just barely permitting a stiff-legged little walk to the edge of the wooden jump platform.

Of course, I'd been told that one hard slap at the palm-sized silver disk strapped across my solar plexus would cause the whole apparatus to peel itself away from me, revealing the underlying parachute ready at my stomach. And my arms, at least, were free enough to make that movement. But it still took faith to jump—blind, unwarranted faith that the mind quite rightly rebelled at. To any creature that thinks and feels and imagines, there is nothing harder than falling off a log.

And so I stood, the rest of the party lined up behind me in similar gear, with Mishima and Foyle at the end to provide a little push if one of the others balked. Ruy Lagado in particular had seemed reluctant, despite our assurances that the devices had always been intended for first-timers just like us.

Most of Arboria was invisible from its top rung, the world all sky and breeze. Maybe that was just as well. There was no perspective, no sense of our true height. Just one moment of empty-bellied doubt.

But the strange contraption worked flawlessly. I pitched forward in the advised lateral dive. The wings unfolded behind and above and to either side. Servomotors in the lower braces reshaped my body to trim as the tailrudder unscrolled to join my legs together. And when I tried the hand control, it worked.

Floating on my stomach in midair, I banked cautiously into a wide circle around the supertrellis. For the first time I noticed that it cast no shadow on the sea—because, of course, this bright sky had no sun. And I'd been right, cables did connect Arboria to the ceiling, though they were slender enough that the eye couldn't follow them very far. I heard the cries of the others only dimly, concentrating on the pull of the wing harness upward, the breeze breaking against my thrown-back head.

I was flying—soon we all were—and in surprisingly little time all sense of the mechanism fell away. The control was simple and intuitive, a glove on the left hand. It responded to the same gesture children use to pantomime the flight of an aircraft: with fingers parallel to the forearm, you fly level; rotate the wrist to bank left or right; pull the fingers back or push them forward to go up or down. Or use the other hand to hit the red button on the back of the glove and go to autopilot, free to use both arms for other purposes while continuing in your last set course.

It was also possible to set a course verbally using the helmet of the rig, whose microphone communicated with a guidance computer. The helmet's clear visor was actually a sophisticated scanner, which could superimpose on your current view magnified images of other fliers along with cues to their current location relative to you. Not that the helmets had radar or cameras; the images were clever computer animations, based on information beamed from somewhere else—hidden sensors on the ceiling, or in the sky itself.

The helmet automatically scanned for the nearest objects in the general direction it was pointed, the level of zoom adjusting to the frame of the visor, with a scale reading below. You could get other views with a few verbal commands, as well as lock the wing's guidance computer onto the object pictured. But these features required repetition of the tricky Ur-Linguish consonants in the words we'd been taught. That elected me flight leader.

The glove and the helmet would have been wildly inadequate for controlling a flitter, or even a glider, but this was a different kind of flying. The winged exoskeleton's computers decided how literally to take our commands, keeping us from excessive dive speeds or total stalls, and never even consulted us on the throttle control of the turbines on our backs or the trim of our legs and the jointed wings. But control did not feel secondhand; we went unthinkingly where we wanted to go, as in a dream. Despite a few details that never come up in dream flights—the queasy feeling of the dives, the stiffness in the neck from holding the head back all the time—it was exhilarating. Our low speeds permitted wondrous aerobatics, tight turns and quick rolls, an almost birdlike freedom.

Once we'd pulled away from the great green column of Arboria, most of the others couldn't help playing around a little, veering farther and farther apart to avoid collisions. I yelled at Harry or Foyle when I thought they were swooping and curving too far away, but they rarely heard me. It was partly the white noise of the impeller fans on our backs and partly the thinner air, but voices just didn't carry. Too late now, I wished we'd worked out more hand signals.

It was all happening too fast. While my left hand kept me level, my right tightened on the grip of my loaded crossbow. In the briefing cabin, I'd lectured the party only as long as I dared, afraid of letting the mercs get a lead on us. Had it been enough? Did we really know what we were doing?

"The trick is to remember all the things that I can translate for you, but which none of the mercs will have understood. The warnings, in particular. Stay out of clouds—they're full of dangerous turbulence. Avoid the birds who nest on the pylons we're supposed to be racing around; they'll get aggressive if you come too near. And most important—the referee voice put a lot of stress on this one—check your altitude buckle at all times! If it flashes red, you're in danger of going too high."

"Does the air get too thin or something?" Harry had asked.

"No, that's not a problem here. The danger's more basic than that. Have you noticed that the sky is different over Arboria, more lifelike? Well, in fact that's just another kind of ceiling, and you can crash right into it without seeing how close you are; that buckle is your only warning, so don't forget it."

"Why don't the computers in the wings protect us against these things, if they protect us from falling?" Lagado had complained.

"It's not supposed to be entirely safe," I'd said. "It's an

obstacle course. There are hazards, and goals, too. If we were taking this seriously as a race, we would be competing to see who could collect the gold hoops that dangle off the pylons, and so forth. Only the mechanics of staying in the air have been simplified, so that they won't distract us.''

But it was distracting, all the same, as much fun as perhaps it had been meant to be. Now I tried to put the layout back in perspective. The Hellway was an elongated cavern and we were finally approaching its V-shaped northern limit. Our Arboria had stood at one end of an east-west starting line; there was another Arboria at the other end, out of sight over the horizon. We were racing north-northeast and the mercs were racing north-northwest toward the point of the V.

The intended line of flight wasn't hard to guess, though we had no compasses. There were a few islands in the sea below, dun and green, dappled with rocks and guano, as real as anything in the Hellway—but shaped like the arrows on a street sign. Which is more or less what they were.

Each party would pass six ''pylons'' along the way to the finish line, and then the two paths would converge just past a common seventh one near the end. No party would officially finish until it had collected six gold hoops from the pylons, and the party that returned with the seventh would be the winner of the race, irrespective of finishing time. But of course we didn't give a damn about that part.

The wind sang past me. Not like ballooning, but just as big a kick. Especially now that the others had eased my mind, having found the formation we'd planned. I rested my neck a moment, taking in the unshadowed sea.

Aside from the arrow islands, it was almost featureless, no color bands of varying depths. But it was a real ocean; there was life in it. Shoals of fish could be half-seen sometimes, once the big diving birds had whitely pointed them out. The birds had the wings of Terran fishhawks, but their heads and beaks were square-cornered and ugly, and the calls they threw back and forth were articulated into something like angry words. I hoped the others remembered all my warnings.

Twenty minutes later we caught our first sight of the second type of island we'd been told about. An imitation volcano. The cone shape looked authentic, but it was too small to be the real thing, nor did it smoke at all—real volcanoes are poisonous with flying ash. But there was a red glow inside it, and a visible ripple of heated air dangling above.

"What's the point of them, then?" Ariel had asked. "Just local color?"

"Another hazard," Foyle speculated. "The thermal updrafts?"

"Only a hazard if you go into them without thinking," I said. "Actually, they're meant as a convenience. The referees assume we'll be doing a lot of diving—for fun, I guess. Flying back up under power is slow, so the volcano updrafts are provided as a quick alternative. You spiral around the outside, see—careful to peel away before you get too high."

Harry had laughed. "They're ski lifts!"

"That's about the size of it."

The next tourist attraction did not come from the sea, but from the sky. First it was just a hazy blue shape in the distance, like a child's top. Then it became a small hill, upside down. Then a top-heavy mountain of rock and steel, terraced with plants—but still floating in midair. From its downward-pointing peak, a gold hoop dangled like an elephant's earring.

So this was a pylon, actually a huge artificial stalactite hanging down from the underworld's true ceiling. But the bright blue plane of false sky cut off sight of the connection above.

Of all the wonders of the Hellway, this seemed most surreal and poetic, this inverted aerial island. Here the universe had shrunk to the scale it had had in my childhood. When my parents had told me of other planets, I'd imagined them something like this, as if I could sail a catboat to one, and dock there.

And that was only the first pylon. The next, twenty minutes further on, was just as extensive but less massy, full of cutouts, wide caves you could see through to the other side. More elaborate plant life filled the outer terraces, and within the holes the big birds had made nests over a meter across, where we could see and hear their young squalling for food like human babies. Here the gold hoop did not dangle from the bottom, but from the end of a pole that jutted to one side so that it could be hooked by a flier without disturbing the birds.

"These hooks are works of art," Foyle had said sadly. "Robots didn't carve these."

It was true. The hooks were wrought of a black hardwood,

each nearly the size of an umbrella. The catching ends were carved with the heads of birds and snakes, lighting bolts, and other decorative motifs, each one different. They were tail ends of a folk history, and it was cruel, what Mishima and I were asking the archaeologists to do.

But we had too few weapons, and so the hunting knives were brought out to whittle the curved ends down and make them weapon-sharp. After she had thought it over a moment, Foyle also suggested putting grooves in the handles and tying towlines to them; she'd salvaged several spools of supercord from Mothland. "Swinging these things like flails would be useless. And we don't want to fight in that close, anyway. We want to throw or tow the hooks into their wings."

"Do we?" Ruy Lagado had asked softly. In the end, I had given him Foyle's spear for last-ditch defense; no flyer, he knew he'd never be able to maneuver one of the tow-hooks. Surprisingly, Ariel had felt the same way, and had taken the other ski pole. "These things aren't like flitters," she'd said, shaking her head. "Not my kind of flying." And in a way, Harry's misplaced boot-camp enthusiasm for his wings and hook was even more alarming, more desperate. But I had to make the most of it.

"We have to be prepared for the worst," I had said. "With luck, with our superior understanding of the game, we'll reach the exit long before they do, no problem. But remember what the colonel said: if we do encounter them, they'll show no mercy. They've gone through a worse hell than we have—no idea what's going on, half their party slaughtered, and all our fault, sort of. The only thing they do know is this: if we reach that exit first, we'll raise an alarm against their military operation and have them put on trial for treason on top of everything else."

"No quarter. No prisoners," Mishima had said—of them, or us. He'd been given the most powerful weapons, mainly because they were also going to be the trickiest to handle. Foyle had learned from my use of her chemical pack; when she'd left most of her things behind, she'd kept two of the vials, filling them with an especially incendiary mixture of the celluloid and acetone combination she'd had to take such care of back at the dig. Mishima had been able to rig them as grenades with fuses from his utility belt, but they were untested and quite possibly worthless.

I had found myself staring into his eyes. And how would he kill the other two he'd promised me? I was suddenly sure that the extra twenty minutes we'd spent preparing for this fight weren't just wasted, but fatal; that we would have avoided the enemy entirely if we'd simply flown.

Was that right? I'll never know. I don't even know how long the racecourse was, or how fast we were going; there were no marks to judge by. But the minutes—an hour, then the better part of another—streamed past. We held our formation. I in front, scanning; Foyle and Harry higher up, hooks streaming, waiting for me to point out targets; Ariel and Lagado trailing a little, defensively close together, with Mishima covering them from slightly behind. The birds waved whitely in passing, small clouds sailed by like clippers, and the mercs cut across the narrowing V to intercept us at the fifth pylon.

Chapter Twenty-six

AT FIRST I hoped they were a lone pair, two white-winged men in green fatigues. I ordered my helmet to give me a zoomed view. The leading merc carried a strangely bulky handgun, his companion a crossbow. The rims of their visors were a dead black, meaning that they weren't even trying to use the tricky verbal controls of their scanners.

And so I considered letting them pass to one side of us on their present course. Always a chance we wouldn't be seen. But suddenly the lead merc's head jerked up, and he fired his pistol—away from us.

It was a flare gun, streaking orange fire; these two scouts were out to summon the whole wolf pack.

But the damage wasn't necessarily done, not if they couldn't use the scanners. One flare might go unseen. But the man who'd fired it had to be stopped now—which meant that the trooper who was covering him, the crossbowman, had to be taken out first.

My hand signal had been anticipated. I hadn't realized how far ahead of me Foyle had gotten, at her higher level. And, too late, I was learning one of the basics of flying. Her downward course was inescapably faster than my level one; I wasn't going to close the gap in time to give her the support she'd expect. My engine dragged me forward at its usual pace, and I could do nothing but watch.

Foyle came down on her target at a raking diagonal. It must have been a preset course, because she needed both hands to make her strike. The winged trooper saw her at the last second and turned into the line of attack, just as she'd intended—a fish into her hook. He sheered off as she overflew him, but the grapnel had been thrown and had caught, somewhere in the rear of one wing close to the body. She deliberately pulled up into a near-stall, and seconds later her victim hit the end of the supercord line.

I saw him wrenched sideways, but the image was flickering as my helmet tried to keep all the actors in the frame—because the victim's buddy, the one with the flare pistol, had circled back into view, leveling in on Foyle. And perhaps he would have struck her if the yank on the hook-line hadn't pulled her up like a kite, out of his path.

But he had an instant at close range, and rolled over in passing to fire the flare gun at her as if it were a weapon. He was quick, and as I watched the flare streak upward I feared he might be lucky, too . . .

But then the three of them shrank to dots as my helmet picked up something nearer, more imperative, and my steering hand automatically banked my wings before I'd registered what had been coming down on me. A hawklike shadow of camouflage color slashed high, then low, spiraling far to my left, the advantage of height gone, looping away for another try again later. I focused on this new enemy before he was too far away to worry about, and ordered a zoom.

Bad news: this one's scanner was lit—after all, you didn't have to be a linguist to use it, just a quick study at repeat-after-me—and he carried what appeared to be a rifle. I assessed the new facts, though it was like trying to file papers in a dust devil. Our seven enemies were apparently organized as three buddy-pairs and one rover—the latter probably their leader, with his helmet and superior weapon.

The computer gave me a better view, and now there was no doubt. I saw the black bloodstain on one leg, a lock of orange hair escaping from the helmet. Principato. He hadn't had that superior weapon the last time I'd seen him; he must have commandeered it from a lower-ranking merc. My opposite number, he might also become my responsibility, but first I had to see to Foyle.

I resumed my original course, with a slight climb. My scanner couldn't find the flareman again, but picked up Foyle immediately. The trooper she'd hooked was doing tight circles below her, standing on one wing as he tried to dislodge the grapnel. But that was the least of her worries. Her own wings were on fire.

The flare must have started it. I caught sight of her at the moment the smoldering crossed some heat threshold and mushroomed outward in red and yellow.

Flicker zoom, shutter back; no, I was still hundreds of meters away, could only watch the jiggling image.

Nothing to see but a ball of pale fire. But before the shock of her death could register on me, she dropped back into the world of the living. She'd hit the emergency release buckle at her chest just in time, and the heat of the burning wings carried them up and away from her. For an instant the slender figure was etched against the empty blue of free fall, her hair streaming like a last lick of red flame as she began to drop . . . and I was thinking, Smart girl, wait to pick up some speed before deploying your parachute—but, incredibly, she had something else in mind.

For as the hooked merc below her tried to fly clear of his kill, he once again jerked into a sideways stall, and the line of Foyle's fall broke just as violently—into a downward slant straight toward him.

She'd never dropped the supercord—or her attack! But it was just as well that she didn't quite have the momentum to crash into him bodily, instead grabbing one of his legs from below as she tumbled past. That split the last of the air from under his wings, and the two of them spun away in a falling-leaf pattern, wrestling in midair. I thought I saw the flash of a knife blade before I lost them again in flickering planes of focus.

Where was I? Within a hundred meters of them, I thought, and most likely above. At the moment I saw nothing but blue sea and sky, and I came around in a tight loop for fear I'd overshot. That saved my life.

My visor went black for an instant, overzooming, then flickered into a windowpane view of a flier coming at me head-to-head, only fifty meters away. It was the merc with the flare gun. He must have been coming up behind me, hoping to attain the same point-blank range that had served him so well against

Foyle. But our wings were as maneuverable as they were slow; my double-back had been too tight for him follow.

And now—thirty meters distant—he knew I'd seen him, and he had to fire before I could jink away. He went into a slight climb to bring his head and arms down into a more familiar position. Then he disengaged the steering hand to brace it against the arm that held the flare pistol. I flinched to see the gun spit gray smoke, and—ten meters—instantaneously felt a little tug at my own gun arm, too soon for him to have hit me, his wavering flare going wide anyway, but something had in fact passed between us in that instant: a straight black bolt that struck past the merc's helmet into the base of his throat—

—and then I snapped out of it, rolling to one side just in time to avoid colliding with him.

He passed over me like a sailboat's boom, with the same sound and shadow and swash of air. Out from under, I dove forward to pick up a little speed, then executed a passable Immelmann turn to face him again. But there was no reason to hurry.

He remained in that upward slant, his engine revving higher in support of a course that would not change—a course fixed, like his life, on the point of an arrow.

I hadn't even been aware of pulling the trigger. But that was what had made the shot good. He was the one who hadn't had a chance, thinking and aiming as if he were using a handgun on the ground. In the air, our only good chance to hit each other with light arms was to direct the shot straight ahead along the path of flight. I'd achieved it without thinking, carrying the crossbow that way because it offered the least wind resistance. And even my freezing up had helped me, preserving the true line. But luck wouldn't be good enough next time; I wasn't the only one learning these lessons.

A sailboat, abandoned at sea, will tack back and forth as if someone were at the helm. The dead merc kept flying in that way, arms and legs swinging limply from side to side in unison, while a black plume of blood waved from his throat until it was too thin, too far away, to see.

I disengaged my steering long enough to reload the crossbow with one of the spare bolts stored behind a rubber stopper in its hollow butt. But first I set myself in a tight circle until I had a new line on my comrades.

Scanning, zooming . . .

Just a glimpse of crumpled white wings, smeared with red,

before they crashed into the sea far below. Foyle's adversary, I could only hope—and there! there was a parachute that might be hers. And it looked like a parafoil, maneuverable. If she could find some updrafts to ride, it would give us a little longer to reach her with a towline. But where were the others?

Blue sea and sky, white cloud and spray. Landmarks: a few dun patches of phony island in the distance below, and the Magrittesque hulk of a floating pylon in another direction, another dimension. Pan, zoom, shutter back . . . looking for wings, fooled once by a few of those big birds.

How had we come to be so separated? The battle to date had lasted only a few minutes. Yet the sole figure my scanner could lock onto was that Flying Dutchman, the merc I'd killed myself, far above me now and drifting higher, higher . . .

There was a great flash of silver light, accompanied by a noise like a thousand canvas sheets tearing apart. I could only stare as the merc's feet followed his legs and body into the silver flame, and it went out, leaving nothing behind.

The dead man had flown too high. He'd hit the upper limit, the blue plane we saw as "sky," and had come to the end we'd been warned against. Disintegration? Electrocution? I glanced at my own altitude buckle, then began to search for the others again.

I finally found something. A group of three dots strung out vertically, lower than me and not too far away. Something about the way the upper one was swooping down made me zoom on the one in the middle.

It was Ariel, her tidy figure recognizable even in the computer mockup. But the next instant a gaping hole appeared in one of her white wings and she was torn out of my sight.

My scanner picked up another object coming into frame. It was the merc flyer from above, leveling after his successful dive attack. He carried a short-barreled shotgun, and I swore at it: the perfect weapon for imperfect aiming. I locked a computer course onto the gunman. No one could rescue Ariel until he was taken out.

My legs floated up; my wings shifted forward; I began to fall toward my enemy. As the breeze in my face freshened, I brought my crossbow up into firing position. Now I had a few seconds. Scan down, find Ariel's dot a hundred meters lower.

Zoom, and it was her. Ejected, thank God, the parachute already in full bloom. But her ski-pole weapon was gone, and a second attacker, the third dot, was barreling in from the side with a crossbow perfectly aligned. Her parafoil was maneuverable, but unpowered. She couldn't evade him.

The air moaned in my wings.

And then, at the last second, when the bowman had to fire or slam into her, she made her move: a violent yank on a single shroud line of her chute. It collapsed, all its air spilt—and she plummeted out of the bowman's line of fire, silk streaming behind her like a flag.

I saw the bowman overfly where she'd been and yank off a shot downward. But before I could see whether her chute had reopened safely a new image eclipsed the whole scanner view. I'd overtaken my original target.

I'd hoped to come in from above and behind, the shotgunner's blind spot. But he'd banked into a tight downward spiral in pursuit of Ariel, wings nearly straight up and down. A glance to one side let him spot me.

I leveled off to save the advantage of greater height. I'd overfly him in a moment . . . But he snapped over onto his back, matching my horizontal course on his lower level, still leading me as the shotgun swung up to draw a bead. What now?

And in one icy splash it came to me, like the rhyme that brings two lines together in a terminal couplet, the unexpected cleverness that seems so much like fate.

I rapped out an order to the helmet, one that committed me to an interception course.

It was a dive—an overdive, technically, steep enough to send waves of panic fluttering in my belly—and as my feet lifted higher, I disengaged the glove's steering control and aimed the crossbow with both hands. He was close enough to see that, but I'd guessed his response correctly. He disengaged himself in turn, freeing his steering hand to steady the short barrel of the shotgun.

I hurtled toward him, cocked and aimed, but I don't think he was afraid of a civilian like me. A professional, he would have seen the difficulty of shooting away from his angle of flight, and he was experienced and cool enough to wait for point-blank range instead. He knew my course was locked; he held his fire confidently as I plunged closer, closer . . .

I cleared my mind. Nothing left but a target in the blue, and the wind and keening of gathering speed, and my image of myself as a spear-shaft extending back from the cutting-edge shape of the crossbow. Always aiming just ahead of him, allowing for his motion . . . Down and down, faster and faster, and hell, the timing was wrong, those were the whites of his eyes, he would surely fire, but *Now!* I heard it—

—that skirl along my wings—

—and squeezed the trigger in that last instant—*Got you!*—before the wing computer overrode my orders, as I'd known it would have to, and pulled me out of the too-dangerous dive. At my unexpected change of course the gunman did yank his own trigger. But it was already too late, probably just a reflex twitch as the crossbow bolt hammered into him like a tent peg. I heard the bang, loud, but the cloud of pellets went wild, a gray smear in the air I may just have imagined.

Shuddering with reaction, I banked to one side and looked back. I saw a twirling twig: the shotgun, dropped. The gunman himself was only a ghost; he sailed west on spectral wings, a stake through his heart.

Everyone else was lost again.

I had to reload the crossbow before toggling the steering; it took both hands to set the new bolt and crank the string back to cocked position. I banked sharply, circling back to Ariel—but back where? No locations in midair.

I scanned and scanned, fighting desperation, then found three new dots, reasonably close together. The largest one proved to be Ariel's parachute, functional again. She looked unhurt, tugging on her shroud lines, trying to steer the parafoil's glide.

And Mishima circled her protectively. I remembered his promises. A closer view of the third dot indicated that he was making good on them.

It was a ball of fire, and in the center of it writhed a man-sized silhouette that had to be a trooper, presumably the bowman Ariel had spilled to avoid.

So the first of Mishima's incendiaries had worked—better than we'd dared hope; we hadn't known how flammable the wing plastic was. Even as I watched, though, the brightness died, the blackened human husk dropped from sight, and the morbid spell was broken.

Three down. Incredibly, we were holding our own. But how to find the Lagados, or Foyle? *Concentrate!*

Well, Foyle would be at a low altitude now, in her parachute—and yes, combat would tend to drive all fliers lower, as they grabbed at the extra speed they got from descent. I looked downward for flecks of white against the sea, saw a few whitecaps—and found Foyle.

She was still a few minutes from splashing down, but it took me nearly that long to reach her. The descent felt good, like a ski run, and at the bottom I burst into a different zone of air, cooler, the ocean smell suddenly rich and tasty, wave chop and bird cries loud enough to hear despite a stronger churning from my engine.

I had to circle Foyle twice before she was ready to be towed. We'd rationed out the supercord so that everyone had a length for this purpose. The trick was to fly on my back beneath her, close enough to see the thin stuff dangling and find the button she'd tied on the end to give it weight. Then I briefly disengaged my steering hand to grab it.

I rolled over and got ten or twenty yards ahead of her before she stopped giving me slack. When the line went taut, she began to rise like a kite while I nosed down. But it worked better when I went onto my back again, and it didn't take long for my wing computers to adjust to the drag; our engines were safety-designed, with power to burn.

I had to wrap my end of the line a few times around the butt of the crossbow to free the steering hand and take the piano-wire pull more comfortably. But then I saw how hard this would make it to aim—too late.

Our other mistake had been not making the towline between us as long as possible. The white of my wings and her parafoil so close together had made us easy for Principato to spot. But at least I saw him, too, flying on my back.

Curving in from the west, Principato soon matched our northward course perfectly, higher, but not too high. Smart. Whether he'd seen my last attack or not, he knew his computer would override him if a steep dive went on too long. And *he* could afford to drive his shot all the way home. This time I was the one who would be firing away from his own flight line, almost certain to miss.

I zoomed on Principato. The computer-synthesized image was clearer than any telescope view. I'd been wrong before; his weapon wasn't a rifle. That pump slide along the bottom of the barrel jogged my antiquarian memory. Skeet gun. The deadliest weapon he could have had: shot-pellet spread and precise aim, too.

I looked back at Foyle. We had no hand signal for this, even if I'd had a free hand, but I got the idea of a follower across with jerks of my head. She nodded. At least I'd towed her to a decent altitude for now.

Principato tipped over into his dive. The zoomed image foreshortened to a dark circle, with the smaller circle of gun barrel somewhere near its center. I could feel its aim, like a coin of ice pressed to my forehead. I wrestled the crossbow into firing position, let him see that I, too, had disengaged steering, and he kept coming . . . built up speed, committed to his line, became a sharp image at close range—

And then I released the supercord towing Foyle.

Relieved of that drag, my engine jerked me forward even as Foyle stalled backward, and Principato sliced down harmlessly between us. Variation on a theme: once again, I'd broken course without using the steering controls. I hoped Principato caught the same wisp of Foyle's jeering laughter I heard as he swooped back and around into a slow climb.

I didn't want to go head-to-head with the skeet gun. I banked and turned after Principato, hoping to get on his tail and stay there, but he broke off in a new direction. On a hunch, I scanned the vista ahead of him.

Flecks zoomed to become flyers. There was Ariel, safe, and Mishima towing her. And what was that to the side? Another blazing corpse; another merc victim of our own merc colonel. No wonder Principato considered Mishima the more urgent target.

I looked back at Foyle, thinking she was safe enough for now, Ariel needed me, and so forth. But the redhead recalled me to the part I'd somehow agreed to play. She pointed, with exaggerated jerks, to another part of the sky.

I scanned in that direction and swore. She'd found the Lagados, father and son, and I was obliged as our team's rover to go to their defense, leaving Ariel to another man's protection.

The direction was more west than north. I saw a mock volcano some hundreds of meters farther on and a pylon floating beyond that, each providing a little dark contrast for white wings in the foreground.

Scan, close-up.

I caught Ruy Lagado for just a moment, wings already lost, a fleshy ball suspended from a parachute. And then he was gone forever, his head red wreckage, bloody spatters to his waist, arms jerking on control lines in a last spasm. His chute spilled and became a shroud for a quick burial at sea.

I could only keep coming, in steady descent. I appreciated Principato's problem now, always playing catch-up. Maybe that's why I felt so sure it would come down to him and me in the end . . .

I had the scanner widen frame, trying to get a line on Ruy's killer. It pulled too far back. It showed me two mere specks, no detail, but they were approaching each other at top speed and soon the computer focused in again.

Here was a shotgunner, taking a hard bank away from the line that had just ended in Ruy's death. And here, from the opposite direction, headed straight at him before he could reload, flew Ruy's son, Harry, sharpened wooden hook upraised to throw. They came together so close it seemed they would have to collide, but passed each other by. My computer view flickered backward again as the gap widened. Harry didn't have the hook anymore.

An invisible cord snapped taut between them, and both were hit with the impact of our top speed times two. Harry's wings jerked straight up and down, stalled, and began to drop—and the merc, his shotgun spinning loose out of sight, was ripped out of his wings entirely.

The hook had caught the merc in the midsection—not his belly, but the parachute strapped over it. Even as Harry settled back into flight, the merc went straight down to dangle from the boy like an anchor.

One of Harry's own wings showed signs of whiplash, no longer smoothly curved, as if some of its internal shapers had been knocked out of commission. But he settled into a lopsided climb away from me, the merc dangling behind.

I was finally closing with them, ready to help if Harry's wings failed entirely. I saw Harry's body shuddering and thought he might be wrestling the line into position for cutting. But then the purposeful way he held his direction despite wing trouble registered on me. Those shudders were sobs of pain and rage, and the man who had killed Harry's father was being taken, very deliberately, for a ride.

I followed them toward the volcano.

The merc was too high to risk a fall into the sea. He knew it, too. He'd pulled the long-shafted hook free of the parachute in order to get at the cord, which he'd begun to slowly climb. Even though he appeared to have gloves, the fine line must still be murder on his hands. Tough customer. Maybe he even had a plan, to force the kid to land at knife-point or something.

As they passed over the stage-set island cone they hit the updraft, air so hot it visibly rippled. A ski lift, Harry had called it, and he did ride up. His wings looked worse than ever, but by stalling and nearly falling into the center of the column, he reached a point where the merc's weight stabilized him like the tail of a kite; he spiraled around tightly without being moved from that center and the two of them quickly rose.

When I reached the volcano, they were already high above me. My first attempt to enter the updraft was a failure. A huge but gentle hand simply lifted me to one side, where I stalled, for a net loss of height. The trick was to head in and down, and hold the falling and lifting in balance, like keeping a boat's sail from luffing. And when I found the angle, it had something of the thrill of sailing, this continuous circular swoop. But the air I rode was hot and dry, not cool and wet, as I stared down into the heat source—a receding circle of what looked like molten metal.

It was still Harry's play. I craned my neck painfully to follow the action and saw the merc clambering upward hand over hand, closer and closer to the boy, like a marionette in revolt.

"Cut the line!" I shouted. What was the kid waiting for? Couldn't he see or feel the climbing? Had he forgotten what would happen if we soared too high?

Zoom view. *Harry had no knife*, that was the problem. Spinning dizzily, he was trying to untie the tiny knot that secured the ultra-thin cord to his belt. Another moment would be too late; the merc was almost close enough to grab his ankle. I shouted at him to let the whole belt go—*déjà vu*, hadn't I yelled that to Hogg-Smythe once for some reason?—but I couldn't be heard. The boy drew his legs up out of reach. And the merc heaved himself closer—and the boy's face changed expression, let me see what he'd intended all along, as his feet hammered down at the head finally within range.

I caught the flicker of the merc falling past me down the center of the updraft, faintly heard the cross-section of a long scream. He dwindled to a dot in the center of the orange glow beneath us and vanished in a puff of greasy black smoke.

I rolled over onto my back and let the heat wave shoulder me aside into cooler air, looking for the boy to do the same. But he couldn't. His twisted wings—or their confused computers—kept him in a tight spin, like a leaf in a drain but upward, and twice as fast now that his anchor was gone. I heard my own voice shouting meaninglessly as he shot up the invisible pipe. The seconds hurtled past, ran out.

I was dazzled by the silver light, deafened by the infinite shearing sound. Harry had hit the barrier where the sky ended.

Chapter Twenty-seven

FEAR FOR THE others kept me going.

I'd lost all sense of direction, going round and round the volcano's airspout. But I remembered the nearby pylon as having been past the volcano, and put my back to it now as I scanned the lower distance.

Nothing on the first swing. My wings hummed softly as I took a slower second look. In the back of my mind, something else was going on, a headcount. Was it just wishful thinking? Mishima had only taken two of his promised four scalps, but I had matched him, and Foyle and Harry had contributed one apiece. If I'd been right about the original number of mercs, there remained only—

Tiny hailstones spattered against the calf of my left leg, just a faint coldness. But hot pain followed a moment later like the simultaneous sting of a half dozen hornets. I turned hard into a new course and went over onto my back.

Principato straightened from a bank that had matched mine. Of course; the flare of Harry's passing would have drawn his eyes in this direction. Now he'd achieved the classic aerial kill position, above and behind me. Even as I watched, he fired the skeet gun again.

After a moment's lag, I heard a faint chittering sound from my left wing, felt it dip only slightly with the hit. Apparently his ammo was just the small birdshot characteristic of the gun. But that would be enough, if I started catching full bursts.

The scary thing—as I rolled back on my belly and began jinking from side to side—was that he'd hit me twice in two shots, without the advantage of a dive-bomb attack. He was evidently more than proficient, and had picked a range great enough to take advantage of the spreading of the pellets.

Damn! I'd got into a rhythm, and he'd anticipated my bank. Another faint wing-hit.

I flew on, twisting and turning, trying to stay in a broad circle around the area where I believed the women to be, its northern boundary newly marked by an east-west drift of cloud. The next few shots—I could just hear the reports—were misses, but I wasn't encouraged. My zoom-view of Principato had shown a bandolier of ammo. He could take his time. Eventually, partial hits would destroy the control structures in my wings, and once I was reduced to a parachute I'd be helpless.

The fear-sweat was hot on my ribs, cold on my forehead. Principato was far enough away that he couldn't stay on my tail if I doubled back sharply. But the maneuver would only put me broadside to one of his blasts, then give him a chance to punch one big hole in my head instead of a lot of little ones in my tail.

I held the next bank a moment or two longer, trying to be unpredictable. I'd thought the bastard had to disengage steering to shoot, but the blasts were coming too often for that. Firing one-handed? He had to reload the pump periodically. That might give me a few seconds for radical action, but meanwhile I had a reload problem of my own. I was down to my last crossbow bolt.

No choice but to use it. Without doubling back, I couldn't fire *forward* along my line of flight, but there was one other way to stay aligned.

I climbed slightly in order to dip slightly, tucked my chin hard to my chest, and aimed the crossbow straight back between my toes. Principato's image seemed to hang motionless "above" the ankle-to-ankle horizon of my tailwing, perfect, but the bow bobbed with my breathing—God damn it, I was *panting*—and once, twice, three times I had to hold my fire at the last instant. And if I maintained a straight course much longer I'd get lost in the cloud bank ahead. Steady, steady . . .

Then Principato's position shifted and I had to jink up and down again to bring him back into my sights, the cloud wall that much closer. And yet, when I finally squeezed the shot off, it felt so orgasmically right I couldn't imagine it missing.

Which it did, by a good five meters. Only then did I realize, in a sickening rush, just how much beginner's luck had contributed to my first two shootouts. And now my last arrow was gone, even as another smear of birdshot howled past, snapping and snarling along my left wing.

Panic hammered at the mind's portal, not to be put off much longer. My engine seemed much louder, as if compensating for something. Were my wings already so ragged I was losing lift? I couldn't tell how bad they were from my angle, though I could see a few shreds and flaps marring the front edge of the fabric. I only knew I had to peel Principato off, and fast; I couldn't last much longer.

And suddenly the cloud ahead seemed like the only possible haven; the sound of Principato's latest shot drowned the warning voices in my head, the memories of the holo briefing; I dove in.

At first the cloud seemed to part for me: the nearest meter of vapor was transparent. My tail still felt exposed, but then I looked back and saw the whiteness closing behind me.

I was alone in my own world.

The cloud was something like ground fog, cool and soft and placid. But there was nowhere to stand, no reassuring sight of grass or smell of earth below, only the same luminous whiteness as above. The single variation in color lay ahead, toward the center of the great massless mass: a not-white, white's shadow, more like blindness than like anything seen.

I could hear myself think again, but didn't like what I heard. I was out of ammo and lost. While Principato wasn't likely to follow me into the cloud—he wouldn't have understood the Ur-Linguish warnings in the briefing, but he could see that the vapor would blind him—he could use the time to pick off Ariel or Foyle instead. I didn't even know if Mishima was still protecting them, maybe dead, maybe knocked down to a parachute; in any case, he'd used up his incendiaries. At least in the clear I could have decoyed Principato away, but now—

One moment I was cruising north through the universal mist, faint hurt cries coming from my wings where the breeze hit them. Then, without warning, the air quit holding me, as if a whirlpool had opened below.

Wind shear! I fell helplessly, spinning end over end, my wings offering no resistance at all. Fifty, sixty, maybe a hundred meters down a greased tunnel of empty white, and then, with a terrifying whipcrack sound—droplets of condensation bursting from me in all directions—the wing computers found purchase in the air again, let me slice down into a stable glide, not quite a dive.

But within seconds I encountered a rising column of air as solid as a piston, and was hurled upward farther and faster than I'd fallen. I hit an air pocket above and tumbled down again—to be batted up, and to one side, and down once more, a hoarsely shouting shuttlecock. But the watchful computer had the sense to furl my wings, protecting them, until I'd lapsed back into a natural fall. Soon, the rough air past, I found myself gliding safely on my back, swearing as if praying while I clutched my empty cross.

I was adrift in cold white nothingness. And fear. Very like a place I'd been before, perhaps had never left. The suspend-sleep tank, that magic mirror that always asks the same primal questions: *Who are you really? And where?*

You are not a fighter pilot. You are not a match for murderers. That was just a part you played on the other side of the white curtain. You are really just a dreamer from Wayback who loved women and the stage and the secrets of the old tongue. And where you are is a world woven of just those secrets. In this lies your only possible advantage, in your wits the only weapon. It is Principato who must be drawn into one of the traps the old tongue warned you against—a warning he could not have understood.

Now my scanner made signs to me. I wasn't blind after all; the device, which did not depend on lenses, was still receiving information from its mysterious source. It cast pictures of various distant objects against the cloud's white screen.

I struggled to supply a context. There was the volcano where Harry had died. Higher, at a right angle from the line I flew, was a pylon, probably the seventh and last. And finally, far above but matching my course exactly, flew Principato.

Yes, he could scan me, too—or at least some representation of my position and bearing—despite the white vapor. Having never lost sight of me, he'd had no reason to risk the unknown territory of the cloud. Instead he'd climbed over it, following me at that altitude, ready to stoop and pounce whenever I made my exit. Now that the cloud had softened me up—and burdened my wings with water—he could move in for the kill: one last dive-bomb attack, one tight grouping of shot in my heart or my head.

But I knew myself now, felt my old powers as I moved the plot elements around on the blank white page before me. I saw how to bring things to a close: win or lose, a spectacular finish.

I scanned for my objective, and rounded into its direction at a slight climb. Having passed the turbulent middle of the cloud, I could hope to hold this line unbrokenly, Principato shadowing all the way.

There was only one unknown. I could scan solid objects outside the cloud, but I couldn't get a fix on the empty place where the cloud ended, couldn't judge how far it would be until I emerged. My objective, zoomed, did not appear to be inside the cloud—it was not dripping with condensation as I was—but I didn't know how much open space I'd have to cross to reach it. Too little or too much and my plan would end in disaster.

But I soared forward anyway; my fear felt more like stage fright now, at least half exhilaration. *Here it comes! Props ready?* I pried the heavy almond-shaped rubber stopper from the storage hole in the crossbow's stock and held it between my teeth. *You're on!*

I came up out of the white vapor like a cannonball, so close to the enormous rock mass of the pylon—only a score of meters away, a few seconds' flight—I had to pull back and stall to avoid smashing into it.

The floating island nearly filled my sky from side to side, and wider as I looked higher, up to the razor-sharp line where it appeared to end. Below me, where it tapered, a broad cave cut through to a far hole of blue, and in that first impression—everything in high contrast and high color after the white void—I made out the oversized bird nests inside the tunnel, and white bodies roosting. Another fifty yards lower the pylon ended in a point, but the gold hoop was not visible, apparently fixed to the opposite face.

I twisted my body so as to fall sideways and rightward, not stall onto my back, and looked up the left wing as I went over to see if Principato was making his move. Yes! He'd seen me hanging there so teasingly and now he was locked on, roaring down like a thunderbolt.

Had to stay ahead of him just a little longer. But the holes in my wings didn't slow me much going down, and that was my aim, a steep dive straight at the lower part of the pylon.

The rock wall surged toward me. I could make out green vines in the crevices, could even smell wet earth. I was on line with the cave opening below, but it was going to be close; I couldn't tip any steeper without scaring the wing computers into pulling me up—and dashing me against the wall. But I couldn't shear away and let Principato make his strike, either. Down, down, listening for that fatal moan from my leading edges. *The only way out is—*

Through the opening, with sickening lurches from side to side as I flattened out and hit the expected turbulence, an airstream shaped by the tunnel. Hand-steering all the way in the semi-darkness, cold rock and the stink of guano all around, the exit circle my only hope. I tried to keep close to the curved rock ceiling, as far from the bird nests ten meters below me as I could.

But there was an air cushion along the ceiling; I would hit it and bounce down, alarming the scores of birds below, and at least once overcorrected for it, crashing my engine up against the rock with a terrible scraping noise.

That was too much for some of the birds. They came after me just as I cleared the lip of the exit cave. Now!

It was all one move, the dip forward, chin down, looking back between my toes—and *yes!* Principato hadn't gone the long way around when he was so close to nailing me; he was still on my tail, unaware of what we'd been warned against—as my arm snapped down and hurled the crossbow backward at the hawk-like pursuer. The bow was another bird shape, coming back at them low and aggressively, and they were sure the nests were under attack now, and I was retreating, no danger, but Principato was deep in the tunnel when the whole flock rose up and went for him.

Powerful pinions drove the hunters' beaks and talons. Their battle cries were like knives against stone wheels, sharpening, sharpening. Principato vanished in an angry whirlwind of white and red.

You're the one with the birdshot, Killer.

I pulled up and away, jinking from side to side and flailing with my free hand to discourage the one or two birds still following me, until they returned to the nests. I hadn't covered much distance when Principato broke free.

I suppose the romancer in me had expected them to tear him to shreds, like piranha fish. In fact, they didn't even follow him too far from their cave. But his face and body were bloodied, his wings torn. And he'd lost the gun.

None of which stopped him from locking onto my course and closing with me, drawing a short machete from a sheath on one thigh. Vengeance? Military professionalism? Or a superman's need to win at all cost? I'd planned for it, that was the important thing.

And when he reached my altitude I turned head to head with him and locked in as my free hand took the rubber stopper from between my teeth. There was no help for it. I had to let him get close. Almost—but not quite—as close as he wanted to. Because I, too, had always suffered from a sense of destiny—I, too, was willing to end the contest with one cast of the dice.

And so he came to me, pointing like an avenging angel with his outstretched steering hand, chopping blade upraised in the other. To change the angle, face his whole body and not just the top of it, I broke off into a steep climb that turned into a stall.

He swooped up to match me exactly. For a moment we were face to face at full-length, only a few meters apart, and before he could throw the machete—he was mad enough to do it, his white teeth bared in a contorted, blood-spattered mask of a face—I hurled the rubber stopper at him.

He had a champion's reflexes; the machete arm went sideways to protect his face, and as the stopper bounced harmlessly off his chest instead, I heard his bark of contemptuous laughter.

It drowned the click that came from my target, the silver disk at the yoke of his wing harness.

I will never forget his look of shock and horror as his wings unstrapped themselves, peeled back, and shot away from him. For an instant he seemed to hang in the void, stalled as I was stalled. Then I dipped and caught the air, while he went down like a brick. He finally did throw the machete, too late, but with all his strength; I didn't see where it went, but the action changed his course, put a slant on it. As the green figure shrank against the distant background of the sea, it also skimmed ever closer to the rock wall of the pylon island we'd just left.

And so he hit the long pole jutting from the side of the pylon, the one with the gold hoop on it. His body jackknifed with the impact, whipped around the pole and down again, and spun head over heels all the rest of the way.

He never released his parachute. Five seconds later, quite a long time, a tiny white circle blossomed on the sea. It opened up and became a hollow pale wreath, into which, a moment later, the gold hoop also disappeared.

I went south, climbing slowly over the cloud on my tattered wings, scanning downward on the other side. I found my party alive and well, with Mishima still under wings, towing both women, making slow time.

I glided back to them. The trivial birdshot wounds in my leg ached dully. The savage satisfaction I'd felt at my own lethal cleverness had passed. Moral hangover had set in.

Was it incredible that the mercs should lose to us? But we'd taken losses, too. And we'd had Mishima and Foyle, professional soldiers of a high caliber. And I, of course, had cheated the mercs at every turn—I'd used my brain.

I was glad we couldn't talk when I joined up with the others, though I signaled that all was clear, and felt their relief and pleasure at seeing me alive. I took Ariel's towline from Mishima's hand and shared the duty. Tired and torn up, I just wanted to finish.

The remaining trip north took an hour, the last hour of the day. It was an eerie and valedictory experience, as if careless stagehands had started to take the set apart before the actors had quite reached the end of the play. We were finally approaching the apex of the V-shaped Hellway cavern, which meant that its walls were becoming visible through the blurring of the atmosphere. At first we saw them only to the far left and right, a column of gray tile on either side. But the columns widened and flattened toward the middle of our view until foreground and background reversed.

Now there was only one column, consisting of blue haze, directly in front of us as the enormous wall tiles passed flatly on either side. And in the center of this dimming column of daylight glowed an orange patch, like a setting sun behind light clouds, and I somehow knew this would be the exit. As we got closer it dazzled us and retreated, became a fading orange tunnel. We flew into it, and onward.

Orange subsided to shades of red and violet. *We* were the setting sun; we were going where a sun goes, rolling up into a new country; and the Hellway was behind us at last, gone down into night, a dream.

Part Three

The Mirror

Chapter Twenty-eight

THE REST IS mist. We flew and we flew . . . Possibly we were drugged. I have a vague impression of a gray fog, anesthetically cold . . .

And we finished in a whirlwind.

It was a fraud, a wonderful melodramatic trick, but for a moment I thought it was real, the four of us spaced around a circle facing each other in midair, slowly whirling, coldness blasting in our faces—the roar of great winds everywhere, annihilating thought. Some invisibly fine web at our backs was really holding and directing us, though, not the dark tornado column we thought we could see above and below us through gray rings of simulated dust. Part of it may have been real, spun out of some sort of mesh, but most of it must have been a holographic projection.

In any case, we whirled in perfect safety, the men in wings and the women without. The parachutes which would have complicated the situation had been conveniently removed during the lost, blacked-out minutes.

As soon as we had time to grasp what was being simulated—an ascent via whirlwind to a higher world—the mists beyond the dust rings faded away. We could see the "landscape" we were supposed to be rising from, a golden harvest country of china-blue streams and gentle hills. White temples stood here and there on hilltops. Next to them human figures in togas or chitons were consigning part of their meal to a fire, as if in sacrifice. Wraiths of white smoke ascended from these circles, gathered speed and shape, and passed us going upward. I recognized various characters from Roman mythology: Hercules in a lionskin, Ulysses with an oar on one shoulder.

So we, too, were joining the Olympians, as heroes—was that it? I tried to decide whether this told me anything new about the enigmatic Elitists, their goals and values. But I was too weary.

And then the gray curtains closed again and new forces affected our motion, my comrades swirling below me at different altitudes until we were in single vertical file. Suddenly something cold and hard and unyielding pressed against my back, something that magnetically gripped my wings and stopped me in place. The wing-release mechanism triggered itself; I cried out as I slipped down; but then my feet met resistance and I found myself standing on a rocky ledge.

I looked down. Far, far below . . .

Wait a minute.

The mountain face we clung to was not really as steep as the holographic scenery made it appear. But with that yawning chasm "below," one could not help but take one's time creeping along the narrow ledges upward.

I was the first to reach the cave mouth. It opened nearly two meters above the level of my feet, and I had to reach up and pull myself in. I helped the others up as they arrived: first Ariel—a quick kiss from her in passing, almost an afterthought—then Foyle.

Mishima could doubtless have heaved himself up without help, but I knelt down and grabbed him by belt and armpit anyway, and brought him to his feet. It was an interesting moment.

He stepped away from me and brushed himself off, as if embarrassed. Perhaps he was thinking that he hadn't kept his end of our bargain, hadn't taken the four scalps promised. But that didn't matter now. We had pulled through anyway, most of us.

Now that we could hear one another again, I had to supply the details of what had happened to the Lagados. The others took it expressionlessly. Perhaps they felt as I did, washed out.

There was a brief silence. A door began sliding down to convert the "cave" into a room, and before we lost all the light from outside I found a bank of switches against one wall and lit the overheads.

"Is this it?" Ariel said. "What a disappointment."

Just a round room with doors and a few open archways, like the statue chamber, but smaller. Artificial light, canned air. Nothing of interest.

"What could we expect?" Foyle replied. "This is where we break with the pilgrims. Those kids had their people to meet them, to give them gifts and lead them through that final affirmation maze."

She pointed to an archway at the far end of the room, the largest, marked with the sign of the fasces. "There's a glimpse of open sky somewhere in there, the only time an Elitist child would ever see the real thing in his life. And then the trip back to the parents and brothers and sisters, celebrations and solemnities. But that's all ghost stuff. It's not for us."

Even the stolid Mishima looked depressed.

"We have our own celebration ahead of us," I said quickly, "if we can get the word out to the satellites in time to stop them from being taken over. Break up a senator's assassination and we'll be feted as heroes, never fear. Let's get on with it."

"Foyle," Mishima said, "didn't you say you would have a way of contacting your ship if we reached this point?"

Foyle's answer sounded hollow, guarded. "All I meant was, if we could break out to open sky, we ought to be able to rig some sort of radio transmission to my ship. Its orbit will bring it directly overhead, and it has standing orders to scan for low-power distress signals from me."

"I see. I thought you had more direct means at hand. Very well." Mishima thought a moment. "All right, this was one of the control centers of the colony. If there was any provision at all for contacting their scout ships in space, its transmitter would be here, far from the main population, for security. All we have to do is find it."

"The sooner the better," Ariel suggested. "We'll have to split up."

"Agreed," I said. "Pick your doors."

"I'll find the upper exit in the maze," Foyle offered. "We'll need to know where it is in any case."

Ariel's door revealed a passageway, and an arrow-shaped sign cryptically marked CRANK ROOMS. Mishima took an elevator. I was left alone with Foyle.

"Mishima's pretty sure you have a transmitter on you," I said. "Theoretically, we're all on the same side, but I think I'll stick close to you. Just in case."

"Besides," she said after a moment, suddenly smiling. "You have to see the affirmation maze. You want the complete experience, don't you?"

"Guilty. And it's not as though we *need* to find another transmitter. Do we?"

She pulled the aqua pendant from within her jumpsuit and rubbed it like a lucky charm. "No," she admitted. She looked at it closely, read something in its chatoyance. "Still at least an hour before my freighter is overhead. I don't think this is a puzzle maze. We should solve it in plenty of time."

We stared up at the Elitist fasces over the entryway, the birch rods for whipping children, the squat little axe for executing enemies of the state. "The sign of over-mastery," or whatever the phrase had been.

"I say 'solve' it," Foyle went on. "But I don't suppose we ever will. Not without those people to meet us, not without knowing what was in their hearts . . . They're still a thousand years away, and always will be, now. Older than the Green Church and the Kanalists, and more secret. Closer to Old Earth than to us . . . It's not fair. We've made it. We are adults of their tribe now. We were meant to understand them, their history."

"That's not what initiations promise," I said gently. "To know *ourselves*, that's the promise. I don't think the secrets of Elitism would have helped either of us with that."

"No."

We entered the foyer of the maze, passing a little curtained-off nook with speakerholes in it. "A singer would have been here, during the affirmation walk," Foyle suggested. "Or maybe a Questioner, after the style of Masons or Kanalists."

The walls were dark and featureless. At the first branching Foyle went unhesitatingly to the right, following the turns of that passage as if she knew where she was going. But we soon reached a dead end.

"Not even a picture to look at," she said.

"What was that all about?" I asked as we returned to the fork.

"Just a whim. Didn't matter which way we went. Thought I'd start out like a Kanalist. Silly. A salute to my husband's sad old cult."

"Okay, but that would be this way, to the left," I said as we took that branch.

She laughed. "I forgot your literary theories. In the Larkspur play, it *is* to the left, isn't it:

The Questioner begins to sing,
'Nothing is left—but *everything*.'

However, in an actual initiation—"

"The actual path is the one encoded in *The Enchanted Isle*," I said. "Your husband's chapter must not have used a canonical maze." How could I put this, and still stay in character? "My own initiation may have been Reform, but it was held in the maze at Nexus University, the oldest known. Trust me, it starts with a left."

"Nexus?" she repeated as we turned a forced corner. "You went—"

We came to a dead halt, staring.

The gleaming point of the arrow was aimed in our direction. Drawn to the furthest, the bow did not even quiver in those powerful arms. The eyes behind it did not blink, despite their anger and the long, long wait for us.

"It's . . . not . . . *possible*," Foyle whispered.

But there he stood, in rags, aiming the great bow that only he could draw, ready to fire through the row of double axes the drunken suitors had set up for him as a target.

Odysseus's homecoming. The first mosaic on the Shining Fare. *Nothing is left—but everything* . . .

Foyle shook her head and tried to speak again.

"That's the left turn," I heard myself say, in a strange, creaky voice. "And the next one is a right." And I took her unwilling arm, and pulled her along the path, hearing the turn in the lines I said aloud:

> "The wanderer, his end in view,
> Will thread the shining axes through.
> Like him, you must return. Take aim.
> You have your own birthright to claim."

The coding gets more subtle after that, but I had no trouble following it, turn for turn and strophe for strophe.

The story of Odysseus comes first, of course. It always did. You know that one. The crafty man, the enduring man. The man who gets home.

My voice echoed as a Questioner's would have, bringing the pictures to life for Foyle as we passed. We'd seen such images in the Hellway, too, but under the spell of the fasces had taken them for Roman lore, not the Greek the Romans copied.

And so we treaded my measures, and read the walls, all the archetypal tales. Persephone—not Proserpine—accepted the seeds from Hades, as her mother arrived too late: Hephaestus—not Vulcan—displayed Aphrodite and Ares under the net, and the other gods laughed at him; Pandora opened the box; Orpheus looked back . . .

And I was in the moment, lost to Time entirely. It was as if my whole tortuous life had reraveled to this. I didn't know or care how I had come to the Shining Fare again. A true Kanalist knows that he can *always* return, always be reborn, it's merely a question of admitting his own freedom to affect the current moment. That's why our proper peers are gods and goddesses—because we can create worlds when we choose.

Foyle followed me as if we were dancing, occasionally looking from the mosaics to my face as I interpreted a particularly arcane directional clue . . . but never less than entranced, a true participant in the rite.

Up the stairs, to the second level.

We shuttled through the final twists and turns, ignoring the dead ends where the Midases and Minoses were pictured in their self-inflicted misery.

The story of Daedalus, the talented man, comes near the end.

We see him as a brilliant young inventor and artist, devising statues that talk and paintings that weep. Then older, jealous of the rising generation, he throws his talented apprentice Talos from the roof of the Acropolis, murdering him.

Banished, Daedalus finds work as architect for King Minos of Crete. To hide the shame of Minos's queen, her monstrous Minotaur offspring, Daedalus builds the great Labyrinth at Knossos. But his sympathy for the loves of women leads him back through his own maze to full humanity. Young men from Athens are being sacrificed to the Minotaur; it is Daedalus who shows Princess Ariadne the secret of the maze, to save them.

The Minotaur is killed by Ariadne's lover Theseus, and Daedalus is imprisoned. He has his own son now, Icarus, and they escape from Crete on wings of wax and feathers—but the boy flies too high—*Of course! But we warned Harry, it wasn't our fault, or his, or the builders', just bad luck*—and falls to his death, like Talos.

Daedalus, chastened and enlightened, lives out his life in Sicily, as tutor to its royal family. He teaches his arts instead of hoarding them, achieving greater wonders than ever before.

Minos still searches for him. He offers a golden reward for anyone who can draw a linen thread through the secret inner windings of a triton shell. Daedalus rises to the challenge because he cannot do otherwise; he must be his best.

Why hadn't I recognized this picture before, in bas-relief at the entrance to Slugland?—the ant emerging from the gastropod shell with a thread tied to one leg, lured through the maze by the honey on Daedalus's fingers . . .

The reward is claimed, and Daedalus's location is revealed. But the last scene is not of his death. For when wrathful Minos arrives, the rising generation of Sicily acts to protect the tutor they love, and it is the great king of the Mediterranean who is cast down. He becomes the chief magistrate of hell, for he is the personification of the state, while Daedalus . . . There is no final view of Daedalus. Perhaps he never dies.

Then a golden thread appeared in the carpet, and the way became straight.

We followed it past unadorned panels. In the distance the destination shone, the mirrored wall, the sacrificial emblem balanced against its own reflection there, the graven words I was remembering before I was quite close enough to see them—*You have found the right passage, So ends the Shining Fare*—but I held myself in the moment with my own lines from ten or a hundred years before, the Chorus of Parents:

The Maze is ending. You know where you are headed.
The unwound way, no longer recondite,
Will wend until the higher axe is threaded,
But the axis that you tread has turned to light.

The Masque has ended. We pass the world to you,
Complete with costumes, props, and cardboard throne.
Have fun. Play all its gaudy parts, but when you're through,
Perform these lines for children of your own.

The Mirror *never* ends, a wall that fades
Away, our past your future, all of Time
Balanced between these two unblooded blades.
Your lives are now your own. Echoes, a rhyme,
A memory—We are no more, mere air.
But look into the mirror. Aren't we there?

We stand before the mirrored wall, Foyle and I, two tough and cynical people in their thirties, with the wondering faces of children. Nearby, a fountain, whose two copies I remember from Nexus University, sings quietly; its name was the Pierian Spring.

YOU HAVE CHOSEN THE RIGHT KANAL

"It's German for 'channel.' As simple as that."

"Of course," Foyle says.

SO ENDS THE HELLER WEG

"The 'Heller' Way?"

" 'Bright,' " I say. "Shining. Of course."

The fasces? Gone, for it is not the sign of 'overmastery to come,' it is the sign of 'mastery to overcome'—the stage of absolute authority that children and criminals might have needed over them, but adults and citizens must outgrow. The once-bundled birch rods lie scattered, each broken in the middle like Prospero's staff. And the short, cruel chopper has grown into a long-handled thing of art, a ritual weapon only, its Cretan double blade rising from the burst bundle like a butterfly from the cocoon.

It props up its reflection in the infinite mirror, past and future, one blade whetting the other.

"It was all very obvious, wasn't it? Were we just too close to see it?"

"Can you see the workings of your own heart?"

She shakes her head, tries to say something else, and fails.

"Look at this," I say.

In a corner opposite the mirrored wall, a hand-painted map depicts a hemisphere of Old Earth, featuring Southern Europe, Northern Africa, and Asia as far as China. A transparent glass case overlies the map, and the jewels inside the case—the scarf-pins, badges, and whistles of the Questioner and other ritual attendants—serve to mark the sites of the earliest Earth civilizations. Although there was never anything like this at Nexus, I know where I will find the most important piece, precisely where Summerisle told me to look, *Near the Labyrinth, in a mountain cave, on the isle of Crete, on Earth* . . . It glitters back at me from the painted Mediterranean: the Master's ring.

THESE ARE THE ORIGINALS.

So says the golden plaque. Some of the words are German, but I translate them without thinking; this part I have never seen but I can guess the essence of what it will say:

WE WILL TAKE COPIES WHEREVER WE GO,
MAKING MORE AS NEEDED,

AND MAZES FOR THE DANCE.
YOU MAY WISH TO DO THE SAME,
IF YOU FIND YOURSELVES HERE.
JUST REMEMBER,
IT IS NOT THE RITUAL,
IT IS NOT ONE HOLY PLACE,
OR A CHOSEN PEOPLE—
IT IS THE WILL TO KNIT TOGETHER
THAT FINDS THE GOLDEN THREAD.
WE HAVE FOUND THE WHOLENESS
THAT CAME APART
IN DISTRIBUTORS AND
MERITOCRATS.
IT IS ALL WE WILL TAKE BACK
TO THE WORLDS OF MEN.
IT IS ALL WE LEAVE BEHIND
FOR YOU:
STRANGERS, FRIENDS.
IT IS ALL THERE IS.
FAREWELL.

"They've adopted us," Foyle says. "Even us. The way the Kanalist elite was always adopting the brightest people they met, wherever they came from. That's why the 'desirable mix of classes' in the Hellway teams: so that poor kids could make a name for themselves, and rich families adopt them. *That's* what their tombstones were trying to tell me—not that children were lost and sacrificed, that they were adopted and lifted up."

"Up?" I say. "Up. There's more."

I find the velvet tassel, like a bellpull, and the staircase comes down at my tug. We ascend.

The stars.

Arctic air, of course, so near the north pole, and high. A husk of natural wall holds back the wind in three directions, but this is still the top of the mountain, on a world without smog, and even in twilight there are millions of stars, so bright they burn. And one bright enough to stand out from the rest, at their hub. The polestar, the closest. The one the Elitists must have stared at most longingly, decade after decade, knowing that the folk in orbit around it were their kin. The one they finally left for.

"At Nexus U.," I said, but breathlessly, heart pounding, "we just wound up on the roof; went down by a fire escape to come in through the side door. There was a final mosaic there, the marriage of Earth and Heaven, but it was wrong, we knew it, an anticlimax; something important to the meaning had been lost . . ."

"*Catharensis.*" Foyle gazed at the star. "Catharensis Five. So they got there after all."

"But even on a new world, they had the sense to stay underground," I said. "It was a century or more before something called 'Kanalism' seeped into the mainstream. It looked freshly made up then.

"Because they'd kept it fresh. They'd kept their priorities. It would be, what? . . . two or three centuries more before the Federal Alignment was founded, but the creed lasted long enough to make that happen. And longer, for centuries of freedom after that. Not the usual quick decay, Foyle—a thousand years since Avalon! The Elitists didn't die, and *they never sold out*."

There were tears of something like joy on Foyle's face, but what she said was—"Until our century, you mean."

"No, you don't believe that. You and I can never be sure of that again." I held her cold hand in the dark. "A thousand years makes them different from any who've passed before. They've just gone underground again, that's all. To them—to us—only individuals matter; those Column Kanalists can call themselves anything they like so long as there are individuals out there, somewhere, who live the true creed. The members of the underground Old Rite lodges you told me about. You yourself.

"Our time can always come again, because even in the worst of times, not everyone sells out. Your husband never sold out. I never sold out."

"That's right, isn't it?" she whispered, staring back at me. "*Evan Larkspur* never sold out."

Chapter Twenty-nine

"YOU CAN'T EVEN deny it, can you?" she said, laughing raggedly. "My God, it's true."

It took me by surprise.

And I found I could not deny my name. Not so soon after being rebaptized, not under these stars. "You can't—"

"Know? But I can. You don't even bother to hide it—the old-fashioned accent, the way you talked about flitter controls, your knowledge of the verses, a hundred giveaways—even the magic tricks! And yet *you're safe*. Everyone always says that Larkspur could still come back, but no one really believes—"

"You can't—"

"One mistake, but you couldn't have known. You see, the Kanalist maze at Nexus University was burned to the ground during the Ratification Riots. Ninety years ago . . . But you were initiated there, all right. It's true, isn't it? Admit it."

I found myself nodding my head. I took a deep breath of the frigid air, and found I'd lost none of the previous moment's exaltation. I could not fear the future in this timeless place.

She cocked her head. "You don't look much like Schaelus's bust of you, though."

"I've been taking hormones."

She laughed again, almost giddily, hugging herself against the cold.

"It's crazy. I always knew you were a ringer, but . . . It's like catching a burglar, and finding out he's also the Archangel Michael."

"Thanks."

"This, and the Shining Fare, it's too much to take in, it's like a dream. What are you doing here? What . . . what *happened* to you?"

At long last a chance to tell someone about it, to get it off my chest.

I told her as much as I could in a few words, and only up to the point where I'd returned to the human sphere. All the bumming around I'd done since, my sordid arrangement with Condé, and so forth . . . Dramatically, it was better to end with the *Barbarossa*.

". . . The worst thing is that I'll never know everything. The memories aren't missing, they're distorted, all jumbled up now with the dreams and the wishes and the fears."

"And you felt you couldn't announce your return?" she asked.

"It would be suicide. People would kill me for the *Barbarossa*'s data record—which is in fact worthless, so I'd have no fortune to protect myself with. Meanwhile, the rulers of the Column are my worst enemies. They couldn't let an Old Rite Kanalist with millions of admirers come back to life now. They might even remember that I was Summerisle's best friend and think that I had his Vice Book, full of potent material to blackmail them with. I'd have to fight every minute just to stay alive.

"Nor would I have anything to gain by the name. The boy who wrote Larkspur's plays died in the suspend-sleep tank. I can't summon up anything like his talent. I can't even be sure I *am* Evan Larkspur. Maybe that's just a fantasy an amnesia victim pieced together after a flitter crash on a remote planet. Maybe there was a bust of Larkspur in my hospital room, and that's all."

"That's crap. You know things only he could know."

"So you say. But there's another possibility. I could be the real Larkspur, but *you* could be a fantasy. Suppose they never did get me out of that suspend-sleep tank. Suppose this is just a dream that goes on and on."

"That's crap, too, and you know it."

"No, I *don't* know it. This is not philosophical bullshit, it's a real possibility I have to live with every day—the most believable hypothesis.

"You see, with no role to play, no place to fit, I've done nothing for eight years but test the limits of experience. I've taken risks I would never take if I really believed this was my life—and I've always lucked out, like the hero of a cheap thriller. Look, just on this planet! Think about it. It's as if the whole place had been designed, authored, to bring me to this revelation under the stars, a Kanalist reborn. I love it, it moves me, but can I *believe* in it?"

"Oh, and I'm a part of your dream, too, I suppose."

"You and Ariel are just the sort of women I dream of, as a matter of fact."

"Don't you know that *everybody* has that feeling sometimes?"

"Does everybody have my reasons?"

She looked into my eyes, shivering. "No, I suppose not. Then again . . .

"Ten years ago, my husband started a guerrilla war to keep Vesper from being colonized. When it was all over, when he and most of the rest were dead, I negotiated the peace. I always felt like a sellout for that. Roger would have told me to shrug those feelings off. He was a Larkspurian, of course, and an Old Rite Kanalist, and he'd have said, '*This* is the only real moment, you are born into a new world to start over, again and again, anything is possible.' I'd closed my heart to that voice.

"But now I've been led through the mysteries he told me about—shriven and initiated—by Evan Larkspur himself! And you think this world was tailor-made for *you*? No. It's just that it's true, that's all. Anything *is* possible. It's true."

I think I laughed.

"To think that you ever criticized *me* for taking too dark a view," she went on. "What evidence do you have that you willfully abandoned your mates? Why assume the worst of yourself, when what you actually remember is fighting a hijacker for them?"

I shook my head. "What I 'remember' is a childish fantasy. The agent of a dire conspiracy steals a whole ship by taking it into praeterspace without a target star—magically stranding it *outside* space-time, see, in a sort of—"

"Bubble universe?" she said.

I stopped, thunderstruck. She eagerly repeated the phrase.

"There is no such thing," I said. "I searched the literature again and again. In the hundred years since I left, no shred of evidence that such a thing—"

"Can be," she told me, gently but firmly. "The Titans knew of it. It's one of the few big secrets of their physics that the Elitists were able to figure out. 'The way in and out of bubble universes in praeterspace.' It was the most tantalizing hint in their data bank's description of the White Codex, the treasure they took with them when they went to Catharensis Five. I wish I could tell you that they left the details behind. They didn't. But I can show you the reference, at least. Bubble universes are *real*, you didn't make them up. Anything . . . is . . . possible!"

I just gaped at her, thinking, thinking . . .

"Anything!" she went on. "Look at what you've already done. A Shadow Tribune of the Column! How many years, how many risks has it taken you to establish that identity? Seeming to work for them, just so that sometimes you can slip in something against them, like keeping a reformist senator alive. All the time maintaining this false front of a charming, self-centered lightweight. Where do you find the dedication? Where do you find the courage?"

Her eyes were shining. Her lips were parted. I could scent the vapor of her breath. There was nothing else I could say:

"*Somebody* has to do it."

She nodded, smiling, and reached for the collar of her jumpsuit. "So let's do it."

"What, right here?"

"Let's signal the senator's people." She had removed that pendant again, and was reading something from it.

"Oh."

"Early Sunday morning," she said. "Has so little time really passed?"

The calculation brought us back to reality with a wrench. It had been late Sunday afternoon when I'd spied on Pro and Contra, the mercs, and overheard them planning to attack the construction camp before the senator arrived. Pro had said he'd take a week to set it up.

"Sunday night, we were in the mirror maze," Foyle said. "The next night we camped out on the plain of moths."

I counted by nights. "Tuesday night, I slept in the eel-balloon. Wednesday, on vines in Slugland. Thursday, oh, between clean sheets in the lighthouse. Friday—God, if the Valley Backstage was just yesterday, then Friday I slept, uh—"

"In good company," Foyle said. "But spare me the details. So Saturday night just ended, and it's not quite a week yet."

"The pendant is a comm-link to your freighter, isn't it?"

She nodded.

"Why so secretive about it?"

"Most places, port authority doesn't allow you remote control once you've parked. Besides . . . Well, I know all *your* secrets; I guess I can tell you. It's a computer, too, and much more than that. I could never afford to buy a device as powerful as this one, if humans even make such a thing. It's an alien artifact."

"And you've never reported it."

A sidelong glance. "I'd have to turn it in. And it's my personal guarantee of freedom. It's scannerproof—same reason the EMP in the elevator shaft didn't affect it—and Customs officials take it for a junk jewel, but I can run my whole ship with it, at a distance. That's saved my neck plenty of times."

"How so?"

"I have a one-seat shuttle. No fuel to spare, but it can just manage to retrieve me from a planetary surface and achieve orbit. From there on, the freighter has to complete the pickup. It's a risk, but I take it when I have to."

"Nice."

"Used to be. Port authorities have heard about that model now. The senator's people reprogrammed the shuttle doorlock when they checked me in; without a password from them I can't use it. So we're restricted to sending a warning by radio."

"Did I ever tell you about the merc spies on the satellites?"

"Yes. But I have enough power to beam a few compressed data bursts. The satellites may not even monitor them. Then my ship's computer can decompress them and transmit the warning in an endless loop to the ground camp."

"And that little thing can reach a ship in orbit?"

"Well, only when it's overhead. And—" She consulted the link, though I could not see what she was reading. "And it won't be overhead for another twenty minutes. I've already recorded the warning message; I had plenty of time, hiking. So there's nothing else we can do out here just now. Except freeze."

"Okay. Let's check in with the others. Maybe they've found hot food. We can get back here in minutes, now that we know the way."

We were back in the junction room, standing next to the bank of switches that controlled the overhead lights. "Now, didn't one of these bring an elevator for Mishima?" Foyle asked.

"Let's try this door first," I said. "It's where Ariel went."

We entered the passageway with the arrow-shaped sign.

" 'Crank Rooms,' " Foyle read. "What could that mean? It's not another one of those Deutsch puns, is it?"

"I don't think it would be spelled that way." We turned a corner. "There is a German word *krank*, means 'sick,' and I suppose a 'krank' room could be—"

Footsteps, as Ariel met us, her face aglow.

"It's the infirmary," she said.

She grabbed my hand, and would have dragged me if I hadn't run. Foyle followed without comment.

"I told you, I told you," she was saying, "the Elitists weren't monsters. *Look!*"

Harry Lagado. Helen Hogg-Smythe. Alive.

We leaned against a glass wall, staring at them where they lay, in hospital beds. A robot tended them. They looked fine, but couldn't see or hear us, even when we pounded on the wall.

"Don't bother," Ariel said. "The door's around the next corner. I need one of you to get in, someone who can talk the door's language. Alun."

"Foyle, you try," I said. "I want to collect Mishima. No reason for us not to stick together now. I'll be back as soon as I can."

Their excited voices faded behind me as I closed the door to the junction room. It took me a while to get the elevator button to work, as though it were stopped on override. And then it lit up and indicators at the shaft door followed its rise.

Foyle joined me, closing the passage door behind her. "I got her in," she said. "Then I had a bad feeling. Two of the other hospital beds have been slept in."

The elevator opened before her words could register. Three men stepped out. I felt Foyle stiffen next to me.

"Thought they were supposed to shoot you if you didn't have an identification code, Colonel," I said.

Mishima smiled.

One of the mercs was tall and vaguely familiar, the other short. Their uniforms were reasonably clean. The short one carried a knife. The tall one cradled a curious two-shot weapon: not just two arrows, but an extra bow stacked on top of the first, and two triggers to work them independently.

A double crossbow.

"I was lucky," Mishima answered. "My brothers here are still recovering from the poison your treacherous friar spilled into their food; they say the robots had them in intensive care for days. I was able to surprise them and establish my rank. I've established a number of things, in fact.

"There is a communicator down there. An intercom to a number of key city centers. Including Level Null, where my brothers are headquartered.

"I've spoken to the main force. It seems that when the search party failed to return, their commander got nervous and moved up his schedule for the attack.

"It's all over. They took the construction camp without firing a shot, and secured the satellites yesterday morning. Prisoners have been cooperative; when the senator arrives, he will be greeted with all the right codes. The trap should work."

"Except that you're calling it off," I said, playing out the hand. "That was our agreement."

"An agreement is not binding if it is secured by fraud," Mishima said gently. "My lieutenant here"—and he gestured at the taller merc, whom I suddenly, sickeningly recognized as Contra, the ranking officer of the search party—"has clarified your role in this matter, *Commissioner*. I no longer believe that the Column has any inkling of Sir Max Condé's plans to dethrone the Consultant. I don't believe the great families of the Column will care, either, once he agrees to be their satrap. And I'm told he even has backing among a secret faction within the top levels of the navy—"

" 'The Few'?" I said—and Mishima's face registered the lucky hit. "So that was true, too. They *do* exist!"

Mishima must have thought I was trying to con him again. "True? Everything you've told me has been a lie. That being the case, my union can afford to take a fee for helping to bring Condé's coup about. For one thing, the Column doesn't even have to know. Our role will end when his militia navy uprising begins. And there aren't going to be any witnesses to say we were ever here.

"Anything to say? Anything at all? You've always been so good with words . . ."

Chapter Thirty

FOR SOME REASON I'd always fascinated Mishima. Even now, the commonsense order to shoot me wouldn't come—I saw questions in his eyes instead. But you must never give even a minor poet the time to take a breath; we can spin whole worlds on those diamond points.

I opened my mouth as if to speak, my hands obediently at my sides—and threw my whole body out of the line of fire and into the panel of light switches. Blackout. Managing to find Foyle's arm in the first flush of darkness, I yanked her up after me. Wordless shouting. One of the mercs almost immediately found the door to the infirmary and opened its light onto the intersection but by then we'd reached the maze, and vanished into it.

The lights went on, then off, then—after a few moments of muffled argument in the distance—on again. I'd counted on memory to let me solve the maze in the dark, but Mishima had the sense not to try following that way. It didn't make any difference, though; all we had to do was move quietly, give them no cues. We lost them in seconds, and proceeded to the end, the center.

Foyle and I found ourselves once more beneath the true sky. Catharensis, polestar for refugees, glowed like a votive candle, light-years too far away.

"Mishima should find this exit in twenty or thirty minutes," I said. "The maze is complicated, but not large. All you need is a system." I explained the ancient trail-one-hand-against-the-wall technique. "If he's never heard of it, he'll figure it out for himself. He has that sort of mind. He pares problems down."

She shivered and hugged herself in the arctic air. "It doesn't matter anyway," she said. "There's no one left to radio."

"What about your shuttle?" I asked. "If you could get back to your freighter, you could try to intercept the senator's ship before it arrives."

"I told you. The senator's people reprogrammed the shuttle doorlock so I can't use it while I'm here. I could bring it down, but I'd never get in without something like—"

"A skeleton coder?" I said. Handing her one.

She gaped at me.

"It's Mishima's," I explained. "He used it to sabotage the Otis system, and other things. I've always thought it would be less dangerous, and more useful, in my possession. Do you remember that touching moment, after the whirlwind, when I helped him over the ledge? Think of it as sleight-of-hand."

She laughed, shaking her head. "Okay. But the mercs have the defense satellites now. My escape shuttle is tiny, but not invisible. Safe enough coming down, probably, but then the observers'll compare notes and lock onto it as it comes back up."

However, she squared her chin and produced the pendant again. After whispering something briefly to it, she aimed it into the sky for a few moments.

I waited, shivering, while multicolored pennons of aurora waved between the stars.

Then Foyle's pendant changed color and she put it away.

"Might as well risk it," she said, "if Mishima doesn't get here first. And we might be able to hold that trap door against him, if he does."

But even as she spoke, I moved along the platform's west wall to the open edge that looked north, and surveyed what I could of the steep mountainside beneath us. "I think we can do a little better than that."

She joined me. Hope warred with reason in her voice. "You mentioned something about a stairway, before. But—even if there is, even if there is a door somewhere down there and it works . . . What's your plan? To get behind them? They already expect that; they're in a maze. And we'd still be unarmed."

"Here's the staircase," I said. "It's tricky to make out in this twilight. See how this"—I patted the rock wall—"extends downward, in a sort of spiral ridge?"

"Maybe," she allowed.

"The Elitists made the steps uneven, to fit into the contours of the rock. And there's some ice and weathering, that's why they're not flat. But if you assume we take a big step down, right here, look—you can keep going, down and clockwise. They're steep, but they're still just stairs."

She hugged herself again, rubbing her upper arms vigorously. "What about that ice?" she asked doubtfully. "And what I said before—What would we gain even if we made it?"

"Remember what *I* said before," I replied, removing from my belt the coil of ultrafine cord I'd saved from confetti-moth country. "About how I never understood the way the lodge ceremony on Nexus ended, the fire-escape descent—never saw the point to it, ritually? It seemed like such an anticlimax, to get to the bottom of the stairs and open the door, only to see one more mythological painting. After you'd already ascended to the heavens. The subject of the painting was wrong, too, didn't belong at the end of the story. But now we know that the lodge ceremony was just a pale copy of the original ritual. Beyond the door at the bottom of *these* stairs is the real icon, which could only be hinted at on Nexus—something awesome, the Elitist holy-of-holies."

"And what did you say the painting was again?" she asked with just a touch of irritation.

"The marriage of Gaea and Uranus—Earth and Heaven."

"I don't get it."

"And it had a title, was never referred to by any other name . . . 'The Great Coupling.' "

She looked blank, but only for a second. "The *control* coupling," she said. "In that heroic statue at the entrance to the city—the governor for the planetary magnetic field! Of course. As you said, almost a religious icon to the Elitists . . . Well, okay. Clever of you to realize. But so what?"

I laughed at her—a rare pleasure, to run ahead of someone you suspect is smarter than yourself. "You're like Mishima. A simplifier. But a magician knows when it's more useful to complicate. Think of the Great Coupling as a big switch, hooked into all the complexity of earth and sky—what happens if we *throw* that switch?"

"Move the cable back into the Titans' governor, you mean? Well . . . assuming we could do it, the magnetic field would start to grow stronger again. Gradually, I guess; we don't have any idea how it works. Are you thinking it will signal something to the senator before he lands?"

"Naah," I said. "I agree with you, the field figures to change only gradually. But it's still a *huge* change, because it ripples across a million kilometers of space . . . Come on, class, what do we call this?"

"A magnetic storm!" She shook her head, swearing—then surprised me with a kiss on the cheek.

"With a little luck," I said, "it *might* screw up radio, radar, everything. Communication reduced to tight beams. False images all over the scanners—"

"And my shuttle slipping away in the general confusion—scot-free!" She laughed delightedly. "It's a lousy bet, of course; I can think of a half-dozen things that might go wrong. But I don't care. At least this way we play to win."

"I think we've got a shot," I said. "We've already told your escape shuttle our location, and if you want to give it an extra fix at the last minute, that's line-of-sight stuff, the storm probably won't affect that."

"But if Mishima gets here first—"

"No problem, except for those last few minutes. Up until then, we'll be down the mountainside, out of sight. He'll stick his head up and see no one. Maybe he'll keep looking elsewhere. Remember, he doesn't know about the shuttle—or any other reason for us to wait in this cold." I took the long step down to the first stair and turned to face the mountain, groping across the rock face.

"What are you looking for?" Foyle asked.

"If the stairs ice up now, then they probably always did. There's got to be someplace to tie a safety line, maybe here on the side . . . something low down . . . Damn!" I crouched and spat on my hand.

"Problem?"

"I found it, but my skin stuck to it. I'm loose now. It's a metal loop, it'll be good. You're the pro with knots, why don't you do this?"

Five minutes later we were properly yoked up, one end of the fine unbreakable cord tied to the metal loop, the coil held in my hand, and the other end knotted around and through my belt across to Foyle's empty backpack harness, with two meters' slack between us. We would now be fully exposed to the wind. Foyle had a hood to raise against it. I didn't. But my tunic and hers had pockets, and after I showed her the trick of ripping out the linings to make gloves, she suggested tearing a big interior swatch from where the double-breast of my uniform overlapped, and tying it around the top of my head.

Without that protection, I wouldn't have lasted ten minutes.

Ice, snow, hail—they're all visible, they force us to allow for them. But cold by itself is a killer we don't figure on. Foyle and I hadn't gone a dozen steep meters before I realized we might not make it up again, not unless there really was a door we could open at the bottom, a chance to restore body heat. The winds run high at the top of an Earthlike world, and when the sun is just a faint glow on the horizon the chill is like ice-water, then ice-needles. You finally pass through numbness to the other extreme, a sensation more like burning. Without the heaviest clothing, life is measured in minutes.

Your eyes may adjust to the polar twilight, but less blood reaches hands, feet—and brain: the other mountains in the distance become hazy and unreal, a jagged purple jumble, while nearby details take on portentousness and mystical clarity, each sight perhaps the last you'll see. A cranny of ice in the gray grain of the rock face, a vein of white marble that echoes it. The hypnotic swirl of loose threads edging the cloth that wraps your hand, the meatlocker blue-pink of the naked wrist below that . . .

Fortunately, the climbing wasn't mechanical; it was treacherous enough to keep resharpening mind and senses, even as they weathered away. Foyle would take each new step first. I'd hold her wrists and then lean backward, letting her put her weight down gradually, testing, testing . . . At these polar temperatures, ancient ice would feel just like rock, providing if anything more friction, until the temperature change of a boot's pressure turned it slick and slippery a second later. And at one point a clear stair, wind-scoured, gave way beneath Foyle—the rock itself crumbling beneath her. If I hadn't dropped to my knees I'd have lost my grip, and we'd have found out how strong the line and my broad uniform belt really were. But we didn't fall, and we made the stair below that. I just don't remember how . . .

The fire escape on the lodge building at Nexus University had been only two stories tall, but—not for the first time—I'd relied too heavily on a metaphor. Now we'd run nearly to the end of my cord, an estimated sixty meters. True, I might have left a little slack behind us as we went along, but I couldn't guess how much; all but the nearest meter of the ultrathin line was invisible in the twilight. I was just about to ask Foyle whether we should proceed without line—a grim prospect, but so was the twenty minutes back up, our strength gone—when she spoke. "I think we've made it."

The step just below her was broader than the others, a ledge, and she said she could see a door facing it. I delivered her there, but could feel the weight of the line tugging back now, wrapped maybe a twentieth of the way around the narrow peak and riding up as the slack disappeared. "I've reached the end of the line," I said, and the words sounded odd on various counts, odd and thin in the jeering wind.

She looked up, and her hood blew back. Her hair showed only an underpainting of red in the dimness, but her face was angled to catch what light there was, and shone palely. Taut, lineless, the eyes sharply slanted. She'd hit her limit, but she'd hit it strongly, quite beautiful in an inhuman way. She untied herself.

"Stay secured . . . until I get it open," she said. "I'll feel stronger then . . . more help for each other." I understood what she meant, even if the words didn't make much sense.

The wind let up for a second and I took in the view. It was savagely unreal, shadowed gulfs and sharp masses that faded in and out of perspective. And above—was that the aurora, or eye fatigue? Stick to business, look at Foyle.

I had a one-quarter view of her standing a few meters below

me and to the side. She was facing inward, her makeshift glove poking at something chest-high and out of sight. Her lips moved and I caught the word "frozen," and then she pounded at the unseen door controls with the heel of her fist. And something happened.

A wave of dull red light swept across the ledge, then rose up her legs and body to the top of her head, and she looked over to me, yelling, "It's open!" But even as I fumbled at the restraining cord around my belt, a sharp-edged shadow descended over her face once more, and she hit the controls frantically, crying, "It's closing again—can't stop it!"

"Get inside!" I called out. "Handle it from in there!"

"But you—"

"Don't be stupid!"

She didn't wait for further permission, but ducked into what remained of the red glow, and a moment later I was alone on the mountain face. But not for long.

I'd been hearing crackling noises for some time; presumably echoes of icefalls from the valleys around us. But this one sounded more immediate. I looked up the rough-hewn stairs to where they curved out of sight and saw Ken Mishima come around the bend, less than ten meters away.

He was wearing work gloves and extra shirts, perhaps taken from the other mercenaries, and some sort of headband as well. He carried no safety rope, but he'd evidently made better time that way; his boots gleamed with the ice-gripping strap-on cleats he'd taken from the equipment shelf before the Backstage climb and he moved with Zen assuredness. He'd commandeered the double crossbow I'd seen before, and now, without raising to aim or otherwise telegraphing his intent, he fired.

The bolt whiffled past my cheek and off the edge of the world.

"Missed!" I shouted, flattening against the mountain wall, behind the protection of its curve; the bow's lower cross was still loaded and cocked.

"Sorry!" Mishima called back. "Windage. I'll try to make a clean job of it next time." Something—the cold, victory, malice—put a harsh edge on his usual tone of philosophical detachment, but he went on conversationally, "How far down do these stairs go?"

"All the way to the bottom," I said. "Why not let us chance it? You can't follow much longer—you'll freeze, too."

"But why would you be going down, then?" he asked. I heard confused scraping noises. His voice sounded no closer.

"Perhaps to suck you in. It's the only way I can take you with me, isn't it?" I risked a glance and saw that he was having trouble with the stair that had crumbled away. The necessary slide would be much riskier without a safety line. Hence this conversation; he'd be just as glad to stall me in place.

For my part, I gave up the panicky tugging at Foyle's impeccable knot. If she got the door open, I could always unbuckle the belt itself—even my increasingly numb fingers could manage that—but in the meantime, with nowhere to go and my strength dwindling, I was better off secured. I could play Mishima's game, and stall.

"Think about it," I went on. "I just have to stay a little bit ahead of you, always around the bend, and you won't get a shot. Maybe you can resist hypothermia longer than I can—but twice as long? When I finally fade, you still have to make it all the way back up. It may already be too far. I may already have won."

"I don't think so," he said. "You underestimate the powers of a directed spirit. And I no longer overestimate you. Your little tricks."

I stuck my head back out again, still hugging the mountain, and discovered I could watch him with impunity for a while; he was not in firing position, his free hand extended for balance. One boot tested the stub of the missing stair. "Do I detect a note of pique?" I asked. "That's it, isn't it? You have to finish me off personally, because you think I've made a fool of you."

"Nonsense," he said. "It's my duty because I'm in charge. Because the others refused to believe that these were stairs, or that anyone would use them. The lower ranks see only what they want to, and never volunteer." Yes, he was clearly padding his lines; it would be the simplest solution, if he could keep me listening until I dropped. "But I have a responsibility to tie up loose ends," he went on. "Nothing *personal* about it. It's just neatness—completeness . . ."

"Like leaving Lagado to die when you were teamed with him—Ariel, too, on a crumbling stair like the one that's about to kill you—" He didn't turn a hair, though, just kept probing. "At that point you still didn't know how badly your brothers had compromised the union, or what you'd have to do to clean up the mess. But whatever else was true, civilian witnesses to Brotherhood involvement were an unwelcome complication. I guess you didn't need any more motive than that, in your line of work. Especially since you wouldn't have to raise a hand yourself, just let the Hellway do the killing. Until you saw Wongama take out your fellow mercenary, that is. I recognized your knife in his back, you see, because I've always taken a keen interest in the tools on your belt—looking for the skeleton coder. Why'd you kill him, after cutting a deal with me? Force of habit?"

"I thought you'd died in the earthquake," he said. "That voided my agreement to protect the others. Otherwise I would certainly have kept it. But I don't expect you to understand what it means to follow a clear line of duty."

"By killing your own brothers for me, for instance, later on," I said. "Yes. It may have been your duty, but won't it grieve your comrades on the grievance committee, when you make your report? They'll also wonder why you failed to eliminate me when I first arrived on Newcount Two. You couldn't quite guess my true role, but you should have simplified me out of the situation anyway. The flitter crash wouldn't have had any political blowback—if you'd made it work. But it was stupid to use the same skeleton coder you'd already used on the Otis. Not as undetectable as you thought, which made your denial later pretty pointless . . ."

Speaking of pointless, though, why the delay? Why didn't he just use my own safety line, if not to climb down with, to yank me up with? But of course—wrapped low against the mountain all the way down, it was neither visible nor underfoot. Which explained why his underlings had doubted that the stairs were in use.

"The truth is this," I went on. "As a troubleshooter, you haven't hit a proper target yet. Mainly your own men, just because I told you to. And who am I?"

"You're *nothing*!" he said. "An empty mask. I admit it, you fooled me for a long time. There are so few real warrior spirits in any age. We look to each other as to candles in the dark. We welcome any chance to learn from a peer, especially from a spirit with its own style, a centered master."

This was stalling, too, but deplorably sincere. I kept glancing back at the ledge, looking for the red light that would spill across it if the door opened again.

Mishima had reached his peroration. "But there's another archetype we may encounter, Parker. The trickster. At first he appears to be a master in disguise, but he is only a master of appearances, the center of attention. To such as you, *everything* is personal, ego is all. You had a direction to follow, Condé's commission, and you went back on it—for what? The good opinion of women? A distaste for dirty work? Do you even know?

"I do. Ego is a vortex, and you are slipping down its funnel. Even the tricks have dwindled, Parker—'The stairs go all the way.' 'I'm sucking you in,' 'Don't slip, now!' Pathetic. A balanced spirit doesn't have to rely on tricks. Watch."

He held the bow sideways above his head, flexed his knees—and *skated* down the broken rock incline to the next complete stair, sparks streaming off his crampons like shooting stars. He came to a stop without jerking or bobbing, just straightened up. The wind moaned in wonderment. His next step down was confident, another meter closer, and he lowered his weapon into firing position. I glanced back at the ledge—no glow, no escape—and gripped my belt with both hands; everything seemed to be receding from me, darkness and emptiness in all directions.

"That was no trick," he said. "No ego trip. Just balance, Parker. That's all. We've reached the end together. Nothing personal."

The end of the line, the end of all tricks? But I know more directions than your simple compass-points, Colonel. And while life lasts, I have the death card yet to play—not necessarily a loser, for it is the ace of spades.

I backed to the outer edge of the stair as if to give Mishima a better shot, and from there, with a jump, into the vast gulf behind, beyond, below.

Chapter Thirty-one

I'D PUSHED OFF as hard as I could, but still experienced only a moment of free-fall—mountain flying up before me, the skull's smile of an ice river kilometers below—and then the line yanked back at my belt. At first I was swung sideways more than anything, spiraling outward, as the cord unreeled invisibly from the rough staircase above. But then there came the sharp but yielding tug that must have been the line catching Mishima at ankles or knees and hurling him off the edge.

I didn't even see his death scene, just felt the jerk as my swing changed to downward and inward. I braced myself for the first impact. With the line connected near my belt buckle, my feet came forward naturally, and when they hit the dark mountain-face I let my knees bounce like springs. But my lateral momentum was too great; I went into a helpless spin on the rebound, and as I swung in again there was nothing I could do but protect my head as I slammed at full length against the rock, only to bounce sideways and hit again, and a third time, skipping along as if I'd been thrown onto a highway from a moving vehicle.

But only the first smash was at full speed—that was the one that must have cracked a few ribs on my left side; the rest just left superficial bruises and abrasions, and a strained wrist from fending off once—and oh yes, a hoarse throat from the screaming.

Could have been worse, in other words. Could have let Mishima have the satisfaction of shooting me. Worse still, I could have missed my chance to send him ahead of me to hell through wishful thinking—if I'd tried the cord-swipe from where I stood, yanking with my hands, both angle and force would have been insufficient. At least this way, dangling against a cold rock wall, I could die the relatively painless death of freezing: not much left to it but going to sleep.

Climbing the cord was out of the question—it was too fine, would slice through my frozen hands like piano wire. And the wall before me was too smooth for fingerholds. But the wind kept blowing, stinging, hurting. It wasn't getting any easier, this death business. And I found myself drawing my feet up again, scrambling and swinging to make wider and wider arcs sideways, looking for a crevice I could grab with my hands, chasing the dream of a series of crevices all the way back up to the stairs.

I didn't find a one. But I burned off the adrenaline the jump had engendered, and when I finally swung to a halt I was truly finished, twisting in the wind—black mountain, blue night, black mountain, blue night. It was soon after that when I began to hear the voice.

"I have aged, I have aged internally . . ."

Ur-Linguish. I tried to translate in the light of a flickering mental candle. The hallucination's style was conversational, everyday but somehow oblique, vaguely reminiscent of—

"I grow old, I grow old, I shall wear out batten-lines, if triple-rolled. . . ."

Scribbles of a student night, fragments from one of the ancients I'd had to give up on, ironic cadences too brittle for translation—

"And there will be time, there will be time . . . The evening is spread against the sky like a point array, or simple two-D table . . ."

"Uh, help?" I called. Sounds of fairy pickaxes and power drills offstage. Possibly what happens when frozen eardrums crack. But then the creaky metallic voice began again:

"No, I am not presentient, nor was meant to be . . . Automatic, cautious, and meticulous . . . Almost, at times, a tool . . . I have measured out my line in coffer spools . . ."

But it was real, some strange shape had eclipsed the stars above me. "Help! I'm down here!" I cried, and did it again in the old tongue, remembering to sound the *h*'s, the *l*, the *w*.

And faintly, faintly, far above, Foyle's answering voice, a command. "That's him, that's him, bring him up!" And from somewhere between us:

"Shall I port a stair behind? Do I dare to make a reach? I have heard the humans calling, each to each! . . . Should I, now I see how caked the ice is, halve the length to solve a momentary crisis? . . . I should have had a pair of rubber claws . . ."

And then it was upon me, still muttering dementedly to itself, a steel spider more than two meters in diameter. It descended from directly above to block all view, its batten arms manipulating shiny metallic support-lines as they unreeled from internal spools. Now its spindly jointed legs extended to bracket me, tipped with tiny drillheads that whined and drove securely into the solid rock on either side. The headbox eyed me with penlights and cameras; scanners whirred and clucked.

"There will be time, there will be time," the robot assured me, even as terrifying shears emerged from its body to clip the cord I hung from. *"Let us go, then, you and I."* I heard my line snap, but instead of falling I was caught and drawn into a possum-pouch in the machine's thorax, where I curled up in darkness and warmth. I felt a great lurch, a smooth ascent, a bobbing traverse; heard Foyle's voice, too faint for words, and then the robot's, all around me, "*Glad to be of use*"; wondered when I'd really blacked out; and blacked out.

* * *

"Hell and back in half an hour," Foyle was saying. "Or forty minutes, anyway. Lucky if you don't throw up—I did."

She was in a crouch; I lay at full length with my head in her lap. Beneath us was an open-grill catwalk, and empty space. Stone walls loomed dim in the distance, indirectly lit in red and marked with heavy dark lines and squares. The air was warmer, and dry—and in gentle motion, back and forth, like breathing. Strange.

Foyle was wearing a heavy hooded parka, and in her right hand she brandished the hypodermic airneedle she'd just injected me with. I felt as though she'd changed my blood to brandy.

"What is this stuff?" I asked.

"I don't know. One hell of an upper. Three minutes from now you're going to think you've had ten hours' sleep and twenty cups of coffee. But we'd better accomplish our business as fast as we can, because when we come down, we're going to come down hard."

"Where . . . did you get it?"

"A kit inside the rescue robot. And don't worry, there's a fresh inspection sticker on it—all pharmaceuticals have been replaced since we put the Hellway into use again."

". . . Rescue robot?"

"Oh God, did you hit your head when you fell? You told me a minute ago about your ribs—do you remember that?"

"No. But I remember I hurt them. And I didn't fall, I jumped. And I remember the robot rescuing me. In a surreal sort of way . . . You found it here? 'Here' being the inside of the mountain?"

"That's it, now you're tracking. When I ducked in, either the door clipped my head or I just passed out and hit the floor. Anyway, the robot came and gave me an injection. Then I had some trouble getting it to understand there was someone trapped outside—the language barrier. But I just enunciated letter for letter, and finally it showed me where the warm coats were and opened the door again. When I realized you'd gone over the side—what do you mean, 'jumped'?"

"Mishima was going to shoot me anyway. Thought I'd take him with me. Sweep him off with the safety line, see." But she didn't see. I explained it in more detail, but she just stared at me sympathetically.

"Are you really sure any of that happened?" she asked. "Couldn't it have been a hallucination—or a blackout dream?"

"Don't . . . *ever* ask me that, about *anything*," I told her, and she looked back, scared.

"I'm sorry. I forgot."

"I'm sorry, too. And the answer is, I don't know." I found I could sit, now, and even stand. She had described the stimulant's effect precisely. Aside from some throbbing ribs, and a vague desire to puke, I felt dangerously terrific.

The spider robot sat at one end of the catwalk, crouching complexly. I approached it, saying, "Lucky for us it was here."

"Not luck," Foyle said. "Ariel was right about the philosophy behind this place. You go down the stairs with nothing but a safety line, because the danger is fun, but no one's supposed to die just for slipping. This machine's the safety net."

"Am I right that this thing talks a lot?"

"Certainly kept trying to report to me," she replied. "I couldn't make much out, of course."

I had a brief conversation with the device in my halting Ur-Linguish. It was indeed eager to make reports, and concerned that it was not maintained often enough—some of its parts were in need of replacement, and so forth. It formally requested a lexical update because it could hardly understand my companion. A smart, adaptable machine. The voice was as I remembered it, but uttered nothing suggestive of either insanity or Imagism. I had to wonder if Foyle was right, if I'd hallucinated Mishima, too.

I conferred with it another few moments, then turned to Foyle. "No problem," I said. "We're back on course. When you're ready to go up and meet your shuttle, this thing can carry you to the top in a minute. I didn't try to explain the cops-and-robbers aspect of the situation—that's beyond its ken. But I can't believe the mercs have been waiting for us out-of-doors, not all this time, and if you just park our friend here on top of the trap door, that should keep them from making an appearance while the shuttle comes down."

"Excellent!"

"So if your forty-minute guess is anywhere near right, we still have enough time to replug the Great Coupling first. But I'm afraid this machine doesn't know anything about that—the Coupling's location, for instance."

Foyle's end of the catwalk ended in a set of lockers, a control turret, and what I assumed to be the door to the outside, currently shut. In the spider's direction, the catwalk faded off into darkness.

"Oh, you were right about that, the Coupling's right here," Foyle said. "We're on the viewing stage, I guess. Wait a second . . . I found the switch before . . ." She reached for one of the controls, and a moment later spotlights came on.

We were suspended in the middle of a vertical shaft, narrower than the lake elevator, but bottomless. The catwalk we stood on bisected it, and the far side, past the spider, led to a steep ladder that ended in a small steel door. The rescue robot had confirmed that its relief and maintenance robots came from beyond that, presumably the control levels beneath the infirmary and maze. So much for the human superstructure; the rest of what we saw was Titanic, a million years old.

The Great Coupling itself was lit up for drama's sake, looking much as it had in the bronze statue at the city entrance: a half-meter-thick serpent extending horizontally along the wall, then bending upward from its former socket to a new socket almost two meters higher. Just below was the scaffold the humans must have bolted into place to facilitate the work. A side ladder, I saw, could be unfolded from our catwalk to the scaffold. A piece of cake.

"You had this lit before?" I asked. "Why did you turn it off again?"

"Didn't like the scenery," she said shortly, gesturing downward.

With the spotlights on, one had an attenuating view of the seemingly infinite drop beneath us. And there was something oppressive and dwarfing about the details of the walls, too. Other cables, and sockets, and larger but equally simple structures, traced geometric patterns all the way around and down, a vertiginous spiral.

"I suppose it must hit the roof of the Hellway, eventually," I said.

"I think we're just north of that. I don't like to think how far down it might go."

"I don't care anymore," I said. "All normal fear of heights has been burned out of me. Ever since the shuttle from orbit, Newcount Two has been one long fall, with occasional breaks for lunch."

She laughed, and I realized we were both a little high. "But I don't like any of it," she said. "Know what it reminds me of? Artifacts from the days before organic cybernetics—as though we were grains of dust on the side of a silicon chip. And listen."

". . . I don't hear anything," I lied.

"High and faint in the background. Like breathing, all around us. Wouldn't be so bad if we could get the whole place really bright, but this fading off into the unknown—"

"Yeah, well, that's enough of that," I interrupted. "Help me get this ladder unfolded."

A minute later we crossed over to the scaffold and stood beneath the Coupling. "Looks simple enough," I said. "May be heavy, but you probably don't need the six people we saw in the statue. That was just ceremonial choreography."

"If you say so."

"See, I think if you stand just one step behind me here, your right shoulder behind my left, our necks will bracket it, and we can ease it down by bending our knees. It'll want to haul back, so prepare to lean forward, pushing at the flange here."

"How do we release it?"

"Looks to me like we just push the studs. How did the friar describe it? Just a scaled-up version of the sort of connector you'd see in a small machine. I can push two, and you can push two, and that's where we hold it."

"Look," she said. "Are you sure you want to do this? We got our information from the equivalent of a child's schoolbook. You can't just replug planetary electromagnetism into some sort of transformer and step it up or down, it's crazy."

This wasn't like her—it was the stimulant talking. "No, it's what you said before, Foyle," I told her. "We're on the chip. Only it's not one micropulse of electricity in this circuit, more likely billions of data strands inside the cable, and I don't know what the data relates to or what vast mysterious thing the couplings do with it. But it's supposed to affect the field, and nothing else matters. If we can't foul up the surveillance net, you don't get away. If you don't get away, Condé wins and all of us are eliminated as witnesses; other planets will be enslaved or even exterminated. If replugging this thing is a colossal mistake, and turns Newcount Two into a fireball or a pumpkin, it's the same death for us, but it at least ruins his plans, and saves those people . . . Would you find this speech more eloquent in verse?"

"No, that's all right." She braced her shoulder behind mine. "The threat is enough."

But she'd spooked me with her misgivings. I told her we'd hit the studs at the count of three, but delayed after two, and found myself whispering the last word.

The studs resisted for an instant, then slipped all the way

down. The cable was heavy, but we were braced against its backward pull. Silence rolled over us in a great cold wave.

Was I imagining it, or had the cosmic breathing stopped?

Bending our knees in unison, lining up the cable-end with the socket, driving it forward like a ram . . . we did it with desperate quickness, and above the sound of the studs snapping back up, retainer bolts springing into place, came a high-pitched, all-encompassing gasp—and the breathing noise was back, perhaps a little different, a little stronger.

"Please," Foyle said. "Let's get the hell out of here."

There were actually two doors between us and the surface, forming a long airlock through a wall six meters thick. I stood next to Foyle on the ledge at the foot of the great stone stairs, looking out over the jagged valley as the rescue robot came up behind us. It wasn't so cold, knowing I could duck back inside.

"Wait a minute," I said before Foyle could step into the machine's carrying pouch. I pointed at an object on the staircase and ordered the spider to retrieve it, which it did with a speed and dexterity that must have relieved Foyle.

"What is it?" she asked me as the machine handed it over.

Mishima's crossbow.

"The line must have caught him very low," I said. "Maybe ankle-high. Natural for him to drop the bow and make a snatch for the edge as he went over. But he must not have made it, or he wouldn't have left this . . . I think it was the only weapon the mercs had. Now I'll go back in, across the catwalk, and come up on them from below."

"Good luck," was all she said, pressing my hand. She'd withdrawn into her own future now, and I couldn't blame her. The robot bore her away, and as I looked up after them I saw the aurora. It had grown larger, a blanket rather than a pennon, and was still billowing out, its chatoyant folds shimmering with new power. Had we done that, with the coupling?

I hefted the crossbow. It had discharged when it fell, but I found some spare bolts in a compartment in the stock. Mishima was going to save my life one last time.

I'd seen a lot of deaths, living on the run in the ragged fringes. Few had been worse or more gruesome than Friar Francisco's, for instance, but it suddenly struck me that Mishima's was one of the scariest, because the purest. Death distilled. One minute you're standing there on the upper stair, full of purpose, knowing exactly what's going on and prepared to enjoy it. And then you're not. Just thrown away, into the night and cold—nothing you did, no warning, no time to figure it out. No chance to modify whatever your last words might have been.

Nothing personal.

As it turned out, the rest was easy. After some blind wandering around in an intermediate level, I found an elevator with labeled buttons and ascended to the infirmary floor. Ariel met me with kisses at the door, putting aside a weapon she'd made from a chair leg. She told me that Mishima and the mercenaries had never returned from the maze, though she'd occasionally heard voices from within it. It figured; Mishima must have ordered them to wait for him, just beneath the trap door, and they would have cleared off only after the robot's arrival changed the situation. I didn't go in after them, but waited for them to come out instead, sitting inside the recess next to the entrance, behind the semitransparent curtain, where the Questioner used to sit as he chanted.

I heard the voices, too, occasionally. The two mercs were apparently lost; Mishima had not explained his system to them. But eventually they found their way out. They were if anything more formidable-looking without the shirts they'd loaned to Mishima. I eased past the curtain into position behind them. On the basis of experience and general psychology, I aimed at the one who was shorter than average height.

"It's all over," I said. "Nobody has to get hurt."

"Hey sure, no problem," said the one I was aiming at as they both turned, and his hand made a few flickering motions, so I shot him.

I'd had plenty of time to nerve myself to the likelihood, sitting and waiting. He pitched over backward, the bolt I'd aimed at his belly lodged in his shoulder. Contra, the taller one, was already three steps into the split-up-and-flank routine his buddy must have signaled—but as I locked onto him, one cross still loaded, he dropped to his knees and bent his hands in front of his forehead, open palms facing me. "Okay?" he asked. "Pax?"

"Okay."

"That was stupid, Rolf," he told his friend.

Stripped of its rhetorical flourishes, Rolf's reply expressed basic agreement, regret, and discomfort. Maybe I should have guessed that this sort of weapon would throw high at short range, but I was just as pleased with a nonfatal result.

"Look, guys," I said, "let's wrap this up. You got a message off by intercom. We just got a message off by shuttle. Larger forces are going to fight, and nothing we can do inside this mountain will affect that. Whichever side wins will rescue us. So if you give me your full parole, we can put weapons aside, get the medical robots to work on Rolf, and wait out the war. Winners will swear that the losers were model prisoners. Fair enough?"

"Hell, yes," said Contra.

"Sure," agreed Rolf. "Don't know what I was thinking of. You were the colonel's responsibility anyway, he said so. That is the bow he made us give him, isn't it?"

" 'Fraid so."

He sat up, nodding, already very pale. "What did I tell you?" he said to his friend as we helped him to his feet. "Fucking union is a fucking joke."

The mercenary guilds have a tradition of scrupulous parole; otherwise, no government would bother holding a union's prisoners for exchange. Rolf and his leader, whose real name was Achmed, gave us no trouble at all during the next few days, and it was only to humor Ariel that I found a way to lock them in a room of their own at night.

I crashed pretty hard when the emergency stimulant wore off, just as Foyle had predicted, and the medical machines did good work on my ribs, cuts, and frostbite lesions while I slept. The next day the mercs and I went down and put the Great Coupling back the way it had been. Foyle had either gotten clear or not by then, and I thought we'd be better off in some contingencies if normal radio conditions were restored. But the disturbance I'd started would be a long time fading; in the radio monitor room we still heard nothing but static. No one had ever returned to Level Null's intercom post. We could do nothing but wait.

Helen Hogg-Smythe and Harry Lagado occupied themselves with reading texts from the old Elitist computer library on their bedside terminals. The old woman was almost fully cured, though she'd apparently been in terrible shape when the watchers rescued her from the wrecked eel-balloon; her blood had been cleansed of contaminants, and the damage these had done her liver and kidneys was being repaired.

Harry had broken one leg in the confusion when his wings burst through the sky barrier, which had been no more than an electrostatic illusion. A robot device had caught the wings before they could smash into the true ceiling above, but Harry—thinking it was attacking him—had twisted in his harness and hurt himself.

I think he'd been hoping that his father would be resurrected like Helen, but had known better. He was bearing up well. He read quietly or listened, with his apparently genuine historical interest, to Helen's reminiscences about the days of her youth—the early decades of the previous century.

For my part, I found it hard to concentrate. Bad futures loomed. A week before, making our plans in the cemetery, we'd only needed to get word to the construction crew in the satellites, and the mercenaries' attack would have collapsed before it could begin. But now that the mercs owned the satellites, it was not clear what Foyle could do; we hadn't had time to discuss it. I believed she'd make it back to her freighter—and even pull the freighter out of orbit—without opposition, but then the mercs would be on to her. There were message boats on those satellites; if any of them were armed, they could follow and harry her.

If she sunplunged, and took word back to authorities in the Column's central worlds, she and the senator would cross like letters in the space mails, and Mehta would be captured anyway. The fence sitters in the higher circles of the Column would probably just accept the fact of Condé's victory and cut a deal with him. But if she didn't sunplunge, her only chance was to intercept the senator's vessel soon after it emerged into this system—at an unpredictable point in tight solar orbit, where communications would be lousy—and warn him to turn back before her merc pursuers blasted him. Little time in which to maneuver, and too much distance. The more I thought about it, the less chance I thought we had.

I didn't burden Ariel with my thoughts, but my attitude depressed her anyway. I was not acting cheerful and righteous as a white-uniformed hero should. She took me aside on the third day and asked if it was really necessary for me to play cards with the mercenaries.

It was, actually. I'd lost a few hundred munits—on paper—but in the meantime, when Ariel was not around, had managed to brainwash them into accepting the "political agent" story again. Clever, wasn't it, how I'd infiltrated Condé's operation as an actor . . . easy to convince him I could impersonate a government official, since I really was one . . . not good form to discuss these operational details when the civilians are listening, of course, but have you guys ever considered the advantages of government service? That sort of thing, a form of mental needlework: patching the old cover.

"Oh, they're not such bad guys off-duty," I said. "And it keeps their hands occupied. Speaking of which, if you're bored, there are some romantic little nooks in the maze . . ."

But this didn't go over either. I could see from the half-horrified, half-baffled look in her eyes that full female sexual amnesia had set in. The old malady. The most passionate woman in the world need only go forty-eight hours without it, and she may suddenly and entirely forget what it's like, or that she enjoys it. Some bizarre psychobiological short-circuit takes place, causing her to mistake the subject under discussion for something else, satisfying, but too taxing: something no one could expect to do very often at all, or within anything except the cleanest and most quiet surroundings, or at less than a peak of mental and physical readiness—i.e., childbirth.

This confusion always passes in time, of course. Maybe the delay is its only evolutionary purpose—to winnow out the men who won't be around next year, next month, next week. The unreliables, the pretenders. The butterflies.

"Injustice is relatively easy to bear," said Mencken, a classical sage. "What stings is justice."

Another four days passed.

We didn't hear the rescuers land on the mountaintop above us, but the confused calling back and forth in the maze brought those of us who were ambulatory out to meet them. I shouted directions into the entrance. Achmed stood at my side, waiting to receive the crossbow from me if the next uniforms we saw were Iron Brotherhood or militia navy; meanwhile, Ariel wished audibly for a loyal Column marine.

"It's all over," the first one out said, adding inevitably, "no one has to get hurt." And I handed the crossbow to Achmed, who assured the merc officer we'd been model prisoners.

Chapter Thirty-two

THE VOICE CRACKLED at us from over two million kilometers away. "Code responses all seem to be in order. Has anything changed since my scout checked in with you? Over."

Condé's voice. The trap I'd entered the first time I'd heard it, weeks that seemed like years ago, was only smaller and tighter now.

The Iron Brotherhood's local commander—the major whom I had once mentally dubbed Pro, actually named Dubbs—bent over the radio. "No, Sir Maximilien. Ground camp and satellites still secure. Repairs have been made to the senator's vessel, but I'm afraid his medical condition continues to decline. His own fault for resisting, of course, but . . ."

He let his voice trail off—a rhetorical failure, due to the necessity of adding, "Over." And then there was the time lag; it took the tight beam ten seconds to reach Condé's yacht, and as long for the Knuckle-Cracker's reply to come back to us:

"I want to see the senator alive, one last time. Over."

"So your scout informed us. But even three days ago he was too weak to be moved, and he's worse now. I'm glad you got here before we lost him, Sir Maximilien. Over."

Twenty seconds elapsed. Not a short time.

"You may call me Admiral now, I think. Over." The merc major twisted his face in frustration. At these distances, most people avoid small talk.

"Considering the time factor, Admiral, we expect you'll want to dock directly with the senator's yacht. I am already here. The prize crew will be standing by. Suggest we reconcile orbits when you're somewhat closer. Over."

Another twenty-second lag, and—I reflected gloomily—Condé already thousands of kilometers nearer.

"At my current rate of deceleration, we should be able to dock in just under two hours," he said. "Over and out."

"Base out." Major Dubbs stretched, leaning back in one of

the roomy swivel chairs. The bridge of Senator Mehta's yacht was lit like a nightclub—no overheads, pools of intensity on low surfaces, a colorful central holo tank.

"Well," said the mercenary finally, "he seems to have bought it. Do I get to attend the party?"

A tall figure emerged from the shadows at his side, revealing the uniform of a Column marine colonel. "Sorry, Major," he said. "I'm afraid the senator expects you to spend the rest of your tour in custody. But your boys did well—Condé really grilled them on those passwords. Convincing job."

"He's a cautious old fox," Major Dubbs said. "That's a hopped-up little messenger boat, probably one of those one-man Hermes express jobs. Smarter than coming with the big ship and escorts you expected. Harder to detect. And notice his approach angle? If he'd seen any indication we were responding under duress, he could have screamed past us into a half-orbit slingshot back to the sun."

"You don't have sell me," the colonel said. "Your usefulness has been noted. The playacting's well worth it, if we can net the big fish without having to fight the whole school."

"Damn it," protested Senator Mehta's personal pilot, sitting nearby—a militia navy captain, on loan from the Swathe's Sodality—"There never was going to be any militia uprising behind Max Condé. Aren't my crew proof enough of that?"

"Yeah, for a mixed operation, things have gone very smoothly," the colonel conceded. He nodded a head in my direction. "Of course, the commissioner deserves some credit for the intelligence background."

"Not to mention the whole plan," I said.

"Which has justified my approval," said the colonel. "There you have it, Citizen DeVysse. Condé couldn't pass up the chance to gloat over the senator in person. In two hours we'll have him."

"Terribly exciting," said the most bored voice in the universe, at my side: Senator Delip Mehta's private secretary, a rail-thin fop named Meier DeVysse. The senator had been keeping to his private chambers so far, but he'd sent out his amanuensis to grill that mysterious figure, Sub-Commissioner Parker. "Please finish the story," DeVysse said to me now. "When those Iron Brotherhood uniforms came through the maze, you must have been devastated."

"Deflated, anyway," I said. "But I'd forgotten something I'd learned at the beginning, while eavesdropping in the statue chamber. Condé had managed to plant a Brotherhood lieutenant in each of the two manned defense satellites. When the ground attack began they were supposed to make sure that the satellites didn't get off a distress call, by disabling the message boats in dock.

"Well, when the time came, they succeeded. Their comrades on the ground joined them in captured shuttles, and secured the satellites. At that point, they theoretically had the planet covered. But the magnetic storm we started prevented them from seeing Foyle regain her ship. And after her freighter slipped out of orbit, shields raised, their only chance to stop her was with the station's boats . . ."

"I see," DeVysse said. *"The same boats they'd disabled themselves."*

"Exactly. So she had a clear field, and no trouble intercepting the senator's yacht when it arrived the next day."

"Fortunately, the senator believed her warning. A keen judge of character," he added meaningfully.

I passed over this. "Your replunge, with Foyle in tow, was monitored. Major Dubbs, a practical man, realized that despite his local victory, the game was up. The planned uprising was still months away, and before that could happen the senator would be returning with Column troops. Condé's rebellion was over before it started. Dubbs gave orders to preserve the life of all prisoners, and was quick to find the one best qualified to negotiate a surrender for him—myself. The rest you know."

"Not quite. Who conceived the current plan?"

I shrugged. "The major had volunteered to do anything he could in the way of reparations. I simply restaged Condé's own plan—reversed, as in a mirror. And so it is Condé, not the senator, whom the mercenaries welcome into a trap with all the right recognition codes.

"He sees what he expects. Signs of a battle, because there has been one. And the senator's yacht, just as if captured. The only thing that could have given the game away was an extra Column spacecraft in orbit. But that's the final turnabout. Because a marine troop-carrier is designed to withstand surface gravities, we were able to hide it in Condé's own secret hangar, Level Null under the lake.

"So much for my contributions," I yawned. "You must ask the colonel about the rest."

"But there are still certain questions about your personal role, Commissioner," DeVysse said quietly. "Major Dubbs and the other mercenaries are under the impression that you had been on to Sir Max's operation for some time. Infiltrated it, in fact, so that they thought you were *his* man. But if the Tribunal has been conducting such an important investigation . . . Why is this the first we've heard of it?"

" 'We'?" I said. "Do you hold a rank in one of the intelligence services, Citizen DeVysse? I thought not. If your employer wishes to put questions to me in person, though, I'm at his disposal."

DeVysse smiled as effectively as any puff adder. "I believe I can arrange the necessary . . . disposal, within the hour. Let us say, before the party."

"Very well." An exaggeration. Even if I did manage to spin out another successful installment of *Al Parker, Secret Agent*, I still had to face the senator's dinner party. The entertainment was supposed to be provided by Sir Maximilien Condé, in chains. And once Condé pointed out the actor he'd hired to wear Column whites, told everyone what he knew about my history over the previous year—oh, they might not believe him at first. But they'd have to run an identity check . . .

The same trap I'd started in. But with less chance of getting away.

At least, while visiting the planet surface that morning, I'd been able to recover my wardrobe of uniforms; one should always dress up for a party or a hanging. An intercom in my stateroom informed me that the senator would grant me an audience in an hour. I sat in front of the little nightstand.

In the drawer I found an ink pen and a few sheets of the woodpulp paper rich men use for social notes. I cleared my mind and began to rough out the words I wanted Ariel to remember me by. I had a fair copy in thirty minutes. Pausing only to pick up a heavy leather carrying case I'd had to borrow from the construction camp that morning, I went into the empty corridor.

Directly across the way was the door to Ariel's cabin. The robot lock opened to the sound of my voice—a privilege I hadn't tested since our first night on board. I left the note on her bed and left.

Foyle's cabin was next door. It, too, read NOT AT HOME and LOCKED, but this lock wasn't set to my voice. A good test for the skeleton coder. I fit the end of the device into the lock's computer jack. Days of experimenting on the yacht's comp net paid off; the door opened in seconds. And sure enough, Foyle was not at home.

Shortly afterward I met with Senator Mehta. He was a large, tired-looking man with gray hair, gray skin, gray eyes. But it was the gray of steel, plenty of strength left.

"If what you just said was a Shadow Tribunal password, Senator," I told him, "I don't pretend to know the countersign. I answer to a higher authority, one which I am not permitted to name."

"I'm afraid I need more satisfactory answers than that, Commissioner," he said. "For instance, why wasn't I informed of Condé's conspiracy, once you'd infiltrated it? You knew the Senate was investigating the man's activities—"

"But who knew you weren't a partner in them?" I asked.

He gaped at me.

"Come, come, Senator," I said. "Look at it objectively. Despite your oh-so-public feud, he is your former partner, and was storing matériel of war on a planet owned by you. Matériel which could be used to 'liberate' the Blue Swathe from Column control—and isn't that the same goal you've worked toward, in your neo-Federalist way, for years? Certain influential people suspected you of complicity. The Director of the Shadow Tribunal, for instance."

He was trying to take it in. "Then you—"

"Represent Someone who disagreed. Someone who believes that the Column will only be strengthened, in the long run, by less dictatorial methods of provincial control. This Someone thought you were being framed for treason by the Tribunal, and sent me to Newcount Two to gather evidence that would vindicate you. You may think I played the cards too close to my chest. But don't you see, I *had* to wait until Condé moved against you personally—the only way to prove, no matter what the Shadowmen say, that the arms stockpile and the treason were his, not yours."

"I see," he said finally. He passed a hand in front of his face. "I have long suspected . . . But you insist you can't tell me who your principal is."

The key moment. I locked eyes with him. "Senator . . . I think you *know* who secretly favors your politics. Don't you?"

The pause dragged on for so long I thought the gamble had failed, but then he nodded his head.

"Then you understand why I cannot even speak the name in private."

He licked his lips nervously. "Tell her I understand," he said.

Her? What the hell. It's a good trick that surprises the magician.

"I need to assimilate this." He summoned up a smile. "But I've just been informed that the Knuckle-Cracker will be in custody within the half hour. We can discuss the matter further after the party. I'll join you there shortly."

I nodded, picked up the carrying case, and left, having successfully extended my freedom perhaps twenty minutes. As the senator shook hands with me on the threshold, the marine colonel passed, on his way to the party.

I overtook him, saying, "This is convenient—the senator just asked me to speak to you. A matter of protocol; you know these civilians. The senator wants his guests to see that this arrest is an Intelligence matter, and not just a private vendetta. He requests that when you take Condé into custody, you send the news by military courier, not the intercom, and to me, not him. I will then announce it to the party guests. Silly, I know, but—"

"Damned silly," the colonel grumbled. "More logical for the runner to report to *me*."

"Well, I'm afraid the senator—"

"I could step in front of the flag by the banquet table, and announce it as a sort of a toast. Maybe prepare a few words in advance, humorous but dignified—oh, all right, since you insist. Not the first time I've had to cater to the petty vanity of civilian officialdom. I'll go pass the word now, *sir*."

He stamped back the way he'd come. "Marine," it occurred to me, is an obsolete name; we need something more contemporary and logical—like "Space-taker."

On to the party. The size of the senator's yacht may be imagined by the fact that it had a ballroom. True, the floor curved, but if you didn't look down, spin-gravity would leave you unaware of the fact. Waiters passed around hors d'oeuvres and straightened the white linen on the banquet tables. My friends wandered amid the senator's retainers and hangers-on.

Ariel detached herself from a palm-leaf cluster of admiring military men and came my way diffidently. She'd given me another hero's reward the night we were transferred to the senator's ship, but it had been in the nature of a good-bye, the butterfly spell of our tryst in the arbor-tree long since broken. I wondered if some sixth sense hadn't told her I'd finally given up my secrets—to another woman. Or perhaps she'd noticed the discrepancies in my various stories, and suspected I was a phony. Fair enough; at least I wasn't quite phony enough to try changing her mind. We conversed like cousins. I could tell she hadn't received my note yet.

A moment later I saw her dancing with Wu Arsenovich, the chief contractor. The man had never made such impression on me, but was now a local hero for refusing to collaborate with the mercs. There was a slight bruise on his temple. I recognized the type: the seemingly pointless speaking part from Act One who reappears just before the final curtain to squire away the unattached but deserving heroine. Bit of a cliché, but too late to fix it.

Next I paid my respects to Helen Hogg-Smythe, and shook hands with Harry Lagado. The boy had been marooned by his father's death, but Helen was looking after him, and from what she said after drawing me aside, I gathered that an adoption was in the works. "I have no children," she explained, "only a few years left, and hundreds of thousands of munits I'd rather not leave to the tax man."

"He's a good kid."

"Too good, if anything. Too polite, and a bookworm. But a huge inheritance should ginger him up, if it doesn't ruin him entirely. We all have to pass through the fire."

"It's an easier trip when we're in good company," I said, and lifted her hand to my lips. "Take care."

"You too, dear Commissioner," she replied. "Or whatever you are."

Someone tapped me on the shoulder, and handed me a glass as I turned.

Foyle was a contrary as ever. I'd have bet anything that this prickly and independent woman wouldn't even own an evening gown, much less one that snapped a man's neck around faster than a hangman's knot. It was the same green as her eyes, and set off the dangerous red hair. I'd always considered her handsome, but this sudden outburst of playful sexiness made me feel as if I'd been conned. Even cheated.

Her eyes and lips shone with champagne, professional success—the Newcount Two finds would make her famous—and the enhancement of all pleasures that one feels for a few weeks after not being killed. There was our shared secret, too; she seemed to find everything I said and did ironically amusing now.

"Well, all the players are in place," she said, "save the villain, and he's due to be marched in soon. A little barbaric to greet him this way, but I suppose it's good theater."

I grunted.

She responded more quietly. "Ah, a professional opinion. What does make for good theater, then?"

"The exquisite timing," I said, "of entrances and exits."

The waiter with the bottle passed, and I took it away from him as a gift for Foyle. He made chiding tut-tut noises until it actually passed into her hands, then wisely retreated.

"Thank you! How does it feel to be a hero of the Column—considering?" she asked, and poured herself another.

"Don't you know?"

She laughed. "I'm not even ashamed. After all, what we really did was preserve the Blue Swathe's local freedoms. Very Kanalist of us, to ignore the state structure and liberate from within. And I do feel liberated—the heroine of a Larkspur play, in fact. You've won, I believe it all. Anything is possible, freedom is a state of mind, and we can start fresh every morning if we choose to."

I glanced at my new watch. Five or ten minutes left until Condé's arrival.

Still smiling, she pointed at the carrying case in my hand. "Speaking of which, I have to admit I was a little nervous when you shuttled away with the maze jewels this morning. I can see how you might feel you have a certain personal claim to them. But really, it's not worth throwing away your new identity for. Now that you're a hero, you can do so much more good, on the inside."

I must have looked dubious, though I didn't intend to explain how little job security Sub-Commissioner Parker really had. "Besides," she went on urgently, "the jewels belong to the whole human sphere. I think I've persuaded the senator to put them on traveling exhibit. I'll write the catalog; it could educate people about the real meaning of Kanalism, if I can get it past the censors. And I promise I'll try—but here's the senator now."

And in fact the senator, DeVysse, and most of the other guests were gathering around the pedestal on which the jewels were to be displayed. As we joined them, DeVysse introduced me to the crowd as no more than a sub-commissioner of antiquities—though I could tell by the nasty edge to his voice that if I was just a government agent using archaeology as a cover, he didn't understand the trouble I'd taken over the jewels. But when I had the whole room's attention, I played the curator role to the hilt, lifting my carrying case onto a nearby table with a flourish and pausing dramatically before opening it flat.

The displays it had contained now lay side by side, apparently two puffs of faintly edged air with an identical arrangement of jewelry floating within each. "Instead of using conventional glass for a case," I explained, "I used thin sheets of luminotrope Alpha, virtually invisible, no distraction from the pieces themselves. So one of these slabs is mostly hollow, with the actual jewels fixed between transparent panes and side pieces. The only trick was keeping the joins and angles from reflecting light—that's what took me two hours. The other slab I then cast in less than a minute: a mass of type-Beta glass large enough to produce an interior illusion of the same set of jewels, and a coating of Alpha to square it into the same shape as the real case. This is the copy the senator has graciously permitted me to keep for myself. But can anyone tell which is which?"

Various polite murmurs, no.

"Fortunately, I can point it out," I said. "Let me just make sure I got the dimensions right . . ." I picked up one slab and fit it into the slot at the top of the pedestal.

"Well, let's see," Foyle said. She picked up the slab I'd left on the table. "Since this is relatively light—it must be the thin glass and the real jewels."

She put it down and removed the other slab from the pedestal where I'd just put it. "Unh! And *this*, the heavy one, must be your solid personal copy, Commissioner."

She handed it back to me.

". . . Well, yes," I said. "That's an even better way to tell them apart, yes."

There was a bit of extra color in her face, but an angry warning in the green eyes as well. However, when DeVysse murmured, "You might have turned a nice profit on a mistake there, Commissioner," she bit his head off.

"Nonsense! As I'm sure your patron knows, the jewelry is of little metallic value—low-grade gold and silver, mainly. Without a provenance, it's not worth much."

"What's a provenance?" Ariel asked as I packed my slab back into its case and put the lighter one in the pedestal's slot.

"That data cube you've seen me working on these last few days," Foyle replied. "A fully documented history of the pieces.

I started with the original jeweler's designs from the Elitist data banks, and ended with holograms of their position and appearance when found, and all the other facts needed to confirm authenticity."

"And that's the real treasure," the senator said, more of the politician in his voice than I had heard before. "What viewers can actually take away with them. The history."

Another secret Old Rite man? Could be. Always discreetly defending the old liberties from within the Column's own Senate. Who knew how many of us there might still be out there, in the Hellway of the stars, slowly winding our way back toward the center, and revelation?

As he went on speechmaking, a Column marine sergeant entered the room with a crisp stride. All eyes shifted to him. The senator coolly kept talking, but he did raise his eyebrows when the soldier drew me aside.

"Sir, I was told to inform you that the arrest has been made, in Docking Bay Two. The individual was alone. He's in custody, and we are prepared to bring him here as ordered, in restraints."

I led him a step farther away from anyone else. "Restraints?"

"Handcuffs and leg irons, sir."

"What about the gag?"

"I . . . don't recall that detail of the orders, sir."

"Good God, man, of course he's supposed to be gagged. You may bring him in as soon as you've seen to that."

He saluted smartly, turned to salute the senator, and made his exit. Everyone was looking at me.

"Yes, that was it," I told them. "Sir Max will be joining us in just a moment."

"And what did the sergeant have to discuss with you?" DeVysse asked.

I grimaced and picked up my case. "Intelligence business. First of all, the colonel is insisting that Condé remain gagged, at least until after he's been interrogated."

The senator made a puzzled noise, and I shrugged.

"You know Security types. And apparently they've found something in Condé's little boat they think I should have an immediate look at. It's probably not important, but"—I caught the senator's eye—"I'd like to keep our own record of anything we turn over to the Tribunal. Will you excuse me?"

"Of course, Commissioner, if duty calls." The senator looked just as glad to reclaim the limelight. And as I left, he made a strange sound of contentment with his nose, a loud buzzing snuffle. Whereupon DeVysse, a step or two behind him, flinched like a man under the ten thousandth droplet of a water torture.

But I still couldn't get to Docking Bay Two without passing Condé in the corridor.

The marine colonel had decided that he could cut a dashing figure anyway, by leading the prisoner escort. I told him that the senator had ordered me to search Condé's boat, and he gave me a password to get by the guards. "But look here, before you go," he said, and stepped aside to show me Condé. "What's this gag business? First I've heard of it."

My former employer had been standing with his head bowed, that great shock of white hair in disarray. They'd ripped the militia patches off the admiral's uniform he'd been wearing, and his hands and feet were bound with chains. But now he looked up, his tanned hawk nose extending beyond a tight gag. His eyes grew wide at the sight of me, and he gave a surprised grunt.

"Oh, you don't want to take that off," I said.

"He was quiet enough before."

"That's the way it is with these megalomaniacs. One minute they're quietly sorting through their delusions, and the next they're screaming at the top of their lungs."

Condé tried to say my name, but you can't make a *p* sound in a gag. He bumped into the colonel sideways and jerked his head at me, gargling louder and louder. "I see what you mean," the colonel said, frowning.

Nor an *f* sound. After that, Condé went for sheer unintelligible volume, and made an abortive attempt to butt me in the stomach. "He's a goddamn loon, isn't he?" the colonel marveled as two of his men tried to subdue him.

"Hope you don't have to shoot him," I called back, moving right along. ". . . Not that anyone would blame you, really."

The password got me past the marine guards at the docking bay into Condé's hopped-up Hermes, and I promptly closed all the airlocks behind me, fired up the reactor, strapped in, and opened a link to the yacht's computer net. The master computer told me I couldn't detach the boat. But that was before it had spoken with my skeleton coder.

Twenty seconds later, the little craft rolled out into space, I punched in a provisional course, and the engine kicked in. By this time I was getting baffled and desperate radio calls from the yacht and the defense satellites.

I immediately sent back a clear visual signal of myself, Column uniform angled to the camera, saying something complicated and reassuring with lots of gestures and facial expression, but no sound.

Five minutes of this gave me as much head start as I needed. I switched to autopilot and took the high-g drugs, and when the engines hissed up to full power I was safely unconscious.

I was awakened on schedule, twenty minutes before final solar approach. No one was following me, not within scanner range.

Yawning, I lifted the carrying case into my lap and removed the heavy slab within. Time to jettison the deadweight. Using my elbow, I gently smashed in the small hollow center of the otherwise solid slab.

Foyle had never understood magic tricks—a perfect dupe from the audience, not only buying my story of one entirely genuine case and one entirely solid copy, but helping to sell it to the others, too. In consideration for which, I'd left her most of the real jewelry, in the mostly hollow case she'd correctly judged the lighter. It was only the central tenth of her slab, seemingly containing the best and smallest piece, that was solid simulacrum glass.

I took the prize from my slab, and with the other hand removed from my pocket the data cube I'd rifled from Foyle's room an hour before—the provenance. I gloated over this matched set for only a moment, then couldn't help slipping the original Master's ring of the Kanalists onto my finger and exulting at how well it fit.

No one could make better use of it than I. Foyle had said that there were countless Old Rite lodges underground, awaiting only the appearance of a Master with the True Ring to start Kanalism anew. Who better to play the part than the most famous of Old Rite Kanalists, returned from the dead? What better time to revive the fight for human liberty than now, when the Consultant and the Column had fallen out like thieves?

Besides, the ring was mine by right; Summerisle had willed it to me. To be sure, he couldn't have known that I would stumble upon it by bumming around the freer fringes for seven years, unconsciously searching for my cultural roots. He'd arranged for me to get it another way, the last time I saw him, when we'd met by the fountain at the Great Plaza—when, in fact, he'd told me exactly where to find the Vice Book.

" 'A little learning is a dangerous thing.' Trust me, as Pope of our little order, to do what's best, even if it means

abjuring my mystic Book forever, like Prospero . . . It will be safe for centuries, or until the next Master comes to find it.''

He'd overestimated me. I'd forgotten the name of the fountain inside the Labyrinth, and that was the key to the *Alexander* Pope quotation, which continues, 'Drink deep, or taste not the Pierian spring.' And in *The Tempest*, Prospero vows to 'drown' his book. I was certain, now, that Summerisle's Vice Book was still safe, deep in the base of a Kanalist fountain. Not the fountain in the destroyed Nexus Labyrinth, but the disguised copy in the plaza, which only he had known to be Kanalist. Until he showed it to me—the heir to his Book.

Even if I'd never entered the Blue Swathe, the Book would have led me to Newcount Two, and to the Ring that was waiting for me. Because surely the ''Vice'' Book had once been the ''Weiss''—or White—Codex, and had contained the whole history and technological lore of the Elitists, before we'd added all the scandalous personal secrets of the latter Kanalists.

Summerisle had been bound by oaths not to use the information for blackmail; but he'd hand-chosen a Master who would not be, who could revenge him and our Federal Alignment on the First Columnards—many of whom still lived, occupying key positions of power in their old age. And that wasn't the only weapon against the Column within the Book. Its technological secrets might also turn out to be tremendously potent.

For Summerisle's hokey stories had proven entirely true. Since there *was* a cabal called the Few, who hijacked navy ships and made use of ''secret lore''—read ''Titan technology''—they'd stolen from our Book, what else mightn't the same Book tell me?

If the *Barbarossa* was truly floating in a bubble outside space, wouldn't that make its log readings appear ''globally distorted''—though understandable, once one had the cosmological key? And if it was truly outside time, then wouldn't my mates still be there, no older than when I last saw them—not yet betrayed because I could still rescue them? *Anything is possible. The sun is new every day.*

But first things first. I programmed in a target star: the star circled by Nexus, its plazas and fountains. Then I leaned back and stretched, thinking of the note I'd left Ariel:

BUTTERFLY DREAM

That dawn, the sight of her was all it took
To stun you flat, your wings like flowers clapped
Between the pages of an ancient book
By a little girl. A poet Monarch, rapt.

She wakes. I hold my breath and you your wings.
To save our dream (this bubble world) from Time,
I twine its limbs and leaves (and balancings)
Into an Aerial arbor: rhythmic rhyme.

The hands of all the clocks sow dust and death
Behind us. But what they bury, Art retrieves.
And when we held that world within a breath,
A wingbeat—I pressed a girl between the leaves.

Just verses, not poetry. But the way they'd spilled forth, as if from a full reservoir—that was a new feeling. Or an old one. I remembered the fantasy I'd had in the eel-balloon, *Cyrano On The Moon*; a similar tone might serve . . .

Save it, I thought, feeling a rush of vast, impersonal power coming under my control, like a sailor with a fresh wind rising behind him, strong and true. There will be enough time. That was the message of the old ring. I wound it on my finger, gazing at the maze that was its setting, and in that maze the mirror, and in that mirror the image of a mask so changeable it might even be a Master's face.

It winked back at me, one bright flash, as I pushed the lever forward and plunged into the sun.

About the Authors

A graduate of Harvard University and Mahopac High School, BILL ADAMS is known to readers of mystery fiction as T. M. Adams. He has also been a bonded courier, motel manager, and night dispatcher of everything from grocery trucks to private detectives. During the hours of darkness he produces novels, short stories, verses, computer games—everything, in short, but letters to his friends, some of whom do not know that he now lives in California.

Though a New Englander by nature and nurture, CECIL BROOKS lost a few years in Miami and Chicago, then settled in Harrisburg, Pennsylvania in time to enjoy the meltdown of Three Mile Island. After acquiring a degree in something vague, he has held several paper-marking jobs, cooked in a vegetarian restaurant, perpetrated acts of guerilla journalism and underground publishing, and is locally infamous for his photography and poetry.

MICHAEL McCOLLUM PRESENT'S
HARD CORE
SCIENCE
FICTION